call of adventure

A completely new selection of outstanding children's stories and poems compiled for enrichment reading by a distinguished editorial board of children's librarians.

Series Editor
MARGARET E. MARTIGNONI
Former Superintendent
Work with Children
Brooklyn Public Library

Editor-in-Chief
DR. LOUIS SHORES
Dean, Library School
Florida State University

Managing Editor
HARRY R. SNOWDEN, JR.

Volume Editor
CHARLEMAE ROLLINS
Children's Librarian
Hall Branch
Chicago Public Library

Collier's *Junior* Classics Series

THE CROWELL-COLLIER PUBLISHING COMPANY • NEW YORK

Call of Adventure

Introduction

Collier's Junior Classics Series

We are children only once, and then only for a few brief years. But these are the most impressionable years of a lifetime. Never again will the world and everything in it be so eternally new, so filled with wonder. Never again will physical, mental, spiritual growth be so natural and unavoidable. During these years, habits become ingrained, tastes are developed, personality takes form. The child's whole being is geared toward learning. He instinctively reaches out for truth and, having no prejudices, seizes upon that which is good, just, beautiful. For these reasons, a child deserves what Walter de la Mare has called "only the rarest kind of best."

What do we mean by "best" in a book for children? Best books reflect universal truths with clarity and artistry. Such books reveal that man is essentially good and that life is infinitely worth living. They do not deny the existence of evil, but rather emphasize man's thrilling struggle against evil through faith, courage, and perseverance. They awaken the young reader's imagination, call forth his laughter as well as his tears, help him to understand and to love his fellow man. The reading of such books constitutes a rich heritage of experience which is every child's birthright.

The librarian-editors of *Collier's Junior Classics* have combed the best children's books of the past and present to assemble in a single series a sampling of the finest literature for boys and girls. High standards have been maintained for the art work also, which in most instances has been taken from the original book. No attempt has been made to cover all fields of knowledge or to include factual material for its own sake. The emphasis here is on good literature, chiefly fiction and biography, folk lore and legend, and some poetry. Special attention is given to the American scene and American democratic ideals, but many selections cover other cultures, geographical areas, and historical periods.

The purpose of *Collier's Junior Classics* is to introduce boys and girls to some of the best books ever written for children, to stimulate young readers to seek for themselves the books from which the selections have been drawn as well as other good books of similar appeal, and to encourage children to become discriminating, thoughtful, life-time readers. Author, title, and publisher are given at the foot of the page on which each selection opens. This enables readers to ask for the complete book at a library or bookstore. When necessary, brief introductions set the scene for the selection, while follow-up recommendations, complete with publishers' names, appear at the end of most stories.

Collier's Junior Classics is a series of ten individually indexed volumes. A, B, C: GO! has been lovingly compiled for the youngest, and consists of nursery rhymes, favorite folk tales, best-loved poems, and stories for reading aloud. Four volumes have been assembled for the intermediate group: ONCE UPON A TIME, a wonderous collection of fables, world folk tales, and modern fairy tales; MAGIC IN THE AIR, selections from great masterpieces of fantasy; JUST AROUND THE CORNER, excerpts from warm-hearted stories of other lands; and IN YOUR OWN BACKYARD, selections from stirring books about our own country. Four additional volumes cater to the interests of more mature boys and girls: GIFTS FROM THE PAST, memorable selections from world classics; LEGENDS OF LONG AGO, selections from great myths, epics, and American tall tales; ROADS TO GREATNESS, excerpts from biographies of some of the greatest men and women of the world; and CALL OF ADVENTURE, selections from action and suspense stories of today and yesterday. Finally, and most unusual of all, is the volume entitled HARVEST OF HOLIDAYS, a feast of stories, poems, documents, and factual material about twenty-two American national and religious holidays. Although perhaps of greatest interest to the intermediate group, HARVEST OF HOLIDAYS will intrigue and delight all ages.

The tables of contents for the ten volumes read like an all-time Who's Who of distinguished writers. A brief mention of only a few of these authors would include such names as Lewis Carroll, Kenneth Grahame, Charles Dickens, Mark Twain, Louisa May Alcott, Pearl Buck, Laura Ingalls Wilder, Eleanor Estes, Genevieve Foster, Robert Louis Stevenson, Robert McCloskey, Valenti Angelo, Carl Sandburg, A. A. Milne, Eleanor Farjeon, Elizabeth Enright, and Margaret Wise Brown. Among the illustrators, many of whom are also authors, are to be found the Petershams, the d'Aulaires, Wanda Gág, Louis Slobodkin, Helen Sewell, Lois Lenski, Roger Duvoisin, Maurice Sendak, Kurt Wiese, Marguerite de Angeli, Steele Savage, Howard Pyle, Lynd Ward, James Daugherty, Arthur Rackham, Fritz Kredel, and Gustave Dore.

Collier's Junior Classics is intended primarily for the home, although libraries will find the series valuable for browsing as well as for introducing children to many different books. Because each book is an individual volume, complete with its own index, it can be shelved where the librarian believes it will be most useful to the children.

No pains have been spared to make the individual volumes a series of stepping stones to all that is best in the magic world of children's books.

Margaret E. Martignoni
SERIES EDITOR

Contents

vii

Call of Adventure

We cannot live all lives, nor go to all lands—except in books. In stories we can experience the sacrifice and dauntlessness, the fortitude and the far-seeing courage of many people, far away or near at home. We can live beside ancient rivers, dwell in hidden mountain fastnesses, or huddle in tents on the Great Plains.

From the wealth of stories in CALL OF ADVENTURE, you can choose as wide as the world is wide, as deep as time. You can absorb the weariness and boredom of a young lad keeping his llama flocks in the Andes or suffer the accusation of witchcraft with sixteen-year-old Kit in Puritan New England.

Adventure beckons from the Baker Street office of Sherlock Holmes; it calls from outer-space; it whips through the sails of a listing ship. Adventure is a stormy sea, a duel to death, an unsolved mystery. It is courage in *Lance of Kanana,* cruelty in *Black Beauty,* kindness in *Lassie Come-Home.*

Adventure is life—it is facing tasks which seem impossible, conquering fears that halt our progress, and fighting for what we feel is right. In this volume we invite you to visit with adventure, to see it and feel it in many forms—to share the excitement of a battle with nature, to know the meaning of responsibility, friendship, and growing up. Here, then, is your chance to answer the CALL OF ADVENTURE.

CHARLEMAE ROLLINS
Children's Librarian,
Hall Branch,
Chicago Public Library

Frontispiece by Anton Otto Fischer

Head Winds and a Rough Sea

BY CHARLES BOARDMAN HAWES

Illustrations by Emil Weiss

When Philip Marsham ran away to sea and joined the crew of the frigate Rose of Devon *he expected to find adventure, but hardly to the extent of being kidnaped by pirates. But pirates were everywhere on the high seas during the seventeenth century.*

The Master's Guest

"A SAIL! A sail!"

The seas had somewhat abated and the Rose of Devon was standing on her course under reefed mainsail when the cry sounded.

The vessel they sighted lay low in the water; and since she had one tall mast forward and what appeared to be a lesser mast aft they thought her a ketch. But while they debated the matter the faint sound of guns fired in distress came over the sea; and loosing the reef of their mainsail and standing directly toward the stranger, the men in the Rose of Devon soon made her out to be, instead, a ship which had lost her mainmast and mizzen-mast and was wallowing like a log. While the Rose of Devon was still far off, her men saw that some of the strange crew were aloft in the rigging and that others were huddled on the quarter-deck; and when, in the late afternoon, she came up under the stranger's stern, the unknown master and his men got down on their knees on the deck and stretched their arms above their bare heads.

"Save us," they cried in a doleful voice, "for the Lord Jesus' sake! For our ship hath six-foot water in the hold and we can no longer keep her afloat."

1

In all the Rose of Devon there was not a heart but relented at their lamentable cry, not a man but would do his utmost to lend them aid.

"Hoist out thy boat and we will stand by to succour thee," Captain Candle called. "We can do no more, for we ha' lost our own boat in the storm."

It appeared they had but one boat, which was small, so they must needs divide the crew to leave their vessel, part at one time and part at another; and the seas still ran so high, though wind and wave had moderated, that it seemed impossible they could make the passage. With men at both her pumps the Rose of Devon lay by the wind, wallowing and plunging, and her own plight seemed a hard one. But the poor stranger, though ever and again she rose on the seas so that the water drained from her scupper-holes, lay for the most part with her waist a-wash and a greater sea than its fellows would rise high on the stumps of mainmast and mizzenmast. Her ropes dragged over the side and her sails were a snarl of canvas torn to shreds, and a very sad sight she presented.

Three times they tried to hoist out their boat and failed; but the fourth time they got clear, and with four men rowing and one steering and seven with hats and caps heaving out the water, they came in the twilight slowly down the wind past the Rose of Devon and up into her lee.

The men at the waist of the ship saw more clearly, now, the features of those in the boat, and the one in the stern who handled the great steering oar had in the eyes of Philip Marsham an oddly familiar look. Phil gazed at the man, then he turned to Martin and knew he was not mistaken, for Martin's mouth was agape and he was on the very point of crying out.

"Holla!" Martin yelled.

The man in the stern of the boat looked up and let his eyes range along the waist of the ship. Not one of all those in sight on board the Rose of Devon escaped his scrutiny, which was quick and sure; but he looked Martin coldly in the face without so much as a nod of recognition; and though his brief glance met Phil's gaze squarely and seemed for the moment to linger and search the lad's thoughts, it then passed to the one at Phil's side.

It was the thin man who had been Martin's companion on the road—it was Tom Jordan—it was the Old One.

Martin's face flamed, but he held his tongue.

A line thrown to the boat went out through the air in coils that straightened and sagged down between the foremost thwarts. A sailor in the boat, seizing the line, hauled upon it with might and main. The Old One hotly cursed him and bellowed, "Fend off, fend off, thou slubbering clown! Thy greed to get into the ship will be the means of drowning us all."

Some thrust out oars to fend away from the side of the ship and some held back; but two or three, hungering for safety,

gave him no heed and hauled on the rope and struggled to escape out of their little boat, which was already half full of
water. The Old One then rose with a look of the Fiend in his
eyes and casting the steering oar at the foremost of them,
knocked the man over into the sea, where he sank, leaving a
blotch of red on the surface, which was a terrible sight and
brought the others to observe the Old One's commands.

Some cried "Save him!" but the Old One roared, "Let the
mutinous dog go!"

Perhaps he was right, for there are times when it takes death
to maintain the discipline that will save many lives. At all events
it was then too late to save either the man or the boat, for
although they strove thereafter to do as the Old One bade them,
the boat had already thumped against the side of the ship and
it was each man for himself and the Devil take the last. The men
above threw other ropes and bent over to give a hand to the
poor fellows below, and all but the man who had sunk came
scrambling safe on board.

The Old One leaned out and looked down at the boat, which
lay full of water, with a great hole in her side.

"I would have given my life sooner than let this happen," he
said. "There are seven men left on board our ship, who trusted
me to save them. Indeed, I had not come away but these feared
lest without the master you should refuse to take them. What
say ye, my bawcocks, shall we venture back for our shipmates?"

Looking down at the boat and at the gaping holes the sea
had stove by throwing her against the Rose of Devon, the men
made no reply.

"Not one will venture back? Is there no one of ye?"

"'T were madness," one began. "We should—"

"See! She hath gone adrift!"

And in truth, her gunwales under water, the boat was already
drifting astern. At the end of the painter, which a Rose of
Devon's man still held, there dangled a piece of broken board.

"Let us bring thy ship nigh under the lee of mine," the Old One
cried to Captain Candle. "It may be that by passing a line we
can yet save them."

"It grieves me sorely to refuse them aid, but to approach nearer,
with the darkness now drawing upon us, were an act of folly

that might well cost the lives of us all. Mine own ship is leaking perilously and in this sea, were the two to meet, both would most certainly go down."

The Old One looked about and nodded. "True," said he. "There is no recovering the boat and darkness is upon us. Let us go as near to the ship as we may and bid them have courage till morning, when, God willing, we shall try to get aboard and save them."

"That we will. And I myself will con the ship."

Leaning over the rail, Tom Jordan, the Old One, called out, "Holla, my hearts! The boat hath gone adrift with her sides stove; but do you make a raft and keep aboard a light until morning, when God helping us, we will endeavor to get you aboard."

Perceiving for the first time that the boat was gone and there was no recovering her, those left on board the wreck gave a cry so sad that it pierced the hearts of all in the Rose of Devon, whose men saw them through the dusk doing what they could to save themselves; and presently their light appeared.

Working the Rose of Devon to windward of the wreck, Captain Candle lay by, but all his endeavours could not avail to help them, for about ten o'clock at night, three hours after the Old One and his ten men had got on board the Rose of Devon, their ship sank and their light went out and seven men lost their lives.

The Old One, standing beside Captain Candle, had watched the light to the last. "It is a bitter grief to bear," he said, "for they were seven brave men. A master could desire no better mariners. 'T is the end of the Blue Friggat from Virginia, bound for Portsmouth, wanting seven weeks."

"A man can go many years to sea without meeting such a storm."

"Yea! Three days ago when the wind was increasing all night we kept only our two courses abroad. At daybreak we handed our main course, but before we had secured it the storm burst upon us so violently that I ordered the foreyard lowered away; but not with all their strength could the men get it down, and of them all not one had a knife to cut away the sail, for they wore only their drawers without pockets; so the gale drove us head into the sea and stopped our way and a mighty sea pooped us and filled us and we lay with only our masts and forecastle out of the water. I myself, being fastened to the mizzenmast with a rope, had only my head out of water. Yea, we expected to go straight down to the bottom, but God of his infinite goodness was pleased to draw us from the deep and another sea lifted up our ship. We got down our foresail and stowed it and bored holes between the decks to let the water into the hold and by dint of much pumping we kept her afloat until now. In all we have lost eight lives this day and a sad day it is."

"From Virginia, wanting seven weeks," Captain Candle mused.

Captain Jordan stole a swift glance at him but saw no suspicion in his face.

"Yea, from Virginia."

"You shall share mine own cabin but I fear you have come only from one wreck to another."

The two captains sat late that night at the table in the great cabin, one on each side, and ate and drank. There was fine linen on the table, and bread of wheat flour with butter less than two weeks from the dairy, and a fine old cheese, and a mutton stew, and canary and sack and aqua vitæ. At midnight they were still lingering over the suckets and almonds and comfits that the boy had set before them; and the boy, nodding in uncontrollable drowsiness as he stood behind his master's chair, strove to keep awake.

The murmuring voices of the men at the helm came faintly through the bulkhead, and up from below the deck came the creak of whipstaff and tiller. The moon, shining through the cabin window, added its wan light to the yellow radiance from the swinging lanthorns, and stars were to be seen. So completely had wind and weather changed in a night and a day that, save for the long rolling swell, the great gap where waist and boat and capstan had gone, the hole stuffed with blankets and rugs and hammocks, the stump of a mizzenmast, and the rescued men on board—save for these, a man might have forgotten storms and wrecks.

"You are well found," said Captain Thomas Jordan, tilting his glass and watching the wine roll toward the brim; "yea, and we are in good fortune." His thin face, as he lifted his brows and slightly smiled at his host, settled into the furrowed wrinkles that had won him the name of the Old One.

"We can give such entertainment as is set before you," his host drily replied. Francis Candle was too shrewd a man to miss his guest's searching appraisal of the cabin and its furnishings. In his heart he already distrusted the fellow.

Between Midnight and Morning

Through the main deck to the gun-room and up into the forecastle there drifted smoke from the cookroom in the hold, which was the way of those old ships. At times it set choking the men at the pumps; it eddied about the water cask before the mainmast and about the riding butts by the heel of the bowsprit, and went curling out of the hawse pipes. It crept insidiously into the forecastle, and the men cursed fluently when their eyes began to smart and their noses to sting.

There were seven men in the forecastle and Martin Barwick was one of the seven, although his watch was on deck and he had no right to be there. Philip Marsham, whose watch was below, had stayed because he suspected there was some strange thing in the wind and was determined to learn if possible what it was. Two of the others were younkers of the Rose of Devon, who suspected nothing, and the remaining three were of the rescued men.

There was a step above and a round head appeared in the hatch. The dim smoky light gave a strange appearance to the familiar features.

"Ho, cook!" Martin cried, and thumped on the table. "Come thou down and bring us what tidings the boy hath brought thee in the cookroom. Yea, though the cook labour in the very bowels of the ship, is it not a proverb that he alone knows all that goes on?"

Slipping through the hatch, the cook drew a great breath and sat him down by the table. "She was the Blue Friggat, I hear, and seven weeks from Virginia—God rest the souls of them who went down in her!"

"From Virginia!" quoth Martin. "Either th' art gulled, in truth, or th' art the very prince of liars. From Virginia! Ho ho!" And Martin laughed loud and long.

Now it was for such a moment that Philip Marsham was waiting, nor had he doubted the moment would come. For although
Martin had gone apart with the men who had come from the
foundered ship, the fellow's head, which was larger than most
heads, could never keep three ideas in flourish at the same time.
To learn what game was in the wind there was need only to
keep close at Martin's heels until his blunders should disclose
his secrets.

"The Devil take thee, thou alehouse dog!" the cook cried in a
thick, wheezy voice. "Did not the boy bring me word straight
when he came down for a can of boiling water with which this
Captain Jordan would prepare a wondrous drink for Captain
Candle?"

"And did not I part with this Captain Jordan not— Wow-
ouch!" With a yell Martin tipped back in his chair and went
over. Crawling on his feet, he put on a long face and rubbed his
head and hurled a flood of oaths at the sailor beside him, a small
man and round like an apple, who went among his fellows—for
he was one of those the Rose of Devon had rescued—by the
name of Harry Malcolm.

"Nay," the little round man very quietly replied, "I fear you
not, for all your bluster. Put your hand on your tongue, fellow,
and see if you cannot hold it. I had not intended to tip you over.
It was done casually."

"And why, perdy, did'st thou jam thy foot on mine till the
bones crunched? I'll have thy heart's blood."

"Nay," the man replied, so quietly, so calmly that he might
have been a clerk sitting on his stool, "you have a way of talking
overmuch, fellow, and I have a misliking of speech that babbles
like a brook. It can make trouble."

Martin stopped as if he had lost his voice, but continued to
glare at the stranger, who still regarded him with no concern.

"It is thy weakness, fellow," he said, "and—" he looked very
hard at Martin—"it may yet be the occasion of thine untimely
end."

For a moment Martin stood still, then, swallowing once or
twice, he went out of the dimly lighted forecastle into the darkness of the deck.

"He appears," the little man said, addressing the others, "to be an excitable fellow. Alas, what trouble a brisk tongue can bring upon a man!"

The little man, Harry Malcolm, looked from one to another and longest at Phil.

Now Phil could not say there had been a hidden meaning in the hard look the little man had given Martin or in the long look the little man had given Phil himself. But he knew that whether this was so or not, there was no more to be got that night from Martin, and he in turn, further bepuzzled by the little man's words and after all not much enlightened by Martin's blunder, left the forecastle to seek the main deck.

Passing the great cannon lashed in their places, and leaving behind him the high forecastle, he came into the shadow of the towering poop on which the lantern glowed yellow in the blue moonlight, and continued aft to the hatch ladder. Already it was long past midnight.

He imagined he heard voices in the great cabin, and although he well enough knew that it was probably only imagination,—for the cabin door was closed fast,—the presence of the Old One on board the Rose of Devon was enough to make a man imagine things, who had sat in Mother Taylor's cottage and listened to talk of the gentlemen who sailed from Bideford. He paused at the head of the ladder and listened, but heard nothing more.

An hour passed. There were fewer sounds to break the silence. There is no time like the very early morning for subtle and mysterious deeds.

Boatswain Marsham was asleep below and Captain Candle was asleep aft, when Captain Jordan arose and stretched himself, and in a voice that would have been audible to Captain Candle if he had been awake but that was so low it did not disturb his sleep, vowed he must breathe fresh air ere he could bury his head in a blanket for the night.

Emerging from the great cabin, Captain Jordan climbed first to the poop, whence he looked down on the brave old ship and the wide space of sky and darkly heaving sea within the circle of the horizon. To look thus at the sea is enough to make a philosopher of a thinking man, and this Captain Thomas Jordan was by no means devoid of thought.

But whereas many a one who stands under the bright stars

in the small morning hours feels himself a brother with the most trifling creatures that live and is filled with humility to consider in relation to the immeasurable powers of the universe his weakness during even his brief space of life—whereas such a one perceives himself to be, like the prophets of ancient times, in a Divine Presence, the Old One, his face strangely youthful in its repose, threw back his head and softly laughed, as if there high on the poop he were a god of the heathen, who could blot out with his thumb the ship and all the souls that sailed in her. His face had again a haunting likeness to the devils in the old woodcuts; and indeed there is something of the devil in the very egotism of a man who can thus assert his vain notions at such an hour.

Presently decending from the poop and with a nod passing on the quarter-deck the officer of the watch, he paced for a time the maintop-deck. He pretended to absorb himself in the sea and the damage the storm had done to the waist; but he missed nothing that happened and he observed the whereabouts of every man in the watch.

Edging slowly forward, he stood at last beside a big man who was leaning in the shadow of the forecastle.

"We meet sooner than you thought," he said in a low voice.

"Yea, for we were long on the road and entangled ourselves wonderfully among those byways and highways which cross the country in a manner perplexing beyond belief."

"Saw you your brother?"

"In all truth I saw him—and the Devil take him!"

The Old One laughed softly.

"It is plain thy brother hath little love for a shipwrecked mariner," quoth he, "yet there is a most memorable antiquity about the use of ships, and even greater gluttons than thy brother have supped light that worthy seamen might not go hungry to bed. We will speak of him another time. What think you of this pretty pup we have met by the way?—Ah, thine eye darkens! Methinks thou hast more than once felt the rough side of his tongue."

"He bears himself somewhat struttingly—" Martin hesitated, but added perforce, since he had received a friendly turn he could not soon forget, "yet he hath his good points."

"He was one too many for thee! Nay, confess it!"

"Th' art a filthy rascal!" Martin's face burned with anger.

"I knew he would be too cunning for thy wool-gathering wits. Truly I believe he is a lad after my own heart. I have marked him well."

"But hast thou plumbed his inclination with thy sounding lead?"

"Why, no. At worst, he can disappear. It has happened to taller men than he, and in a land where there are men at arms to come asking questions."

"Hgh!"

"This for thy whining, though: we shall play upon him lightly. Some are not worth troubling over, but this lad is a cunning rogue and hath book learning."

"Came you in search of this ship?"

"It was chance alone that brought us across her course. Chance alone, Martin, that brought your old captain back to you."

Watching Martin, as he spoke, the Old One again laughed softly.

"Yea, Martin, it touches the heart of your old captain to see with what pleasure you receive him."

"Th' art a cunning devil," Martin muttered, and babbled oaths and curses.

"We must sleep, Martin—sleep and eat, for we are spent with much labour and many hardships, and it is well for them to sail our ship for us a while longer. But the hour will come, and do you then stand by."

The Old One went aft. The ship rolled drowsily and the watch nodded. Surveying her aloft and alow, as a man does who is used to command, and not as a guest on board might do, the Old One left the deck.

Head Winds and a Rough Sea

"Lacking the mizzen she labours by the wind, which hath veered sadly during the night," quoth Captain Jordan in a sleepy voice, as with his host he came upon deck betimes.

"I like it little," the master replied.

"It would be well to lay a new course and sail on a new voyage. There is small gain to be got from these fisheries. A southern voyage, now, promises returns worth the labour."

To this Captain Candle made no reply. He studied the sore damage done to the ship, upon which already the carpenter was at work.

"With a breadth of canvas and hoops to batten the edges fast, and over all a coating of tar, a man might make her as tight and dry as you please," said the Old One. He smiled when he spoke and his manner galled his host.

"It was in my own mind," Captain Candle replied, with an angry lift of his head. There are few things more grievously harassing than the importunity and easy assurance of a guest of whom there is no riddance. It puts a man where he is peculiarly helpless to defend himself, and already Captain Candle's patience had ebbed far. "Bid the boatswain overhaul his canvas, mate, and the carpenter prepare such material as be needful. Aye, and bid the 'liar' stand ready to go over the side. 'T will cool his hot pride, of which it seems he hath full measure."

"Yea, yea!"

As the master paced the deck, back and forth and back and forth, the Old One walked at his side—for he was a shrewd schemer and had calculated his part well—until the master's gorge rose. "I must return to the cabin," he said at last, "and overhaul my journal."

"I will bear you company."

"No, no!"

The Old One smiled as if in deprecation; but as the master turned away, the smile broadened to a grin.

Boatswain Marsham and the one-eyed carpenter who wore a beard like a goat's were on their way to the forehold. The cook and his mate were far down in the cookroom. Ten men in the watch below were sound asleep—but Martin Barwick, the eleventh man in the watch, was on deck, *and of the eleven rescued men not one was below.* With Captain Candle safe in his cabin and busied over his journal, there were left from the company of the Rose of Devon eight men and the mate, and one man of the eight was at the helm. These the Old One counted as he took a turn on the quarter-deck.

The Old One and his men were refreshed by a night of sleep and restored by good food. To all appearances, without care or thought to trouble them, they ruffled about the deck. One was standing just behind the mate; two were straying toward the steerage.

"Thy boatswain is a brave lad," the Old One said to the mate, and stepping in front of him, he spread his legs and folded his arms.

The mate nodded. He had less liking for their guest, if it were possible, than the captain.

"A brave lad," the Old One repeated. "I can use him."

"You?"

"Yea, I."

The mate drew back a step, as a man does when another puts his face too near. He was on the point of speaking; but before his lips had phrased a word the Old One raised his hand and the man behind the mate drove six inches of blue steel into the mate's back, between his ribs and through his heart.

He died in the Old One's arms, for the Old One caught him before he fell, and held him thus.

"Well done," the Old One said to his man.

"Not so well as one could wish," the man replied, wiping his knife on the mate's coat. "He perished quietly enough, but the knife bit into a rib and the feeling of a sharp knife dragging upon bone sets my teeth on edge."

The Old One laughed. "Thy stomach is exceeding queasy," he said. "Come, let us heave him over the side."

All this, remember, had happened quickly and very quietly. There were the three men standing by the quarter-deck ladder—the Old One and his man and the mate—and by all appearances the Old One merely put out his hands in a friendly manner to the other, for the knife thrust was hidden by a cloak. But now the mate's head fell forward in a queer, lackadaisical way and four of the Old One's men, perceiving what they looked for, slipped past him through the door to the steerage room, where they clapped down the hatch to the main deck. One stood on the hatch; two stood by the door of the great cabin; and the fourth, stepping up to the man at the helm, flashed a knife from his sleeve and cut the fellow down.

It was a deft blow, but not so sure as the thrust that had killed the mate. The helmsman dropped the whipstaff and, falling, gave forth a yell and struck at his assailant, who again let drive at him with the knife and finished the work, so that the fellow lay with bloody froth at his lips and with fingers that twitched a little and then were still.

The man who had killed him took the whipstaff and called softly, "Holla, master! We hold the helm!" then from his place he heard a sailor cry out, "The mate is falling! Lend him aid!"

Then the Old One's voice, rising to a yell, called, "Stand back! Stand off! Now, my hearts!"

There came a quick tempest of voices, a shrill cry, the pounding of many feet, then a splash, then a cry wilder and more shrill than any before, "Nay, I yield—quarter! Quarter, I say! Mercy! God's mercy, I beg of you! Help—O God!"

There was at the same time a rumble of hoarse voices and a
sound of great struggling, then a shriek and a second splash.
The man at the helm kicked the dead helmsman to one side
and listened. In the great cabin, behind the bulkhead at his back,
he heard a sudden stir. As between the mainmast and the forecastle the yells rose louder, the great cabin door burst open and
out rushed Captain Francis Candle in a rich waist with broad
cuffs at his wrists, his hair new oiled with jessamine butter, and
gallant bows at his knees, for he was a fine gentleman who had
first gone to sea as a lieutenant in the King's service. As he
rushed out the door the man lying in wait on the left struck a
fierce blow to stab him, but the knife point broke on a steel

plate which it seemed Captain Candle wore concealed to foil just such dastardly work.

Thereupon turning like a flash, Captain Candle spitted the scoundrel with his sword. But the man lying in wait on the right of the door saw his fellow's blow fail and perceived the reason, and leaping on the captain from behind, he seized his oiled hair with one hand and hauled back his head, and reaching forward with the other hand, drove a knife into the captain's bare throat.

Dark blood from a severed vein streamed out over Captain Candle's collar and his gay waist. He coughed and his eyes grew dull. He let go his sword, which remained stuck through the body of the man who had first struck at him, clapped his hand to his neck, and went down in a heap.

The yells on deck had ceased and the man who had killed Francis Candle, after glancing into the great cabin where the captain's cloak lay spread over the chair from which he rose to step out of his door and die,—where the captain's pen lay across the pages of the open journal and a bottle of the captain's wine, which he had that morning shared with his guest, Captain Thomas Jordan, stood beside the unstopped bottle of ink,— walked forth upon the deck and nodded to the Old One, who stood with his hand on the after swivel gun.

There were a few splotches of blood on the deck and three men of the Rose of Devon's crew lay huddled in a heap; there were left standing three other men of the Rose of Devon, and sick enough they looked; Martin Barwick was stationed by the ladder to the forecastle, where he stood like a pigeon cock with his head haughtily in the air and his chest thrust out; and the little round apple of a man, Harry Malcolm, who had broken in upon Martin the night before, bearing now a new and bloody gash across his forehead, was prowling among the guns and tapping the breech rings with a knowing air.

The Old One from the quarter-deck looked down at the new comer.

"Rab took the steel," the fellow said.

"Rab!" the Old One cried. "Not Rab, you say?"

"Yea, he struck first but the master wore an iron shirt which turned the point and he was then at him with his sword."

"We have lost nine good men by this devil-begotten storm, but of them all Rad is the one I am most loath to see go to the sharks." The Old One paced the deck a while and the others talked in undertones. "Yea, Martin," he called at last, "nine good men. But we have got us a ship and I have great hopes of our boatswain, who may yet make us two of Rab. At all events, my bullies, we must lay us a new course, for I have no liking of these northern fisheries. Hark! They are pounding on the hatch."

The sound of knocking and a muffled calling came from the main hatch, whereat the men on deck looked at one another and some of them smiled.

"It were well—" the little round man began. He glanced at the huddled bodies and shrugged.

"True, true!" the Old One replied, for he needed no words to complete the meaning. "You men of the Rose of Devon, heave them into the sea."

The three looked at one another and hesitated, and the youngest of the three turned away his face and put his hand on his belly, and sick enough he looked, at which a great laugh went up.

"Go, Harry," the Old One cried to the little round man, "and tell them at the hatch to be still, for that we shall presently have them on deck. We must learn our brave recruits a lesson."

Again a roar of laughter rose, and as the little man went in to the hatch, the others drew about the three who cowered against the forecastle ladder, as well they might.

"Come, silly dogs," said the Old One, "in faith, you must earn your foolish lives. Lay hands on those carcasses and heave them to the fishes."

They looked into the faces of the men about them, but got small comfort as they edged toward their unwelcome task.

"It is hard to use thus a shipmate of three voyages," the oldest of them muttered.

"True," replied the Old One, "but so shall you buy your way into a goodlier company of shipmates, who traffic in richer cargoes than pickled codfish and New England herrings."

The three picked up the bodies, one at a time, each with its arms and legs dragging, and carried them to the waist and pushed them over. But the youngest of the three was trembling like a dead weed in November when they had finished, and the Old One chuckled to see the fellow's white face.

"Have courage, bawcock," the Old One cried; "there shall soon be a round of aqua vitæ to warm thy shaking limbs and send the blood coursing through thy veins. Now, Mate Harry, lift off the hatch and summon our good boatswain and carpenter."

"As you please, as you please," came the quick, gentle voice of the little round man. "But there are two of 'em left still—Rab and the captain—and there's a deal of blood hereabouts."

They heard the hatch creak as the little man pried it off. They heard his quick sentences pattering out one after another: "Hasten out on deck—nay, linger not. The master would have speech of thee. Nay, linger not. Ask me no questions! There's no time for lingering."

Then out burst Phil Marsham with the older carpenter puffing at his heels.

"What's afoot?" cried Phil. "Where's the master?—what— where—"

So speedily had they hurried from the hatch (and so cleverly had the little round man interposed himself between the hatch and the two bodies at the cabin door) that in the dim light of the steerage room the two had perceived nothing amiss. But now, looking about for the source of the fierce cries and yells they had heard, they saw red stains on the deck, and men with scared white faces.

All looked toward the Old One as if awaiting his reply; and when Phil Marsham, too, looked toward him, he met such another quizzing, searching, understanding gaze as he had long ago met when he had taken the words from Martin's lips on the little hill beside the road.

"Why, I am master now, good boatswain."

"But Captain Candle—"

"His flame is out."

The lad glanced about him at the circle of hard old sea dogs— for they were all of them that, were their years few or many— and drew away till he stood with the waist at his back. Laying hands on his dirk, he said in a voice that slightly trembled, "And now?"

"Why," quoth the Old One, "you have sat in Mother Taylor's kitchen and heard talk of the gentlemen. You know too many secrets. Unless you are one of us—" He finished with a shrug.

"You ask me, then, to join you?"

"Yea."

"I refuse." He looked the Old One in the eye.

"Why, then," said the Old One, "you are the greater fool."

The circle drew closer.

"What then?"

"'T is but another candle to be snuffed."

With hand on dirk and with back against the waist, the boatswain looked one and another and then another in the eye. "Why, then," said he, "I must even join you, as you say. But I call upon you all to witness I am a forced man." And he looked longest and hardest at the three men from the old crew of the Rose of Devon.

The Old One looked back at the lad and there was, for the first time, doubt in his glance. He stood for a while pondering in silence all that had taken place and studying the face of his boatswain; but his liking of the lad's spirit outweighed his doubts, for such bold independence, whether in friend or foe, was the one sure key to Tom Jordan's heart. "So be it," he said at last. "But remember, my fine young fellow, that many a cockerel hath got his neck wrung by crowing out of season." He turned to the carpenter. "And what say you? We can use a man of your craft."

"I am thy man!" the fellow cried. The stains on the deck had made him surpassingly eager, and his one eye winked and his beard wagged, so eager was he to declare his allegiance.

"Well said!" the Old One responded. "And now, Master Harry, have them up from below—the sleepers, and the cook and his mate, and all! We have taken a fine ship—a fine ship she will be, at all events, once our good carpenter has done his work—and well found. We needs must sign a crew to sail and fight her."

They heard the little round man calling down the hatch and at a great distance in the ship they heard the voices of men grumbling at being summoned out of sleep. But the grumbling was stilled when one by one the men came out on deck; and of them all, not a man refused to cast his lot with the Old One and the rest. The mere sight of a little blood and of the hard faces that greeted them was enough for most. And two or three, of whom Will Canty was one, must fain perceive how futile would be present resistance. Indeed, in the years since the old Queen had died, and the navy had gone to the dogs, and merchantmen had come to sail from the Downs knowing they were likely enough to meet a squadron of galleys lying in wait fifty leagues off the Lizard, many a sailor had taken his fling at buccaneering; and those that had not, had heard such great tales of galleons laden with treasures of the Indies and with beautiful dames of Spain that their palates were whetted for a taste of the life.

The cook smiled broadly and clapped the boy on the back and cried out that as a little lad he had sailed with John Jennings what time John Jennings's wench had turned his luck, and that having begun life in such brave company, he would gladly end it in a proper voyage if it was written that his time was near. They all laughed to see the boy turn white and tremble, and they huzzaed the cook for his gallant words. But Will Canty met Phil's eyes and there passed between them a look that made the Old One frown, for he was a man who saw everything.

The Rose of Devon, although close-hauled by the wind, rolled heavily, which was the way of those old tall ships; but the adverse winds and high seas she had encountered were of fancy as well as of fact. The sun was shining brightly and sky and sea were a clear blue; but despite sun and sky and sea no weather-wise man could have believed the dark days of the Rose of Devon were at an end. Like so many iron bars the shadows of the ropes fell blue on the sails, and the red blotches on the deck matched the dull red paint of the stanchions and the waist. The carpenter, who had come up with his plane in his hand, fingered the steel blade. The boy turned his back on the bloody deck and looked away at the sea, for he was a little fellow and not hardened by experience of the world.

"Come, my hearts," cried the Old One, and gaily enough he spoke. "We are banded together for the good of all. There is no company of merchants to profit by our labour and our blood. God hath placed in our keeping this brave ship, which will be staunch and seaworthy when our carpenter has done his work. Harry Malcolm is our mate and master gunner as of old, and

Phil Marsham shall continue as our boatswain—nay, grumble not! He came with Martin Barwick and he hath sat in Mother Taylor's kitchen, where may we all sit soon and raise our cans and drink thanks for a rich voyage. There is work to be done, for all must be made clean and tight—yea, and Rab is to be buried."

The little round man was still wandering from gun to gun and smiling because the guns pleased him. They were demiculverins of brass, bored for a twelve-pound ball and fit to fight the King's battles; but alas! they had shown themselves powerless against a foe from within the ship. And as the Rose of Devon rolled along in the bright sun, alone in a blue sea, the body of Francis Candle lay forgotten in the steerage room.

The Dark Frigate *was awarded the Newbery Medal in 1924. Another tale of narrow escapes and foul murder on the high seas by Charles Boardman Hawes is* The Mutineers, *published by Little, Brown.*

Service at the
Point of a Rifle

BY ELIZABETH FOREMAN LEWIS

Illustrations by Kurt Wiese

At first, the city of Chungking seems a fabulous place to the country boy Young Fu, who has been apprenticed to a master coppersmith in order that he might support his widowed mother Fu Be Be. But after learning how the poor and the helpless often suffer at the hands of the powerful, Young Fu sees the city through different eyes.

AUTUMN'S somber days became the darker ones of winter. Rain fell daily. Fu Be Be unceasingly voiced complaints: "True, indeed, is all that I ever heard of this city's weather. In my village I believed with difficulty that rain and mist could fall anywhere without end. But so they do here. As for the sun, I see it so seldom that I jump at the sight of its rays. The very walls sweat dampness, and mildew discolors all of our possessions. To live thus is like dwelling in a grave!"

Her son grinned, "But not so lonely!"

And then, one morning there was a rift of blue in the sodden sky, and beyond the Yangtze the hills stood out in unexpected beauty of detail. Heavier rains followed, but days of glistening sunshine broke their monotony.

At Tang's the quality of weather made little difference. Trade flourished. Constantly, prospective patrons sat at the two square tables in the shop and sipped tea while Small Den ran about displaying selections suited to their demands. Young Fu and Small Li delivered orders, or, accompanied by the accountant, hurried through the streets to wealthy homes whither they had been summoned and, unwrapping their samples in the rooms reserved for tradespeople, awaited the buyer's pleasure. On one or two rare occasions, Tang paid these calls, but usually he trusted the business to the clerk on whose ability to get a fair price he could depend.

For Young Fu these errands were thrilling experiences. He it was who carried the heaviest brasses, he who lifted them about as the patron ordered, he who squatted on his heels in silence while the accountant pursued the delights of bargaining. He would not have exchanged positions with anyone in the Middle Kingdom. This life gave him an opportunity to see marvels that exceeded imagination.

At first he could not conceal his expressions of pleasure. "Certainly, there can be no dwellings finer than these in all the land," he said with an intake of breath.

The clerk lowered one eyelid in disdain. "When you have lived a few more years, you will not make such foolish remarks."

Young Fu said nothing more, but his opinion remained unchanged. Gatemen led them over intricate garden paths to the low, spreading buildings. Young Fu peered through carved lacquer doorways into rooms whose walls were hung with priceless scrolls and tapestries. Ebony tables and chairs, porcelain jars from which flowering trees lifted gnarled branches, tall vases a thousand years in age, vied with one another in attraction. In the spring of his ninth year, his mother had taken him to a temple several li from their farm. For a month afterwards Young Fu had been able to think of little else but the grandeur of the place. Compared with the magnificence of these homes, that of the temple now seemed on a level with his own village hut.

Sometimes it was the women of the household who wished to purchase, and the gateman would lead the tradespeople to the rear wings of the building, and there the eldest mistress of the family would receive them in the servants' gallery. Voices of younger women filtered through the thin walls, but none of these ever appeared to make their own selections. The small satin-clad and jeweled figure designated with a flourish of a tiny pipe what was desired, and in the bargaining frequently worsted Tang's representative. Young Fu, his gaze directed to the ground as was the custom in a lady's presence, found it difficult to control his amusement at such times. These old mothers, for all their wealth, differed not at all from Fu Be Be in her dealings with the shopkeepers.

Children ran along these garden paths, playing at hopscotch with persimmon seeds for counters, or using their toes to kick a feathered shuttlecock an indefinite number of times. At one place a boy of seven was engaged in clownish antics in the effort to entertain a small girl. As the others approached, he stopped and stood in embarrassed dignity. Young Fu's glance roamed from him to the little maid. Her cheeks were streaked and her eyes red from weeping. She sat on a wooden stool and swung her feet mechanically to and fro. They were swathed in bandages that told their own story.

Girls always cried during the tedious moons of foot binding. He had seen them often enough in the village, though a few of the farm women kept their daughters' feet of natural size that they might help in the fields. But this was not common. Everyone agreed that it was better to stand the agony of foot binding than the stigma of possessing large feet. And even though deformed feet permitted a woman to work only around the house, they were important in getting a husband. Ever since that day centuries ago when an Empress had first bound her feet and then named the crippled results Golden Lilies, all of China's women had followed the fashion. He, Young Fu, was glad that his mother's feet were small; that she was not a coolie woman was plain for all to see.

In some of the homes they would find teachers instructing the boys of the family in the Classics. Sometimes these youths attended private schools in the city. Small, ill-lighted rooms set between shops on busy thoroughfares and presided over by one venerable scholar, they offered much the same subject matter and methods that they had used two thousand years before. A hundred feet away, one could determine their location. At the top of their lungs, students memorized and recited lessons, and the noise rose in waves above the other sounds of the street. Young Fu wondered at times what it would be like to have time in which to do nothing but study and play. He did not envy them, but neither did he forget that he had set himself the task some day of learning to read and write characters. It did not occur to him to tell Wang Scholar, whom he met on the curb each evening, that he wished to do books. An apprentice did not trouble a gentleman with such small affairs. Moreover, it was his duty just now to learn all that he could of Tang's business; the other would come in time.

Six months of this life had slipped by when he awoke to the realization that Chungking was not made up of magnificence and entertainment alone. On his way home at dusk one day, he noticed a crowd collected in the hollow space made by an abrupt angle of two compound walls, so built that evil spirits, which are able to travel only in a straight line, might butt themselves against this sudden obstruction and have an untimely end. Everyone knows that devils are stupid and that simple expedients like these often save a whole family from disaster. As he came nearer, the crowd dispersed. Most of them wore frightened faces, and some muttered ominously to one another. Alive with curiosity, he pressed on and found himself almost alone with a half-dozen soldiers.

In their midst was a load-coolie, his back pressed to the wall, his breast pinned by the muzzle of a rifle. His face was ashen as he attempted to reason with his persecutors.

One of the soldiers interrupted him. "I will count ten," he said. "If by that time you still refuse to carry our bedding—" he smiled cruelly.

"I dare not, Honorable Military," wailed the coolie. "I am late with my load for my master. If you do not let me hurry on, he will give me less than my due in payment, and already my family starves for lack of food."

Young Fu's gaze shifted from the miserable man to the paving. There were several bundles of bedding belonging to the soldiers, and close by sat two round baskets filled with rice, on the top of which rested the coolie's carrying pole and ropes.

"One, two, three, four, five," counted the soldier.

The coolie's face was contorted with fear. "Sirs," he begged.

"Six, seven, eight, nine, ten!"

"Sirs! What will you do—" There was a deafening report and the load-bearer's last protest died away in a faint scream. He slid silently to the ground.

Stricken with horror, Young Fu stared at the bundle of reddening rags that only a few seconds earlier had been a man intent on earning food for himself and family. The youth felt suddenly cold; he began to tremble. He wished for nothing save to escape from this revolting scene of violence, but his feet refused to move.

The soldiers were now quarreling over the deed; each blamed the other for the man's death; one in particular seemed worried. He kept murmuring that this had not been necessary, that their captain must not hear of the matter.

He who had done the shooting sneered, "Of what importance is a coolie?"

A coolie, an eating-bitterness man as he was called—what did he matter? The question burned into the youth's numbed mind. But the man had done nothing except to refuse to carry bedding that belonged to these soldiers. He had been delivering rice for his master, and because he would not leave that in the streets and take up this bedding, he had been killed.

Young Fu puzzled over the injustice of the affair. And the soldiers would go unpunished; no one was ever strong enough to punish the military. First they had killed his father by destroying the crops; that had taken several years of exposure and overwork. Now this man had paid with his life, and in less than a minute of time. And if he did not slip away before they awoke to the knowledge of his presence, they might shoot him, also. He took one step when a heavy hand gripped his shoulder.

"What are you doing here?" a gruff voice demanded.

Young Fu winced in terror. "Nothing," he stammered.

"Let the boy go!" commanded the one with the worried expression.

"No," was the reply, "he looks strong. We shall, until we find help elsewhere, have to carry our bedding, but he can bring this fellow's load of rice. We can use that to good advantage."

The youth listened in a daze. He could not carry that rice. It must weigh twice as much as any of the brasses Tang had taxed his strength with, and his muscles had strained under them. "I have not the strength for this," he began, "perhaps, the bedding—"

"Do you wish to be the second to lie there?" The soldier pointed to the body.

Shivering, the boy stooped down, caught up the dead man's pole, slipped the ropes over each end, and tried to lift the baskets clear of the ground. The pole cut into his shoulders and he staggered under the painful pressure. With the unexpected

jolting, a small shower of rice slid from the surface of each basket. His tormentor cursed, struck him across the back with his rifle butt, and dared him to be so careless again.

The worried man interfered, and a bitter quarrel ensued. The others shrugged their shoulders, then cautioning haste, picked up rolls of bedding and started on down the street. Young Fu, hedged in between the brawling men and the grain baskets, sought desperately for a way of escape, but there was none. Behind the baskets rose the stone wall; blocking him in front were the two soldiers. He turned hopelessly to the load.

As he did so, the worried one shook his head, motioned for his antagonist to have his way in the argument, and reached for a roll of bedding. Marshaling every ounce of strength in his young body, the boy at last managed to lift the load from the ground, and the three followed in the path of the others.

Darkness was softening the outlines of the street. It covered from curious eyes a pitiful bundle of rags which lay quietly in the hollow space made by the right angle of two compound walls. The body within the rags would not again handle a load-pole; as for its family—they would have to find some other way of earning rice. Chungking's great wealth did not prevent most of her inhabitants from living always on the verge of starvation.

To the fourteen-year-old boy now attempting to carry the load which the dead man had laid down, each movement was torture. Sweat poured from him, and his heart responded with

increasingly painful thuds. Every few paces he was compelled
to halt, release his neck for the moment from the weight, and
fill his exhausted lungs. Shop fronts were closed and the streets
almost deserted. If it were day, he might appeal for help, though
this was a small hope. Who in this city, however kind of heart,
would consider him of sufficient importance to risk a quarrel
with soldiers about him? Dully he went on, moving more slowly
each moment. At last, the soldier ordered him to stop, and
bowing over his load for this brief respite, Young Fu waited
for the next word.

A loud guffaw roused him to the presence of others. He
looked up to see soldiers all about him. They filled a whole
section of shops, sitting about tables eating, gambling, loud in
discussion. He had heard that the army had quarters in one
end of the city, but he had not seen them for himself. He was
seeing them now and, perhaps, for the last time, for they would
surely kill him—if not by rifle, then by forcing him to bear
burdens like this one.

Several men rose and moved closer. There was more harsh
laughter followed by speech. "Lin steals the newborn from their
mothers to carry grain for him!"

"Where did you find that rice?"

"Look, the babe faints by the load!"

Young Fu struggled to command his senses. His head was
whirling.

"What shall I do with him?" asked Lin, now surly over the
amusement at his expense.

"Do with him? Send him away. Do you think our captain
would let you keep him here for your slave? A year ago, perhaps, but now he wishes to win the favor of the new government at Nanking, and they have foolish ideas about children
and law-abiding citizens. Law-abiding citizens! If I had my
way, these greedy Chungkingese would be relieved of some
of their treasure. Such food as they give—they would starve
their defenders!" The speaker sifted rice through his fingers.
"This is good grain you have brought in, Lin. Where did you
get it?"

"From a grain merchant, naturally."

The youth, strength flowing back into his veins, seethed with indignation. He did not care if they killed him, he would tell where this liar had found the rice. He opened his lips to speak, but a hand pulled him swiftly to one side. In the shadow of a neighboring doorpost, the worried one, who had remained silent throughout this conversation, ordered sharply: "Close your mouth, young fool! I saw what you would do. Do you think it matters to my companions that a coolie died? Or that they would not kill you, if they wished? And had you spoken, your life would have paid for it. They would have feared the tale might later reach the captain, who desires a good name in this city and, in time, Nanking. Run, and run swiftly, before they realize that you are gone!"

For a second Young Fu stood where he was. "Why do you do this for me? Your heart is good!"

The other cursed the delay and pushed the boy along. "Because, fool, I was your age when they tore me from my father's house!" He watched the youth disappear, then stealing quietly away from Lin and the circle about him, he joined a group of soldiers several doors down the street.

After a weary hour of stumbling about unfamiliar thoroughfares, Young Fu found himself once more on Chair-Makers' Way. Before the doorway to Dai's house stood Fu Be Be and Wang Scholar. His mother was crying openly, and the old gentleman greeted him with grave concern. "Thy mother carries a heavy heart," he chided.

"Where have you been?" demanded Fu Be Be.

Her son sank down on the sill. "It was not my fault," he offered by way of explanation, and could say nothing more. He felt deathly sick. He rested his head on his arms and shook with chill.

Fu Be Be hovered above him. "Where is your pain?"

"A bowl of hot tea is what he needs now," suggested the scholar. "Later, he will be able to tell you what happened."

The mother rushed within and returned with the bowl of steaming liquid. Young Fu gulped it down. After a time he ceased shaking and Wang Scholar, aware that he could be of no further assistance, went to his room. In their own quarters the boy told the story. Fu Be Be wept.

When her son was safe in bed, she went through the doorway and down the street to a small, bare space where there was erected a shrine to Kwan Yin, the Goddess of Mercy. On the pungent, gray curls of smoke that ascended from lighted incense, she offered her gratitude to the kindly looking little statue within. In the future she must remember to be more faithful about these offices; experiences such as her son had known this night were common to a great city. How she disliked the place with its crowds and noise!

As for her work with the bristles! She caught her breath. She must not be ungrateful. Her work meant food. And her son was learning fast. The more she heard of his master, Tang, the better satisfied she was about the apprenticeship. And her own unpleasant work was a small affair when she remembered from what grave danger her son had just been saved. She stopped in the middle of the road; she had neglected to ask Kwan Yin's special protection for that soldier. Hastily she retraced her steps to the shrine.

Young Fu of the Upper Yangtze *was awarded the Newbery Medal in 1933. Mrs. Lewis has also written an absorbing story of a modern Chinese girl in* Ho-Ming, Girl of New China, *published by Holt, Rinehart and Winston.*

Alas! Poor Annabelle!

BY CAROL RYRIE BRINK

Illustrations by Kate Seredy

Caddie Woodlawn was a real little girl who grew up on the Wisconsin frontier, riding horseback and making friends with the Indians. Naturally, she was a terrific tomboy, as Annabelle, her stylish cousin from Boston, found out very quickly when she came to Wisconsin for a visit.

THERE were rains after that and things grew green again. And presently it was time for cousin Annabelle to arrive on the Little Steamer. Mrs. Hyman and Katie had come out to help make the girls' new summer dresses, and Clara and Mother had been in their element, turning the pages of the *Godey's Lady's Book* and talking of muslin, bodices, buttons, and braids.

"Of course," said Clara sadly, "anything we can make her will be sure to be six months behind the fashions in Boston, to say the least; and I do wish I might have hoops for every day."

"I don't!" cried Caddie. "Good gracious, every time I sit down in hoops they fly up and hit me in the nose!"

"That's because you don't know how to manage them," said Clara. "There's an art to wearing hoops, and I suppose you're too much of a tomboy ever to learn it."

"I suppose so," said Caddie cheerfully. But to herself she added: "I'm not really so much of a tomboy as they think. Perhaps I *shall* wear hoops some day, but only when I get good and ready."

Then one day Cousin Annabelle came. The Little Steamer seemed full of her little round-topped trunks and boxes, and, after they had all been carried off, down the gangplank tripped

Annabelle Grey herself in her tiny buttoned shoes, with her tiny hat tilted over her nose and its velvet streamers floating out behind. Clara and Caddie had been allowed to come with Mother and Father to meet her, and Caddie suddenly felt all clumsy hands and feet when she saw this delicate apparition.

"Dearest Aunty Harriet, what a pleasure this is!" cried Annabelle in a voice as cultivated as her penmanship. "And this is Uncle John? And these the little cousins? How quaint and rustic it is here! But, just a moment, let me count my boxes. There ought to be seven. Yes, that's right. They're all here. Now we can go."

Father piled the seven boxes in the back of the wagon and Clara and Caddie climbed in on top of them, while Annabelle sat between Mother and Father, her full skirts billowing over their knees. Above the rattle of the wagon wheels her cultivated voice ran on and on. Clara leaned forward to catch what they were saying and sometimes put in a word of her own, but Caddie sat tongue-tied and uncomfortable, conscious only of her own awkwardness and of a sharp lock on one of Annabelle's boxes which hurt her leg whenever they went over a bump.

When they reached the farm Hetty, Minnie, and the boys ran out and stood in a smiling row beside the wagon. Tom held baby Joe in his arms.

"Dear me!" said Cousin Annabelle, "are these children all yours, Aunty Harriet?"

"There are only seven," said Mother, "and every one is precious."

"Of course! Mother told me there were seven. But they do look such a lot when one sees them all together, don't they?"

"I picked you a nosegay," said Hetty, holding out a rather wilted bunch of flowers which she had been clutching tightly in her warm hands for a long time.

"How very thoughtful of you, little girl," said Annabelle. "But do hold it for me, won't you? I should hate to stain my mitts. You've no idea what a dirty journey this has been, and what difficulty I have had in keeping clean."

"You look very sweet and fresh, my dear," said Mother, "but I'm sure that you must be tired. Come in and take a cup of tea."

Caddie stayed outside a moment to put a quick arm about

Hetty's shoulders. "That was an awful pretty nosegay you made, anyway, Hetty," she said.

Hetty's downcast face suddenly shone bright again. "Yes, it was, wasn't it, Caddie? Would you like it?"

"Why, yes, I would. I think it would look real nice here on my new dress, don't you?"

"Oh, it would be lovely, Caddie!"

That evening everyone listened to Annabelle telling about Boston. Mother's eyes shone and her cheeks were pinker than usual. It had been a good many years now since she had seen one of her own kin direct from home. Now she could find out whether Grandma Grey's rheumatism was really better or whether they only wrote that to reassure her. She could find out what pattern of silk Cousin Kitty had chosen for her wedding gown, who had been lecturing in Boston this winter, what new books had come out since the end of the war, why Aunt Phœbe had forgotten to write to her, and a hundred other things that she longed to know, but could never get them to put into letters. From time to time Father glanced at her happy face, over the old newspapers which Annabelle had brought him. It was only at moments such as this that Father understood how much Mother had given up when she left Boston to come with him to Wisconsin.

But after an hour or so of Boston gossip, Tom grew restless. Both he and Caddie were well tired of Annabelle's city airs.

"Well, I guess Boston's a pretty good place all right, but how about Dunnville?" Tom said.

Cousin Annabelle's silvery laughter filled the room. "Why, Tom, Boston is one of the world's great cities—the only one I'd care to live in, I am sure; and Dunnville—well, it's just too quaint and rustic, but it isn't even on the maps yet."

"Why, Tom," echoed Hetty seriously, "you hadn't ought to have said that. I guess Boston is just like—like Heaven, Tom." Everyone burst out laughing at this, and Cousin Annabelle rose and shook out her flounces, preparatory to going to bed.

"But really, Tom," she said, "I want you to show me *everything* in your savage country. I want to be just as *uncivilized* as you are while I am here. I shall learn to ride horseback and milk the cows—and—and salt the sheep, if that is what you do—and—turn somersaults in the haymow—and—what else do you do?"

"Oh, lots of things," said Tom, and suddenly there was an impish twinkle in his eyes.

"And you, Caroline," said Annabelle, turning to Caddie. "I suppose that you do all of those amusing things, too?"

"Yes, I'm afraid I do, Cousin Annabelle," replied Caddie. She tried to avoid Tom's eyes, but somehow it seemed impossible, and for just an instant an impish twinkle in her own met and danced with the impish twinkle in Tom's.

"You must begin to teach me to-morrow," said Annabelle sweetly. "I'm sure that it will be most interesting, and now, if you will excuse me, I am really quite fatigued."

"Yes, of course, dear Annabelle, and you're to sleep with me," said Clara, linking her arm through Annabelle's and leading her upstairs.

The next morning Tom, Caddie, and Warren had a brief consultation behind the straw stack. They ran through the list of practical jokes which they were used to playing when Uncle Edmund was among them.

"We can make up better ones than most of those," said Tom confidently. "It'll do her good."

"Let's see," said Caddie dreamily. "She wants to ride horseback and salt the sheep and turn somersaults in the haymow. Yes, I think that we can manage."

"Golly! What fun!" chirped Warren, turning a handspring.

When they entered the house, Annabelle had just come bouncing down the stairs, resolved upon being uncivilized for the day. She wore a beautiful new dress which was of such a novel style and cut that Mother and Clara could not admire it enough. Up and down both front and back of the fitted bodice was a row of tiny black jet buttons that stood out and sparkled at you when you looked at them.

"Golly!" said Warren, "you don't need all those buttons to fasten up your dress, do you?"

"Of course not," laughed Annabelle. "They are for decoration. All the girls in Boston are wearing them now, but none of them have as many buttons as I have. I have eight and eighty, and that's six more than Bessie Beaseley and fourteen more than Mary Adams."

"You don't say!" said Tom, and once again he and Caddie exchanged a twinkling glance.

"When shall I have my riding lesson?" asked Annabelle after breakfast.

"Right away, if you like," said Caddie pleasantly.

Clara stayed to help Mother, and Minnie was playing with baby Joe, but Hetty came with the others.

"Hadn't you better stay with Mother, Hetty?" said Tom in his kindest voice.

But, no, Hetty wanted to see the riding lesson.

Annabelle chattered vivaciously of how much better everything was done in Boston, while Tom went into the barn to bring out the horse.

"Why, Tom," cried Hetty, when he returned, "that's not Betsy, that's Pete."

Pete was perfectly gentle in appearance, but he had one trick which had kept the children off his back for several years.

"Hetty," said Caddie firmly, "we must have perfect quiet while anyone is learning to ride. If you can't be perfectly quiet, we'll have to send you right back to the house."

"I suppose he bucks," said Cousin Annabelle. "All Western horses do, don't they? Shall I be hurt?"

"He's pretty gentle," said Tom. "You better get on and you'll find out."

"Bareback and astride?" quavered Annabelle. "Dear me! how quaint and rustic!"

Caddie and Tom helped her on.

"He hasn't started bucking yet," said Annabelle proudly. "I *knew* that I should be a good rider!"

"Just touch him with the switch a little," advised Tom.

At the touch of the switch, Pete swung into a gentle canter, but instead of following the road, he made for a particular shed at the back of the barn. It was Pete's one accomplishment.

"How do I pull the rein to make him go the other way?" queried Annabelle, but already Pete was gathering momentum and, before they could answer, he had swung in under the low

shed, scraped Annabelle neatly off into the dust, and was standing peacefully at rest inside the shed picking up wisps of hay.

Annabelle sat up in a daze. The little straw sun hat which she
had insisted on wearing was over one ear and she looked very
comical indeed.

"I don't yet understand what happened," she said politely. "I
thought that I was going along so well. In Boston, I'm sure the
horses never behave like that."

"Would you like to try another horse?" said Tom.

"Oh no!" said Annabelle hastily. "Not to-day, at least. Couldn't
we go and salt the sheep now, perhaps?"

"Do you think we could, Tom?" asked Caddie doubtfully.

"Why, yes, I believe we could," said Tom kindly. "Here let me
help you up, Cousin Annabelle."

"I'll get the salt," shouted Warren, racing into the barn.

Hetty looked on in silence, her eyes round with surprise.
Annabelle rose, a bit stiffly, and brushed the back of her beautiful dress.

"She's not a cry-baby at any rate," thought Caddie to herself.
"Maybe it's kind of mean to play another trick on her."

But Warren had already returned with the salt, and he and
Tom, with Annabelle between them, were setting out for the
woodland pasture where Father kept the sheep. Caddie hastened to catch up with them, and Hetty, still wondering, tagged
along behind.

"Will they eat out of my hand, if I hold it for them?" asked
Annabelle, taking the chunk of salt from Warren.

"Sure," said Tom, "they're crazy about salt."

"But you mustn't *hold* it," said Hetty, coming up panting. "You
must lay it down where the sheep can get it."

"Now, Hetty," said Caddie, "what did I tell you about keeping
perfectly quiet?"

"You do just as you like, Annabelle," said Tom kindly.

"Well, of course," said Annabelle, "I should prefer to hold it
and let the cunning little lambs eat it right out of my hands."

"All right," said Tom, "you go in alone then, and we'll stay
outside the fence here where we can watch you."

"It's so nice of you to let me do it," said Cousin Annabelle.
"How do you call them?"

Tom uttered a low persuasive call—the call to salt. He uttered it two or three times, and sheep began coming from all parts of the woods into the open pasture.

Annabelle stood there expectantly, holding out the salt, a bright smile on her face. "We don't have sheep in Boston," she said. But almost immediately the smile began to fade.

The sheep were crowding all around her, so close that she could hardly move; they were treading on her toes and climbing on each other's backs to get near her. Frightened, she held the salt up out of their reach, and then they began to try to climb up *her* as if she had been a ladder. There was a perfect pandemonium of bleating and baaing, and above this noise rose Annabelle's despairing shriek.

"Drop the salt and run," called Tom, himself a little frightened at the success of his joke. But running was not an easy matter with thirty or forty sheep around her, all still believing that she held the salt. At last poor Annabelle succeeded in breaking away and they helped her over the fence. But, when she was safe on the other side, everybody stopped and looked at her in amazement. The eight and eighty sparkling jet buttons had disappeared from her beautiful frock. The sheep had eaten them!

"Oh! my buttons!" cried Annabelle. "There were eight and eighty of them—six more than Bessie Beaseley had! And where is my sun hat?"

Across the fence in the milling crowd of sheep, the wicked Woodlawns beheld with glee Annabelle's beautiful sun hat rakishly dangling from the left horn of a fat old ram.

If Annabelle had rushed home crying and told Mother, the Woodlawn children would not have been greatly surprised. But there seemed to be more in Annabelle than met the eye.

"What a quaint experience!" she said. "They'll hardly believe it when I tell them about it in Boston." Her voice was a trifle shaky, but just as polite as ever, and she went right upstairs, without speaking to Clara or Mother, and changed to another dress. That evening she was more quiet than she had been the night before and she had almost nothing to say about the superiority of her native city over the rest of the uncivilized world. Caddie noticed with remorse that Annabelle walked a little stiffly, and she surmised that the ground had not been very soft at the place where Pete had scraped her off.

"I wish I hadn't promised Tom to play that next trick on her," Caddie thought to herself. "Maybe he'll let me off."

But Tom said, no, it was a good trick and Annabelle had asked for it, and Caddie had promised to do her part, and she had better go through with it.

"All right," said Caddie.

After all it *was* a good trick and Annabelle *had* asked for it.

"Let's see," said Tom the next day. "You wanted to turn somersaults in the haymow, didn't you, Cousin Annabelle?"

"Well, I suppose that's one of the things one always does on a farm, isn't it?" said Cousin Annabelle, a trifle less eagerly than she had welcomed their suggestions of the day before. The beautiful eight-and-eighty-button dress had not appeared to-day. Annabelle had on a loose blouse over a neat, full skirt.

"Of course, I never turn somersaults in Boston, you understand. It's so very quaint and rustic."

"Of course, we understand that," said Caddie.

"But out here where you have lots of hay——"

"It's bully fun!" yelled Warren.

"Now, Hetty," directed Tom, "you better stay at home with
Minnie. A little girl like you might fall down the ladder to the
mow and hurt herself."

"Me fall down the haymow ladder?" demanded Hetty in
amazement. "Why, Tom Woodlawn, you're just plumb crazy!"

"Well, run into the house then and fetch us some cookies,"
said Tom, anxious to be rid of Hetty's astonished eyes and
tattling tongue. Hetty departed reluctantly with a deep conviction that she was missing out on something stupendous.

When she returned a few moments later with her hands full
of cookies, she could hear them all laughing and turning somersaults in the loft above. She made haste to climb the ladder and
peer into the loft. It was darkish there with dust motes dancing
in the rays of light that entered through the chinking. But
Hetty could see quite plainly, and what she saw was Caddie
slipping an egg down the back of Annabelle's blouse, just as
Annabelle was starting to turn a somersault.

"I can turn them every bit as well as you can already," said
Annabelle triumphantly, and then she turned over, and then
she sat up with a surprised and stricken look upon her face, and
then she began to cry!

"Oh, it's squishy!" she sobbed. "You're horrid and mean. I
didn't mind falling off the horse or salting the sheep, but oh,
this—this—*this* is *squishy!*"

Hetty climbed down from the haymow and ran to the house
as fast as she could go.

"Mother, if you want to see something, you just come here
with me as fast as you can," she cried.

On the way to the barn she gave Mrs. Woodlawn a brief but
graphic account of the riding lesson and the sheep salting.
When they reached the haymow, Annabelle was still sobbing.

"Oh, Aunty Harriet!" she cried. "I don't know what it is, but
it's squishy. I can't—oh dear! I *can't* bear squishy things!"

"You poor child!" said Mrs. Woodlawn, examining the back

of Annabelle's blouse, and then, in an ominous voice, she announced: "It's egg." With a good deal of tenderness Mother got Annabelle to the house and put her into Clara's capable hands. Then she turned with fury on the three culprits. But it was Caddie whom she singled out for punishment.

"Caroline Woodlawn, stand forth!" she cried. Caddie obeyed. "It was only a joke, Mother," she said in a quivering voice. Mrs. Woodlawn took a little riding whip which hung behind the kitchen door and struck Caddie three times across the legs.

"Now go to your bed and stay until morning. You shall have no supper."

"Ma, it was as much my fault as hers," cried Tom, his ruddy face gone white.

"No, Tom," said Mrs. Woodlawn. "I cannot blame *you* so much. But that a *daughter* of mine should so far forget herself in her hospitality to a guest—that she should be such a hoyden as to neglect her proper duties as a lady! Shame to her! Shame! No punishment that I can invent would be sufficient for her."

As Caddie went upstairs, she saw Father standing in the kitchen door and she knew that he had witnessed her disgrace. But she knew, too, that he would do nothing to soften the sentence which Mother had spoken, for it was an unwritten family law that one parent never interfered with the justice dealt out by the other.

For hours Caddie tossed about on her bed. The upper room was hot and close, but an even hotter inner fire burned in Caddie. She had some of her mother's quick temper, and she was stung by injustice. She would have accepted punishment without question if it had been dealt out equally to the boys. But the boys had gone free! All the remorse and the resolves to do better, which had welled up in her as soon as she had seen Annabelle's tears, were dried up now at the injustice of her punishment. Hot and dry-eyed, she tossed about on the little bed where she had spent so many quiet hours. At last she got up and tied a few things which she most valued into a towel. She put them under the foot of her mattress and lay down again. Later she would slip down to the kitchen and get a loaf of bread and Father's old water bottle which she would fill at the spring. At least they could not begrudge her that much.

They would soon cease to miss her. Perhaps they would adopt Annabelle in her place.

Her anger cooled a little in the fever of making plans. It would have been much easier if she had known just where the Indians were. But at this season the woods were full of berries and there would soon be nuts. John's dog would protect her and she could live a long time in the woods until she could join the Indians. She knew that they would take her in, and then she would never have to grow into that hateful thing which Mother was always talking about—a lady. A lady with fine airs and mincing walk who was afraid to go out into the sun without a hat or a sunshade! A lady, who made samplers and wore stays and was falsely polite no matter how she felt!

A soft blue twilight fell, and still Caddie tossed, hot, resentful, and determined. There was the clatter of supper dishes down below, and no one relented enough to send her a bite of bread. A velvet darkness followed the twilight and, through the window, summer stars began to twinkle. Presently Hetty and Minnie came up to bed. Hetty came and stood by Caddie's bed and looked at her. Caddie could feel the long, wistful look, but she did not stir or open her eyes. Hetty was a tattle-tale. It was torture to have to lie so still, but at last the little sisters were breathing the regular breath of sleep, and Caddie could toss and turn again as much as she pleased. She must keep awake now until the house was all still and the lights out, and then she would be free to run away. Her heart beat fast, and with every beat something hot and painful seemed to throb in her head. A cooler breeze began to come in at the window. How long it took the house to grow quiet to-night! How tiresome they were! They wouldn't even go to bed and let her run away!

Then the door creaked a little on its hinges, there was a glimmer of candlelight, and Father came in. He went first and looked at Minnie and Hetty. He put a lock of hair back from Minnie's forehead and pulled the sheet up over Hetty's shoulder. Then he came and stood by Caddie's bed. She lay very still with tightly closed eyes so that Father should think her asleep. It had fooled Hetty, but Father knew more than most people did. He put the candle down and sat on the side of the bed and took one of Caddie's hot hands in his cool ones. Then he began to speak in his nice quiet voice, without asking her to wake up or open her eyes or look at him.

"Perhaps Mother was a little hasty to-day, Caddie," he said. "She really loves you very much, and, you see, she expects more of you than she would of someone she didn't care about. It's a strange thing, but somehow we expect more of girls than of boys. It is the sisters and wives and mothers, you know, Caddie, who keep the world sweet and beautiful. What a rough world it would be if there were only men and boys in it, doing things in their rough way! A woman's task is to teach them gentleness and courtesy and love and kindness. It's a big task, too, Caddie—harder than cutting trees or building mills or damming rivers. It takes nerve and courage and patience, but good women have those things. They have them just as much as the men who build bridges and carve roads through the wilderness. A woman's work is something fine and noble to grow up to, and it is just as important as a man's. But no man could ever do it so well. I don't want you to be the silly, affected person with fine clothes and manners, whom folks sometimes call a lady. No, that is not what I want for you, my little girl. I want you to be a woman with a wise and understanding heart, healthy in body and honest in mind. Do you think you would like to be growing up into that woman now? How about it, Caddie, have we run with the colts long enough?"

There was a little silence, and the hot tears which had not wanted to come all day were suddenly running down Caddie's cheeks unheeded into the pillow.

"You know, Caddie," added Father gently and half-apologetically, "you know I'm sort of responsible for you, Honey. I was the one who urged Mother to let you run wild, because I thought it was the finest way to make a splendid woman of you. And I still believe that, Caddie."

Suddenly Caddie flung herself into Mr. Woodlawn's arms. "Father! Father!"

It was all she could say, and really there was nothing more that needed saying. Mr. Woodlawn held her a long time, his rough beard pressed against her cheek. Then with his big hands, which were so delicate with clockwork, he helped her

to undress and straighten the tumbled bed. Then he kissed her again and took his candle and went away. And now the room was cool and pleasant again, and even Caddie's tears were not unpleasant, but part of the cool relief she felt. In a few moments she was fast asleep.

But something strange had happened to Caddie in the night. When she awoke she knew that she need not be afraid of growing up. It was not just sewing and weaving and wearing stays. It was something more thrilling than that. It was a responsibility, but, as Father spoke of it, it was a beautiful and precious one, and Caddie was ready to go and meet it. She looked at the yellow sunshine on the floor and she knew that she had slept much longer than she usually did. Both Hetty's and Minnie's beds were empty, but as soon as Caddie began to stir around, Hetty came in as if she had been waiting outside the door.

"Oh, say, Caddie," she said, "I'm awful sorry I went and told on you yesterday. Honest, I am. I never thought you'd get it so hard, and I'll tell you what, I'm not going to be a tattler ever any more, I'm not. But, say, Caddie, I wanted to be the first to tell you Father took Tom and Warren out to the barn yesterday afternoon and he gave 'em both a thrashing. He said it wasn't fair that you should have all the punishment when the same law had always governed you all, and Tom said so, too, although he yelled good and plenty when he was being thrashed."

"It's all right, Hetty," said Caddie. "I guess we won't be playing any more silly jokes on people."

"What's this?" asked Hetty, pulling at the corner of a queer bundle that stuck out under the corner of Caddie's mattress. Out came a knotted towel with an odd assortment of Caddie's treasures rattling around inside.

"Oh, that!" said Caddie, untying the knots and putting the things away. "Those are just some things I was looking at yesterday when I had to stay up here alone."

Caddie Woodlawn *was awarded the Newbery Medal in 1936. There are more exciting stories about Caddie in* Magical Melons, *also published by Macmillan, which covers the years 1863 to 1866.*

The Kid from Tomkinsville

BY JOHN R. TUNIS

Illustrations by Jay Hyde Barnum

Roy Tucker, the kid from a small town who was born to play baseball, makes his way up from the rank of a rookie to that of a big-time player in a major league. But Roy discovers that the grind never ends and staying on top is even tougher than getting there.

USUALLY the dressing room before a game was a noisy spot. Not this time. Usually there were shouts of laughter, loud calls for the Doc or old Chiselbeak. Not this time. Usually there was horseplay and wisecracks too. But not that afternoon. Already, an hour before the game, the team had been obliged to fight their way through a mob outside the gates to reach the locker-room entrance, and the ticket sale had stopped at every box office. So it was a grim and tight-lipped crowd of boys who started getting ready for the last game of all, the game on which the season and the pennant depended.

Everyone attended to the business of dressing with determination and despatch. Now they were sitting round, tying the final shoelace and doing those last-minute things that have to be done before taking the field. A few were glancing carelessly at newspapers, others were nervously chewing gum or staring at the floor, a few were rubbing oil into the pockets of well-oiled gloves. Overhead on three sides of the big room where no one who entered could possibly miss them, Chiselbeak had tacked three large printed signs.

"THE TEAM THAT BEATS BROOKLYN WILL WIN THE PENNANT." It was Murphy's wisecrack when the season opened, come back to roost in the visitors' dressing room at the Polo Grounds.

Roy, tense and tightened like the rest, sat on the bench before

46

his locker and tried to read Casey's column in the early edition
of the afternoon paper. The words of the chunky sportswriter
danced before his eyes, and he found himself obliged to read
and reread sentence after sentence to get their meaning.

"Well, lads, you could have knocked me over with a Flatbush
trolley yesterday. The Dodgers are on the move again. More
than that, they come to the final game of the season in the one
place baseball wouldn't expect to find them, half a game behind
Murphy's Giants. Don't ask me how they've done it. The team
that looked like a joke in fourth place a few weeks ago suddenly snapped out of it and started to function. Nothing could
stop them. In succession they whaled the Pirates and then the
Cubs, took two out of three from the Cards and in the last two
games against the league leaders they've battered four Giant
hurlers from one end of the Polo Grounds to the other.

"The Brooklyns are fielding and they're hitting also. Roy
Tucker, for instance. Three weeks ago the Connecticut farm
boy was just another guy named Joe, and then after going fifteen
games without a hit he silenced the fans as he used to, getting
a single and two doubles out of three times at bat against the
Pirates. Since then he hasn't gone hitless in a single game. The
Kid from Tomkinsville is pretty far behind in home runs now,
but he's hitting .325 and he's bringing in runs in that second
slot. So is Swanson, so is big Babe Stansworth, a pretty reliable
man behind the bat.

"The pitchers are all in one piece at last and they are pitching
heads-up ball. Dodger pitching all summer has been good; last
two weeks it's been sensational. That combination of Street
and Davis around second base is just about the best in the
League. You think you've got the team in a hole and then one
of them comes up with a doubleplay ball that nips a rally and
saves another game. This rookie Street is one of the main fac-
tors in the Dodgers' sudden rush to the front. You look up to
see him behind second on one grounder and somewhere back
of third on the next. They ought to put a cowbell on his neck
so folks can tell where he is. Honest, the way this ballclub is
going now would bring tears to the eyes of a rocking horse."

That wasn't all. But the door banged and everyone jumped. It
was Dave followed by MacManus, strangely quiet and calm.

Dave had a ball in his hands, slapping it from one fist to the other as the Kid's paper slid to the floor and he rose with the others, ready to go. MacManus stepped forward. Taking off his eyeglasses, he twirled them in his hand. His voice was low.

"Just want to say one thing. I've been in this game ever since I left college and played semi-pro ball up in northern Michigan, and I never seen a better fight or a finer ballclub than this one. I hope you win today. Gosh, I sure hope you win. I want to see you go in there next week in the Series and trim those Yanks the way you did in the exhibition games last year, and I think you can do it, too. But whether you win or lose this afternoon . . . I'm for you . . . all . . . everyone . . . understand? . . .

"One thing more. The manager of the team we play today doesn't think much of Brooklyn. Maybe you remember the crack he made to Casey the sportswriter several weeks ago when we were in that slump in fourth place. He said . . ." For the first time his voice became vibrant and there was passion in his tone. "He said, 'Is Brooklyn . . . still . . . in the League?'

"Don't forget that crack out on the field today."

There was silence for a few seconds when no one seemed to breathe. Then they turned and went out for the last time, a team that three weeks previously had been in fourth place and now, half a game behind the leaders, was fighting for the pennant.

Clack-clack, clackety-clack, clack-clack their spikes sounded on the concrete runway leading to the field.

The crowd rose with a roar as the first man appeared at the entrance of the runway. There they are, there they are . . . the Dodgers!

Sixty thousand frenzied human beings packed the stands behind the plate, jammed into the upper tier which encircled the playing field, stood up two or three deep in the rear. A sell-out. A sell-out at the Polo Grounds. Not for the Series itself could another person have jammed in. Because sport offers no more inspiring spectacle than the man or the team who comes back, who takes the cracks of fate and pulls together to rise once more. Down-and-out, the Dodgers were on the way back. And the roars of the throng which beat about their ears was proof of the tribute of the fans.

While they spread upon the field, another but a derisive cry arose. It had a jeering, taunting note; it was bitter and it was hostile because it came from the Brooklyn crowd behind third, many of whom had been in line all night. Like a wave it rose, fell, rose again, stomp . . . stomp . . . stomp . . . as the men with GIANTS on their shirts took the diamond.

"IS BROOKLYN . . . STILL . . . IN THE LEAGUE? . . . IS BROOKLYN . . . STILL . . . IN THE LEAGUE? . . ."

A roar of sound swept into the quiet and orderly living room on the farm. It was late September and there was a chill in the air, and Grandma was sitting before the radio with a cup of tea in her lap. Tea without milk, too. Tea without milk in the late afternoon always kept her awake, but that redoubtable old lady felt the need of something strong. Tea without milk was the strongest thing she could think of. That roar filled the room, it swelled and grew, as Grandma, the tea in her lap, her face flushed, rocked back and forth.

The telephone rang.

For a moment Grandma sat there, then with decision marched into the other room and, taking the receiver off the hook, set it face down on the table. The jangling of the bell instantly stopped and a voice from the radio came into the room.

". . . yes, folks, and believe me, that one run looks big, awfully big right now . . . and here comes Tucker, 'Bad News Tucker' as the boys call him because he's been breaking up so many ball games with that little old stick of his; just hear those fans give him a hand; yep, even the Giant rooters . . ." And once again the noise echoed across the room in that little Connecticut farmhouse.

"Moe Kleinert looks round the diamond . . . he brings up his leg . . . throws . . . and it's a strike! Strike one against Roy Tucker, men on first and third, one out and the Dodgers leading by a single run in the first half of the fourth inning, and *is* this crowd nuts? Listen to 'em howl. Half of 'em want Tucker to crack it and the other half don't. There it goes . . . there it goes . . . a beautiful single into right . . . Tucker slaps a single into right sending Davis across with run number two." The noise drowned out his voice, the noise beat against the walls of the little room, and the announcer was silent for several seconds.

"Yeah . . . there he comes . . . there comes Manager Murphy in from third . . . yep, Kleinert's going out . . . Moe Kleinert, the Giant pitcher, is knocked out of the box, as the second Dodger run comes over with Tucker's clean single, the fourth this inning. That means two runs on four hits, both runs earned. Men on third and first . . . and . . . one out . . . le's see who's coming in . . . I think it's Delaney . . . no, it's Honeyman, Sam Honeyman, the star lefty of the Giants who won twenty-two games this season. He's taken four and only dropped one to the Dodgers. But those two runs sure do look big right now . . . here goes Kleinert . . . Moe Kleinert going to the showers . . .

and Red Allen, the Dodger first baseman, swinging two bats in his hand comes to the plate."

Watching the game from the stands, from the press quarters, or from his own box just back of the Dodger dugout, was impossible. The strain was too much, so MacManus paced up and down in a small office back of the press box, which had been assigned him for the three days of the Series. Every once in a while he stepped through a corridor and into the press coop where he looked down over the heads of the newspapermen at work, onto the field. Onto Razzle hitching his trousers and stuffing in his shirt with that familiar gesture, onto Harry Street dancing around at second, and Roy Tucker nervously fingering his cap in right, at Eddie Davis scooping up dirt with his fingers back of second. At Babe behind the plate, at the outfield shifting a little to the left as Dave from the bench moved them around for each batter. He wanted this game, Mac did, he wanted it as he had never wanted anything in his life before. Mustn't let the boys know and that was one reason for keeping away from the field.

". . . so coming into the eighth, and old Razzle looks kinder tired out there on the mound . . . it's two to one for Brooklyn, two men out, men on first and third, and Muscles Mulligan, the Giant first baseman, at the plate." From his little office Mac-Manus snapped the dials of a small portable radio. He could have sat beside the announcer had he wished, but that would have meant being too close. It was easier like this.

"Here's the pitch . . . low and inside . . . ball ONE. The infield's playing a little to the right . . . here it comes . . . IT'S A HIT . . ." The roar drowned his voice; it came over the radio and it also came through the closed door, telling the stocky freckled-faced man of disaster. He stood in the middle of the room, sweat coming out on his forehead. "Mayerson is coming in with the tying run . . . Ronsek going round second . . . coming into third . . . he's going home . . . he's trying for home . . . he made it . . . another run and Muscles takes second on the throw-in."

The noise of sixty thousand insane spectators again blanketed the announcer's voice. The Giants were ahead, three to two, and the man alone in the room passed his fingers across his wet forehead. "And there goes old Razzle . . . the crowd's giving him a great hand . . . but Nugent is tired . . . just plain tired . . . Leonard's pitchers haven't had enough rest these last few weeks, they're beginning to feel the strain . . . and here comes a relief pitcher from the bullpen . . . wait a minute . . . I can't see . . . yes, it's Leonard's star, Elmer McCaffrey, in for Razzle Nugent, with the Giants leading three to two, one out and a man on second, the last of the eighth. We now pause for station identification."

Down on the sunbaked field Roy kept repeating those words he had been saying to himself all through the game. Until the last out . . . on the last afternoon of the season. Ever since he'd heard that sentence on the day Dave took a chance and shoved him into the line-up again, the Kid had repeated it. Dave was right, Dave was certainly right. It was the ninth. One man was out and the Dodgers were a run behind. But the season wasn't over until the last out. . . .

Up and down the dugout their voices came as he walked up to the plate.

"Now, Roy old boy, old kid. . . ."

"You can do it, Roy. . . ."

"Save me a rap, Roy. . . ."

Maguire, the Giant catcher, stood watching and noticed something strange. It looked as if he was whistling. Even through the noise and roar from the stands he heard a distinct whistle. As the Kid came close he heard . . . *Yankee Doodle.* That Dodger rookie must be going nuts!

"Ball one." The welcome words from Stubblebeard behind the bat greeted his ears. He had to get on . . . had to get on . . . had to get on . . .

The next pitch. He took it. Ball two.

But the next was a strike and he stepped back to pick up some dirt and rub it on the moist palms of his hands, whistling as he did so. The catcher looked at him queerly.

"Ball three." Three and one. The cripple. Should he hit? This was the one to hit. What would he do in the pitcher's place—shoot it over, of course. This was the one, the one to hit. . . .

Crack!

He was off, for he felt in that ring a ball that had carry. The roar as he dashed down toward first told him it was safe, and everything he had, every ounce of nerve and sinew, went into his strain for an extra base. Old Cassidy was shouting, urging him on, but as he rounded the bag Muscles crowded him ever so little, gave him just enough of a body-check to jostle him and throw him completely off stride. He stumbled down the base-path, caught himself, and tore for second. Ten feet away he hit the dirt and with a hooked slide went into the bag. The ball was still in the fielder's hands as he rose, and but for Muscles' trick he would have had a good shot at third.

Red Allen came to the plate swinging two bats. Watching, the Kid saw Dave from the dugout give the steal signal with a bunt on the second pitch. Roy had been studying Honeyman all summer with the eyes of a former pitcher. The big left-hander had a peculiar delivery, and whenever he threw a ball to the batter he bent his front knee slightly from the normal position. From his toes, arms outstretched, the Kid concentrated on the man in the box, while the great crowd stood yelling passionately in the stands.

There it was. . . .

Down toward third, as Jerry dropped a slow rolling bunt along the base line. The play he knew would be for the out at first. Then as he dug hard into the dirt, a thought flashed through his mind. Here at last was his chance. Like lightning it came to him, the whole play, and here was the one perfect set-up for the thing he had been working on and waiting for ever since his fight with Muscles. This was the moment to take a chance. He raced round third with Charlie Draper on the coaching lines shouting at him to hold the bag. He was twenty-five feet down the path toward home when Muscles, expecting him as usual to turn and dart back for third, drew his arm to throw. Instead the Kid broke for the plate. Muscles bit completely, fired the ball to third, by which time Roy was almost at the plate. He went over standing up and the score was tied.

In her room on the second floor she sat sewing, the door half open. Downstairs the children had the radio on, but she preferred to be alone. Too much was at stake, too much depended on what happened over in the Polo Grounds that afternoon, and she felt she couldn't endure the strain of listening to the slow drama on the air.

"Mother! Mother!" The voice of a little girl at the foot of the stairs drowned for a moment the excited tones of the announcer.

"Mother! Motherrr . . . Daddy's going in!"

Her sewing dropped to the floor and she rushed downstairs as his voice filled the sunny living room.

". . . and Stansworth is standing there shaking his head . . . the fellow's in pain . . . Babe Stansworth got that foul tip right on the end of his throwing thumb . . . yes . . . he's chucked his mitt into the dirt . . . boy, does he hate to leave this ball game . . . yes, he sure hates to leave . . . and here comes the bat boy with Dave Leonard's favorite mask . . . Leonard, the

Dodger manager, man who pulled the Brooks into this amazing under-the-wire drive for the pennant, is going in. The thirty-nine-year-old catcher will take Stansworth's place behind the bat. . . . Just hear that roar. . . . Those fans are giving Dave a big hand as he slips the chest protector over his shoulders. . . . He pats Stansworth on the back . . . and now McCaffrey is throwing him a couple of balls, there goes a snap throw to second and a pretty good one too. . . . The veteran Dave Leonard, leading his own team at the end of this stirring contest, going into the thirteenth inning with the score still deadlocked at three-three. The whole field is in shadow now . . . this is Luke Cunningham bringing you the crucial game at the Polo Grounds between the Dodgers and the Giants over the Continental Broadcasting System thanks to the courtesy of Starlight Soap, S-T-A-R-L-I-G-H-T. . . ."

As the inning finished and the Kid trotted in from the field, he realized that Dave was right. He was always right, everlastingly right; Dave knew baseball like no one else. The season wasn't over until the last out on the last afternoon. It was the first of the fourteenth, and Roy, leaning on his bat and watching Swanny fly out to the field, realized again that in baseball the impossible could happen. Dave was right.

When he walked to the plate they rose all over the field cheering. Not for him. Why, only three weeks ago they were razzing him, and the boys in right over at Ebbets Field were booing him between innings. Now they were all for him, on account of that play in the ninth which tied the score, so he tipped his cap as he stepped into the box.

The pitcher went into the crouch. Low and inside for a ball. Another pitch, by his cap, and Stubblebeard behind the plate yelled,

"Ball two!"

Was the pitcher weakening? Outwardly Honeyman looked unruffled, but the Kid knew exactly how he felt and wasn't surprised to see a hand go to his hip in a gesture of fatigue. Here it was . . . he swung and missed a curve, a down and inner.

Two and one. The next was on the outside and in the dirt. He looked at it. Three and one; the cripple. The pitcher's leg went up and the ball came . . .

"Ball four." He slung his bat away and trotted to first while behind third the cry came.

"IS BROOKLYN . . . STILL . . . IN THE LEAGUE? . . . IS . . . BROOKLYN . . . STILL . . . IN THE LEAGUE? . . . IS BROOKLYN . . . STILL . . ."

Red Allen up. Old Cassidy back of first gave him the signal to go down on the second pitch. Muscles made no attempt to crowd him, but he took only a conservative lead until he saw that front knee bend, and then . . .

Crack! He was off as the batter swung, rounding second, tearing for third with everything he had. Reaching third he saw them urging him in, so head down he strained for the plate with the run which might win the game. Past third, closer, nearing home, closer, closer, and then ten feet away he saw the catcher waiting, arms open, so he hit the dirt as the ball plunked into the mitt. His momentum carried him ahead into the catcher's legs with such force that they rolled over and over together in the dust. While the ball fell hopping along the grass.

From the bleachers in center came the roar. It echoed back from the stands behind the dugout, bounced across from right field stands to left, fifty thousand humans concentrated on that play. The Kid was yanked to his feet by Harry Street, slapped

on the back by Karl Case, surrounded by the entire team who
emerged from the dugout, dancing and cheering with delight.
But Dave, who missed nothing, was cool in the midst of the
noise and excitement.

"Look at yourself, Roy. Go in and get that fixed quick now."

He glanced down at his trousers. There was a long tear on
one side and warm blood was oozing down his leg. He turned
for the dugout as Doc Masters rushed up and grabbed his arm.

"Come here, we gotta change those pants. Hurry up."

While Red Allen danced off second and Harry came to the
plate, the substitutes leaned around him on the bench and his
trousers were pulled off. Doc swabbed iodine over the wound,
a long nasty-looking cut on the upper part of his leg. Then
slapping a bandage over it, he pasted strips of tape across his
thigh. The cut throbbed painfully, but what did that matter?
They were ahead. Four to three. They were leading the Giants!
A minute later he was walking out to right again for the last
half of the fourteenth.

The first batter grounded out to Eddie who came up cleanly
and smoothly with the ball as if it were the first out of the opening inning. Only two more men to get! Next came a base on
balls. Like Honeyman, McCaffrey was tiring. The Kid knew the
signs and could see weariness in his pitching even from the
field. Why not? The pitcher had been in six games in two weeks,
been pitching for almost seven innings, his second game in
three days. McCaffrey was tiring and Dave realized it too. He
walked down the path in that feverish atmosphere as quiet and
calm as if he had been calling plays at Clearwater in practice.
The two whispered together and Dave went behind the bat.

Crack! On the first ball the batter struck deeply to left. Their
heads in their shoulders the two baserunners rounded the bags,
while Swanny and Karl hustled after the ball and Harry ran
far out behind short. By the time it was back there were men
on second and third and only one out. Now Dave's words came
back with an ominous significance. The race wasn't over until
the last out on the last afternoon of the season.

A roar rose from the stands. McCaffrey was leaving the game.

The big pitcher threw his glove disconsolately into the dirt
and walked in while the crowd stood yelling. Dave slapped him

on the shoulders and then through cupped hands yelled to the
bullpen. Through the din Fat Stuff waddled across the field.

Of all people, Fat Stuff! The Kid suddenly saw baseball as if
for the first time. The slow good-natured man whom he had
always rather pitied because he had only been used this season
as a relief pitcher and was on the way out. All summer he'd
been the man they sent for when star pitchers got into trouble.
Fat Stuff! Old Fat Stuff, the butt of everyone's jokes, patient,
smart, steady, Fat Stuff, of all people! It was Fat Stuff on whom
the whole season depended. Now he realized how important a
relief pitcher was when crisis came, what a vital cog he was in
that machine which is a winning ballclub.

"Foster, No. 6, pitching for McCaffrey, No. 30, for Brooklyn."

It was up to Fat Stuff.

Down above the lower meadow the sky darkened. Through
the kitchen window Grandma could see flashes of lightning in
the sky. She poured herself a cup of tea without milk and took
it back to the living room. The shadows were deepening in the
September twilight, but still that flood of words came from the
radio beside her rocking chair.

". . . friends, right now while Foster is taking his warm-up
pitches is a good time to ask you a question. *Would you turn
your back on a thousand dollars?* Of course not. And ten other
cash prizes of five dollars each. Remember the Starlight soap
contest is open to everyone, to all fans who simply tear off the
cover of a box of Starlight soap and send in the answer in one
sentence. WHY . . . I . . . LIKE STARLIGHT . . . SOAP . . . Because . . ." A terrific peal of thunder startled Grandma. She
jumped in her chair.

"That's all, no fancy writing necessary, anyone can do it. Remember, fans, you all have a chance and don't forget the name,
spelt S-T-A-R-L-I-G-H-T soap. Don't turn your back on a thousand
dollars. Well, here we go back to this great ball game, four to
three for the Dodgers in the last of the fourteenth, Muscles
Mulligan at the bat, the tying run on third, and the winning run
on second. Just hear the Giant fans give Foster the razoo."

Distinctly the noise came into the living room, fifty thousand
pairs of hands together:

Clap-clap, clap-clap, clap-clap, clap-clap.

"And here's the pitch . . . he takes it . . . ball two. Foster can't seem to find the plate." A roar filled the room, a roar that was only louder than the continuous background of sound that had been coming all through the last minutes. "Strike one . . . right . . . down . . . Broadway . . . for a called strike. . . ." Outside the lightning was brighter now and the thunder louder. Grandma looked anxiously round to see if all the windows were closed.

"Mulligan batting from a slight crouch . . . there it goes . . . a high twisting foul behind the plate . . . Leonard is after it . . . back . . . back . . . almost into the Giant dugout . . . the New York players are scattering in front of the bench . . . he has it . . . HE HAS IT . . . a wonderful catch . . . he turns and snaps to Foster at the plate to prevent McKinnon on third reaching home on the play. That was a wonderful catch, what the boys call a 'dilly.' Yessir, that old-timer is still in there. Two out, and the winning run on second, four to three for the Dodgers in the last of the fourteenth . . . and here comes Manager Murphy of the Giants . . . just hear those Dodger fans back of third there giving him the bird."

The cadence entered Grandma's somber living room.

"IS BROOKLYN . . . STILL . . . IN THE LEAGUE? . . . IS BROOKLYN . . . STILL . . . IN THE LEAGUE? . . . IS BROOKLYN . . . STILL . . ."

"Foster looks round . . . Brooklyn infield playing deep . . . the outfield slightly to the left . . . and deep . . . Foster trying to protect his one-run lead . . . here's the pitch. . . .

"Strike one! A beauty, right through the middle, and Murphy didn't offer at it." The roar rose higher. "Guess Murphy didn't think he had the nerve . . . here it comes . . . a ball. One and one. Across the letters, too high. One and one, two out, men on third and second, the last of the fourteenth. . . .

"Oh, it's a hit. It's a hit!" He was yelling, screaming almost, but the tumult was so great he could hardly be heard nevertheless, and Grandma leaned over toward the radio. "It's a hit, IT'S A HIT, IT'S A HIT, a long drive, was that tagged . . . and there goes that old ball game. A deep drive to right center . . . wait a minute . . . Tucker going over fast . . . Tucker back . . . back . . . back against the fence . . . he speared it . . . no . . . he crashed into the fence. . . ."

There was frightful explosion outside and the lights went out, cutting the speaker short.

Rain descended. It poured down against the windows, beat on the roof which Roy had covered with the first money he had earned from baseball. In the Connecticut Hills round Tomkinsville the storm struck furiously, and Grandma sat silently in the dark. While in the murky dusk of the Polo Grounds a boy writhed in agony on the green turf of deep right center.

Dusk descended upon a mass of players, on a huge crowd pouring onto the field, on a couple of men carrying an inert form through the mob on a stretcher, and meanwhile up in the press box, where the lights were on, Jim Casey for the fifth time that afternoon pulled a piece of copy paper from his typewriter and tossed it, a crumpled ball, to the floor. Once again he started a new lead.

"I've followed every game, had thrills, watched last minute finishes in every sport, but the contest at the Polo Grounds between the Dodgers and the Giants yesterday left me with sixty thousand other fans limp, beaten, and exhausted. The Daffy Dodgers are certainly unpredictable. You can never tell what they'll do, but you can be sure it won't be the thing you imagined. Paced by a has-been relief pitcher, Foster, with Dave Leonard, who is old enough to be in the Baseball Museum at Cooperstown, behind the bat, this crazy ballclub scrapped, fought, disregarded every rule of the game by running wild on the basepaths, making impossible stops and catches in the field, and finally nosed out the Giants to enter the Series next week by a score of four to three in fourteen innings. Led by their brilliant youngster, 'Bad News Tucker,' they went ahead in the fourth, were caught and passed in the eighth, tied the game on a foolhardy bit of baserunning in the ninth, and finally won it by Tucker's leap into the right field fence to spike Murphy's homer in the last of the fourteenth.

"Right now they don't know the extent of Tucker's injuries and whether or not he'll be able to play for the Dodgers in the World Series next week. Just the same, I wouldn't bet five cents against this cockeyed ballclub when they meet the Yanks . . ."

There was a clap of thunder. Rain descended upon the Polo Grounds.

Roy Tucker's adventures are continued in The Kid Comes Back *(Morrow). Other fast-paced sports stories by Tunis are* All American *(Harcourt), which deals with football; and* Yea! Wildcats *(Harcourt), a basketball book.*

The Great Tarnov Crystal

BY ERIC P. KELLY

Illustrations by Lewis Zacks

Back in the days of fifteenth-century Poland, Pan Andrew Charnetski flees from the Ukraine with his wife and son, Joseph, and with the great Tarnov crystal hidden in a pumpkin. When the crystal falls into the hands of Pan Kreutz, the alchemist, and his unscrupulous student Tring, the whole city of Krakow is in danger.

I T was late one evening in April, a few weeks after the unsuccessful attack of Peter upon the tower, that the alchemist, Kreutz, and the student, Johann Tring, were sitting upon rude stools in the loft above the alchemist's lodging, arguing with much heat some question that had arisen between them. The day had been sultry for early spring and the sun was setting red over the distant hills, flooding with its crimson the high mound called the Krakus Mound over beyond the river on the road to Wieliczka and the salt mines.

Tring sat where he could see the sunshine through the little window, but the alchemist sat within the gathering darkness of the room. Above their heads on the slanting walls vials and glass tubes of the alchemist's craft gleamed like precious stones, and every now and then some substance lying upon the hot coals of the braziers would hiss up into a little flame and smoke, for all the world like a serpent suddenly raising its slender head and coils above a quiet patch of grass.

"I tell you that I have had enough," the alchemist replied to some remark of the student's. "I am ready to forswear this scientific experiment into which we have so boldly launched and go back to my old studies which are much better suited to a God-fearing man."

Tring laughed, low but maliciously. "So that is where your courage lies," he answered. "That is the crown of valor that you boast in exploring the wonders of the unknown world. Come," he added after a minute, as if changing his tactics in dealing with this man who was now thoroughly in his power, or so he thought, "come and put a better complexion upon things; we are already past the hardest stretch of the road— if there is to be found the solution to that problem upon which we both have spent so much time, it will be found so much the more readily now because of the sacrifices that we have already made for it. Are the trances tiring you beyond endurance?"

The alchemist let his head sink into his hands. "I am tired— I am tired," was all that he could say.

Tring regarded him with disgust, but held back the angry words which sprang to his lips and expressed himself more gently.

"Then if there is a fault it must lie with you, Pan Kreutz," he said. "It is beyond my understanding that such a man as you should find exhaustion in these simple experiments that I have performed. Many another person I have put into trances similar to yours, and for longer periods of time, too, and there has been no harm, nay, nor physical exhaustion from it."

"Alas," the alchemist moaned as if making a confession, "I have been in trances other than those of your making, and almost continually, too."

"What?" Tring leaped to his feet in astonishment. "What do you say? You have been in trances induced by others? Other men share our secrets, then? Who may it be that is also a master of this rare craft? I had thought that no others, save I, in this town were able to bring about such trances." He glared at Kreutz with open hatred and let his fingers stray as well to the handle of a short knife that he carried in his belt, for although he was but a young man, he took his occult powers very seriously. There was as well an element of fear in his emotions, since the civil authorities of that day dealt usually in short and severe fashion with persons brought before magistrates on the charge of indulging in dark or occult practices. Death even was prescribed as punishment for some, although disfiguring, whipping, stocks, and banishment were the most common penalties.

Tring's powers, though mysterious in those days, could be easily explained in ours. The so-called trances into which certain persons have the power to send others we call in these times merely hypnotic sleep. Hypnotism in the days when all men and women were to an extent superstitious was looked upon as one of the very worst works of a malignant devil upon earth. Tring possessed to some extent the ability to summon hypnotic sleep to a willing patient, and the alchemist had become a too willing patient in his endeavor to discover the secret that Tring had made appear so desirable.

And as is the case with most practitioners of hypnotism and their subjects, the hypnotist had gained, little by little, more and more power over his co-worker, until in a few months the alchemist had become merely a tool in the hands of Tring, who, knowing his ability and scholarly accomplishments, did not hesitate to use them for his own ends. He did this, however, with great caution, and enjoined ever upon the alchemist the need for the utmost secrecy, for if it had become known that such tricks were being practiced, the law would make short shrift of both.

"No man," answered the wretched alchemist, "no *man*, but perhaps—devils!"

"Devils?" Tring stood motionless, thunderstruck. Was the alchemist losing his mind?

"Yes, devils. I can stand it no longer." The alchemist rose from his stool and turned upon Tring. "You who have powers greater than man, know most of what is passing in my soul. The secrets of my craft, the sciences of actions and reactions— all these you know. But I hold from *you* one secret, one great secret which has bowed my shoulders with care and blackened my heart with crime. Come, watch, I will show you something that has powers beyond those of which you dream. See . . ."

His accents became wilder and his voice trembled. He shuffled about the attic as if making preparations for some experiment. He set up a tripod in the very middle of the room and linked the top with chains as if he were to set a bowl upon it; he un-

locked a great chest that stood in one corner under the eaves and took from it some object wrapped in black cloths, and this object he placed upon the tripod.

"Now let us have a light," he said.

He shook some powder into a brazier full of coals which suddenly leaped into flame. As the whole room burst into existence with the illumination there appeared most prominently in it the tripod which bore the covered mystery. The alchemist whipped the cloth covering away.

It was as if he had uncovered a diamond of the finest water! Upon the brass top of the tripod gleamed in that instant a very miracle of color and light; the object itself was about the size of a man's head. Upon this exquisite thing no artificial effort of man had been expended; it was as nature had fashioned it in the depths of some subterranean grotto where drops of water falling in steady succession for thousands and thousands of years had slowly created it. The outer layers were clear like the water of a mountain spring; as the eye fell farther and farther within the surface a bluish tint was perceptible and at the very center there was a coloring of rose. Such was its absolute beauty that whoever looked into its depths seemed to be gazing into a sea without limit.

"In the name of Heaven," shrieked Tring, "what is this?"

The alchemist spoke in a low voice as one might speak in a church: "The Great Tarnov Crystal."

"The Great Tarnov Crystal!" repeated Tring. "The Great Tarnov Crystal! . . . Why, that is the stone for which alchemists and workers of magic have been searching these hundreds of years. The Great Tarnov Crystal!" He shouted it almost in high excitement. "Why, man, we have here the greatest scientific treasure of all ages." He began to skip about in transports as the possibilities of the treasure's possession leaped into his mind. "And now I understand," he continued. "Indeed you have been under the hand of a devil if you have been gazing into that thing. Why, do you know that this stone can send a man into a trance in which all manner of truths will be divulged? Do you know that we can learn now for a certainty the very secret that we have been seeking?" And going close to the stone, he gazed into its depths as a thirsty man might gaze into a well of water.

There was this curious property of the Great Tarnov Crystal, and perhaps of all great crystals in the world's history, that it never presented the same vista twice to the man who looked within its depths. Now this may have been due to many things, to the fact that the lights surrounding it were never twice the same, and also perhaps to this, that the crystal had the strange property of reflecting back to the observer the very thoughts that were tucked away deeply in his head. What drew men to the Tarnov Crystal in the beginning was, of course, its beauty, its color, its light, its constantly changing vistas, and besides these, there was that indefinable fascination that all such stones have. Diamonds, as well, possess this fascinating power to a high degree though the diamond is, of course, a small stone, and not large enough to hold the concentrated focus of two eyes for a very long time; the crystal by reason of its size possesses this quality according to its fineness.

The Tarnov Crystal was the finest crystal known to the magicians of the Middle Ages. And although magic was frowned upon by scholars and men of science such as astronomers and alchemists, still there was no distinct line between science and magic, with the result that many of these men found themselves practicing magic when they had intended only to make scientific investigations. It was even so with Pan Kreutz, who ordinarily had but little use for magic or the Black Arts in any form—until now he had come entirely under the domination of the student Tring whose enthusiasm had carried him away.

"I tell you that I have had enough," the alchemist repeated now. "I have perjured my soul to obtain this stone and I am ready to return it to its rightful owners. This stone is a thing of wickedness and blood and it has a woeful history, as old perhaps as the world itself."

"Return it!" shouted Tring. "Return it! Why, Pan Kreutz, listen to my reasoning. I know not how you have come by this thing— I do not ask at present—but you would be scarce the man I took you for did you not use it for the purpose that we need it. After that we many return it—if indeed it has been stolen— or if it sticks within your conscience to retain it now, then perhaps I——"

"Nay, nay, Johann Tring," exclaimed the alchemist emphatically, "to its rightful owners it shall go. Here I have kept the secret to myself knowing that the knowledge would tempt you —and indeed you would not have known now unless the secret had burned so heavily in my brain."

"As you will," said Tring, humoring the alchemist with his concession, though the purpose in his eyes was of different intent, "but first let us learn from it at once how to transmute baser metals into gold; this I am sure we shall do, then we can be independent of these smirking dogs who rule the universities."

"Then let our experiments be brief," said the alchemist. "I have looked too long upon this glittering thing."

"You should have told me before." Tring again adopted the attitude of a kindly adviser.

"But, in truth," went on the alchemist, "I doubt if we can

wring that secret from the crystal. I have now an opinion, though perhaps a wrong one, that the crystal only gives us back our own thoughts. We may not call upon it as upon some friendly spirit to tell us what we do not know—we may not wish and have our wishes fulfilled. I begin to doubt it all." Here he rose to his feet and began to stride about the floor. "It is already having a bad influence upon me. I cannot see straightly in the world of men as once I did. When I have looked into it for minutes and minutes my thoughts come back to me crookedly, and while I have taken much interest in such contemplation, I find that there is too deadly a fascination in gazing into those crystal depths. I have, as I said, found much of interest, and were I alone in the world, I might even pursue these studies to the very limits of human thought, but I some- times feel as if my very soul were getting caught in the rays of that bright thing."

"Might I ask," inquired Tring, unable to restrain his curiosity longer, "how the crystal came into your possession?"

"It was like this"—the alchemist willingly relieved his mind of the secret that he had been bearing alone. "That night when the thieves came here some time ago I entertained them for a bit with some Greek fire and niter."

"Yes?"

"It seems that the crystal was at that time in the possession of the family in the rooms below ours."

"What! The trumpeter and the boy who bear the name Kovalski?"

"Yes, though that is not their name. They are Charnetskis and lived formerly in the Ukraine."

"I see—and the thieves? Tartars and Cossacks who followed them perhaps from the Dnieper country?"

"Yes, the crystal was actually in the hands of the leader when I surprised him with an explosive powder. In the surprise and pain occasioned by my attack he dropped the crystal—the powder blazed about his face and burned his hair—the crystal rolled upon the floor and I pounced upon it."

"But how had it come into the possession of the Charnetski family?" asked Tring eagerly.

"It was in this fashion. When the Tartars devastated the Polish country in the thirteenth century the village that stood where now is Tarnov was inhabited by the Charnetskis, among others, of course. It was Andrew Charnetski of that day who performed heroic feats in the defense of the city against the Tartars, and to him was presented for safe-keeping the great crystal which has come to be known as the Great Tarnov Crystal. It was the chief ornament of the old town, and even kings had come there to see it. For besides its qualities as a thing of rare value and beauty, it had those reputed properties you have mentioned: that a man who looked into it might there read the secrets of the past and the future; that he might find out the intimate thoughts of other men and women; that he might learn to overcome the elements, to fly through the air like a bird, to walk invisibly, to transmute base metals into gold. In those times no man was allowed to look more than three minutes upon it, for even in three minutes a man might find his head swimming and curious thoughts coming into his brain."

"But how did the Charnetskis save it from the Tartars?"

"They fled with it to the Carpathian Mountains and remained there until Batu the Tartar was forced to return to the land of the Golden Horde. Then as it passed from eldest son to eldest son, it went to an ancestor of this Andrew Charnetski who settled in the Ukraine after the country had been put under Polish dominion in the days of Vladislas Jagiello. Of course the name Andrew Charnetski is by no means an uncommon one throughout Poland, so little did I think when this man came into the humble lodgings below that he belonged to the Charnetski family which had possession of the Tarnov Crystal."

"Did he tell you his story?"

"Yes. On the day after the crystal disappeared, he made a confidant of me as one already acquainted with his name and a part of his history."

"But you had heard of the crystal before?"

"What alchemist has not?" he answered. "I knew that it was brought in early days to Egypt from somewhere in the East, and there it stood in a temple for many centuries. When the Romans conquered Egypt, the crystal was taken to Rome. During the years when the Romans were colonizing the lands around the Black Sea a certain Roman officer fell in love with a woman of Transylvania, and being sent there with a legion, stole for her this crystal from a temple in Rome. When his crime was discovered the Emperor sent a detachment of soldiers to bring him back, but he fled to the district which is now Halicz, but which went then under the Roman name Galicia. There he lived with his wife under an assumed name, in a remote village later known as Tarnov, and there the crystal remained up to the time that it passed into the hands of the Charnetskis. Around it grew up a sect of sorcerers, magicians, praticers of the Black Art, astrologers, and alchemists—some sincere, others mere charlatans."

"Surely there have been many attempts to steal the crystal from the Charnetskis?"

"Only one. It seems that men, even alchemists and astrologers, lost for a time the thread of its history, and it was only when a runaway servant of Andrew Charnetski spread the news in the East that it was in his possession that an attempt was made to find it. That attempt, as you know, cost Pan Andrew his house and property in the Ukraine. Who it is that is inciting these robbers I know not, but I have no doubt that the leader of the band was in the pay of some person in high authority."

"Would the robbers taken prisoners say anything?"

"No, they did not know all, I believe. And like most Tartars they would rather die than betray a secret. Torture could not wring it out of them."

"Does Pan Andrew suspect that you have the crystal?"

"Pan Andrew considers me his friend. And at heart I am ashamed and sick that I have not restored it before now."

"But think. If it had not been for you, the Cossack would have escaped with the crystal and it would have been lost forever."

"I know it. Yet that is no justification for me. I stole it if a thief ever stole anything. When I first saw it that night on the floor of Pan Andrew's lodging I would have exchanged my chance of heaven for its possession. When I had obtained it, and the attention of the crowd in the court below was turned to the robbers and to the man escaping over the roofs, I brought it here to the loft, under my coat."

"You did well," said Tring, the wildest impulses of excitement leaping within him. "Look—look at the crystal. It glows and dances and quivers like a thing alive, ready to tell its secrets. Quick, draw your chair near to it as you used to draw your chair to me when I was the master of your trances. Gaze deeply into it"—he fixed the hesitating alchemist with his eyes as a serpent might fix a helpless bird—"and now let us try the greatest experiment of all."

The alchemist pulled his chair close to the crystal as he was bid, and fixed his eyes upon it. Tring watched him closely from a distance. One minute—two minutes—three—the alchemist still looked at the crystal and Tring regarded him as a cat might regard a mouse that it was playing with. Four minutes—five. The alchemist still sat motionless, but his posture in the chair was changing slightly. His arms and neck seemed to be stiffening, his face was taking on the look of an entirely different person; his breath came regularly but in longer and deeper draughts than was his wont. His eyes became wide open and staring.

"Listen," Tring's tone was sharp, commanding.

"I am listening," the reply came instantly.

Tring trembled with excitement. Not only had the alchemist gone into this trance more quickly than he, Tring, had ever been able to send him, but he was still responsive to the student who had feared lest the agency of the crystal might render Kreutz unresponsive to him. But Tring had sent him into trances so many times that now his mind seemed to answer the student's bidding automatically.

"Tell me what you see."

"I can see a huge hall like an alchemist's room, filled with braziers and glass instruments. In these instruments fluids of fire are rushing to and fro and near them are great copper kettles out of which are coming puffs of steam."

"It is the devil's workshop that you are in," said Tring sharply. "Do you see any men at work?"

There was silence a moment as the alchemist's consciousness went roaming through the vast room.

"There is no one here," he said at length.

"Are there any manuscripts there?" demanded Tring.

Silence again. Then—"Yes, on the wall hangs a parchment."

"Take it down."

"It burns my hands."

"Pay no heed to that. Your reward will be greater than your pains."

"It is in my hands."

Tring glanced involuntarily at the hands of the man in the trance. Curiously enough they seemed to be turning red as if exposed to a great heat. "Now read what the parchment says."

The alchemist replied slowly as if reading, and he spoke in the Latin tongue, "HERE MAY ONE FIND THINGS WHICH BE NEITHER GOOD NOR EVIL BUT WHICH ARE SOUGHT OF ALL MEN."

"Good! Now unroll the parchment."

There was another silence. At length the alchemist said, "I have found somewhat."

"Read!"

"Nay, I may not. It is in symbols."

"Then write." Tring deftly slipped a piece of board across

his knees and put into his fingers a kind of pen made of wood and a feather; this he had dipped into a pot of ink as thick as paint, and he guided it in the alchemist's hand until it rested upon a piece of fresh white parchment that he laid upon the board.

The alchemist wrote as follows:

> Per
>
> insert:—art
>
> *Fit Lapis Philosophorum*

"What else?"

The alchemist wrote:

"Quod primum incredibile, non continuo falsum est; crebro siquidem faciem mendacii veritas retinet."

"No. That's nothing. Do you find other formulæ?"

The alchemist looked closely and recited as if reading:

"Thus saith Olimpiodorus of Thebes, Osthanes the Egyptian, Psellos of Byzantium, and Giabr of Arabia: heat the fires upon thy brazier and place thereon a vessel full of yellow sulphur; this thou shalt melt until it gives forth a spirit; when the spirit is departed pour slowly upon the sulphur that quicksilver which has its birth in the planet Mercury. In but the twinkling of an eye this will be reduced from its natural state unto a state that is of the earth, black, without life, dead. Then take this lifeless substance and put it in a closed vessel; heat it and it will suddenly take on life again and become a brilliant red."

"Write it, write it," exclaimed Tring. The alchemist wrote. "And is there more?"

"Much. It saith here that this is the secret of the Seven Golden Chapters, of the Emerald Table, and the Pimander. *Natura naturam superat; deinde vero natura naturae congaudet; tandem natura naturam continet.*"

"No more of that. That is vile philosophy," shouted Tring. "Find and write the completion of the Philosopher's Stone, by which we may convert brass into gold."

The alchemist continued:

"Zosimus the Theban directs that this is the true method of turning brass into gold: To the above heated solution of sulphur and mercury add that pure niter which men find in the heart of India. Into this cast brass and it will in a moment change to gold."

"Quick, to work. Light the braziers and bring out sulphur, quicksilver, and brass," commanded Tring. "Have you any of this Indian niter?"

"I have—a small packet on the third shelf of the closet," answered the alchemist. Tring rushed to get it and set all the materials ready for the experiment. Truly and sincerely did he believe that the alchemist had hit upon the solution of the much desired process of changing base metals into gold, and his own lack of knowledge in the realm of the science of alchemy was responsible for the ignorance with which he ordered the alchemist to compound one of the most dangerous chemicals known to man. The alchemist, on his part, was but acting under the hypnotic suggestion of Tring, and had no opportunity to interpose his normal-self sense between the student's intention and its execution. Indeed the information he had during the trance came from his own fund of learning, although the suggestion of adding niter to the heated compound was but a fancy of a mind grown either tired or weak.

As the student hurried about arranging materials for the experiment Kreutz sang a Latin hymn which extols the practice of alchemy and the alchemist:

> *Inexhaustium fert thesaurum*
> *Qui de virgis fecit aurum*
> *Gemmas de lapidibus.*

"Compound the Philosopher's Stone," commanded Tring.

The alchemist, still in the trance, arose, and leaned over the brazier. Something flaky and white and inflammable was tucked close to the bottom to act as kindling, and a coal brought from a farther brazier and laid upon this. It turned all black for a minute, then sizzled into an intense heat and ignited the brazier's contents. The flame was at first yellow and creeping, then it changed to blue and leaping. Kreutz put a vessel filled with sulphur into the flames, and sure enough in a moment the spirit of the sulphur arose in fumes that filled the room.

Both leaned over the brazier eagerly as the alchemist shook mercury over the melted sulphur. As the parchment had de-

creed, so the reaction followed; in a short time the glittering mercury had mingled with the melted sulphur and became an ugly black substance. Tring handed to Kreutz another vessel which was closed at the top. Kreutz shook the hot material from the first vessel into the second and put the latter back on the brazier. In all his motions he acted mechanically as if he were but working out the will of another. He opened this second vessel after a few seconds and, sure enough, the black substance was becoming a lively red.

"The niter; the niter," exclaimed Tring eagerly at his elbow.

The alchemist took the package from his hands and tossed it into the substance now seething with heat. As he did so, as if obeying some unconscious instinct of self-preservation, he leaped back into the middle of the room and drew Tring with him. The exclamation of anger on Tring's lips was cut in half, for at that instant the loft of the house rocked in a terrific explosion!

"Quick, seize the crystal and descend!" screamed Tring, who was already speeding through the doorway, frantically wiping sparks of fire from his clothing.

The exploding substances had sent their flames into the dry roof and walls of the house, and fire was leaping through them merrily. Everything in the room was beginning to blaze, and in two minutes more it would have been impossible to leave. The alchemist, still in a daze, took the crystal as he had been commanded, and made for the stairway. The stone gleamed in his hands like a million diamonds, rubies, and emeralds where the flames fell upon it, and he clutched it with all the strength of his right hand as he clung to the stair rail with his left, now swaying out over the court like a drunken man, now regaining his hold and descending another stair. But the student had been more nimble, and by the time that the alchemist had descended to the third floor of the house, Johann was down the stairs and through the gate, calling with all his might for the watch to notify the water master that the house above him was in flames. No watch was in sight and so he sought one at full speed, and while he was searching, Pan Kreutz had reached the open door and disappeared in the night, the Great Tarnov Crystal hidden under the folds of his black gown.

But behind him the flames had eaten through the roof of his house and had leaped to the adjoining house. In a few minutes they had bounded clear across an open court near by, and had laid hold of one of the pensions of the university. The wind then veering swept the flames in a seething mass in the direction of the great Rynek, and in less than fifteen minutes after the flight of the two men from the loft of the building, the university section of Krakow was in the grip of a terrible conflagration that threatened to devour the whole city.

Since earliest times Krakow was divided into four sections— the Castle Quarter, the Potters' Quarter, the Butchers' Quarter, and the Slavkov. At the head of each of these districts was a quartermaster who was responsible for everything that went on in his district, the fighting of fires being one of his chief concerns. Therefore the watchman from one of the streets that lay in the districts threatened by the fire went pounding at the gate of the quartermaster's house, shouting "Fire" at the top of his lungs in order to send the servants flying to the master. In a short time the quartermaster was up and dressed, and had sent summons to the water master who had charge of the town reservoir and aqueducts.

The bell meanwhile began to sound clamorously from the tower of the Church of Our Lady Mary, for the watchman there had caught sight of the flames. Cries of "fire" were now being echoed from all sections of the city, and in the red glare which was beginning to illumine all the grim Gothic buildings and churches, a very tumult of confusion was arising. The water master had already set his machinery in motion and drummers were pounding away at their drums in all the city streets in order to awaken the merchants and their apprentices upon whom fell the burden of fighting the flames. All the town guilds were assembling, companies of servants from the palaces were filling buckets of water and taking positions on the roofs of their own houses, and all citizens were busily getting down from the wall, hooks and axes and pails such as the law required them to keep for such emergencies.

A fire of any size in Krakow was a serious thing in those days, for there were hundreds upon hundreds of wooden and part-wooden houses clustered together in the thickly populated streets. In the section about the old university the majority of dwellings were very ancient, dry, and cobwebbed everywhere, and a single spark upon their roofs was enough to turn them in exceedingly rapid fashion into belching furnaces of flame and smoke. As the fire raced through these streets, the inhabitants poured out in panic-stricken confusion; each building was literally teeming with life, and the whole scene, viewed from above, would have resembled a huge ant hill suddenly destroyed or burned out by a careful gardener.

Women and children came out rushing and shrieking. Black-robed students dashed through the streets with manuscripts and parchments in their hands; others came carrying glass tubes or astrolabes or metal dividers; frantic domestics ran here and there with no definite refuge in view save only to escape the heat and terror of the ever-spreading flames. The streets were rapidly filling with furniture, clothing, beds, and personal possessions of every variety, hurled out of casements by desperate owners—and some of this material in the streets had already caught fire from the sparks which were descending like rain in a spring thunderstorm, making the lot of the fugitives even more unendurable. Inside some of the courts those who had preserved presence of mind were combating the fire with much vigor; tubs of water and pails were being pressed into action, and burning walls were already being hauled down.

The water master had marshaled a line of water carts which extended from the burning buildings to the aqueduct; these water carts were usually drawn by horses, and some of them were on this night, but there had been difficulty in getting enough horses quickly, and men and boys were harnessed into the shafts. At the aqueduct men were busy filling the carts with water; as each cart was filled it moved on some little distance to the fire, and there being emptied, swung about into another street and returned to the aqueduct for another filling. The nearest section of the aqueduct was about an eighth of a mile from the point where the fire started.

Forces of men armed with hooks and axes were sent out by the water master to surround the district where the flames were reaching, for the rapid spread of the fire had made it ap-

parent at an early stage that very little could be saved in the
university area. These men were under orders to demolish any
building that seemed to offer a chance for a further spread of
the blaze, whether the fire had already reached it or not. One
detachment formed a line in front of the Church of the Franciscans, another on St. Ann's Street, and another on Bracka.
All these detachments were forced to retreat, however, as the
fire ate its way out of the district where it had started. The
Rynek was the scene of a turbulent mob which had struggled
from the burning section in the Street of the Pigeons, and every
open space was quickly filled with rescued goods. Two families
had even taken possession of the platform where the town
pillory stood and children were being put to sleep there by
mothers thankful to find a place of rest.

Amid all this uproar, an elderly woman, a boy, a girl, and
a dog were fighting their way through the Street of the Pigeons
amidst the débris of furniture and personal belongings that
had been thrown from windows. They had all been sleeping
when the fire broke out, and not having been roused until the
flames were all about them, had been able to rescue nothing
but themselves and the clothes which they wore. The boy was
Joseph, the girl, Elzbietka, and the woman the wife of Pan
Andrew. Wolf, cut loose by Joseph, was the most terror-stricken
of the group, but he followed after them, submissive and
obedient, not knowing exactly what he was expected to do.

Each of them was busy with separate thoughts as they fought
their way through the disorder. Joseph was ever figuring the
quickest route out of the burning district, and this was no easy
task, since the fire was playing so many tricks. It was not
marching ahead in a straight wall of flame but was whirling
about, leaping here and there, skipping this house and fastening
upon that, advancing, retreating, spreading to the flanks, all
with terrific speed and unexpected vivacity. Sometimes the
two roofs just above the heads of the fugitives would shoot up
in flames—passing these with great peril, they would find that
the fire was now behind them and rejoice at the breath of air
that fell upon them; then suddenly without warning the roof
of a building just ahead would belch forth smoke and flame

as if the fire demon were working invisibly, and this new peril must be passed.

At length they reached the place where the Street of the Pigeons is cut by a cross lane, known to-day as Wislna Street, but this lane was already full of smoking beams and fallen timbers; escape that way was impossible. There was nothing to do but to push on through the Street of the Pigeons where it curves to meet Bracka.

Elzbietka was wondering most of all about her uncle; there had been no answer to their hurried calls when they left the doomed house, and, besides, the loft was glowing in red and purple flames of such intensity that no person alive could have been there at that time. Joseph's mother was thinking of the father, wondering if he had left his post at the church to come to his family's aid, and wondering, too, if they could reach him at the tower before he began to suffer too much from anxiety concerning them.

The houses were a little higher in this portion of the street and there was therefore more cool air, in the lower reaches. The fire was still whirling along here but was not taking hold quite so fast as it had done down below, and consequently the fugitives made better progress. The only difficulty was the ever-increasing crowd that now swept in from three directions, making it hard for the three to keep together. Finally they locked arms and literally fought their way through the crowd. All about them the scenes were heart-rending, men and women fleeing with but few possessions from the only homes they had ever known, children lost in the mad scramble who set up shrill cries and tried to keep their feet as the crowd pushed ahead. Sick persons were brought into that raging torrent of humanity, carried on the shoulders of their relatives or perhaps stretched upon cots. Here was one old man who sat astride a young fellow's neck like Anchises on the back of Æneas fleeing from the burning city of Ilium.

At length they stood where the fire had not reached, much more fortunate in that than many other people that night. Joseph waited only until they caught their breath, though he, too, felt like throwing himself down upon the ground and resting, and then started forward again through Bracka in the direction of the Rynek. In his heart he hoped that when he had settled Elzbietka and his mother in the tower where his father was on duty, he might come back with the apprentices and help fight the fire, for there is that in a youth which draws him into such fighting. As they went along Bracka he heard the sound of horses' hoofs from the direction of the Wawel.

"Wait," he said, drawing the women back on a footpath, "here come soldiers from the castle to preserve order."

He spoke truly, for the next moment a great troop of cavalry wearing mail armor and carrying spears rode into Bracka Street from below and began to deploy in lines that marked the district immediately threatened by fire. A few minutes later foot soldiers and artisans began to appear and, joining with the watch, pulled down buildings at the edge of the fire. Siege machinery was also drawn up into Bracka and the buildings just outside the reach of the fire began to crumble under its pounding.

"This will prevent the spread of the flames," thought Joseph.

They went ahead again toward the church, but while they were still in the Rynek they saw a company of soldiers dragging forward a prisoner whom they had taken in the burning district.

"A thief," said the boy.

"Bless us," exclaimed the mother. "It is not possible that men could be so cruel as to steal from poor folk driven mad with terror."

As the company came near and the torches fell upon the face of the prisoner, Joseph let out a cry of amazement.

"Why, mother, that is Peter of the Button Face, the leader of the men that attacked our house. That is the man who met us on the first day we were in Krakow. He it was who tried to make us prisoners in the church tower. . . . See how he struggles—but they are holding him tight for all that. And mother, it is not the city watch that has taken him. It is the King's own guard. Do you not see the royal crown on their helmets, do you not notice the richness of their clothing? I wonder what it can be about."

Joseph spoke truly. Peter had at last fallen into the hands

of guardians of the law, and this time it was the King's own men that held him. It was evident, too, from the way they held him that they thought they had a prize. They did not stop at the Town House where offenders against municipal law were kept but marched straight along Castle Street in the direction of the royal castle on Wawel Hill.

At the church they found Pan Andrew in a very sweat of anxiety and fear lest something of harm had befallen them. He caressed them all one after another and then said to Joseph earnestly:

"I want you to remain here and sound the Heynals for the rest of the night. There is much work to be done in the quarter where the fire is, and every man's hand is needed to stay the flames. . . . I see that Pan Kreutz is not with you. He stayed, too, I presume, to work with the rest of the men?"

"Indeed, father, I know not. We called many times, but his loft was a mass of flames like to a roaring furnace, when we were driven down the stairs."

"I must see, then, if I can find aught of him. He has been on a previous occasion our very great benefactor and it would but suit us ill not to seek at least his body in the ruins. Should he not have perished, as I pray God he has not, then we can offer him shelter here until such time as he can find a roof again."

But when Joseph told him of the capture of Peter he looked very serious and said that if such people were in the city then he had better not leave his wife and the young people. On second thought, however, it seemed right for him to go, for the city was now lighted by flames and it would be easy to summon aid if they were attacked.

And so he, with thousands of other valiant men, fought the fire in Krakow that night. They formed in a ring about the conflagration and tore down all the buildings across which it might run. The Collegium Minus was the last building to catch on the side toward the city wall, and then the fighters tore down the houses near the old Jew Gate and stopped the fire there. The flames swept around the other buildings of the university, destroyed one or two, though not all, and were finally halted on the second street above St. Ann's. Sweeping in the other direction, the fire had early in its progress destroyed the monastery and adjoining houses of the Church of the Franciscans, and had crossed over to Castle Street where it burned flat a whole line of buildings.

On these and the other edges of the district a wide belt of destruction was created by the fighters. This belt, the tradesmen, running to and fro with water wagons filled constantly at the aqueduct, wet down and soaked until it was almost a water wall. So furiously had they worked that the main progress of the fire was checked in seven or eight hours, and although certain buildings and ruins smoked and even blazed for several days afterward, yet the great danger passed when this well-soaked belt of destruction was completed.

When Pan Andrew returned to the tower in the full blaze of the morning sun, nearly one third of the city of Krakow lay in ruins. Fortunately it was not the better portion of the city, and many of the old wooden-built hovels had been there since before the days of Kazimir the Great; that monarch had successfully converted about one half the city of Krakow from wood to stone more than one hundred years before; had he not done so it is probable that the fire of 1462 might have utterly consumed it.

Elzbietka and Joseph's mother were asleep on the trumpeter's bed clasped in each other's arms. Joseph sat outside the compartment with the hourglass before him on a beam, gazing out over the smoking ruins of the university quarter.

"Is the city saved?" was the first question he asked his father.

"It is not now in danger," answered Pan Andrew. "But there are many homeless souls in the city this day."

"Did you see the alchemist?"

"I did not. He has disappeared as if he had flown away on the clouds of smoke that covered the city."

"Poor Elzbietka," exclaimed Joseph.

The girl inside the compartment moaned slightly as her name was spoken, although she was deep in a heavy slumber.

"I wonder if he was caught in the loft?" mused Pan Andrew. "It was in the very center of the burned district."

The answer to his question came with sudden unexpectedness. There was a sound of footsteps on the stairs and Jan

Kanty's head appeared from below. The scholar was leading another man by the arm, a man who had been in the fire—his charred clothes and blackened face showed it; around his shoulders and falling to his waist was all that remained of what had once been a black robe. He kept his hands beneath this robe.

"Pan Andrew," whispered Jan Kanty softly, "I have found in the street—Pan Kreutz." And, checking the other's startled exclamation, he explained, "He is not in his right senses. Something has affected his brain. But he has here something of interest to us all."

Pan Andrew turned toward Kreutz—he never would have recognized him had not Jan Kanty identified him; Joseph felt his eyes glued with strange eagerness upon the eerie, blackened figure and the mysterious folded hands beneath the robe; it had been a scholar's robe once.

"Ha, ha, ha!" laughed the alchemist suddenly, "up to heaven goes everything in fire and yet no gold is found anywhere. Johann Tring!" he looked about anxiously. "Where is Johann Tring? He answers me not. He is lost in the flames, the flames that came so red and purple when niter mixed with charcoal. Oho, Johann Tring! Come, Johann Tring, and see what I have carried this whole long night for you."

Throwing back the black robe, he held up the object that he had been concealing there, and at the same moment the sun, streaming in through the little window on the east side, fell full upon that object; fell upon it and made it sparkle like the myriad of dew diamonds shining upon a morning lawn new-mowed; sparkled like the thousand chandeliers in the King's great hall in the palace on the Wawel Hill; sparkled like the rubies and emeralds that gleam in the Queen's crown; sparkled like the wondrous thing that it was, all touched by the red rays of the morning sun—the Great Tarnov Crystal!

"Now whence has that come?" shouted Pan Andrew so loudly that the sleepers in the next room awoke. "Where by all that is good and holy in the world have you found the gem which has been in my family for years and years, which all my ancestors and I have sworn to guard forever and to surrender to no person except to the King of Poland? How has it come into your hands after it was stolen from me, and my heart was nearly broken? Did you get it perhaps from that ruffian who has been captured by the King's guards? Did you find it perhaps in the ruins of the town? Did you perchance ——" The truth suddenly flashed upon him and he was speechless.

"It is an accursed thing," cried out the alchemist suddenly, reeling in Jan Kanty's arms as if he were gone faint. "There is blood upon it, and fire! It has lured princes and kings to their destruction! It has made men's brains mad with lust for want of it! It has caused good men to steal, and evil men to kill. I will have none of it. I will have none of it, I say." He was growing almost boisterous, yet there was something in this attack of madness that had much of reason and determination in it. "I will have no more of it," he repeated, "and no more of Johann Tring."

At that he fell fainting to the floor.

Jan Kanty raised him, and Elzbietka who had run out from the trumpeter's room rushed to him and kissed and fondled his blackened hands.

Pan Andrew picked up the Great Tarnov Crystal and held it at arm's length with a smile.

"Now may peace come upon us all," he said, "for I may fulfill the oath that my family has taken and deliver this to the King. While the secret of its hiding place remained with me I might keep the crystal as long as I chose, but now that the secret is out, there is but one place where it may be guarded safely and that is in the palace of the King. Pan Kreutz is right. This jewel has already done too much harm in the world."

Eric Kelly's tale of fifteenth-century Poland, The Trumpeter of Krakow, was awarded the Newbery Medal in 1929. The author has also given us a thrilling tale of the sixteenth century in At the Sign of the Golden Compass, also published by Macmillan.

Adventure in Sheridan Square

BY VALENTI ANGELO

Illustrations by the author

Twelve-year-old Joey Enrico lives on Bleecker Street in New York City. Because his father is away at war, Joey is often in trouble. But Joey and his friends are normal, happy boys who manage to have a lot of fun. As, for example, the time they were confronted with the problem of what to do with a dead cat that was sadly in need of a decent burial.

I T was a sad day, the day that Mimi, Peggy di Lucca's Persian cat, died. The children sat in Peggy's backyard and discussed the matter of its disposal. Mimi had been placed in a large paper box, and her limp body was surrounded with sprays of leaves, mixed with marigolds, which Joey had clipped from his mother's flowerpots. Peggy sat beside the box. Now and then she touched the white silken fur gently and her face saddened. A soft warm breeze stole into the dingy yard and lazily fanned the wash on the line. The distant sound of a radio playing *Rhapsody in Blue* echoed over the neighborhood.

Joey sat cross-legged beside Peggy, his chin cupped in both hands. He said, "We just can't put Mimi into the ash can and have the garbage man take her away."

"I should say not," said Peggy. "My cat's not going to be dumped into a garbage can. Not if I can help it." She rearranged a marigold in the box. "We've got to think of something better'n that."

"We sure do," said Joey.

Peggy's brother David looked at Pete the Squeak and said, "What's on your mind?"

"Oh, just thinkin'," replied Pete the Squeak.

Joey turned his eyes toward Michael and saw that Michael's eyes were searching Peggy's. He thought, "I guess he's in love."

In his cage up on the fire escape Peggy's parrot plucked its feathers. Every now and then the parrot looked down upon the group and screeched, "Peggy's got a sweetheart! Scat. Hurray!"

The music on the radio came to an end. A commentator's voice informed the neighborhood of the latest news.

Pete the Squeak was thinking very hard. Suddenly he snapped his fingers. "I've got it. I've got it," he cried.

"Yeah? Let's hear it," Michael said. "It better be good."

"How about a funeral for Mimi?" said Pete the Squeak.

All were speechless except Peggy. Her face brightened for the first time since Mimi's death.

"It's a wonderful idea, Peter! Don't you think so, Michael?" she asked sweetly, her doelike eyes searching his.

The others waited for him to answer. Michael looked at Joey and Joey looked at Tony. While Tony passed his look on to David, Pete the Squeak suppressed a giggle. Michael stretched out his legs and fidgeted under Peggy's questioning gaze.

Pete the Squeak went on talking about a nice wooden box, flowers, a procession, and many other things needed to make Mimi's entry into cat heaven a most elaborate affair.

Peggy turned her eyes away from Michael. She bowed her head and looked at her hands. "You think Peter's idea is silly, don't you?"

Michael's face reddened. "Oh, no, Peg. Really, Peg, I don't think anything of the kind. I think it's a swell idea. Don't you, David?"

Sensing Michael's predicament, David came to his rescue. "Sure, we'll do it," David said. "And we'll bury Mimi right here in our own backyard."

"Oh, no, David," said Peggy. "We've got to find a better place. This old yard? I wouldn't think of it! Besides, I'd—"

"We could bury Mimi in my backyard," Joey interposed. "It's much larger, and we've got a tree and some grass. I'm sure my mother wouldn't mind."

Peggy said, "I will *not* have Mimi buried in a backyard!"

"But, Sis," cried David, "what else can we do? It's as good a place as any. It's better'n giving Mimi to the garbage man, isn't it?" He turned to his companions and shrugged his shoulders. "Gee, I don't know. You fellows have any ideas?"

"What's the matter with Joey's backyard?" growled Pete the Squeak. "It's a swell place, Peggy. I buried Micky, my fox terrier, there. And if it's good enough for my dog, it ought to be good enough for your cat."

"Sure, why not?" the boys said.

"I'll not have Mimi buried in a backyard and I mean it!" She eyed them one by one for a full moment, then continued, "I want Mimi's grave to be in Sheridan Square. And I know just the spot."

"Sheridan Square?"

"You mean, Sheridan Square?"

"You're crazy!" said Pete the Squeak.

"What a brilliant idea!" said Tony.

"You don't really mean it," said Joey.

"I do. You heard what I said."

The boys groaned. They moaned. They shook their heads. When finally they recovered from the shock, they repeated,

"Sheridan Square? Bury a cat in Sheridan Square? Oh, no! Not me! Nothing doing!"

They discussed the matter at great length. Michael and David tried to change Peggy's mind. The more they argued, the more stubbornly she insisted. Pete the Squeak told her she might as well make something really big out of Mimi's death and bury her in a real honest-to-goodness cemetery for cats and dogs. "I've heard of 'em. But you have to have money."

Joey insisted, "My backyard is as good as any cat-and-dog cemetery. In fact, much more private, and it wouldn't cost anyone a cent." He urged Peggy to accept the idea. "If we have a funeral, there's the place for your cat."

Peggy, her lips pursed, stroked Mimi's fur. She turned Mimi's limp body into a more comfortable position. She rearranged the scattered leaves and marigolds.

"I've made up my mind on Sheridan Square, and I intend to keep it that way," she said, and her words were decisive.

Joey, David, and Michael pleaded, "We're bound to run into a mess of trouble."

Pete the Squeak said, "Of that I'm sure."

"Sheridan Square—I want her buried there."

"For heaven's sake, Sis!" cried David, dismayed at his sister's behavior. "Please try and think of some other place. But *not* Sheridan Square!"

"All right then," said Peggy. "How about Washington Square?"

"Suffering cats! Do you want us to end up in a reform school or jail or something? Have some sense," cried David. He knelt down and put his arm around his sister. "Gee whiz, Peg. Listen. We'd like to do it, see? But . . ." He stood up and looked to Michael for help.

Peggy sprang to her feet. She faced them.

"All right then," she said. "If you're afraid to do it, I'll do it myself." She picked up the box and waited.

When she saw they had no intention of changing their minds, she called them " 'fraidy cats." "*I'll* bury Mimi in Sheridan Square. *I'll* go there and do it tonight when nobody's around. That's what *I'll* do." She turned and started for the back stairs.

The boys hung their heads. None of them spoke. They watched Peggy out of the corners of their eyes and with their hands in their pockets went about the dingy yard kicking at imaginary things. Finally Michael started toward Peggy. He caught up with her.

"Aw, gee," he said with great discomfort. He took the girl's arm gently and held her back. His voice was so hoarse it sounded like a distant foghorn. With no little effort he blurted out, "Listen, Peggy. Golly, I—I'm awfully sorry." The tears in her eyes made him lose his voice altogether. His hands trembled. He gulped and tried to find the proper voice, the voice that would express his feelings. Peggy remained silent. Finally she looked him squarely in the eyes. At last Michael found his voice. He turned and called, "Hey, fellows, if we do it late at night, it'll be a cinch!" He laughed. "Why didn't we think of it before?"

Pete the Squeak looked at Joey. "I knew he'd fall for it," he said.

Peggy retraced her steps. After placing the box on the ground she smiled. "You mean—you mean you'll do it then?"

Michael kicked an empty flowerpot absent-mindedly. He glanced at the others. "Sure, Peg. We'll be glad to do it for you. Won't we, fellows?"

"It's okay by me," said David.

"You can count on me," said Joey, "but I have to be home by ten, or else."

Pete the Squeak and David said they would stand guard.

"We're all set for tonight then?"

Joey said, "Okay, Michael. You and I better go to my father's shop and make the box. It's nearly dinnertime and we haven't a minute to lose."

They trailed out of the yard through an underpass leading to the street. The parrot pecked at his cage and called after them. "Hurry, hurry, hurry. Peggy's got a sweetheart! Scat! Hurray!" The radio which had echoed over the neighborhood most of the afternoon was no longer heard. In the west the sky hung low, heavily laden with dark, threatening thunderheads, whose edges sparkled with the brilliancy of shining brass. Peggy lifted the box carefully and, after hiding it in a safe place, climbed the back stairs leading to the di Luccas' flat.

Mrs. di Lucca opened the window and set the clothesline screeching. As she took the dry wash off the line she sang "O

Sole Mio." Now and then the parrot, imitating the voice of a high-pitched tenor, accompanied her.

It was nine o'clock by the bell of Our Lady of Pompeii. The sky was starless, and a dense, sultry blanket of clouds hung low over the roofs. Occasionally the distant, muffled roll of thunder was heard. With the exception of a few men and women standing in doorways, Bleecker Street was deserted. The boys turned off Bleecker into Seventh Avenue. Michael carried the small wooden box containing Peggy's cat. Joey limped along. The small coal shovel he had stuck down his trouser leg caused him no end of trouble. It kept sliding down over the top of his shoe. Tony and Pete giggled as Joey hopped along. Every now and then Pete the Squeak said, "There's another cop." A few drops of rain splattered the sidewalk. The splattering was followed by a sudden flash of lightning, which brightened the sky, outlining the buildings along the street.

Michael said, "If we get a good storm everything will be in our favor. We can do it quickly and no one will see us." He shifted the box to his right arm.

Joey said, "Don't worry, it'll storm. Let's hurry up. I have to be home by ten."

They entered Sheridan Square unnoticed. Keeping under cover of a tall evergreen, they stood huddled in conversation.

Michael set the box down and told David and Pete the Squeak to keep their eyes peeled. "If you see anyone who looks nosy, give us the signal. You know what I mean?"

"Sure I do," replied Tony. "Listen. Hoo-Hoooooo-Hoo."

"Okay," said Michael, "that'll do."

"I can imitate a sparrow," said Pete the Squeak. "You want to hear me?"

"Not now. We'll have to find the lilac bush Peggy told us about. It's supposed to be somewhere near the statue. She wants us to bury the box right near it." He looked cautiously around. "Let's go, Joey. Where's your shovel?"

"It's here under my jacket. I'm darned glad to get it out of my pants leg. There's a swell bruise all the way up and down my shin. And it isn't funny."

Michael laughed softly. "That's too bad. It won't take long

once we locate the lilac bush. Gee, just what I'd hoped for. It's starting to rain."

"It's pouring," said Joey, rolling up the collar of his jacket. "Here's the statue. Now which one of these things is a lilac bush?" He turned and saw Pete the Squeak behind him. "Weren't you supposed to keep watch with Tony and David?"

"I want to see you bury the cat. I'll keep a good lookout from here."

"Okay," said Joey, "but keep your eyes open and don't make any noise." A loud crack of thunder overhead drowned out his voice. After that the rain swelled into a deluge.

"Is this a lilac?"

"I don't think so," said Michael. "It looks more like a barberry bush."

"Ouch! It is!"

"Maybe this is it," said Pete the Squeak. "It smells nice."

"That's a dogwood tree, you dope."

A flash of lightning lit up the Square. Through the downpour came a faint sound, as if an owl were hooting. Michael, Pete the

Squeak, and Joey scurried under cover of the dogwood tree. The owl sound continued.

"I guess somebody saw us," said Michael, peeking through an opening under the tree.

"I can't see anything," Pete the Squeak giggled. "I don't think anyone could see us in this storm. Golly, listen to it rain."

"Listen to it?" said Joey. "What do you mean? I'm soaking wet."

Pete the Squeak whistled like a sparrow. He stopped suddenly for Michael's hand had found his face. "You little trouble-maker. Do you want us to get caught?"

"Oh, no one can hear a sparrow in a storm like this."

"Just the same, don't do it again, understand?"

"All right," said Pete the Squeak. "Don't be mad at me."

They listened for the owl-hoot signal and heard nothing but the rain, which poured down in torrents. The bronze statue near by glistened with each flash of lightning. The muffled roar of taxicabs and buses along Seventh Avenue echoed in the Square.

"I guess the coast is clear. I don't hear any more signals," said Michael. "Let's find the lilac bush and get it over with. I hope Peggy will appreciate what we're going through."

"She will," said Joey, looking at a plant. "I'm not sure but I think this is what she meant. Oh, let's bury it here anyway," he added impatiently. "I'm soaking wet. What's the difference? One plant is as good as another. Peggy insisted on Sheridan Square and here we are. So what?"

"Take it easy, Joey," said Michael. "Here, you hold the box and give me the shovel. We'll be through in a few minutes."

Pete the Squeak sat under the dogwood and watched them. Now and then he rose to his feet and, parting the heavily foliaged dogwood, looked out in every direction. David and Tony, standing guard near the Square, began to hoot frantically. Pete the Squeak whistled. It was not the soft twittering sound of a sparrow. He had placed his thumb and first finger in his mouth and was signaling with all his might. He rushed up to Michael and Joey. "Hey, beat it! Here comes a cop!" He flew past them like a frightened sparrow and disappeared in the dark.

Michael and Joey took one glance at the approaching form.

They dropped their work and scrambled through the shrubs after Pete the Squeak.

The rapid crunching sound of the officer's shoes over the graveled walk mingled with that of his whistle. A loud roll of thunder swallowed them both. The officer stopped a moment and flashed his light. After picking up Joey's shovel, he gave chase.

The boys united on the run, outside the Square, as though it had been prearranged. The power of the storm muffled their steps. They raced down Grove Street toward the Avenue of the Americas. Michael carried the box under his arm. All of them were drenched to the skin. The sound of the police whistle grew fainter and fainter. Breathless, they hurried up the wide avenue. Joey was glad when Michael led them into the dimly lit entranceway of a store. It wasn't long after that a policeman carrying a small coal shovel hurried by. Tony was so relieved that he began to hoot softly. Pete the Squeak, sitting in a dark corner behind Michael, twittered with joy.

"Boy, that was a close shave," declared Joey, still panting. "What'll we do now? I'm not taking any more chances like that."

"Nor me either," Tony put in. "Life's too short."

David said, "Peggy's going to be very disappointed. You don't know my sister as well as I do. She'll raise an awful fuss."

Pete the Squeak giggled. "We could try to bury the cat in Washington Square."

A sudden scuffling sound was heard in the corner. "Come on, stop it. Ouch, you're hurting my arm. I didn't mean it."

Tony said, "Leave Pete alone, Michael."

"Just the same, this is no time for kidding," Joey retorted.

The storm cleared as quickly as it had come. A nearby street light shone into the entranceway and lit up the display windows of the store. Tony, who was looking at the contents of the window over David's shoulder, laughed. "What is this place anyway, a zoo?"

"It's called a taxi-der-must," said Joey.

Tony said, "Now, aren't you smart!"

"Well," said Joey, "that's what it is. Isn't that right, Michael?"

Michael didn't answer. He was enraptured by the graceful appearance of a stuffed cat mounted on the limb of a tree. He pressed his nose against the glass and, shading his eyes with one hand, leaned this way and that.

"Sure," continued Joey. "And I know the man who owns this place. He let me watch him stuff a deer once. It was a beautiful deer, and—" Joey stopped to count the bell of Our Lady of Pompeii. "Golly! It's eleven o'clock. I better scram."

"Me too," said Tony. "Come on, Joey. I'll walk part of the way home with you."

"Wait a minute," called Michael.

"I'm not burying any more cats tonight," warned Joey.

"Neither am I," Tony replied.

"Listen," said Michael. "I've thought of something that'll please Peggy a hundred times more than burying her cat in Sheridan Square."

"It better be better'n burying it," they said.

"Let's have the taxidermist stuff Mimi, and we'll give her to Peggy as a Christmas present. What do you say?"

"It's a good idea."

"Not bad."

"I'm willing to pay my share."

"Me too. It's worth it."

"So will I."

Pete the Squeak yawned. "Boy, am I sleepy. Come on, let's all go home."

Valenti Angelo is a talented author-artist who has given us other good stories, including The Marble Fountain, *about two Italian war orphans, and* Nino, *a tale based on the author's memories of a boyhood in Tuscany at the turn of the century. Both books are published by Viking.*

Johnny Tremain

BY ESTHER FORBES

Illustrated by Lynd Ward

Johnny Tremain's mother had told him to go to Mr. Lyte for help only if there was nothing left and God Himself had turned away His face. Unable to find work because of a badly injured hand, Johnny remembers his mother's words. The story is laid in Boston during the days of Paul Revere.

IT was past dawn when he woke, his feeling of contentment still in him. He was no longer his own problem but Merchant Lyte's. Tomorrow at this time what would he be calling him? "Uncle Jonathan?" "Cousin Lyte?" Perhaps "Grandpa," and he laughed out loud.

Only imagine how Mrs. Lapham would come running, dropping nervous curtsies, when he drove up in that ruby coach! How Madge and Dorcas would stare! First thing he did would be to take Cilla for a drive. He'd not even invite Isannah. But how she would bawl when left behind! And then . . . his imagination jumped ahead.

At the Charlestown ferry slip he washed in the cold sea water, and because the sun was warm sunned himself as he did what he could to make his shabby clothes presentable. He combed his lank, fair hair with his fingers, cleaned his nails with his teeth. Of course now he could buy Cilla that pony and cart. And Grandpa Lapham . . . oh, he'd buy him a Bible with print an inch high in it. Mrs. Lapham? Not a thing, madam, not one thing.

Christ's Church said ten o'clock. He got up and started for Long Wharf where his great relative had his counting house.

On his way he passed down Salt Lane. There was the comical little painted man observing Boston through his tiny spyglass. Johnny wanted to stop—tell that fellow—that Rab—of his great connections, but decided to wait until he was sure of his welcome into the Lyte family. Although half of him was leaping ahead imagining great things for himself, the other half was wary. It was quite possible he would get no welcome at all—and he knew it.

He walked half the length of Long Wharf until he saw carved over a door the familiar rising eye. The door was open, but he knocked. None of the three clerks sitting on their high stools with their backs to him, scratching in ledgers, looked up, so he stepped inside. Now that he had to speak, he found there was a barrier across his throat, something that he would have to struggle to get his voice over. He was more excited than he had realized. But he was scornful too. These three clerks would not even look up when he came in today, but tomorrow what would it be? "Good morning, little master; I'll tell your uncle—cousin—grandfather that you are here, sir."

Finally a well-fed, rosy youth, keeping one finger in his ledger, swung around and asked him what he wanted.

"It is a personal matter between myself and Mr. Lyte."

"Well," said the young man pleasantly, "even if it is personal, you'd better tell me what it is."

"It is a family matter. I cannot, in honor, tell anyone except Mr. Lyte."

"Hum . . ."

One of the elderly clerks laughed in a mean way. "Just another poor suitor for the hand of Miss Lavinia."

The young clerk flushed. Johnny had seen enough of Madge and Dorcas and their suitors to know that the gibe about poor boys aspiring to Miss Lavinia had gone home.

"Tell him," snickered the other ancient spider of a clerk, "that Mr. Lyte is—ah—sensible of the great honor—ah—and regrets to say he has formed other plans for his daughter's future. Ah!" Evidently he mimicked Mr. Lyte.

The young clerk was scarlet. He flung down his pen. "Can't you ever forget that?" he protested. "Here, kid," and turned to

Johnny. "Mr. Lyte's closeted behind that door with two of his
sea captains. When they leave, you just walk in."

Johnny sat modestly on a stool, his arrogant shabby hat in his
good hand, and looked about him. The three backs were bent
once more over the ledgers. The quill pens scratched. He heard
the gritting of sand as they blotted their pages. There was a

handsome half-model of a ship on the wall. Sea chests, doubtless full of charts, maps, invoices, were under the desks.

The door opened. Two ruddy men with swaying walks
stepped out and Mr. Lyte himself was shaking hands, bidding
them success on their voyaging, and God's mercy. As he turned
to go back to his sanctuary, Johnny followed him.

Mr. Lyte sat himself in a red-leather armchair beside an
open window. Through that window he could watch his
Western Star graving in the graving dock. He would have been
a handsome man, with his fine dark eyes, bushy black brows,
contrasting smartly with the white tie-wig he wore, except for
the color and quality of his flesh. It was as yellow as tallow.
Seemingly it had melted and run down. The lids were heavy
over the remarkable eyes. The melted flesh made pouches beneath them. It hung down along his jawbone, under his
jutting chin.

"What is it?" he demanded. "Who let you in? What do you
want, and who, for Heaven's sake, are you?"

"Sir," said Johnny, "I'm Jonathan Lyte Tremain."

There was a long pause. The merchant's glittering black eyes
did not waver, nor the tallow cheeks redden. If the name meant
anything to him, he did not show it.

"Well?"

"My mother, sir." The boy's voice shook slightly. "She told
me . . . she always said . . ."

Mr. Lyte opened his jeweled snuffbox, took snuff, sneezed
and blew his nose.

"I can go on from there, boy. Your mother on her deathbed
told you you were related to the rich Boston merchant?"

Johnny was sure now Mr. Lyte knew of the relationship.
"Yes, sir, she did, but I didn't know you'd know."

"*Know?* I didn't need to *know*. It is a very old story— a very
old trick, and will you be gone—or shall I have you flung out?"

"I'll stay," Johnny said stubbornly.

"Sewall." The merchant did not raise his voice, but instantly
the young clerk was on his threshold. "Show him out, Sewall,
and happens he lands in the water, you—ah! can baptize him
with my name—ah . . . ha, ha!"

Mr. Lyte took up a handful of papers. The incident was over.

Sewall looked at Johnny and Johnny at Sewall. The young man was as kind as his cherubic face suggested.

"I can prove to you one thing, Mr. Lyte. My name is Jonathan Lyte Tremain."

"What of it? Any back-alley drabtail can name her child for the greatest men in the colony. There should be a law against it, but there is none."

Johnny's temper began to go.

"You flatter yourself. What have you ever done except be rich? Why, I doubt even a monkey mother would name a monkey child after you."

Mr. Lyte gave a long whistle. "That was quite a mouthful. Sewall!"

"Yes, sir."

"You just take this monkey child of a monkey mother out, and drown it."

"Yes, sir."

Sewall put a soft hand on the boy's shoulder, but Johnny fiercely shook himself free.

"I don't want your money," he said, more proudly than accurately. "Now that I've met you face to face, I don't much fancy you as kin."

"Your manners, my boy, are a credit to your mother."

"But facts are facts, and I've a cup with your arms on it to prove what I say is true."

The merchant's unhealthy, brilliant eyes quivered and glittered.

"You've got a cup of mine?"

"No, of *mine*."

"So . . . so you've got a cup. Will you describe it?"

Johnny described it as only a silversmith could.

"Why, Mr. Lyte, that must be . . ." Sewall began, but Mr. Lyte hushed him. Evidently not only Mr. Lyte, but his clerks had heard of this cup. Johnny was elated.

"My boy," said the merchant, "you have—ah—brought me great news. I must see your cup."

"Any time you say, sir."

"My long-lost cup returned to me by my long-lost little— ha-ha—whatever you are—kerchoo!" He had taken more snuff.

"Bring your cup to me tonight. You know my Beacon Hill house."

"Yes, sir."

"And we'll kill the fatted calf—you long-lost whatever-you-are. Come an hour after candles are lit. Prodigal Son, what? Got a cup, has he?"

Although Johnny might have been more cordially received by Merchant Lyte, he was satisfied enough with his welcome to build up air castles. He really knew they were air castles, for at bottom he was hard-headed, not easily taken in even by his own exuberant imagination. Still, as he trudged up Fish Street, turned in at the Laphams' door, in his mind he was in that ruby coach. Money, and a watch in his pocket.

He had hoped to slip to the attic and fetch away his cup without being noticed, but Mrs. Lapham saw him enter and called him into the kitchen. She said nothing about his shoes. Evidently the girls had told her his story and she had believed it.

"Johnny, you come set a moment. No, girls, you needn't leave. I want you to hear what I'm going to say."

Johnny looked a little smug. Had he not (almost) arrived in the Lyte coach?

"Grandpa says as long as he lives you are to have a place to sleep. But you've got to go back to the attic. Mr. Tweedie's to have the birth and death room, and you can have a little somewhat to eat. I've agreed that's all right. I'll manange *somehow*."

"Don't fret . . . I'm going for good."

"I'll believe that when I see it. Now, mind. I've two things to say to you."

The four girls were all sitting about, hands folded as though they were at meeting.

"First. You shan't insult Mr. Tweedie—least, not until he has signed the contract. No more talk of his being a spinster aunt dressed up in men's clothes. And NO MORE SQUEAK-PIGS. He's sensitive. You hurt his feelings horribly. He almost took ship then and there back to Baltimore."

"I'm sorry."

"Secondly. There's to be no more talk of you and Cilla. Don't you ever *dare* to lift your eyes to one of my girls again."

"*Lift* my eyes? I can't see that far down into the dirt even to know they are there."

"Now, you saucebox, you hold that tongue of yours. You're not to go hanging 'round Cilla—giving her presents—and dear knows how you got the money. I've told her to keep shy of you. Now I'm telling you. You mark my words . . ."

"Ma'am, I wouldn't marry that sniveling, goggle-eyed frog

of a girl even though you gave her to me on a golden platter. Fact is, I don't like girls—nor"—with a black look at his mistress —"women either—and that goes for Mr. Tweedie too."

He left to go upstairs for his cup.

When he came down, the more capable women of the household were out in the yard hanging up the wash. Cilla was paring apples in that deft, absent-minded way she did such things. Isannah was eating the parings. She'd be sick before nightfall.

Cilla lifted her pointed, translucent little face. Her hazel eyes, under their veil of long lashes, had a greenish flash to them. There never was a less goggle-eyed girl.

"Johnny's mad," she said sweetly.

"His ears are red! He's mad!" Isannah chanted.

These words sounded wonderful to him. He was happy because once more they were insulting him. They were not pitying him or being afraid of him because he had had an accident.

"Goggle-eyed, sniveling frogs!"

With his silver cup in its flannel bag, he set off to kill time until he might take it to Mr. Lyte.

He spent a couple of hours dreaming of his rosy future. And the tears in Merchant Lyte's unhealthy, brilliant black eyes— the tremor in his pompous "ah-ha-ha" manner of speech as he clutched his "long-lost whatever-you-are" to his costly waistcoat. Even if he did not like women, Miss Lavinia, he decided, was to kiss him on the brow. Through this dreaming he felt enough confidence in his good fortune at last to stop in to see "that Rab." There had not been a day since the first meeting that he had not wanted to.

Rab showed no surprise either over his return or the strange story that he proceeded to pour out. It was nightfall and, as Johnny hoped, Uncle Lorne and the little Webbs were gone. Rab was waiting for the ink to dry on the *Observer* so he could fold it. He sat with his long legs stretched before him, his hands clasped behind his neck.

"Lyte's crooked, you know," he said at last.

"I've heard that before."

"He's sly. When the merchants agreed not to import any English goods until the Stamp Act was repealed, he was one of the first to sign—then imported secretly. Sold through another name. Made more money. Sam Adams spoke to him privately —scared him. He says he won't do that again. He's trying to ride two horses—Whig and Tory."

Johnny's life with the Laphams had been so limited he knew little of the political strife which was turning Boston into two armed camps. The Whigs declaring that taxation without representation is tyranny. The Tories believing all differences could be settled with time, patience, and respect for government.

Rab obviously was a Whig. "I can stomach some of the Tories," he went on, "men like Governor Hutchinson. They honestly think we're better off to take anything from the British Parliament—let them break us down, stamp in our faces, take all we've got by taxes, and never protest. They say we American colonies are too weak to get on without England's help and guidance. But Governor Hutchinson's a good man. Of course we'll destroy him. We've marked him down. Sam Adams is already greasing the ways under him. But I can't stand men like Lyte, who care nothing for anything except themselves and their own fortune. Playing both ends against the middle."

"I'd never have picked him for a relative. But beggars can't be choosers—and happens I'm a beggar. It's on to time to get ready to go to him."

Understanding Johnny's unspoken desire not to appear too meanly before the great gentleman, Rab went to the attic above the shop where he slept and came down with a clean shirt of finest white linen and a fawn-colored corduroy jacket with silver buttons.

"It's too small for me. Ought to about fit you."

It did.

Almost miraculously—for Johnny had not seen where it came from—bread and cheese were on the counter. It was his first food since yesterday's gorging.

With the straight, fair hair well brushed and tied behind with taffeta, the handsome jacket, the frilled, immaculate shirt, Johnny did cut a very presentable figure.

By the printing-shop clock the sun had been set for almost an hour. Rab was folding newspapers.

"You can sleep here," he said, "if they don't offer you anything. But . . . good luck, bold fellow."

Standing on Beacon Hill, so far removed from the hurly-burly of the wharves, shops, markets of town, Johnny hesitated. Should he, as a poor out-of-work apprentice, go around back, or should he, as a long-lost something-or-other, raise that gleaming brass knocker on the paneled front door? The silver buttons and Rab's "bold fellow" heartened him. The knocker fell, and instantly a maid was bidding him enter, curtsying, asking his name.

"I'm Jonathan Lyte Tremain."

The front hall was very large. From it rose a flight of stairs, taking their time in their rising, taking all the space they needed. Along the walls were portraits: Merchant Lyte in his handsome, healthy youth; Lavinia, painted long before in London, as regal a child as now she was a young woman. Time blackened old things, already a hundred years old. Was it their long dried blood which now ran red and living in Johnny's veins?

To the left was the drawing room. The tinkle of a spinet, low voices, laughter. Could it be they were laughing because the maid was announcing him? He wished he had called himself merely Johnny Tremain.

"Ah-ha-ha." That was Merchant Lyte. "Fetch him in, Jenny. Just a little family party. All want to see him, eh?"

Johnny's first impression was of dozens of wax candles lighting the long, dove-colored and lavender-and-yellow room. They were reflected in mirrors, silver, gleaming floors and mahogany. A dozen people were gathered together in the far end of the room.

Johnny stood a moment, anxious to do nothing wrong, conscious that the new shoes he had been so proud of did not much resemble the little black buckled pumps on the gentlemen.

"Well," said Mr. Lyte, rising, but not approaching him. "So . . . here we are?"

"Yes, sir."

"Lavinia, Cousin Talbot, Aunt Best, how do you like his looks?"

Aunt Best, a horrifyingly ugly, cross old woman with two gold-headed canes, vowed through her whiskers and toothless gums that he looked just as bad as she had expected.

Lavinia turned from the spinet. She had on a stiff, turquoise-blue dress that suited her marvelously. She looked at the boy with her head tipped sidewise as Johnny had seen other ladies look at silver teapots before they bought.

"At least, Papa, he's a deal handsomer than most of my relatives. Isn't he, Cousin Sewall?" It was the rosy clerk, lovelorn Sewall, who was turning her music for her.

"Yes, daughter." Mr. Lyte's eyes flickered over Johnny. "Quite the little gentleman—from the waist up. Silver buttons, eh? Ruffled shirt?"

His eyes slid over his "little family party." He addressed them in so low a voice he seemed to ignore Johnny standing at the far upper end of the long room.

He had been expecting some such apparition from the past ever since last August. In spite of family efforts to keep certain things dark, he had reason to believe certain things were well known, even among the—ah—lower classes. Then he called to Johnny.

"Now, boy, you brought your cup?"

"It is here—in this bag."

"Very good. Will you—and all of you—please to step into the dining room?" This took some time, for Aunt Best had to be pulled in front and pushed from behind before she was balanced on her two gold-headed canes. She scolded, muttered, and shook her whiskers at everyone, including her famous nephew.

Only Lavinia, still at the spinet, and Cousin Sewall bending over her, did not go into the dining room.

There on the sideboard were three standing cups. They were identical with Johnny's. Silently he took his from its bag, set it with the other three, then stood back to look at the silken, bejeweled, perfumed folk crowding about him.

Mr. Lyte took up the cup, studied it, compared it with one of his own. Silently he handed it to a plainly dressed, thick-set gentleman who thus far had said nothing.

"I think," said Mr. Lyte quietly, "all of you ladies and gentlemen will agree that this cup our—ah, cousin, is it?—has brought back tonight is one of this set?"

There was a murmur of assent. Johnny could hear the tiny tinkle, seemingly far away, of Miss Lavinia's spinet.

"It is perfectly obvious that this cup now stands where it belongs. The question is how was it ever separated from its fellows?"

Johnny felt that everyone there except himself knew the answer to this question.

"In fact," the merchant's voice was smooth as oil, "I declare this to be the very cup which was stolen from me by thieves. They broke through yonder window on the twenty-third of last August. Sheriff, I order you to arrest this boy for burglary."

The thick-set plain man whom Johnny had already noticed, put a heavy hand on his shoulder. His formal words flowed over him.

"Johnny Tremain, alias Jonathan Lyte Tremain . . . apprentice to Ephraim Lapham . . . name of King and Bay Colony . . . standing cup . . . taken away the twenty-third day . . . month . . . year of our Lord one thousand seven hundred and seventy-three."

"This is not true," Johnny said.

"You can explain to the Judge."

"Very well, I can and will." The full horror of the accusation (for a boy might be hanged for stealing a silver cup) froze him into seeming nonchalance. This coolness made a bad impression. Aunt Best was poking at him with one of her canes. She hoped she'd live long enough to see him hanged. He was a perfect little viper—and he looked it. A florid woman was flapping a pink feather fan. She thought he had one of those falsely innocent little faces that are such an aid to evil boys.

"No," someone else was saying, "he has a shifty eye."

Aunt Best croaked, "Look at those silver buttons on his coat. I'm sure he stole them."

Mr. Lyte said, "Boy, where did you get that coat?"

"It was lent me."

"Lent you? By whom, pray?"

"A printer's boy. I don't know his last name. Down at the *Observer* office . . . He's called Rab."

"That coat is worth money. Do you think someone whose last name you admit you don't know would *lend* you a coat?"

"It doesn't sound likely—but happens it's true."

"Sheriff, look into this."

"I certainly will, Mr. Lyte."

"I sent Sewall over to the Laphams—a very respectable, humble, pious, poor sort of folk. Mrs. Lapham swore this boy never owned a thing but the clothes he stood in. As for his name, she showed Sewall the papers of his indenture, signed by his dead mother. She put him down as Johnny Tremain, no Jonathan Lyte about it. And Mrs. Lapham believed that lately he had taken to evil ways—stealing shoes and little things. She swore he never owned a cup. And Mr. Tweedie, a partner of Mr. Lapham, said the boy was a notorious liar, and of most evil report."

The sheriff was taking out handcuffs, snapping them on Johnny's wrist and his own.

"Soon's I get this scamp locked up, I'll be back for that bowl of punch you promised, Mr. Lyte," he called cheerfully as he left. The last sound Johnny heard was the fairy tinkle of the spinet.

The chain clanked. The sheriff said nothing until they had reached the stone jail in Prison Lane. Then, as the jailer was writing down Johnny's name in his book, the sheriff said kindly:

"Now, boy, you've got some rights. Who do you want notified? Got any kin except the Lytes, eh? How about old Mr. Lapham?"

"He's my master no more. He dismissed me months ago."

"Relatives? Parents?"

"I've nothing. But will you please tell that boy down at the *Observer*? He's a tall boy, and dark—all I know is that his name is Rab."

"The one you stole the coat off, hey? I was going to look him up tonight."

Oddly enough, Johnny slept well on his straw pallet in the jail. The night before, lying and weeping among the graves of Copp's Hill, he had reached bottom. He could not go lower

than that. No matter what happened, he could not help but
now go up. He knew Isannah's childish squeals were nothing
compared to the serious charge Mr. Lyte had brought against
him, but the squeals had just about broken his heart. The accusation of burglary he could take. He felt tough enough and
hard enough to take anything. But he could not help but think
of the gallows, just beyond the town gates, how they had
loomed up at him through the dark of the night like a warning.

Before he had finished his breakfast of corn gruel, Rab arrived. Johnny had known he would come. He brought blankets,
books, food. Seemingly, by the nonchalance of his manner,
nothing was more usual than to find one's friends in jail. About
his muscular, brown throat Johnny could see a medal hung
upon a string. On it was engraved a Tree of Liberty. So Rab
was one of the semi-secret famous Sons of Liberty, those carefully organized "mobs" who often took justice into their own
hands. They frightened royal officers out of Boston, stopped
British admirals from impressing Yankee seamen, as they were
impressed in England. They could at will paralyze trade,
courts, government. Many a night Johnny had heard their
whistles, conch shells, and cries of "town-born, turn out," the
running of their feet. And next day had seen the effigies they
had hung, the Tory fences they had torn down or windows
broken, and heard that Royal Commissioner So-and-So had
been frightened out of Boston. Or such-and-such a merchant
had wept when haled before the Liberty Tree and sworn never
to do trade with England until all grievances had been righted.
The Laphams had hated such lawless seizure of government
by the Sons of Liberty. Johnny had not thought much about
it. Seeing the medal at Rab's throat made him think it might
be fun to be out with them.

The medal did its work, for both the turnkey and the jailer
were also "Sons." Johnny was given a neat, private room on
the ground floor. Such rooms were usually reserved for gentlemen jailed for debt.

Here he told Rab his entire story. Rab had already found
out that the case would come up on the following Tuesday,
before Mr. Justice Dana. If Mr. Justice thought there was not
sufficient evidence to hold him for a higher court and a jury

trial, he would immediately release him. Then he asked if Johnny had shown his cup to any living soul sometime before August twenty-third. Such a witness would prove that Johnny had owned a cup, before Mr. Lyte's had been stolen.

"Why, of course—Cilla Lapham. That was July. Come to think, it was the very day Mr. Hancock ordered his sugar basin. It was the second day of July—that was a Tuesday."

"That's all you'll need. Mr. Lyte was a fool to bring so flimsy a charge against you."

"What do you suppose he meant when he said he had expected something like me turning up as soon as that cup was stolen?"

"I don't know what goes on in that clever, bad head, but perhaps he thinks you are an impostor and stole the cup first to back up some claim of kinship. Of course Cilla will come to court for you?"

"She will. If her mother will let her."

"Would Mrs. Lapham give you a good character?"

"No. She thinks these days I'm bad enough to steal a wig off a parson's head."

Next day Rab was back at the same time. He was a little perturbed. Mr. Lyte himself had been to the Laphams (in the ruby coach) and ordered a dozen silver spoons, a tea caddy, and, *if all went well,* would order a silver tankard a foot high.

"A bribe?"

"Cilla says he paid in advance. Then it was Mrs. Lapham said she would not have her girl mixed up in such a disgraceful case. She promised Cilla would spend next Tuesday under lock and key."

"I could hang first?"

"And she is determined to please that Mr. Tweedie too. If he won't sign that contract and get right to work, she can't get Mr. Lyte's silver made. Poor old Mr. Lapham won't do anything but read his Bible. Says he hasn't long to prepare to meet his Maker. By the way, Mr. Tweedie just about hates you. Says you called him a squeak-pig. He didn't like it."

"Of course, I called him a squeak-pig. Don't see why he cares."

"Well—you go around calling people squeak-pigs and you've

just about got to take it when they hit back. Not with their tongues—mostly they're not quick enough—but like this. Tweedie saw his chance to get back at you. He says if Mrs. Lapham lets Cilla testify for you, he'll take a ship back to Baltimore. Says he's sensitive and a great artist and he can't be upset by thieves and brawlers. Well . . . never mind. But I don't see the point of going around and . . ."

"Oh, forget those squeak-pigs, for Heaven's sake." Johnny was sulky.

"Now for a lawyer. I've talked to Josiah Quincy. He often writes for the *Observer*. He says if you want him, he's ready."

"Josiah Quincy? But . . . Rab, you tell him not to . . ."

"You don't want him? He's the best young lawyer in Boston."

"I could never pay him."

"You don't understand. He'll give you his time for nothing. He's coming to see you this afternoon. And I'm meeting Cilla, sort of behind her mother's back, to make plans."

"It all depends on Cilla, doesn't it?"

"Well . . . pretty much."

"And Mrs. Lapham and the squeak—I mean Tweedie—say they'll lock her up?"

"Lock her up so I can't get her out? Boy, I could get her out of this jail. Get her out of the Tower of London. And that girl would testify for you, even if it cost her her life. What's her real name?"

"Priscilla."

"Well, may Priscilla be on my side if ever I'm accused of anything. What about the little girl—is she really as bright as she looks?"

"No, I don't think so. She's just sort of a parrot. She's always going around repeating what Cilla or anyone else says to her as if she had thought it all up herself."

Mr. Justice Dana was a stout and florid man, dressed in a black silk robe and a great woolly white wig.

Johnny sat close to Mr. Quincy, watching the Justice's nervous, taut hands, listening to his "What have we heres" and quick questions to the men and women shoved up before him. Some people he dismissed, some he ordered fined, or whipped,

or set in the stocks, or held for a higher court. Johnny knew
when his own case would soon be called because he heard
the Justice tell a beadle to run down to Long Wharf and tell
Merchant Lyte to present himself in half an hour.

Once again Johnny squirmed about, studying every face in
the courtroom. Rab and Cilla were not there and he was
frightened.

Mr. Quincy whispered to him.

"Rab said he'd get her here by eleven. Rab's never slipped
yet."

Johnny liked his young lawyer. A frail man, flushed with
fever. His cough was prophetic of an early death. That was
how Johnny's mother had died—burned up by fever, coughing
herself to death. The man had a mobile, passionate face, handsome except for one wall eye.

Mr. Lyte arrived, escorted by his poor relative and clerk,
Sewall. He entered as though he owned the court, calling a
cheery good morning to Mr. Justice, interrupting the mumbled
explanation of a shabby bakeress accused of selling mouldy
bread. Next there was a rattle of light gig wheels, a jingle of
horse gear, and to the intense pleasure of everyone Miss Lavinia Lyte entered and, as modestly as she was able, took a
seat near the door.

Even the Justice straightened the bands at his throat. Sewall
blushed. The bakeress forgot what she was saying as she turned
to gape at the beautiful, dark woman, darkly dressed. Restless,
easily bored, Miss Lyte often did unexpected things.

"Jonathan Lyte *versus* Johnny Tremain, alias Jonathan Lyte
Tremain."

Mr. Quincy gave him a secret pat on the knee. Johnny knew
he must now step forward, take his oath on the Bible to tell
the truth, the whole truth—so help him God. He was frightened, for as he stepped forward he was conscious that these
might be the first steps toward those gallows—waiting in the
dark beyond the town gates.

Next Mr. Lyte was called and was taking the same oath.
Mr. Quincy's one good eye caught Johnny's. He was forming
words on his lips. The clock had indeed struck eleven and there,
standing in the doorway, were Rab and Cilla. Rab, enigmatical,

dark, capable, looked as always. Cilla had on a hood that half-covered her face.

Mr. Lyte was talking as informally as though he and Mr. Dana were alone together, sitting at a tavern, cracking walnuts, drinking Madeira. He told how his great-grandfather, Jonathan Lyte, Mayor of Causeway, Kent, England, had had six identical cups made—one for each of his sons. Four of these cups had come to this country and these he himself had owned until last August. On the night of the twenty-third, a thief or thieves had broken a pane out of his dining-room window. The space was too small to admit a grown man, so it was a half-grown boy who had slipped in and taken only one of the famous cups.

Then he snapped his fingers at Sewall, who stepped forward and set four silver cups on the table before the Justice.

"This is the stolen cup," Mr. Lyte said confidently. "I've tied a red ribbon on it." Then he went on to tell, with considerable humor and a bright sparkle in his slippery black eyes, about Johnny's visit to his shop, his claims of kinship, and how he had lured him to his house with the stolen cup.

The Justice said: "Mr. Lyte, could it not be possible that this boy is related to you? Could his story be true?"

No, no, it was impossible. Would Mr. Justice Dana be so good as to glance at this indenture—which the boy's erstwhile master, Mr. Lapham, had been so kind as to lend him? The name was put down as Johnny Tremain—nothing about Lyte. Undoubtedly older heads than this boy's had egged him on to this wretched, scurvy trick, but Mr. Lyte had no wish to go into the matter beyond the recovery of his own property. He did not wish to suggest in any way that the Laphams had any part in the imposture—they were very humble, honest, pious folk. He believed that the case of the theft, all that interested him at the moment, was "dead open and shut against the boy." And might he ask the death penalty? There was too much thieving going on in Boston. Poor apprentices were getting out of hand. The gallows had been too long empty.

"That's for the court to say," said the Justice sourly. He took snuff and Mr. Lyte took snuff. They sneezed together.

Mr. Quincy led Johnny on to tell his own story. The boy

spoke confidently, now that Rab and Cilla were there. He had never had an audience before and he felt the courtroom hanging on his words, believing him. He spoke better and better. He told how his mother had given him the cup, the little that she had told him. She had bidden him not to part with the cup—ever. Nor ever go to the Lytes unless he had come to the end of everything. Then he spoke simply and easily of his accident, his hunt for work, his despair—and arrest. There was a murmur almost of applause.

"Johnny," said Mr. Quincy, "did you obey your mother—never show your cup to anyone?"

"Once I disobeyed. It was the second day of last July. I forgot—or didn't heed. I told my master's daughter, Priscilla Lapham, what my mother said was my true name, and about the cup. She wanted to see it. It was just dawn—that is, the dawn of the third of July. Tuesday it was."

Cilla was called. Johnny had always thought her a shy girl, but she stood up straight before the Judge, speaking in her clear, low voice. He was proud of her. And he had always thought her a skinny, plain girl. She looked at the moment just about beautiful to him.

As she finished, there was a sensation in the courtroom that outweighed the arrival of Mr. Lyte and even his handsome daughter. Isannah, her bright curls in wild array, flew into the courtroom, seeming, like a mouse, to run without feet. She stopped for no oath, no formalities, but flung herself upon Mr. Justice Dana, telling over again Cilla's story. Johnny knew she had been sound asleep when he had told Cilla. She had even been in bed when he had actually shown the cup to her older sister. He was amazed at the vividness of her jumbled recital and touched by the virtues she attributed to himself. Yet she was making it all up.

In vain Mr. Justice Dana's "What have we here?" and "I cannot accept this as testimony," and Cilla's attempts to quiet her. She was so enchanting, so seemingly come from another world, she had her say.

"Bless me!" said Mr. Justice, blowing his nose. "And how old might you be?"

"Eight, sir, going on for nine."

"There now—be a good girl—here, you take this piece of licorice I have in my pocket and sit down quietly and eat it. There!"

Almost immediately he dismissed the case. There was not the slightest evidence, the Justice was saying, that the accused had stolen a cup, nor that the cup with the red ribbon, now illegally in the possession of Mr. Lyte, was the same one as was stolen from his house last August. Evidence was against that. For these young Lapham misses had proved to his satisfaction (and might he point out to Mr. Lyte his own testimony about the high character of honesty and piety the Laphams enjoyed?) that, unlikely as it might seem, the apprentice had possession of a silver cup, undoubtedly one of the original six ordered by the Mayor of Causeway, Kent. He bade Johnny Tremain take the one with the red ribbon. It was his own. If he liked, he might even bring a suit against Mr. Lyte. Didn't recommend it—Mr. Lyte was too powerful.

Johnny took the cup. In a moment he and Mr. Quincy, Rab and Cilla, were standing in the sunshine of the street outside the courthouse. They were so happy they could only laugh. The lawyer said now they would all go together, as his guests, to a tavern, to eat at their leisure, and drink a health to Johnny from the cup. But where was Isannah?

She was standing with a tiny hand in one of Miss Lyte's gloved ones, gazing up at her in adoration.

Cilla called her crossly. Miss Lyte stepped up into her high gig. It was a long step, but she was a lithe, long-legged woman.

"She said," panted Isannah, "she had never seen anything like me . . . not even in some lane in London."

"Drury Lane," said young Mr. Quincy dryly. "I was thinking of that myself."

"Rab," said the little girl, "was I really all right?"

"Just about perfect. Only some of it you put in the first person, so it wasn't quite the truth, but . . . you'll never starve."

Then she tried to kiss Johnny, but he thought it beneath his dignity to be kissed on the street.

"You're too mussed up with licorice," he said.

She bent and kissed his burned hand.

He said nothing. He was suddenly afraid he might cry.

Johnny Tremain was awarded the Newbery Medal in 1944. The author, Esther Forbes, has also written a splendid biography entitled America's Paul Revere, illustrated by the distinguished artist Lynd Ward, and published by Houghton Mifflin.

The Lance of Kanana

BY HARRY W. FRENCH

Illustrations by Wilfred Jones

Sometimes a mild manner and an aversion to violence cover a strength and courage that wait only to be tested. So it was with Kanana, the chieftain's son who ignored the jeers of his countrymen and saved fourth-century Arabia from her invaders.

1: The Coward of the Beni Sads

KANANA was an Arab—a Bedouin boy of many years ago, born upon the desert, of the seed of Ishmael, of the tribe of Beni Sad. It seems well-nigh impossible that the Bedouin boy could have lived who was not accustomed to the use of the sword and lance, long before he reached the dignity of manhood.

The peculiar thing about Kanana was that he never held a lance in his hand but once; yet many a celebrated sheik and powerful chieftain of his day lies dead, buried, and forgotten long ago, while the name of Kanana is still a magic battle cry among the sons of Ishmael, and his lance is one of the most precious relics of Arabia.

The old mothers and the white-haired veterans love to tell the story of the lance of Kanana; their black eyes flash like coals of fire when they say of it that it rescued Arabia.

The Beni Sads were a powerful tribe of roving Bedouins. Kanana was the youngest son of the venerable chief; the sheik who in the days of his strength was known from the Euphrates to the sea as the "Terror of the Desert."

By a custom older than the Boyhood of King David it fell to the lot of the youngest son to tend his father's sheep. The

The Lance of Kanana, by Harry W. French, is published by Lothrop, Lee & Shepard Company.

occupation was not considered dignified. It was not to Kanana's liking and it need not have lasted long; for the Terror of the Desert thought more of making warriors than shepherds of his sons, but greatly to his father's disgust Kanana refused to exchange his shepherd's staff for a warrior's lance. It was not that he loved the staff, but that he objected to the lance.

The tribe called Kanana effeminate because he was thoughtful and quiet, where other boys were turbulent, and as he grew older and the boyish fancy became a decided conviction against the combats constantly going on between the different tribes, they even called him a coward and said that he did not dare to fight.

There is but one name more bitter than "coward" to the Arab. That name is "traitor," and after being called a coward almost all his life, the very last words which Kanana heard from the lips of his countrymen came in frantic yells, calling him a traitor.

Today, however, it is always with throbbing hearts and flashing eyes that they repeat the story of the Lance of Kanana that rescued Arabia.

Until he was five years old, Kanana rolled about in the sand and sunshine, like the other children, with nothing on him but a twisted leather cord, tied round his waist.

Then, for five years, according to the custom of his people, he helped the women of his father's tent; shaking the goatskin filled with cream till it turned into butter; watching the kedder upon the fire, drying the buttermilk to be ground into flour, and digging kemma, which grow like truffles, under the sand.

After he was ten, for three years he watched the sheep and

goats and the she-camels. That was the regular course of education through which all Bedouin boys must pass.

When he reached the age at which Ishmael was sent away with Hagar by Abraham, he was supposed to drop all menial labor and take his place among men; making a position for himself according to the fighting qualities which he possessed.

Kanana's fighting qualities, however, were only exhibited in the warfare which now began between him and his father.

There were at that time very few occupations open to the Bedouin boy. The tribe was celebrated for its men of learning and boasted the most skillful physicians in all Arabia; but they had won all their first laurels with the lance, and none of them wanted Kanana.

Three times his father came to him with the question: "Are you ready to be a man?" and three times Kanana replied, "My father, I cannot lift a lance to take a life, unless it be for Allah and Arabia."

How he came by a notion so curious no Arab could tell. The lad well knew the old decree that the hand of the Ishmaelite should be against every man, and every man's hand against him. He knew that every Arab of the desert lived by a warfare that was simply murder and robbery. Was he not an Arab, and an Ishmaelite?

Alone, among the sheep and camels, he had thought out his own theory. Kanana said to himself, "I am taught that Allah created these animals, and cares for them, and that I cannot please him if I allow them to suffer; it must be surely that men are more precious to Allah than animals. Why should we kill one another, even if we are Arabs and Ishmaelites?"

The menial tasks still allotted to Kanana grew more and more irksome. His punishment was far more keen than the tribe supposed; no one dreamed of the sharp cringe of pain with which he heard even the children call him a coward.

There were some faculties which Kanana possessed that made the warriors all envy him. He had a remarkable power over animals. No other Beni Sad could ride a camel or a horse so fast as Kanana. The most refractory creature would obey Kanana. Then, too, Kanana was foremost in the games and races. No other shepherd's eye was nearly so quick as Kanana's to detect an enemy approaching the flocks at night. No other young Bedouin, watching the ripening grain, could throw a stone from his sling so far and so accurately at the robber birds.

These accomplishments, however, only made his father the more angry that Kanana would not turn his gifts to some more profitable end.

Every year for three months—from planting to harvest-time—the Beni Sads encamped upon a river bank, on the outskirts of the Great Desert. The encampment numbered nearly five hundred tents set in four rows as straight as the arrow flies. These tents, of black goat's-hair cloth, were seven feet high in the center and five feet high on the sides. Some of them were twenty feet broad, and each was divided by a beautiful hanging white Damascus carpet. The men occupied one side, and the women and the children the other. The favorite mare and the most valuable of the camels always slept by the tent, and the master's lance stood thrust into the ground at the entrance.

Far as the eye could reach, up and down the sluggish river, a field of ripening grain filled the narrow space between the yellow water and the silver-gray of the desert sand.

Here and there, through the grainfield, rose curious perches —platforms, constructed upon poles driven into the ground. Upon these platforms watchers were stationed when the grain began to head, and there they remained night and day till it was harvested, frightening the birds away.

Once a day the women brought them food, consisting of buttermilk, dried and ground and mixed with melted butter and dates; these same women renewed the supply of stones to throw at the birds.

The watchers were old men, women who were not needed in the tents, and little children; but all alone, this year, upon the most distant perch, sat Kanana.

There was not one of the tribe but felt that he richly deserved this disgrace; and Kanana could see no way to earn their respect, no way to prove himself a brave fellow. He was glad that they had given him the most distant perch, for there he could bear his hard lot, away from jests and jeers.

The women who brought the food stopped for a long time

at some of the perches reporting all the news, but they never troubled themselves to relieve Kanana's solitude. The perches were too far apart for conversation. Kanana had always time enough to think, and as the grain grew yellow this year, he came to two positive conclusions. He firmly resolved that before the reapers entered that field he would do something to convince his people that he was not a coward; failing that, he would hang his head in shame, acknowledge that they were right, and fly forever from their taunts.

2: The Old Sheik's Promise

The sun was beating fiercely down upon Kanana's perch, but he had not noticed it. The stones piled beside him for his sling were almost hot enough to burn his hand, but he did not realize it, for he had not touched them for a long time. The wooden dish of paste and dates stood in the shadow of the perch. He had not tasted them.

The pile of stones grew hotter and hotter. The hungry birds ate and quarreled and ate, with no one to disturb them. The Bedouin boy sat cross-legged on his perch, heedless of everything, twisting and untwisting the leather cords of his sling, struggling to look into the mists that covered up his destiny.

"Hi, there! You slothful son of a brave father! Look at the birds about you. Are you dead, or only sleeping?" sounded the distant but shrill and painfully distinct voice of an old woman who, with two children much younger than Kanana, occupied the next perch.

Kanana roused himself and sent the stones flying from his sling till there was not a bird in sight. Then he sank into deep thought once more; with his head resting upon his hands he became oblivious to everything.

Suddenly he was roused by the sound of horses' hoofs upon the sandy soil, a sharp rustling in the drying grain. He looked up, as thoroughly startled as though he had been sleeping, to see approaching him the one person than whom he would rather that any or all of the tribe of Beni Sad should find him negligent at his post of duty.

It was his father.

"O Kanana! O Kanana!" cried the old man, angrily. "Thou son of my old age, why didst thou come into the world to curse me? When thou shakest the cream, the butter is spoiled. When thou tendest the sheep, they are stolen! When thou watchest the grain, it is eaten before thy face! What shall a father do with a son who will neither lift his hand among men nor bear a part with women? And now, when all the miseries of life have taken hold upon me and the floods cover me, thou sittest at thine ease to mock me!"

Kanana sprang down from his perch. Kneeling, he touched his forehead to the ground.

"My father, slay me and I will take it as a mercy from thy hand. Or, as I am fit for nothing here, bid me go, and among strangers I will beg. But thou shalt not, my father, speak of me as ungrateful, unfilial. I know of no flood of sorrow that has come down upon thee."

"Thou knowest not what they all know?" exclaimed the old man fiercely.

"I know of nothing, my father. Since I came into the field, three weeks ago, no one has spoken to me but to chide me."

"Then know now," replied the sheik reproachfully, "that of thy two brave brothers who went with the last caravan, one has returned, wounded and helpless, and the other, for an old cause of blood between our tribes, has been made a prisoner by Raschid Airikat. The whole caravan, with the white camel at its head, Raschid has taken, and he has turned with it toward Damascus."

"Thy part of the caravan was very small, my father," said

Kanana. "Only four of the camels were thine, and but for the white camel they were all very old. Their burdens, too, saving my brothers, were only honey and clay dust, of little value."

This was the simple truth, and evinced at least a very practical side to Kanana's mind; but it was not the kind of sympathy which the sheik desired, and his anger burst out afresh against Kanana.

"Ay, thou tender of flocks, and sleeper!" he cried. "Wouldst thou teach me the value of camels and merchandise to comfort me? And hast thou fixed the price of ransom which Airikat will

demand, or slay thy brother? And hast thou reckoned up the value of the white camel which could not be bought for gold, as it brought to thy father and thy father's father all their abundance of good? Answer me, if thou art so wise. Oh, that I had a son remaining who could lift a lance against Airikat as bravely as he hurls his empty words at an old father!"

"My father," said Kanana earnestly, "give me a horse, a sack of grain, a skin of water, and I will follow after Raschid Airikat. I will not slay him, but, by the help of Allah, I will bring back to thee thy white camel with my brother seated upon his back."

The old sheik made a gesture of derision: "Thou wisp of flax before a fire! Thou reed before a whirlwind! Get thee back to thy perch and thy birds, and see if thou canst keep awake till sundown. Harvesting will begin with the daylight tomorrow. See that thou workest then."

Kanana rose to his feet. Looking calmly into the old sheik's angry face, he replied:

"My father, I will watch the birds till sundown. Then let others do the reaping. Kanana, whom thou scornest, will be far away upon the desert, to seek and find his brother."

"Did I not say I would not trust a horse to thee?" exclaimed the old man, looking at him in astonishment.

"These feet of mine can do my bidding well enough," replied Kanana. "And by the beard of the Prophet they shall do it till they have returned to thee thy son and thy white camel. I would do something, O my father, that I, too, might have thy blessing and not thy curse. It is the voice of Allah bids me go. Now say to me that if I bring them back, then thou wilt bless me, too; ay, even though still I will not lift a lance, unless it be for Allah and Arabia."

The aged warrior looked down in scornful pity upon his boy, standing among the stalks of grain; half in jest, half in charity, he muttered, "Yes, *then* I will bless thee," and rode away.

The harvesting began, as the old sheik had said, with the next daylight, but Kanana was not among the reapers.

Few so much as missed him, even, and those who did miss him supposed that he had hidden himself to avoid their jests.

Only the sullen sheik, bowed under his affliction, thought often of Kanana as he rode up and down the line. He remembered his looks, his words. He wondered if he could have been mistaken in the boy. He wished he had given him the horse and that he had blessed him before he went away.

3: At the Foot of Mount Hor

The moment the sun sank into the billows of sand Kanana had left his perch.

From the loaded stalks about him he gathered a goat's-hair sack of grain and fastened it upon his back. There was no one to whom he need say farewell, and, armed only with his shepherd's staff, he started away upon the desert, setting his course to the north and west.

Before he had gone far he passed a lad of about his own age who had come from the encampment to hunt for desert rats. Had Kanana seen him he would have made a wide detour, but the boy lay so still upon the sand that the first Kanana knew of his presence was when a low sarcastic voice uttered his name.

"Kanana!" it exclaimed. "Thou here! Dost thou not fear that some rat may bite thee? Whither darest thou to go thus, all alone and after dark, upon the sand?"

Fire flashed from Kanana's eyes. His hand clutched his shepherd's staff and involuntarily he lifted it; but the better counsel of his curious notions checked the blow. It was so dark that the boy upon the sand did not notice the effect of his taunts and knew nothing of his narrow escape. He only heard the quiet voice of Kanana as presently it meekly replied to his question:

"I go to Mount Hor."

It was an answer so absurd that the boy gave it no second thought and by the time that the footsteps of Kanana had died away the rat-hunter had as utterly forgotten him as though he had never existed.

To Mount Hor?

Kanana had only the most imperfect information to guide him. He knew that the Beni Sad caravan had been for some days upon the road southward to Mecca, when it was captured by Raschid Airikat and turned at an angle, northward toward Damascus.

Seen from a great distance over the sea of sand, the solitary peak of old Mount Hor, where Aaron, the great high priest of Israel, was buried, forms a startling beacon. By day or night, it rises clear and sharp against the sky, guiding the caravans northward from Arabia to Jerusalem and Damascus, and southward from Syria to Medina and Mecca; while the fertile oasis about it is the universal resting-place.

Kanana was not at all sure that the caravan would not have passed Mount Hor long before he could reach it; but if so, it must in time return that way, and, in any case, of all Arabia Mount Hor was the one spot where he could be sure to gather further information from passing caravans.

He knew his path upon that shifting sand as well as an Indian knew his way through the trackless forests of New England. With the sun and stars above him, any Arab would have scorned the idea of being lost in Arabia, and through the long night with strong and steady strides Kanana pressed onward toward Mount Hor.

As the harvest moon rose above the desert behind him, the Bedouin boy was softly chanting from the second *sura* of Al Koran:

"God, there is no God but him;
The living! The Eternal!
Slumber doth not overtake him,
Neither Sleep.
And upholding all things,
To him is no burden.
He is the Lofty and the Great."

His long black shadow fell over the silver sand, and, watching it, he chanted the Koran again:

"God is God. Whatever of good betideth
thee cometh from him.
Whatever of evil is thine own doing."

Suddenly a speck appeared upon the distant horizon. None but the keen eye of a shepherd would have seen it in the night, but Kanana watched it as it quivered and wavered, disappearing as it sank into a valley in the rolling sand, appearing again, like a dory on the ocean, each time a little nearer than before.

Kanana noted the direction the speck was taking, and he made a wide path for it; he crouched among the sand shrubs when it came too near.

First a small party of horsemen passed him, the advance guard of a moving tribe. Then came the main body of men upon camels and horses; but the only sounds were made by the feet of the animals and the clanking of the weapons.

The she-camels with their young followed; then the sheep and goats driven by a few men on foot; next, the camels laden with the tents and furniture; last of all, the women and children of the tribe accompanied by another armed escort.

From all that company there was not a sound but of the sand and the trappings. There was nothing but shadows, swinging, swaying shadows, moving like phantoms over the white sand, as the trailing train went gliding on in that mysterious land of shadows and silhouettes.

There was nothing in it that was weird to Kanana, however. He hid himself simply as a precaution. He had often been a

part of such a caravan, and he knew from experience that if a solitary Arab were found upon the desert, he would very quickly be forced to help drive the sheep and goats, and kept at it until he could make his escape. Any Arab boy would have hidden himself.

Long before Kanana's next halt the sun was pouring down its furious heat. To his great good fortune he came upon a bowlder rising out of the sand; there he quickly made a place for himself where the sun could not reach him and, lying down, slept until night.

Only one who has walked upon a desert hour after hour, parched with thirst and utterly exhausted in the fierce glare and heat, can properly appreciate the Bible picture of "the shadow of a great rock in a weary land."

Had he not found this rock, Kanana would simply have dug a hole in the sand and forced himself into it.

Here and there as he pressed on, Kanana saw grim skeletons of men and animals as they lay whitening among the sand shrubs, but he paid them little attention. Before the sun had set upon the second day, he beheld the distant summit of Mount Hor cutting sharply into the blue sky.

This sight renewed his strength. Hour after hour he pressed onward, with his eyes fixed upon the tomb of Aaron, a white monument upon the summit of the mountain, flashing like snow as the moon rose in the clear, blue-black sky.

Kanana did not pause again until he fell upon his knees beside the stream which rises in a spring upon Mount Hor, to die in the sand, not far from its base. He plunged into the water; then, dressing himself again, he lay down upon the bank to sleep. He awoke with the first gray lighting in the east, when the air of a desert is almost cold enough to freeze.

He had now nothing more to do till he could obtain some information from passing caravans. It would soon be sunrise, the hour for morning prayer, and, to warm himself while he waited, he walked along the banks of the stream. They were blue as the very sky with masses of forget-me-nots.

Suddenly Kanana paused. He started back. His eyes dilated, and his hand trembled till the shepherd's staff fell, unheeded, to the ground. The next moment he dropped to the ground to examine the place more carefully.

What was it? Only some marks upon the grass where a caravan had camped. The herbage was matted here and there where the camels lay, and cropped short in little circles about each spot where they had eaten it as far as they could reach.

Caravans were continually resting for the day under the shadow of Mount Hor. There was nothing remarkable in the fact that a caravan had camped there and had gone. They always move at night; not so much because it is cooler as because a camel will not eat at night, no matter how hungry he may be, and must be given the daylight or he will deliberately starve.

A moment later Kanana was upon his feet again with a triumph in his eyes which clearly indicated his satisfaction.

The grass about the spot was unevenly cropped; there were straggling spears of green left standing in the center of each mouthful which the camel had taken. Upon one side the bees were clustering on the matted grass. A multitude of ants appeared upon the other side. The imprint left by the forefoot of the camel showed that it had been extended in front of him, instead of being bent at the knee and folded beneath him.

All this meant to the young Arab that the camel was old, that it was lame in the left knee, that it had lost a front tooth, that its burden on one side was honey, on the other the dust of river clay to be used in the manufacture of stucco.

Had one of his father's camels stood before him, Kanana could not have been more sure. Nothing more was needed to

assure him that Raschid Airikat, with the stolen camels, had
left Mount Hor the night before, upon the trail leading southward into Arabia.

His eyes flashed with excitement. "My brother and the white
camel are not ten hours from here, and they are on the road to
Mecca or Medina," he exclaimed as his fingers tightened about
the staff. His white teeth glistened in a smile, as he added, "They
are mine, or I am a coward!"

He stood there motionless for a moment, his dark eyes instinctively turning southward. The magnitude of his task lay
vividly before him. He recalled his father's words: "Thou wisp
of flax before a fire! Thou reed before a whirlwind!" They
served to strengthen him.

The first step which lay before him was enough to test the
courage of a brave man, and yet it was only a step toward a
grand destiny.

Suddenly starting from his reverie, Kanana exclaimed:

"I will do it! Or I will consent to be known forever as the
coward of the Beni Sads!" and turning he ran up the rocky sides
of old Mount Hor, toward the white tomb of Aaron, whence he
knew he could see far away over the great ocean of sand.

It might be there would yet appear a speck upon the distant
horizon, to guide him toward the retreating caravan.

4: The Promise

Up the steep sides of Mount Hor Kanana climbed, without
waiting to look for a path. He saw nothing, heard nothing. He
was all eagerness to reach the summit, in the faint hope that
it might not be too late to see the departing caravan of Raschid
Airikat.

Unless a camel is fresh, unusually large and strong, or constantly urged, it rarely makes more than two miles an hour. It
was not over ten hours since the robber sheik had left the oasis,
and some of the camels were very old and exhausted. It was
a foolish hope no doubt, and yet Kanana hoped that anything
so large as a great caravan might still be distinguishable.

Up, up, up he climbed—as fast as hands and feet could

carry him. He no longer felt the cool air of early morning. He no longer looked about him to see the new sights of a strange oasis.

He did not even pause to look away over the desert as he climbed. The highest point was none too high. He did not care how far he could see until he had gained the white tomb of Aaron, upon the very crest.

Had he not been too thoroughly occupied with what was above him to notice what transpired about him and down below, he would have seen five Arab horsemen reach the stream by which he slept, almost as he began to climb.

They were Mohammedan soldiers, thoroughly armed for war, and had evidently come from the northern borders of Arabia, where the victorious Mussulmans were planting the banner of Islam.

They had been riding hard, and both men and horses were exhausted. They hurried to the water. The men hastily ate some food which they carried, and tethered their horses in Arab fashion, by a chain, one end of which is fastened about the forefoot of the animal and the other end about the master, to prevent their being stolen while the master sleeps. The moment this was accomplished, the five men rolled themselves in their mantles, covering their faces as well as their bodies, and lay down upon the grass to sleep.

They were skilled in the art of making long journeys in the shortest possible time, and were evidently upon important business; for an Arab is never in haste unless his mission is very important.

Before Kanana reached the temple the men were soundly sleeping, and the horses, lying down to rest themselves, were still eating the grass about them, as a camel eats.

Panting for breath, trembling in eager haste, Kanana reached the tomb of Aaron: an open porch, with white pillars supporting a roof of white, like a crown of eternal snow on the summit of Mount Hor.

Between the snowy pillars Kanana paused. One quick glance at the sky gave him the points of the compass, and, shading his eyes from the glowing east, he looked anxiously to the south and west.

Sand, sand, sand, in billows like great waves of an ocean, lay about him in every direction. Far away there were low hills, and a semblance of green which, to his practiced eye, meant a grove of date palms upon the banks of a stream. But nowhere, search as he would, was there the faintest speck to indicate the caravan.

He was still anxiously scanning those distant hills when the first rays of the rising sun shot from the eastern horizon, flashing a halo of glory upon the snow-white crown of old Mount Hor, before they touched the green oasis lying about its base.

Never, in all the ages, had the sun rising from the Arabian desert seen such a tableau as his first beams illumined at Aaron's tomb.

All absorbed in his eager search, Kanana stood upon the very edge of the white porch. One hand was extended, grasping his shepherd's staff, the other was lifted to shade his eyes. In his eagerness to reach forward, one foot was far before the other, and the knee was bent as though he were ready to leap down the steep declivity before him.

His turban, a large square piece of cloth, was bound about his head with a camel's-hair cord; one corner was thrown back over his forehead, and a corner fell over each shoulder like a cloak. His coat was sheepskins, stitched together. Summer and winter, rain and sunshine, the Bedouin shepherd wears that sheepskin coat, as the best protection against both sun and frost.

His bare feet rested firmly upon the white platform, and the arm that held the shepherd's staff was knotted with muscles which a strong man might have envied him.

His beardless face was dark, but not so dark as to hide the eager flush which heightened the color in his cheeks, and his chest rose and fell in deep, quick motions from his rapid climb.

His lips were parted. His dark eyes flashed, while the hand which shaded them stood out from his forehead as though trying to carry the sight a little farther, that it might pierce the defiles of those distant hills and the shadows of the date palm groves.

The sun rose higher, and its full light fell across the young Ishmaelite. It was the signal for the morning call to prayer, and from the minaret of every mosque in the realm of Islam was sounding *La Illaha il Allah Mahamoud rousol il Allah.* Kanana did not need to hear the call, however. He instantly forgot his mission, and, a humble and devout Mohammedan, laid aside his staff and reverently faced toward Mecca to repeat his morning prayer.

Standing erect, with his open hand beside his head, the palms turned forwards, he solemnly began the *Nummee Allah voulhamda.* With his hands crossed upon his breast he continued. Then he placed his hands upon his knees, then sat upon the floor. Then with his open hands upon the floor he touched his forehead to the platform as he repeated the closing words of the prayer.

In this position he remained for some time, whispering a petition for strength and courage to carry out the task he had undertaken.

There was something so solemn and impressive in the deathlike stillness of the early morning, upon that solitary peak, that it almost seemed to Kanana that, if he listened, he should hear the voice of Allah, answering his prayer.

Suddenly the silence was broken by a sharp cry, and another and another in quick succession mingled with savage yells.

It was not the voice of Allah, for which he had been waiting, and Kanana sprang to his feet and looked anxiously about him.

The mountains of Arabia are not high. Among real mountains, Mount Hor would be but a rocky hill. Looking down for the first time, Kanana saw the stream below him in its border of blue forget-me-nots, and could clearly distinguish the five soldiers who had so quickly fallen asleep upon its banks.

It was a fearful sight which met his eyes. The five men were still lying there, but they were no longer sleeping. They were dead or dying; slain by three Bedouin robbers who had crept upon them for the valuable prize of their horses, and who did not dare attempt to steal the animals while the masters were alive.

It was almost the first time that Kanana's eyes had rested upon a scene of blood, common as such scenes are among his countrymen, and he stood in the porch benumbed with horror, while the robbers tore from the bodies about them such garments as pleased them; then took their weapons, mounted three of the horses, and leading two rode away quickly to the north.

There was no assistance which Kanana could render the unfortunate men. The caravan was already a night's march ahead of him and every moment that he lost must be redeemed by hurrying so much the faster under the burning sun, over the scorching sand, when, at the best, it was doubtful if flesh and blood could stand what must be required of it.

With a shudder he turned from the terrible scene and began to descend the mountain. Soon he was upon the bank of the stream and passing close to the spot where the five bodies were lying. He would not run, but he hurried on with his eyes fixed on the ground.

A faint sound caught his ear. He started, clutched his staff, and turned sharply about, thinking that the robbers had seen him and returned. It was only one of the unfortunate soldiers who had been left for dead. He had raised himself upon his elbow, and was trying to attract Kanana's attention.

"Water! Water! In the name of Allah, give me water!" he gasped, and fell back unconscious.

For a moment Kanana was tempted to hurry on. He did not want to go there, any more than he wanted to delay his journey; but something whispered to him of the promises of the

Koran to those who show mercy to the suffering: that Allah would reward even a cup of water given to the thirsty.

It required no little courage of the Bedouin boy, all alone under Mount Hor, but he resolutely turned back, filled with water the wooden cup which a shepherd always carries at his girdle, and poured it down the parched throat of the almost insensible man.

"Bless God for water!" he gasped. "More! Give me more!"

Kanana ran to the brook and filled the cup again, but the poor man shook his head. It was too late. He was dying.

Suddenly he roused himself. He made a desperate struggle to call back his failing senses, and, for a moment, threw off the hand of Death. He had almost given up, forgetting something of great importance. Steadying himself upon his elbow, he looked into Kanana's face and said:

"You are a beardless youth, but you are an Arab. Listen to me. The mighty Prince Constantine, son of the Emperor Heraclius, is soon to leave Constantinople, at the head of a vast army of Turks and Greeks and Romans, like the leaves of the forest and the sand of the desert. He is coming to sweep the Arab from the face of the earth and the light of the sun. We were bearing a letter to the Caliph Omar, who is now at Mecca, telling him of the danger and asking help. If the letter does not reach him, Arabia is lost and the Faithful are destroyed. Would you see that happen?"

Too frightened to speak and hardly comprehending the situation, Kanana simply shook his head.

The man made another effort to overcome the stupor that had almost mastered him. He succeeded in taking from his clothing a letter, sealed with the great seal, and gasped:

"In the name of Allah, will you fly with this to the great caliph?"

Hardly realizing what he said, Kanana solemnly repeated: "In the name of Allah, I will."

He took the letter and was hiding it in his bosom when the soldier grasped the cup of water, drank ravenously, and, with the last swallow, let the cup fall from lifeless fingers.

Minute after minute passed, but Kanana did not move a muscle. His hand still touched the letter which he had placed in his bosom. His eyes still rested upon the lips that would never speak again.

His sacred promise had been pledged to fly with that letter to the great caliph at Mecca. It had been made in the name of Allah. It had been given to the man now lying dead before him. There was no power that could retract it. It must be performed, and until it was, no other consideration could retard his steps or occupy his thoughts.

His lips parted and he muttered angrily: "Is this my reward for having given a cup of water to the thirsty?" Then it suddenly occurred to him that the caravan which he longed most of all to follow was also upon its way southward, and that, for the present at least, for either mission the direction was the same, and the demand for haste was great.

He caught his staff from the ground and set his face toward Mecca, pondering upon the dying statement of the soldier till word for word it was fastened in his memory, and the thought that his mission was for Allah and Arabia urged him on.

It was an easy task to follow the trail of the caravan. The Bedouin would be a disgrace to the desert, who could not recognize in the sand the recent footprint of one of his own tribe or of a camel with which he is familiar, and who could not tell by a footprint whether the man or camel who made it carried a burden, often what that burden was, always whether he was fresh or exhausted, walking leisurely or hurrying.

So Kanana hurried on, daily reading the news of the caravan before him as he went, testing his strength to the utmost before he rested, and starting again as soon as he was able; over the sand and over the hills, through groves and villages and over sand again; always toward Mecca.

5: Led by a White Camel

In the world-famous city of Mecca, two men stood by the arch that leads to the immortal Caaba.

They were engaged in an earnest conversation, heedless of everything about them, when the distant cry of a camel driver sounded on the still air.

Both of the men started and looked at each other in surprise. One of them said:

"A caravan at the gate at this time of day!" for it was several hours past midday and a caravan, in the ordinary course of things, reaches a city gate during the night or very early in the morning.

Arabia was seeing troubled times, and every one was on the alert for anything out of the accepted rule.

The camel-driver's cry was repeated. The first speaker remarked:

"They have left the burdened camels at the Moabede gate and are entering the city."

With an anxious look upon his face the elder of the two replied, "Either they have been hard pressed by an enemy or it is important news which brings them over the desert in such haste, in this insufferable heat."

The two men were evidently of great importance in the holy city. They were surrounded by powerful black slaves, who had all that they could do to keep the passers-by from pressing too close upon the elder man, in a desire to touch the hem of his garment. Many, in passing, knelt and touched their foreheads to the ground. Thus they waited the coming caravan.

The first camel of an important caravan is led by a man who walks before it through the narrow streets of a city, and his cry is to warn the crowd to clear the way; there being no sidewalks, and, indeed, but very little street.

"There it comes," said the younger of the two, as the long line of drowsy camels appeared, swinging, swinging, swinging along the narrow street.

"Led by a white camel," added the elder, and they both looked down the street.

The lead-camel was larger than the rest—much larger, and very much lighter colored; a sort of dingy white, like a sheep before shearing. The chief of the caravan sat upon his back, as unmindful of everything as though he were still upon the trackless sand.

It is not impossible that the sheik was really sleeping, and unconsciously grasping his ugly lance, while his Damascus blade hung ready by his side.

He roused in a moment, however, for with many a grunt and groan the great, ungainly, and yet very stately, ships of the desert came slowly and drowsily to anchor in the court before the Caaba.

"*Haji*," a naked little urchin muttered, looking up from his play; but he should have known better. *Haji* means pilgrims, and these were no pilgrims.

There are seasons when this city is one mass of humanity. Haji by hundreds and thousands throng the narrow streets, but these are Bedouins of the desert, bound upon some other mission than worshiping before the Caaba, kissing the Black Stone, or drinking the holy water of Zemzem.

The leader of the white camel gave a peculiar pull to the rope hanging over his shoulder, attached to the animal's bridle, and uttered a short, sharp word of command.

Slowly, very slowly, the dignified, dingy creature, towering high above him, acknowledged the receipt of the order, but he gave no evidence that he was making any arrangements to obey.

His response was simply a deliberate grunt and a weird and melancholy wail that came gurgling out of his long, twisting throat. He would not have hurried himself one atom, even for the sheik upon his back.

A white camel is to the Arab what a white buffalo is to the Indian and a white elephant to the Ceylonese, and he fully appreciates his importance.

He deliberately turned his woolly head quite about till his great brown eyes, with the drooping lids almost closed over them, could most conveniently look back along the line of lank, inferior camels and gaunt and weather-beaten dromedaries, which had patiently followed him, day after day, to the temple court of immortal Mecca.

He was so long about it that the leader repeated the command, and very slowly the camel brought his head back again, till his languid eyes looked drowsily down in a sort of scornful charity upon the insignificant mortal at the other end of his halter.

He had stood in the court of Mecca long before that man was born and would doubtless guide caravans to the same spot long after he was buried and forgotten.

"You may be in haste, but I am not," he seemed to say, and dreamily turned his eyes toward the black-curtained Caaba, as if to see how it had fared since his last visit.

That Caaba, the Holy of Holies of the Mussulman, is the most revered and possibly the most venerable of all the sacred buildings on the earth; but the gentle, wistful eyes of the white camel were more practically drawn toward two or three date-palm trees then growing beside it. When he had satisfied himself that the only green thing in sight was quite beyond his reach, he deliberately lowered his head, changed his position a little, and with another grunt and another melancholy wail sank upon his knees, then upon his haunches. With a deep sigh he lifted his head again still high above the head of his driver, and his drowsy eyes seemed to say to him: "Poor man! I kept you waiting, didn't I?"

Then he quickly turned his head to the opposite side, deliberately poking his nose into the passing throng, till, with a grunt of recognition, it touched the garment of one who was hurrying on among the crowd.

It was evidently a Bedouin, but the wings of his turban were drawn together in front, so that no one could see his face. He responded to the greeting of the white camel, however, by laying his hand upon the creature's nose as he passed. It was a motion which no one noticed, and a moment later he was out of sight.

He was following a boy who had led him directly to the arch, where the boy paused, pointed to the elder of the two men standing there, briefly observing: "It is he."

The Bedouin paused for a moment, as if struggling to collect his thoughts, then hurrying forward was the next to prostrate himself before the venerable man. As he rose he handed him a package, simply observing: "A message to the Caliph Omar."

The great caliph quickly broke the seal and read.

Then, turning to the bearer, he asked sharply, "Who art thou?"

"I am Kanana, son of the sheik of the Beni Sads," replied the Bedouin boy, letting the wings of his turban fall apart that Omar might see his face.

"A beardless youth!" exclaimed the caliph. "And dost thou know aught of the import of this letter?"

Kanana repeated the dying words of the Arab soldier, which had so often escaped his lips as he urged his weary feet toward Mecca.

" 'Tis even so," replied the caliph. "And how came living man to trust a boy like you to come alone through the streets of Mecca with such an errand?"

"I came alone with the letter from the oasis at Mount Hor," replied Kanana, straightening himself up with very pardonable pride before the astonished eyes of the great caliph.

Then he related, briefly, how the letter came into his keeping, and the dangers and escapes of the three long weeks during which he carried it in his bosom; each rising and setting sun finding it a little nearer to its destination.

"Thou art a brave youth," said the caliph, "a worthy son of the Terror of the Desert. Would to Allah that every Arab had thy heart, and Heraclius himself, with all the world behind him, could not move the Faithful from their desert sands. And they shall not be moved! No! By the beard of the Prophet, they shall not be moved! Hear me, my son; I will see more of thee. This is no place for conversation, where the wind bloweth into what ears it listeth. One of my slaves shall conduct you to my house. There I will meet you presently. Go, and Allah go with you."

Indicating the slave who should take Kanana in charge, the Caliph Omar turned abruptly away and showed the letter to the man with whom he had been conversing.

Guided by the black slave, Kanana passed out again under the arch, and walked the streets of Mecca, caring less and

thinking less concerning what transpired about him than anyone, before or since, who for the first time stood in the holy
city.

He found the narrow streets densely crowded. Soldiers and
merchants, Bedouins and city Arabs mingled with an array of
every tribe Arabia could furnish. There were venders of all
things pertaining to the necessities or luxuries of life; water
carriers with goatskins on their shoulders; fruit criers with
wooden trays upon their heads; donkeys laden with cumbersome baskets, beneath which they were almost lost to sight;
camels carrying packs of a thousand pounds' weight upon
their backs, as though they were bundles of feathers; everything hustling and jostling, men and boys shouting and pushing for the right of way.

They all turned out as best they could, however, for the
savage black slave of the great caliph, and by keeping close
behind him Kanana always found an open space where he
could walk without fighting for room.

It was almost the first experience of the Bedouin boy in real
city life, and the very first time that his bare feet had ever
touched the beaten sand of the unpaved streets of his most
sacred Mecca.

He turned from the arch, however, without once glancing
at the black-curtained Caaba, the Beitullah, or House of God,
toward which three times a day he had turned his face in
reverent devotion ever since he had learned to pray.

He followed the black slave onward through the streets,
without so much as looking at the walls of the houses that
crowded close on either hand.

He had fulfilled his vow. The packet he had sacredly guarded through many a hardship and danger and narrow escape
was safely delivered. Now he was free to carry on the work
for which he left the perch and the birds in the grain-field of
the Beni Sad.

Sometimes he thought of the black slave before him, and
wondered if, after all, he was quite free. And the thought
troubled him.

It seemed as though long years had passed since the day
when his father met him with the news of Raschid Airikat's

capture of his brother. He had suffered privations enough for
a lifetime since then. More than once his life had hung by a
slender thread. He could hardly imagine himself again sitting
up on the perch, frightening the birds away, his life had so
entirely changed; his determination to keep the vow he made
his father had grown stronger every day; only he realized more
the magnitude of the task he had undertaken; and he appre-
ciated his father's words: "Thou wisp of flax before a fire!
Thou reed before a whirlwind!" Still he gathered hope, because he was beginning to understand himself.

The dangers and hardships of one enterprise he had met
and overcome, and under the very shadow of the Caaba the
great caliph of Mecca had called him brave.

Now he was eager for the next. There was no vital need of
another interview with the caliph, and Kanana thought that
if he could only escape from the black slave, by darting into
a crowded alley, he could go at once about his own important
business.

For the first time Kanana looked about him. At the moment
there was no opportunity, and while he watched for one, the
slave turned suddenly into a great gate, crossed a court paved
with limestone, lifted a reed curtain, entered one of the most
substantial stone structures of Mecca, and indicated to Kanana
the apartment in which he was to wait for the caliph. It was
too late to escape. With all the patience and dogged submis-
sion to destiny so strongly developed in the Bedouin, Kanana
sat down upon a rug. There were luxurious ottomans about
the room, and divans taken from the palaces of Persian princes,
but the Bedouin boy preferred the desert seat. Much as though
he were still upon the perch, he laid his staff beside him and
buried his face in his hands. The magnificence in this chamber
of Omar's official residence only disturbed his thoughts.

He became so deeply buried in his plans that he had entirely
forgotten where he was, when the rattle of the reed curtain
aroused him and, starting from his dream, he found the great
caliph entering.

Reverently touching his forehead to the floor, Kanana remained prostrate until the caliph was seated. Then he rose
and stood leaning upon his staff while the old ruler silently

surveyed him. It seemed to Kanana that his very heart was being searched by those grave and piercing eyes.

Upon the shoulders of the Caliph Omar rested the fate of Islam for future ages; his word was law wherever Mohammed was revered. He could have little time to waste upon a shepherd boy; yet he sat for a long while, silently looking at Kanana. When he spoke, it was only to bid him repeat, at greater length, the story of how he came by the letter and how he brought it to Mecca.

"My son," he said, when Kanana had finished, "thou hast done what many a brave man would not have ventured to attempt. Ask what reward thou wilt of me."

"I would have the blessing of the Caliph Omar," Kanana replied.

"That thou shall have, my son; and camels, or sheep, or gold. Ask what thou wilt."

"I have no use for anything. I ask thy blessing, my father, and thy word to bid me go."

"Thou art a strange lad," replied the caliph. "Thou art like, and yet unlike the Terror of the Desert. I command thee, my son, say what I can best do for thee."

"Give me thy blessing, then let me go, my father," repeated Kanana, kneeling. "More than that, if I took it, I should leave at thy gate."

Omar smiled gravely at the boy's obstinacy.

"If I can do nothing for thee, there is yet something which

thou. canst do for me. Kahled is the greatest general who fights for the Prophet. He will soon reach Bashra, with thirty thousand warriors. He will turn to enter Persia, but these letters must reach him, with my orders that he go again to Syria. Bashra is three weeks from here, and a company of soldiers will start tonight to carry the messages, while I send far and wide for the Faithful to join him. It would be well, my son, for thee to go with the soldiers, to give the story to Kahled by word of mouth."

"The way is hard. The sand is deep and dry between Mecca and Bashra," said Kanana. The caliph looked in some surprise upon the hardy Bedouin boy.

"Hardship should not be hard to thee; but thou shalt be carried as one whom the caliph would honor."

"The way is dangerous. Robbers and hostile tribes are like the sand about Bashra," added Kanana, who had often heard of the countries along the eastern borders of Arabia.

Surprise became astonishment. The caliph exclaimed:

"Thou! Son of the Terror of the Desert, speaking of danger?"

"My father, I spoke for thy soldiers," replied Kanana, quickly. "Before they reach the sands of Bashra they will be with the five who started with this letter. Dost thou believe that Kanana spoke in fear or cowardice? If so, give him the letters, and with thy blessing and the help of Allah, he will deliver them to the Kahled, though every river run with fire, and the half of Arabia stand to prevent him!"

"Beardless youth!" cried the caliph. "I am too old for mockery."

"My father, without a beard I brought that letter here, and He who guarded me will guard me still."

"Wouldst thou dare to go without an escort?"

"I would rather have a sword I could not lift than have an escort," replied Kanana.

"By the beard of the Prophet, my son, there is both foolishness and wisdom in thy words. Thou shalt take the messages by one route, and by another I will send the soldiers with copies. It may be that Allah guides thy tongue. When wilt thou start?"

"Now," replied Kanana.

"That was well spoken," said the caliph. "What camels and servants shall be provided?"

"My father," said Kanana, "as I came a little way with the caravan which arrived today, I noted the white camel that took the lead. I never saw so great power of speed and endurance in a camel of the plain. The man who led him knew him well and was easily obeyed. I would have the two, none other, and the swiftest dromedary in Mecca, with grain for fourteen days."

The caliph shook his head: "It will be twenty days and more."

"My father, the burden must be light that the sand lie loose beneath their feet, and small that it tempt no envious eye." Then, in the direct simplicity resulting from his lonely life, Kanana added, "If it is a three weeks' journey for others, in fourteen days thy messages shall be delivered."

The caliph summoned an officer, saying, "Go to the caravan at the Moabede Gate. Say that Omar requires the white camel and the man who leads it; none other. Bid Ebno'l Hassan prepare my black dromedary and food for the two for fourteen days. Have everything at the gate, ready to start, in half an hour." Then to a slave he added, "Give to the son of the Terror of the Desert the best that the house affords to eat and drink."

Without another word the caliph left the room to prepare the messages. The slave hurried to produce a sumptuous feast. The officer left the house to execute the orders of the man whose word was law.

Alone, Kanana sat down again upon the mat and buried his face in his hands, as though he were quietly preparing himself to sleep.

Only a whisper escaped his lips. The words were the same which he had angrily spoken under the shadow of Mount Hor, but the voice was very different: "This is my great reward for giving a cup of water to the thirsty. *La Illaha il Allah!*" The slave placed the food beside him, but he did not notice it. Not until the caliph entered again did he suddenly look up, exclaiming, "This shepherd's coat would not be fitting the dignity of the white camel. I must have an *abbe* to cover it, and a mantle to cover my face, that Mecca may not see a beardless youth going upon a mission for the great caliph."

They were quickly provided. The camel and its driver were at the gate, with the black dromedary. All was ready, and with the mantle drawn over his beardless face, and the *abbe* covering his sheepskin coat, Kanana knelt and received the blessing of the Caliph Omar.

As he rose from his knees, the caliph handed him first the letters, which Kanana placed in his bosom, and next a bag of gold which Kanana held in his hand for an instant; then, scornfully, he threw it upon the mat, remarking, "My father, I have already received a richer reward than all the gold of Mecca."

The caliph only smiled: "Let each one dance according to the music which he hears. My son, I see the future opening before thee. This is not thy last mission. I read it in thy destiny that thou wilt succeed, and succeed again, until the name of Kanana be written among the greatest of those who have lifted the lance for Allah and Arabia. Go now, and God go with thee."

7: *A Prize Worth Winning*

There was a group of several people standing about the caliph's gate as Kanana emerged. They were apparently waiting in careless curiosity to see the white camel start, and learn what they could of what was going on in official departments.

The information they received was very meager, yet it proved sufficient for more than one. They saw the white camel rise, with the veiled messenger of Omar upon its back. As the driver looked up to receive his first command their necks were bent in a way that betrayed their eagerness to hear. Only one word was spoken, however. It was "Tayf," the name of a city a short distance to the east of Mecca.

The camel-driver's cry sounded again through the streets, but the twilight shadows were gathering. There were few abroad, and the cries were not so loud or so often repeated as in the afternoon. When they ceased altogether, Kanana had turned his back upon Mecca forever.

The night wind blew cool and refreshing from the surrounding hills as the little caravan moved out upon the plain, but Kanana was ill at ease.

It was still as death in the valley. Far as the eye could pene-
trate the darkness they were all alone, except for five horsemen
who left the gate of Mecca not long after the white camel,
and were now riding slowly toward Tayf, a short distance behind it.

Ever and again Kanana looked back at them. The faint shadows, silently moving onward through the gloom, were always
there; never nearer; never out of sight.

Leaning forward, he spoke in a low voice to the driver, "You
walk as though you were weary. The dromedary was brought
for you. Mount it, and follow me."

"Master," replied the driver, "the white camel is obstinate. He will only move for one whom he knows well."

"You speak to the wind," muttered Kanana. "Do as I bid thee. Hear my words. Yonder black dromedary has the fleetest foot in Mecca. He is the pride of the Caliph Omar. Mount him, and if you can overtake me while I drive the white camel, you shall throw the dust of the desert in the face of Raschid Airikat, and have the white camel for your own."

The driver started back, and stood staring at the veiled messenger of Omar. The word, "Mount!" was sternly repeated. Then he quickly obeyed, evidently bewildered, but well satisfied that he would have an easy task before him, from the moment the white camel realized that a stranger was in command.

Kanana spoke, and the camel started. The dromedary moved forward close behind it without a word from the driver. The horsemen had approached no nearer while they waited, though Kanana had purposely given them time enough to pass had they not halted when he halted. They were still five silent shadows upon the distant sand.

"Faster," said Kanana, and the long legs of the white camel swung out a little farther over the sand and moved more rapidly in response.

The dromedary immediately quickened its pace without urging, and, a moment later, from far in the distance, the night wind brought the sound of horses' hoofs through the silent valley.

It was very faint, but distinct enough to indicate that the shadows behind them had broken into a canter.

The camel driver gave little heed to his surroundings. He was too thoroughly engrossed in the prospect of owning the white camel to care who might be coming or going in a way as safe as that from Tayf to Mecca. Kanana, however, who could walk through the streets of the holy city without so much as knowing what the houses were made of, would have heard the wings of a night moth passing him, or seen a sand bush move, a quarter of a mile away.

His life as a shepherd had, after all, not been wasted.

"Faster," said Kanana, touching the camel's neck with his shepherd's staff, and without even the usual grunt of objection, the animal obeyed. The sand began to fly from his great feet as they rested upon it for an instant, then left it far behind; the Bedouin boy sat with eyes fixed on the path before him, and his head bent so that he could catch the faintest sounds coming from behind. The mantle that had covered his face fell loosely over his shoulder.

The dromedary lost a little ground for a moment, but gathering himself together, easily made it up. The driver was too sure of the final result to urge him unduly at the start. Soon enough the white camel would rebel of his own accord, and till then it was quite sufficient to keep pace with him.

The sound of horses' hoofs became sharper and more distinct, and Omar's messenger knew that the five shadows were being pressed to greater speed, and were drawing nearer.

"Faster!" said Kanana, and the white camel broke into a run, swinging in rapid motions from side to side, as two feet upon one side, then two on the other were thrown far in front of him and, in an instant, left as far behind.

Still the dromedary made light work of keeping close upon his track, evidently realizing what was expected of him; but the driver saw with dismay how quickly the camel responded to the word of his rider, how easily the man sat upon the swaying back—how carefully he selected the best path for the animal, and how skillfully he guided him so that he could make the best speed with the least exertion.

Many a night Kanana had run unsaddled camels about the pastures of the Beni Sads, guarding the sleeping sheep and goats, little dreaming for what he was being educated.

The sound of horses' hoofs grew fainter. They were losing ground, but now and then the listening ear caught the sharp cry of an Arab horseman urging his animal to greater speed.

"They are in earnest," muttered the Bedouin boy, "but they will not win the race."

"Faster!" said Kanana; the camel's head dropped till his neck lost its graceful curve, and the great white ship of the desert seemed almost flying over the billowy sand.

For a moment the dromedary dropped behind. The driver had to use the prod and force him to the very best that was in him, before he was able to regain the lost ground.

The sound of hoofs could no longer be heard, and Kanana was obliged to listen with the utmost care to catch the faintest echo of a distant voice.

"They are doing their best and are beaten, but we can do still better," he said to himself with a deep sigh of relief, as he watched the desert shrubs fly past them in fleeting shadows, scudding over the silver-gray sand.

The music of the sand, as it flew from the camel's feet and fell like hail upon the dry leaves of the desert shrubs, was a delightful melody, and hour after hour they held the rapid pace; over low hills and sandy plains; past the mud village and the well that marks the resting place for caravans, a night's journey from Mecca, without a sign of halting; and on and on, the dromedary always just so far behind, always doing his best to come nearer.

If by urging he was brought a little closer to the camel, the driver heard that low word, "Faster!" and in spite of him the camel gained again. Would he never stop?

The sounds from behind had long been lost when, far in advance, appeared the regular caravan from Tayf. They approached it like the wind. Only the mystic salaam of the desert was solemnly exchanged, then, in a moment, the trailing train as it crept westward was left, disappearing in the darkness behind them.

When it was out of sight the white camel suddenly changed its course, turning sharply to the north of east and striking directly over the desert, away from the hills and the beaten track of Tayf which he had been following.

The driver could not imagine that such a man as sat upon the white camel had lost his way. He silently followed till they passed a well that marked the second night's journey from Mecca toward Persia. The driver and dromedary would very willingly have stopped here; but the camel glided onward before them through the changing shadows of the night, as though it were some phantom, and not a thing of flesh and blood.

By dint of urging, the driver brought the dromedary near enough to call: "Master, we are not upon the road to Tayf."

"No," said Kanana, but the camel still went on.

Driven to desperation, as the eastern sky was brightening the driver called again:

"Master, you will kill the camel!"

"Not in one night," said Kanana; "but if you value your own life, come on!"

Faster still and faster the white camel swept toward the glowing east, but the dromedary had done his best. He could not do better.

More and more he fell behind, and in spite of every effort of the driver, the pride of the caliph was beaten.

Fainter and fainter grew the outline of the white camel against the morning sky, ever swinging, swinging, swinging, over the silver-gray sea of desert sand, with a motion as regular and firm as though it had started but an hour before.

As the red disc of the fiery sun rose out of the desert, however, the driver saw the camel pause, turn half about till his huge outline stood out in bold relief against the sky, and then lie down.

Quickly Kanana dismounted. He caressed the camel for a moment, whispering, "We are two days and a half from Mecca! Thou hast done better than I hoped. Thou didst remember me yesterday in the temple court. Tonight thou hast cheerfully given every atom of thy strength to help me. Tomorrow we shall be far apart. Allah alone knows for what or for how long; but if we ever meet again thou wilt remember me. Yes, thou wilt greet thy Kanana."

The boy's dark eyes were bright with tears as he gave the camel the best of the food provided for him; then, with sand instead of water performing the morning ablution, he faced toward Mecca.

When the dromedary and his rider reached the spot, the veiled messenger of Omar was solemnly repeating his morning prayer.

8: *To Seek the Beni Sads*

All in vain the camel driver sought to obtain one glimpse beneath the mantle, to see the face of the caliph's messenger or to learn anything of their destination. He prepared their very frugal breakfast without a fire, and, when it was eaten, in the humble, reproachful tone of one who felt himself unjustly suspected, he said:

"My master, why didst thou deceive me, saying we should go to Tayf? Didst thou think that I would not willingly and freely lead the white camel anywhere, to serve the great caliph?"

"There were other ears than yours to hear," replied Kanana.

"There were only beggars at the gate, my master. Dost thou believe I would be treacherous to a servant of Omar and the Prophet?"

"I believe that every child of Ishmael will serve himself," replied Kanana; "but that had nothing to do with what I said. Before we start tonight, I will lay out your path before you, to the very end. As for the beggars, where were your senses? For three days, in disguise, I journeyed with the caravan of Raschid Airikat, as it came to Mecca. I saw in him a treacherous man, and when he yielded to a command he must obey and gave me the white camel and his driver, I knew that he would take them back again by stealth and treachery, if he were able to. Have I no eyes, that I should spend three days with the caravan and then not recognize the servants of Airikat, though they were dressed as beggars and slunk away, with covered faces, into the shadows of the caliph's gate? They did not cover their feet, and by their feet I knew them, even when they deceived you, one of their own. To them I said, 'Go, tell your master that his white camel is on the way to Tayf.' "

"My master," said the driver, respectfully, "the sheik Airikat is as devout as he is treacherous and brave. He gave the sacred camel and thy servant willingly, at the command of Omar, for the service of Allah and Arabia. I do not think he would deal treacherously."

Kanana did not reply, for far away over the desert, to the east, there was a little speck of dark, like a faint shadow upon the sand. He sat in silence watching it through the folds of his mantle as it grew larger and larger, and a long caravan approached.

The camels were worn out from a long journey. Their heads hung down, and their feet dragged languidly over the sand. Their slow progress had belated them, and the sun would be several hours above the desert when they reached the oasis by the well, which the two had passed before daylight.

As they drew nearer it could easily be seen that the camels bore no burdens but necessary food, in sacks that were nearly empty, and that their riders were savage men from the eastern borders of Arabia.

"Master, do they see us?" muttered the driver.

"They have eyes," replied Kanana. They had. A fresh dromedary and a white camel alone upon the desert were a tempting prize.

They evidently determined to appropriate them; for, leaving the main body of the caravan standing in the path, twenty or more turned suddenly, and came directly toward them.

"Master, we must fly from them," whispered the driver.

"If they were behind us I would fly," replied Kanana, "for every step would be well taken; but my path lies yonder." He pointed directly toward the caravan. "And I would not turn from it though devils instead of men were in the way."

"It is the will of Allah. We are lost," muttered the camel driver, and his arms dropped sullenly upon his knees in the dogged resignation to fate so characteristic of the Bedouin.

Kanana made no reply, but, repeating from the Koran, " 'Whatever of good betideth thee cometh from Him,' " he rose and walked slowly to where the white camel was lying.

Upon the high saddle, which had not yet been removed, hung the usual lance and sword, placed there by the officer of the caliph.

Leaning back against the saddle to await the approach of the caravan, the Bedouin boy threw his right hand carelessly across the hilt of the Damascus blade, exposing, almost to the shoulder, the rounded muscles of the powerful arm of—a shepherd lad.

The caravan drew nearer and finally halted when the leader was less than ten paces from the white camel.

His envious eyes had been gloating over the tempting prize as he approached; but gradually they became fastened upon that hand and arm, while the fingers that were playing gently upon the polished hilt seemed to beckon him on to test the gleaming blade beneath.

He could not see the beardless face, protected by the mantle. How could he know that that hand had never drawn a sword?

The whole appearance indicated a man without one thought of fear, and the savage chief realized that before the white camel became his prize some one beside its present owner would doubtless pay a dear price for it. He was still determined to possess it, but the silent figure demanded and received respect from him.

Instead of the defiant words which were upon his tongue, he pronounced the desert greeting.

Kanana returned the salutation, and immediately asked, "Did the dust from Kahled's host blow over you when your foot was on the sand of Bashra?"

The sheik drew back a little. It was a slight but very suggestive motion, speaking volumes to the keen eye of the Bedouin boy. He had been leaning forward before, more than is natural even to one tired out with sitting upon a camel's back. It was as if in his eagerness he was reaching forward to grasp the prize. Now he seemed suddenly to have lost that eagerness.

Quickly, Kanana took advantage of the hint. He drew from his bosom the letter of the caliph, sealed with the great seal of Mohammed, which every Mussulman could recognize, and calmly holding it plainly in view, he continued:

"The beak of the vulture has whitened, instead of the bones he would have plucked. The tooth of the jackal is broken, and not the flesh he would have torn. Raschid Airikat is neither at Damascus nor Mecca. Tomorrow morning he will be at Tayf. He would have you meet him there. Say to him, 'The fool hath eaten his own folly. The veiled messenger of the Prophet, sitting upon the sacred camel, glides with the night wind into the rising sun; for the fire is lighted in Hejaz that at Bashra shall cause the camels' necks to shine.' "

A decided change came over the savage face of the Arab sheik. He sat in silence for a moment, then, without a word, drove the prod into his camel. There was a grunt and a gurgling wail, and the tired animal was moving on, followed by all the rest.

Kanana and his camel driver were left alone. When they were well out of hearing the driver prostrated himself before Kanana, touching his forehead to the ground, and asked:

"Master, who was that sheik with all his warriors, and who art thou that they should cower before thy word?"

"I am no one to receive your homage. Stand upon your feet!" almost shouted Kanana. "I never saw nor heard of them until today."

He breathed a deep, quivering sigh, and leaned heavily upon the saddle; every muscle in his body shook and trembled as the result of what had seemed so calm and defiant. He tried to replace the letter in his bosom, but his hand trembled so that he was obliged to wait.

"Thou knewest that he was of the tribe of Raschid Airikat, and that he came from Bashra," said the driver.

"I knew nothing," replied Kanana, petulantly, in the intense reaction. "How long have you been a man, well taught in killing other men, not to see what any cowardly shepherd boy could read? Were not their lances made of the same peculiar wood; and their camel saddles, were they not the same, stained with the deep dye of Bashra? Who should come out of the rising sun, with his camel licking the desert sand, if he came not from Bashra? Who should be going toward Mecca at this season, without a burdened camel in his caravan, if he went not to meet his chief for war? Why did Airikat crowd his caravan, day and night, if he expected no one?"

"But, master, Airikat is at Mecca, not at Tayf," said the driver.

"Bedouin, where are your eyes and ears?" exclaimed Kanana, scornfully. "Your paltry beggars at the caliph's gate carried my message swiftly. We had not left the gate of Mecca out of sight when on the road behind us came Airikat and four followers. While you were struggling to reach the white camel they did their best to overtake us both, but we outstripped them. We kept upon the way till we had passed the nightly caravan. They would have to rest their horses at the well, and the caravan would halt there, too. They would inquire for us, and the caravan would answer, 'We passed the white camel running like the wind toward Tayf.' Enough. Airikat with his horsemen cannot reach there before the next sunrise, and when he learns the truth he will be five days behind us. From him and yonder caravan, by the help of Allah we are safe. If you would learn a lesson, by the way, let it be this: that man can conquer man without a sword or lance. Sleep on it."

Setting the example, Kanana removed the camel's saddle, fastened his hind foot to his haunch with the twisted rope so that he could not rise, and sank upon the sand beside him, laying his head upon the creature's neck. The last words he heard from his driver were: "Master, thou art mightier than Airikat and all his warriors."

The sun beat fiercely down all day upon his resting place; but Kanana's sleep was sweeter than if the cool starlight had been over him, or a black tent of the Beni Sads; because, for that one day at least, his head was pillowed upon the white camel's neck.

It was late in the afternoon before he woke, and the sun was setting when the little caravan was again prepared to start.

They were ready to mount when the driver came to the white camel. He laid his hand upon the dingy haunch, and said, in a voice that was strangely pleading for a fierce Bedouin:

"Master, do not crowd him overhard tonight. He obeys too willingly. He is tired from a long journey. It is four weeks since he has rested. I would rather you would kill me than the white camel."

Kanana thought for a moment, then taking his shepherd's staff from the saddle, he replied: "You can tell better than I how he should be driven. Mount him, and I will ride the dromedary."

To the driver this was only Arab sarcasm, and he hesitated till Kanana silently pointed his staff toward the saddle, and the driver was more afraid to refuse than to obey.

Kanana turned and mounted the dromedary.

As the camel rose to his feet, a strange temptation sent the blood tingling to the driver's finger tips. The dromedary was unarmed. The messenger of Omar held only a shepherd's staff. Almost unconsciously his hand clutched the hilt of the Damascus blade, betraying the fact that it was better used to holding such a thing than the rope that led the white camel through Mecca.

Quickly the driver looked back, to see Kanana quietly watching him. Instantly his hand dropped the hilt, but it was too late. Scornfully Kanana said:

"Lo! every child of Ishmael, from the devout Raschid to the faithful camel driver, will serve himself. Nay, keep the hand upon the sword. Perchance there will be better cause to use it than in defying me. From here our paths must separate. I promised that tonight I would lay out your course for you. It is northward without swerving, for ten nights at least."

"And whither goest thou, my master?"

"That only Allah can direct from day to day. *La Illaha il Allah!*"

"And what is my mission to be?" asked the driver, anxiously.

"It is to seek the Beni Sads; to find the aged chief, the Terror of the Desert; to say to him, 'Kanana hath fulfilled his vow. He hath not lifted the lance against Airikat; but thy white camel is returned to thee, bearing thy first-born upon his back.' Go, and God go with thee!"

"Who art thou?" cried the man upon the white camel, starting from his seat as the dromedary gave the usual grunt in answer to the prod, and moved away.

The Bedouin boy turned in the saddle, tore off the *abbe* and the mantle that covered him, and clad in the sheepskin coat and desert turban answered:

"I am thy brother Kanana, the coward of the Beni Sads!"

9: . For Allah and Arabia

"Kanana! Our Kanana!" cried the brother, striking the camel's neck. The dingy dignity of the great white camel was ruffled by the blow received, and he expressed his disapproval in a series of grunts before he made any attempt to start.

"Kanana! Kanana!" the brother called again, seeing the dromedary already merging into the shadows; but the only response he received was from the shepherd's staff, extended at arm's length pointing northward.

"My young brother shall not leave me in this way. He has no weapon of defense and only a little of the grain."

Again he struck the camel a sharp blow as the animal began very slowly to move forward. The black dromedary was hardly distinguishable from the night, and was rapidly sinking into the deepening shadows before the camel was fairly on the way.

"Go!" cried the rider savagely, striking him again, and the camel moved a little faster; but he made slow and lumbering work, for he was not at all pleased with his treatment.

The rider's eyes were fixed intently upon the dim outline sinking away from him. The last he saw of it was the hand and arm, still holding the extended shepherd's staff pointing to the north. Then all was lost.

He kept on in that direction for an hour, but it was evident that he had begun in the wrong way with the camel, and that he was not forcing him to anything like his speed of the night before.

It was beyond his power to overtake the dromedary, and doubly chagrined he gave up the race and turned northward.

The path before Kanana was the highway between Persia and

Mecca. At some seasons it was almost hourly traversed, but at midsummer only absolute necessity drove the Arabs across the very heart of the desert.

In the height of the rainy season there were even occasional pools of water in the hollows, here and there. Later there was coarse, tough grass growing, sometimes for miles along the way.

Little by little, however, they disappeared. Then the green of each oasis shrank toward the center, about the spring or well; and often before midsummer was over, they too had dried away.

The prospect of loneliness, however, was not at all disheartening to Kanana. He had no desire to meet with anyone, least of all with such parties as would be apt to cross the desert at this season.

If a moving shadow appeared in the distance, he turned well to one side and had the dromedary lie down upon the sand till it passed.

The black dromedary was fresh, and the Bedouin boy knew well how to make the most of his strength while it lasted; but it was for Allah and Arabia that they crossed the desert, and Kanana felt that neither his own life nor that of the dromedary could be accounted of value compared with the demand for haste.

He paid no heed to the usual camping-grounds for caravans, except to be sure that he passed two of them every night till the dromedary's strength began to fail.

Each morning the sun was well upon its way before he halted for the day, and long before it set again he was following his shadow upon the sand.

More and more the dromedary felt the strain. When twelve nights had passed, the pride of the caliph was anything but a tempting prize, and Kanana would hardly have troubled himself to turn out for a caravan even if he had thought it a band of robbers.

The Bedouin boy, too, was thoroughly worn and exhausted. For days they had been without water, checking their thirst by chewing the prickly leaves of the little desert vine that is the last sign of life upon the drying sand. No dew fell at this season, and Kanana realized that it was only a matter of hours as to how much longer they could hold out.

Morning came without a sign of water or of life, as far as the eye could reach.

The sun rose higher, and Kanana longed for the sight of a human being as intensely as at first he had dreaded it.

Nothing but the ghastly bones of men and animals bleaching among the sand shrubs showed him that he was still upon the highway to Bashra.

Out of the glaring silver-gray, the fiery sun sailed into the lusterless blue of the dry, hot sky leaving the two separated by the eternal belt of leaden clouds that never rise above a desert horizon and never disperse in rain.

Kanana halted only for his morning prayer, and, when it was finished, the petition that he added for himself was simply, "Water! Water! O Allah! give us water."

Each day the heat had become more intense, and today it seemed almost to burn the very sand. As Kanana mounted again and started on, his tired eyes sought anxiously the glaring billows for some sign of life; but not a living thing, no shadow even, broke the fearful monotony.

There were gorgeous promises, but they did not deceive the eyes that had looked so often along the sand. There were great cities rising upon the distant horizon, with stately domes and graceful minarets such as were never known throughout the length and breadth of Arabia. And when the bells ceased tolling in Kanana's ears, he could hear the muezzin's call to prayer. Then the bells would toll again and he would mutter, "Water! Water! O Allah! give us water."

He had no longer any heart to urge the tired dromedary to a

faster pace. He knew that it would only be to see him fall the sooner upon the sand. The tired creature's head hung down till his nose touched the earth as he plodded slowly onward.

The sun rose higher. It was past the hour when they always stopped, but neither thought of stopping. Waiting would not bring the water to them, and the Bedouin boy knew well that to lie on the desert sand that day meant to lie there forever.

The dromedary knew it as well as his master, and without a word to urge him, he kept his feet slowly moving onward, like an automaton, with his nose thrust forward just above the sand, as though he too were pleading: "Water! Water! O Allah! give us water!"

His eyes were closed. His feet dragged along the sand. Kanana did not attempt to guide him, though he swayed from side to side, sometimes reeling and almost falling over low hillocks which he made no effort to avoid.

Kanana could scarcely keep his own eyes open. The glare of the desert was blinding; but their last hope lay in his watchfulness.

He struggled hard to keep back the treacherous drowsiness, but his head would drop upon one shoulder, then upon the other. He could have fallen from the saddle and stretched himself upon the sand to die without a struggle, had it not been for the caliph's letter in his bosom. Again and again he pressed his hand upon it to rouse himself, and muttered, "By the help of Allah, I will deliver it."

Each time that this roused him he shaded his eyes and sought again the sand before him; but glaring and gray it stretched away to the horizon, without one shadow save that of the forest of low and brittle sand shrubs.

The burning sky grew black above him, and the desert became a fiery red. The dromedary did not seem like a living thing. He thought he was sitting upon his perch in the harvest field. The sun seemed cold as its rays beat upon his head. He shivered and unconsciously drew the wings of his turban over his face. No wonder it was cold. It was early morning under Mount Hor. Yes, there were all the blue forget-me-nots. How the stream rippled and gurgled among them!

He started. What was that shock that roused him? Was it the

robbers coming down upon him? He shook himself fiercely. Was he sleeping? He struggled to spring to his feet, but they were tangled in something.

At last his bloodshot eyes slowly opened and consciousness returned. The dromedary had fallen to the ground, beside—an empty well.

Kanana struggled to his feet and looked down among the rocks. The bottom was as dry as the sand upon which he was standing.

He looked back at the dromedary. Its eyes were shut. Its neck was stretched straight out before it on the sand, its head rested upon the rocks of the well.

"Thou hast given thy life for Allah and Arabia," Kanana said, "and when the Prophet returns in his glory, he will remember thee."

He took the sack of camel's food from the saddle and emptied the whole of it where the dromedary could reach it. Then he cut the saddle-straps and dragged the saddle to one side. It was all that he could do for the dumb beast that had served him.

Suddenly he noticed that the sun was setting. All the long day he must have slept, while the poor dromedary had crept onward toward the well. It had not been a healthful sleep, but it refreshed him, and combined with the excitement of waking and working for the dromedary, he found his tongue less parched than before. Quickly he took a handful of wheat and began to chew it vigorously; a secret which has saved the life of many a Bedouin upon the great sea of sand.

For a moment he leaned upon the empty saddle chewing the wheat, watching the sun sink into the sand and thinking.

"Thirteen days," he muttered. "I said fourteen when I started, but we have done better than three days in two. If we did not turn from the way today, this well is but one night from Bashra. *O Allah! Mahamoud rousol il Allah!* give thy servant life for this one night."

The dromedary had not moved to touch the food beside him, and there was no hope left of further help from the faithful animal. Kanana stood beside it for a moment, laid his hand gratefully upon the motionless head, then took up his shepherd's staff and started on.

Sometimes waking, sometimes sleeping as he walked, sometimes thinking himself far away from the sands of Bashra, sometimes urging himself on with a realization that he must be near his journey's end, he pressed steadily on and on, hour after hour.

Sometimes he felt fresh enough to start and run. Sometimes he wondered if he had the strength to lift his foot and put it forward another time. Sometimes he felt sure that he was moving faster than a caravan, and that he should reach Bashra before morning. Sometimes it seemed as though the willing spirit must leave the lagging flesh behind as he had left the dromedary, and go on alone to Bashra.

Then he would press the sacred letter hard against his bosom and repeat, "By the help of Allah I will deliver it!" And all the time, though he did not realize it, he was moving forward with swift and steady strides, almost as though he were inspired with superhuman strength.

Far away to the east a little spark of light appeared. It grew and rose, till above the clouds there hung a thin white crescent; the narrowest line of moonlight.

Kanana gave a cry of joy, for it was an omen which no Arab could fail to understand.

Then the air grew cold. The darkest hour before the dawn approached, and the narrow moon served only to make the earth invisible.

The dread of meeting anyone had long ago left Kanana's mind. First he had feared it. Then he had longed for it. Now he was totally indifferent. He looked at the sky above him to keep his course. He looked at the sand beneath his feet; but he did not once search the desert before him.

Suddenly he was roused from his lethargy. There were shadows just ahead. He paused, shaded his eyes from the sky, and looked forward long and earnestly.

"It is not sand shrubs," he muttered. "It is too high. It is not Bashra. It is too low. It is not a caravan. It does not move. It has no beginning and no end," he added, as he looked to right and left.

"It is tents," he said a moment later, and a frown of anxiety gathered over his forehead. "Have I missed the way? No tribe so large as that would be tented near Bashra. If I turn back I shall die. If I go on—*La Illaha il Allah!*" he murmured, and resolutely advanced.

As he drew nearer, the indistinguishable noises of the night in a vast encampment became plainly audible, but he did not hesitate.

Following the Arab custom for every stranger in approaching a Bedouin camp, he paused at the first tent he reached, and standing before the open front repeated the Mussulman salutation.

Someone within roused quickly, and out of the darkness a deep voice sounded in reply.

Then Kanana repeated:

"I am a wanderer upon the desert. I am far from my people." And the voice replied:

"If you can lift the lance for Allah and Arabia, you are welcome in the camp of Kahled the Invincible."

"*La Illaha il Allah!*" cried Kanana. "Guide me quickly to the tent of Kahled. I am a messenger to him from the great Caliph Omar."

The earth reeled beneath the feet of Kanana as the soldier led the way.

The general was roused without the formality of modern military tactics or even Mohammedan courtesies. A torch was quickly lighted. Kanana prostrated himself; then rising, he handed the precious packet to the greatest general who ever led the hosts of Mohammed.

Kahled the Invincible broke the seal, but before he had read a single word, the Bedouin boy fell unconscious upon the carpet of the tent.

As the soldiers lifted him, Kanana roused for an instant and murmured:

"By the dry well, one night to the southwest, my black dromedary is dying of thirst. In Allah's name, send him water! He brought the message from Mecca in thirteen days!" Then the torchlight faded before his eyes, and Kanana's lips were sealed in unconsciousness.

A vast Mohammedan army, with its almost innumerable followers, was marching toward Syria to meet the hosts of the Emperor Heraclius.

Like a pillar of cloud the dust rose above the mighty throng Armed horsemen, ten thousand strong, rode in advance.

A veteran guard of scarred and savage men came next, mounted upon huge camels, surrounding Kahled the Invincible and his chief officers, who rode upon the strongest and most beautiful of Persian horses.

A little distance behind were thousands of fierce warriors mounted on camels and dromedaries. Then came another vast detachment of camels bearing tents, furniture, and provisions of the army; these were followed by a motley throng, comprising the families of many of the tribes represented in the front, while still another powerful guard brought up the rear.

Behind the bodyguard of Kahled and before the war camels rode a smaller guard, in the center of which were two camels bearing a litter between them.

Upon this litter lay Kanana, shielded from the sun by a goat's-hair awning; for almost of necessity the army moved by daylight. It started an hour after sunrise, resting two hours at noon, and halting an hour before sunset. It moved more rapidly than a caravan, however, and averaged twenty-five miles a day.

Close behind Kanana's litter walked a riderless dromedary. At the start it was haggard and worn. Its dark hair was burned to a dingy brown by the fierce heat of the desert; but even Kahled received less careful attention, and every day it gathered strength and held its head a little higher.

The black dromedary was not allowed to carry any burden, but was literally covered with gay-colored cloths; decorating the pride of Omar the Great, that had brought the good news from Mecca to Bashra in less than thirteen days.

Nothing pleasanter could have been announced to that terrible army of veterans surrounding the valiant Kahled, than that it was to face the mightiest host which the Emperor Heraclius could gather in all the north.

There was not one in all that throng who doubted, for an instant, that Kahled could conquer the whole world if he chose, in the name of Allah and the Prophet.

Many of the soldiers had followed him since the day years before when he made his first grand plunge into Persia. They had seen him made the supreme dictator of Babylonia. They had seen him send that remarkable message to the great monarch of Persia:

"Profess the faith of Allah and his Prophet, or pay tribute to their servants. If you refuse, I will come upon you with a host that loves death as much as you love life."

Once before they had seen him summoned from his triumphs in Persia, because all the Mohammedan generals and soldiers in Syria were not able to cope with the power of Heraclius. They had seen him invested with the supreme power by the Caliph Abu-Bekr, Omar's predecessor, and watched while, single-handed, he fought and conquered the great warrior, Romanus.

Most of them had been with him before the walls of Damascus, when he besieged that magnificently fortified city upon one side, and fought and conquered an army of a hundred thousand men upon the other side, sent from Antioch by Heraclius for the relief of the great city. Then they witnessed the fall of Damascus, and followed Kahled as he attacked and put to flight an army outnumbering his by two to one, and equipped and drilled in the most modern methods of Roman warfare.

They had fought with him in the fiercest battles ever recorded of those desert lands, and they knew him only as Kahled the Invincible.

After Abu-Bekr had died and Omar the Great had taken his place, the proud soldiers saw their general unjustly deposed and given such minor work as tenting about the besieged cities, while others did the fighting, until he left Syria in disgust.

No wonder they were glad to see him recalled to take his proper place. They jested without end about the cowards who were frightened because Heraclius had threatened to annihilate the Mussulmans. And the march was one grand holiday in spite of heat and hardships.

As Kanana lay in his litter and listened to these bursts of eloquence in praise of the general, he was often stirred with ardent patriotism and almost persuaded to cast his lot among the soldiers; but the same odd theories which before had prevented his taking up a lance restrained him still.

On the fourth day he left the litter and took his seat upon the black dromedary. Kahled directed that costly garments and a sword and lance be furnished him, but Kanana prostrated himself before the general and pleaded: "My father, I never held a lance, and Allah knows me best in this sheepskin coat."

Kahled frowned, but Kanana sat upon the decorated dromedary precisely as he left the perch in the harvest field. He expected to take his place with the camp followers in the rear, but found that he was still to ride in state, surrounded by the veteran guard. Indeed, he became a figure so celebrated and conspicuous that many a warrior in passing, after prostrating himself before the general, touched his forehead to the ground before Kanana and the black dromedary.

It might have made a pleasant dream while sitting upon the perch in the harvest field, but the reality disturbed him, and again he began to plan some means of escape.

He carefully computed the position of the Beni Sad encampment, and determined the day when the army would pass but a few miles to the east of it.

One who has not lived upon the desert and seen it illustrated again and again, can scarcely credit the accuracy with which a wandering Bedouin can locate the direction and distance to any point with which he is familiar; but even then Kanana was at a loss as to how to accomplish his purpose, when the whole matter was arranged for him and he was supplied with a work which he could perform for Allah and Arabia, still holding his shepherd's staff and wearing his sheepskin coat.

The army halted for the night upon the eve of the day when it would pass near the encampment of the Beni Sads. The tent which Kanana occupied was pitched next that of Kahled.

He sat upon the ground eating his supper. All about him was the clatter and commotion of the mighty host preparing for the night, when he heard an officer reporting to the general that in three days the supply of grain would be exhausted.

"My father," he exclaimed, prostrating himself before the general, "thy servant's people, the Beni Sads, must be less than a night's journey to the north and west. They were harvesting six weeks ago, and must have five hundred camel loads of grain to sell. Bid me go to them tonight, and with the help of Allah, by the sunrise after tomorrow it shall be delivered to thy hand."

Kahled had formed a very good opinion of the Bedouin boy. He had noticed his uneasiness, and suspecting that he would make an endeavor to escape, he had been searching for some occupation that should prevent it by rendering him more content to remain. He felt that a time might come when Kanana, with his sheepskin coat and shepherd's staff, might be of greater value to him than many a veteran with costly *abbe* and gleaming sword.

The result was an order that one hour after sunset Kanana should start, at the head of a hundred horsemen, with ten camels laden with treasure for the purchase of grain, with twenty camels bearing grain-sacks and one with gifts from Kahled to the Terror of the Desert, in acknowledgment of the service rendered by his son.

When he had purchased what grain the Beni Sad would sell, he was to continue in advance of the army, securing supplies to the very border of Syria.

Kanana was no prodigy of meekness that he should not appreciate this distinction. A prouder boy has never lived in Occident or Orient than the Bedouin shepherd who sat upon the black dromedary and publicly received the general's blessing and command of the caravan.

In any other land there might have been rebellion among a hundred veteran horsemen, when placed under command of a boy in a sheepskin coat, armed only with a shepherd's staff, but there was no man of them who had not heard wonderful tales of Kanana's courage; and the shepherd who had left the harvest field six weeks before, known only as the coward of the Beni Sads, set his face toward home that night, followed by a hundred savage warriors who obeyed him as one of the bravest of all the Bedouins.

As the caravan moved rapidly over the plain, bearing its costly burden, it is hardly surprising that the beardless chief recalled his last interview with his angry father, when that veteran sheik refused to trust him with a single horse to start upon his mission; but he was none the less anxious to reach his father's tent and receive his father's blessing.

11: The Sacred Girdle

Shortly after midnight five horsemen who rode in advance returned to report a large encampment, far away upon the left. Then Kanana took the lead as a brave Bedouin chieftain should, and, followed by the caravan, approached the smoldering fires which betrayed the location of the camp.

He rode directly toward the tent of the sheik, which always stands in the outer line, farthest from a river or upon the side from which the guests of the tribe will be most likely to approach.

As he approached, a shadow rose silently out of the shadows. Then there was a faint grunt of satisfaction and the shadow sank down into the shadows again.

Kanana slipped from the back of the dromedary without waiting for him to lie down, and running forward to the white camel, whispered, "I knew that thou wouldst know me."

The Terror of the Desert appeared at the tent door with a hand raised in blessing.

Kanana ran to his father with a cry of joy, and the white-haired sheik threw his arms about the neck of his son and kissed him, saying:

"Forgive me, Kanana, my brave Kanana! I said that thou hadst come to curse me with thy cowardice, and lo! thou hast done grander, braver deeds than I in all my years! Verily, thou hast put me to shame, but it is with courage, not with cowardice."

Kanana tried to speak, but tears choked him. All alone he could calmly face a score of savage robbers armed to the teeth, but suddenly he discovered that he was only a boy after all. He had almost forgotten about it. And in helpless silence he clung to his father's neck.

The old sheik roused himself.

"Kanana," he exclaimed, "why am I silent? The whole tribe waits to welcome thee. Ho! every one who sleepeth!" he called aloud, "Awake! Awake! Kanana is returned to us!"

Far and near the cry was repeated, and a moment later the people came hurrying to greet the hero of the Beni Sads.

Not only had the brother returned with the white camel and a glowing account of his rescue by the veiled messenger of the caliph, but a special officer had come by a passing caravan, bearing to the Terror of the Desert a bag of gold and the congratulations of Omar the Great, that he was the father of such a son.

Now the gifts from Kahled the Invincible arrived, and the hundred horsemen obeying the voice of Kanana. The Beni Sads could scarcely believe their eyes and ears.

Torches were lighted. Fires were rekindled and before sunrise the grandest of all grand Bedouin feasts was in full glory.

Vainly, however, did the old sheik bring out the best robe to put it on him; with a ring for his hand and shoes for his feet; in a custom celebrating a son's return which was old when the story of the Prodigal was told.

Kanana only shook his head and answered, "My father, Allah knows me best barefooted and in this sheepskin coat."

The Bedouin seldom tastes of meat except upon the occasion of some feast. When a common guest arrives, unleavened bread is baked and served with *ayesh,* a paste of sour camel's milk and flour. But Kanana was not a common guest.

For one of higher rank, coffee and melted butter are prepared, but these were not enough for a welcome to Kanana.

For one still higher, a kid or lamb is boiled in camel's milk and placed in a great wooden dish, covered with melted fat and surrounded by a paste of wheat that has been boiled and dried and ground and boiled again with butter.

Twenty lambs and kids were thus prepared, but the people were not satisfied. Nothing was left but the greatest and grandest dish which a Bedouin tribe can add to a feast in an endeavor to do honor to its noblest guest. Two she-camels were killed and the meat quickly distributed to be boiled and roasted. All for the boy who had left them, six weeks before, with no word of farewell but the parting taunt of a rat-catcher.

While the men were eating the meat and drinking camel's milk and coffee, the women sang patriotic songs, often substituting Kanana's name for that of some great hero; and when the men had finished and the women gathered in the maharems to feast upon what was left, the Terror of the Desert, roused to the highest pitch of patriotism, declared his intention to join the army of Kahled, and nearly two hundred of the Beni Sads resolved to follow him.

It was nearly noon when Kanana and those who were with him went to sleep in the goat's-hair tents, leaving the whole tribe at work, packing the grain sacks, loading the camels, and cleaning their weapons for war.

Kanana performed his mission faithfully, little dreaming that Kahled's one design in placing it in his hands was to keep him with the army for services of much greater importance.

The time which the general anticipated came when the hosts of Kahled, joined by the Mohammedan armies of Syria and

Arabia, were finally encamped at Yermonk upon the borders of Palestine.

Kanana was summoned to the general's tent and, trembling like the veriest coward in all the world, he fell upon his face before the man to whom was entrusted the almost hopeless task of rescuing Arabia. To Kahled alone all eyes were turned, and Kanana trembled, not because he was frightened, but because he was alone in the tent with one who seemed to him but little less than God himself.

Kahled's words were always few and quickly spoken.

"Son of the Terror of the Desert," said he, "many conflicting rumors reach me concerning the approaching enemy. I want the truth. I want it quickly. What dost thou require to aid thee in performing this duty?"

Kanana's forehead still touched the ground. Overwhelmed by this sudden order, an attempt to obey which meant death without mercy, without one chance in a hundred to escape, he altogether forgot to rise.

Kahled sat in silence, understanding human nature too well to disturb the boy, and for five minutes neither moved. Then Kanana rose slowly and his voice trembled a little as he replied, "My father, I would have thy fleetest horse, thy blessing, and thy girdle."

Kahled the Invincible wore a girdle that was known to every soldier and camp follower of the army. It was of camel's-skin, soft-tanned and colored with a brilliant Persian dye which as far away as it could be seen at all no one could mistake.

It was part of a magnificent curtain which once hung in the royal palace of Babylon. It pleased the fancy of the fierce warrior, and he wore it as a girdle till it became his only insignia. There was not a color like it within hundreds of miles at least, and when the people saw it they knew that it was Kahled.

"Take what horse thou wilt," replied the general. "I give thee, now, my blessing." Then he hesitated for a moment. Had Kanana asked a hundred camels or a thousand horsemen he would have added, "Take them." As it was, he said a little doubtfully, "What wouldst thou with my girdle?"

In all the direct simplicity which clung to him in spite of

everything, Kanana replied: "I would hide it under my coat; I would that it be proclaimed throughout the army that someone has fled to the enemy with the sacred girdle, and that a great reward be offered to him who shall return to Kahled any fragment of it he may find."

Without another word, the general unwound the sacred girdle, and Kanana, reverently touching it to his forehead, bound it about him under his sheepskin coat.

Kneeling, he received the blessing, and leaving the tent, he selected the best of Kahled's horses and disappeared in the darkness alone.

The next morning an oppressive sense of inaction hung about the headquarters.

The only order issued accompanied an announcement of the loss of the sacred girdle.

Every soldier was commanded to be on the watch for it, to seize and return at once to Kahled even the smallest fragment which might be found. For this the fortunate man was promised as many gold coins as, lying flat, could be made to touch the piece which he returned.

12: Kanana's Messengers

Far and wide the impatient soldiers asked, "Why is the army inactive?"

"Is not the motto of Kahled 'Waiting does not win'?"

"Has he not taught us that action is the soul and secret of success?"

"Does he not realize that the hosts of Heraclius are bearing down upon us, that he leaves us sitting idly in our tents?"

"Is Kahled the Invincible afraid?"

Such were the questions which they put to their officers, but no one dared carry them to the general, who sat in his tent without speaking from sunrise to sunset the first day after the girdle disappeared. "Is it the loss of his girdle?" "Did he not conquer Babylonia without it?" "Does he not fight in the name of Allah and the Prophet? Could a bright-colored girdle give him strength?"

Thus the second day went by.

Kahled the Invincible was silent and sullen, and the impression grew and grew that in some way the safety and success of the whole army depended upon the recovery of that girdle.

So intense was this sentiment, that when at midnight after the third day it was reported that a fragment of the girdle had been captured by some scouts, and was then being taken to the general's tent, the whole army roused itself and prepared for action.

Not an order had been issued, yet every soldier felt instinctively that the coming morning would find him on the march.

It was midnight. For a day Kahled had not even tasted food. He sat alone in his tent upon a Persian ottoman. A bronze vessel from Babylonia, filled with oil, stood near the center of the tent. Fragments of burning wick floating in the oil filled the tent with a mellow, amber light.

There was excitement without, but Kahled did not heed it till a soldier unceremoniously entered, bearing in his hand a part of the curtain from the palace of Babylon.

With a sudden ejaculation Kahled caught it from the soldier's hand, but ashamed of having betrayed an emotion, he threw it carelessly upon the rug at his feet, handing the soldier a bag of gold, and bidding him see how many pieces, lying flat, could touch it.

The soldier worked slowly, carefully planning the position as he laid the pieces down, and Kahled watched him as indifferently as though he were only moving men upon the Arab's favorite checkerboard.

When every piece that could was touching the camel skin, the soldier returned the bag, half-emptied, and began to gather up his share.

Kahled deliberately emptied the bag, bidding him take the whole and go.

He was leaving the tent when the general called him back. He had picked up the skin, and was carelessly turning it over in his hand. It was neatly cut from the girdle, in the shape of a shield a little over a foot in width.

"How did you come by it?" Kahled asked indifferently.

"We were searching the plain, a day's journey to the north,"

the soldier answered. "We were looking for travelers who might bring tidings of the enemy. We saw four strangers, Syrians, riding slowly, and a shepherd who seemed to be their guide. Upon his horse's front, hung like a breastplate where every eye could see, was yonder piece of the sacred girdle. We dashed upon them, and the cowards ran. The shepherd was the last to turn. I was ahead, but not near enough to reach him, so I threw my lance. He fell from his horse and—"

"You killed him?" shrieked the general, springing to his feet and dropping the camel skin.

"No! No!" gasped the frightened soldier. "I only tried to. He wore a coat of sheepskin. It was too thick for my lance. He sprang to his feet, tore the lance from his coat, and ran after the rest faster even than they could ride, leaving his horse behind."

"'Tis well," muttered the general, and he devoutly added, "Allah be praised for that sheepskin coat!"

The soldier left the tent, and going nearer to the light, Kahled examined the fragment of the sacred girdle. It was double. Two pieces had been cut and the edges joined together.

He carefully separated them, and upon the inner side found what he evidently expected.

These words had been scratched upon the leather, and traced with blood: "Sixty thousand from Antioch and Aleppo, under Jababal the traitor, encamp two days from Yermonk, north, waiting for Manuel with eighty thousand Greeks and Syrians, now six days away. Still another army is yet behind. Thy servant goes in search of Manuel when this is sent."

"Allah be praised for that sheepskin coat!" Kahled repeated, placing the fragment in his belt and walking slowly up and down.

"Jababal is two days to the north," he added presently. "A day ago Manuel was six days behind him. He will be still three days behind when I reach Jababal, and while he is yet two days away, the sixty thousand in advance will be destroyed."

An order was given for ten thousand horsemen and fifteen thousand camel riders to start for the north at once. The soldiers expected it, and were ready even before the general.

Four days and a night went by, and they were again encamped at Yermonk; but Jababal's army of sixty thousand men was a thing of the past.

Again a strip of the girdle was discovered. This time it hung upon the neck of a camel leading into the camp a long caravan laden with grain and fruit.

The camel driver reported that one had met them while they were upon the way to supply the army of Manuel. He had warned them that Manuel would simply confiscate the whole and make them prisoners, and had promised that if they turned southward instead, to the camp of Kahled, with the talisman which he hung about the camel's neck, they should be well received and fairly treated.

From this talisman Kahled learned that the army of Manuel was almost destitute of provisions, and that a detachment with supplies was another five or six days behind. The general smiled as he thought how the Bedouin boy had shrewdly deprived the hungry enemy of a hundred and fifty camel loads of food, while he secured for himself an excellent messenger to his friends.

During the night Manuel's magnificent army arrived, and encamped just north of the Mohammedans. Manuel chose for his citadel a high cliff that rose abruptly out of the plain between the two armies, and ended in a precipitous ledge toward Arabia.

Standing upon the brow of this cliff, a little distance from the tent of Manuel, one could look far down the valley over the entire Mohammedan encampment.

When morning dawned, the prince sent for the leading Mohammedan generals to confer with him concerning terms of

peace. He offered to allow the entire army to retire un-
molested, if hostages were given that the Arabs should never
again enter Syria.

The Mohammedan generals, who had been thoroughly dismayed at the sight of the Grecian phalanx, thanked Allah for
such a merciful deliverance, and instantly voted to accept. The
real authority, however, rested with Kahled, who replied,
"Remember Jababal!"

With so many in favor of peace, Manuel hoped for an ac-
ceptance of his terms, and proposed that they consider the
matter for a day.

Kahled, with his hand upon the camel skin in his belt, replied again: "Remember Jababal!"

He realized that his only hope of victory lay in striking a
tired and hungry enemy, and that each hour's delay was dangerous. Less than half an hour later he was riding along the
line of battle shouting the battle cry: "Paradise is before you!
Fight for it!"

The soldiers were ready, and there began the most desperate
struggle that was ever waged upon the plains of Syria.

All day long the furious conflict raged. Three times the
Bedouins were driven back. Three times the cries and en-
treaties of their women and children in the rear urged them to
renew the fight, and again they plunged furiously upon the
solid Grecian phalanx.

Night came, and neither army had gained or lost, but among
the Bedouin captives taken by the Greeks were several who
recognized Kanana. They saw him moving freely about the
enemy's camp. They learned that he was supposed to be a servant who had fled with other camp followers at the time of
the slaughter of Jababal's army. They could see in it nothing
but cowardly desertion. They said:

"He was afraid that we should be conquered and instead of
standing by us to fight for Arabia, he ran to the enemy to hide
himself"; and in their anger they betrayed him. They reported
to the Greeks that he was a Bedouin of the army of Kahled,
not a Syrian servant of Jababal.

Kanana was quickly seized, bound and dragged into the
presence of the prince. Manuel had suspected that some one

had betrayed both Jababal and himself to Kahled, and, chagrined at the result of the first day's battle, he fiercely accused
Kanana.

Calmly the Bedouin boy admitted that it was he who had
given the information, and he waited without flinching as
Manuel drew his sword.

"Boy, dost thou not fear to die?" he exclaimed, as he bran-
dished his sword before Kanana.

"I fear nothing!" replied Kanana proudly.

"Take him away and guard him carefully," muttered the
prince. "Dying is too easy for such as he. He must be tortured
first."

The second day and the third were like the first. The army
of the Prophet fought with a desperation that never has been
equaled. The Ishmaelite counted his life as nothing so that he
saw a Greek fall with him. It was the fate of Allah and Arabia
for which they fought, and they stood as though rooted to the
ground, knowing of no retreat but death.

Again and again their general's voice rang loud above the
clashing arms: "Paradise is before you if you fight! Hell waits
for him who runs!" And they fought and fought and fought,
and not a man dared turn his back.

Again and again the Grecian phalanx advanced, but they
found a wall before them as solid as the cliff behind them.

When a Bedouin lay dead he ceased to fight, but not before;
and the moment he fell, another sprang forward from behind
to take his place.

13: *The Lance of Kanana*

The army of the Prophet had not retreated one foot from its
original position, when night brought the third day's battle
to a close.

Kahled sank upon the ground among his soldiers, while the
women from the rear brought what refreshments they could
to the tired warriors.

All night he lay awake beside his gray battle horse, looking
at the stars and thinking.

Flight or death would surely be the result of the coming day. Even Kahled the Invincible had given up all hope of victory.

He was too brave a man to fly, but he was also too brave to force others to stand and be slaughtered for his pride.

It was a bitter night for him, but as the eastern sky was tinged with gray, he at last resolved to make the sacrifice himself, and save such of his people as he could.

The women and children, with the wounded who could be moved, must leave at once, taking all that they could carry with them, and scatter themselves in every direction.

When they were well away, he, with such as preferred to stand and die with him, would hold the foe in check while the rest of the army retreated with orders to march at once to Mecca and Medina, and hold those two sacred cities as long as a man remained alive.

He breathed a deep sigh when the plan was completed, and rising, mounted his tired charger, to see that it was properly executed.

It was the first time in his career that Kahled the Invincible had ordered a retreat, and his only consolation was that he was neither to lead nor join in it.

In the camp of Manuel the same dread of the coming day clouded every brow. Food was entirely exhausted. Horses and camels had been devoured. They had neither the means with which to move away nor the strength to stand their ground.

Their solid phalanx was only what the enemy saw along the front. Rank after rank had been supplied from the rear till there was nothing left to call upon.

All that remained of the eighty thousand iron-hearted fighters—the pride of the Emperor Heraclius—as they gathered about the low camp fires confessed that they were overmatched by the sharper steel of Mohammedan zeal and Bedouin patriotism.

Manuel and his officers knew that for at least three days no relief could reach them; they knew, too, that they could not endure another day of fighting.

"If we could make them think that their men are deserting and joining us, we might frighten them," suggested an officer.

"Send for the spy," said Manuel quickly, "and let it be proclaimed to the other prisoners that all who join us shall be set
free, and that those who refuse shall be slaughtered without
mercy."

Haggard and worn Kanana stood before him. For fifty hours
he had lain bound in a cave at the foot of a cliff, without a drop
of water or a morsel of food.

"I am about to torture thee," said the prince. "Thou hast
wronged me more than thy sufferings can atone, but I shall
make them as bitter as I can. Hast thou anything to say before
the work begins?"

Kanana thought for a moment, then, hesitating as though
still doubtful, he replied:

"When the tempest rages on the desert, doth not the camel
lay him down, and the young camel say to the drifting sand,
'Cover me; kill me, I am helpless'? But among the captives
taken by the prince, I saw an old man pass my cave. He is full
of years, and for him I would part my lips. I hear that the
prince will have the prisoners slain, but it is not the custom
of my people to make the women, the old men, and the children suffer with the rest. May it please the prince to double
every torture he has prepared for me and in exchange to set
that old man free?"

"Who is he?" asked the prince.

"The one with a long white beard. There are not two," replied
Kanana.

"And what is he to you?"

Kanana hesitated.

"He shall die unless you tell me," said the prince, and Kanana's cold lips trembled as he whispered:

"He is my father."

" 'Tis well," said Manuel. "Let him be brought."

The old man entered, but paused at the opposite side of the
tent, looking reproachfully at his son. He had heard from the
other captives how they had discovered Kanana, a deserter in
the hour of danger, living in the tents of the enemy. Even he
had believed the tale, and he was enough of a patriot to be
glad that they betrayed his son.

"Is this thy father?" asked the prince. "He does not look it in his eyes."

Kanana simply bowed his head.

That look was piercing his heart far deeper than the threats of torture; but Manuel continued:

"You have offered to suffer every torture I can devise if I will set him free. But you have not compassed your debt to me.

You gave to Kahled the information by which he conquered Jababal. You gave him information which prevented his making terms of peace with me. But for you, I should be on my way to Mecca and Medina to sweep them from the earth. But I like courage, and you have shown more of it than Kahled himself. It is a pity to throw a heart like yours under a clod of earth, and I will give you an opportunity to save both yourself and your father. Stand upon the brow of the cliff yonder, as the sun comes up. There, according to the custom of your people, wave this lance above your head. Shout your own name, and your father's, so that all of your people can hear, and tell them that in one hour thirty thousand Arabs will draw the sword for the cause of Heraclius. Then throw the lance, and if your aim be good, and you do kill an Arab, that moment I will set thy father free and thou shalt be made a prince among my people. Do not refuse me, or, after I have tortured thee, with red-hot irons I will burn out thy father's eyes, lest he should still look savagely upon thy corpse!"

He had scarcely ceased speaking when the old sheik exclaimed:

"My son! My Kanana, I have wronged thee! Forgive me if thou canst, but let him burn out my eyes! Oh! not for all the eyes that watch the stars would I have a son of mine a traitor. Thou wouldst not lift a lance before. I charge thee now, by Allah, lift it not for any price that can be offered thee by this dog of an infidel!"

Kanana did not look at his father. His eyes were fixed on Manuel, and when all was still, he asked: "Will the prince allow his captive to sit alone till sunrise and consider his offer?"

"Take him out upon the cliff and let him sit alone," said Manuel; "but have the irons heated for his father's eyes."

Kanana chose a spot whence he could overlook the valley, and whatever his first intentions may have been, he changed them instantly with his first glance. He started, strained his eyes, and looked as far as his keen sight could pierce the gray light of early morning.

Then his head sank lower and lower over his hands, lying in his lap, till the wings of his turban completely covered them. He did not move or look again.

In that one glance he had recognized the result of Kahled's last resolve. In the gray distance he saw that laden camels were moving to the south. He saw the dark spots, most distant in the valley, suddenly disappear. They were folding their tents! They were moving away! Kahled the Invincible had ordered a retreat.

Kanana knew that to retreat at that moment meant death to Arabia, but he did not move again till an officer touched him on the shoulder and warned him that in a moment more the sun would rise.

With a startled shudder he rose and entered Manuel's tent.

"Is the word of the prince unchanged?" he asked. "If I speak the words and throw the lance and kill an Arab, that moment will he set my father free?"

"I swear it by all the powers of earth and heaven!" replied the prince.

"Give me the lance," said Kanana.

His father crouched against the tent, muttering: "For such an act, Kanana, when I am set free I will find first a fire with which to heat an iron, and burn my own eyes out."

Kanana did not heed him. He took the lance, tested it, and threw it scornfully upon the ground.

"Give me a heavier one!" he exclaimed. "Do you think me like your Greek boys, made of wax? Give me a lance that, when it strikes, will kill."

They gave him a heavier lance.

"The hand rest is too small for a Bedouin," he muttered, grasping it; "but wait! I can remedy that myself. Come. Let us have it over with."

As he spoke he tore a strip from beneath his coat, and, turning sharply about, walked before them to the brink of the cliff, winding the strip firmly about the hand rest of the lance.

Upon the very edge he stood erect and waited.

The sun rose out of the plain, and flashed with blinding force upon the Bedouin boy clad in his sheepskin coat and desert turban, precisely as it had found him in the porch of Aaron's tomb upon the summit of Mount Hor.

His hand no longer held a shepherd's staff, but firmly grasped a Grecian lance that gleamed and flashed as fiercely as the sun.

Upon Mount Hor he was bending forward, eagerly shading his eyes, anxiously looking away into the dim distance, searching the path of his destiny.

Now there was no eagerness. Calmly he stood there. Vainly the sun flashed in his clear, wide-open eyes. He did not even know that it was shining.

Not a muscle moved. Why was he waiting?

"Are you afraid?" muttered the prince, who had come as near as possible without being too plainly seen from below. "Remember your old father's eyes."

Kanana did not turn his head, but calmly answered:

"Do you see yonder a man upon a gray horse, moving slowly among the soldiers? He is coming nearer, nearer. That man is Kahled the Invincible. If he should come within range of the lance of Kanana, I suppose that Manuel would be well pleased to wait?"

"Good boy! Brave boy!" replied the prince. "When thou hast made thy mind to do a thing, thou doest it admirably. Kill him, and thou shalt be loaded down with gold till the day when thou diest of old age."

Kanana made no reply, but standing in bold relief upon the cliff, watched calmly and waited, till at last Kahled the Invincible left the line of soldiers, and alone rode nearer to the cliff.

"Now is your chance! Now! Now!" exclaimed the prince.

Slowly Kanana raised the lance. Three times he waved it above his head. Three times he shouted:

"I am Kanana, son of the Terror of the Desert!" in the manner of the Bedouin who challenges an enemy to fight, or meets a foe upon the plain.

For a moment, then, he hesitated. The next sentence was hard to speak. He knew too well what the result would be. It needed now no straining of the eyes to see his destiny.

All the vast army down below was looking up at him. Thousands would hear his words. Tens of thousands would see what followed.

"Go on! Go on!" the prince ejaculated fiercely. Kanana drew a deep breath and shouted:

"In one hour thirty thousand Arabs will draw the sword in the army of Heraclius!"

Then gathering all his strength, he hurled the lance directly at the great Mohammedan general, who had not moved since he began to speak.

Throughout those two great armies one might have heard a sparrow chirp, as the gleaming flashing blade fell like a meteor from the cliff.

The aim was accurate. The Bedouin boy cringed, and one might have imagined that it was even more accurate than he meant. It pierced the gray charger. The war horse of Kahled plunged forward and fell dead upon the plain.

A fierce howl rose from the ranks of the Ishmaelites. Men and women shrieked and yelled.

"Kanana the traitor! A curse upon the traitor Kanana!" rent the very air.

Such was the confusion which followed that, had the Greeks

been ready to advance, a thousand might have put a hundred thousand Bedouins to flight. But they were not ready.

Kanana stood motionless upon the cliff. He heard the yells of "Traitor!" but he knew that they would come, and did not heed them.

Calmly he watched till Kahled gained his feet, dragged the lance from his dying horse, and with it in his hand, hurried toward the soldiers. Only once he turned, and for an instant looked up at the solitary figure upon the cliff. He lifted his empty hand, as though it were a blessing and not a malediction he bestowed upon the Bedouin boy; then he disappeared.

With a deep, shivering sigh, Kanana pressed one hand beneath his sheepskin coat. A sharp contortion passed over him, but he turned about and stood calmly, face to face with Manuel.

"You did well," said the prince, "but you did not kill an Arab. It was for that I made my promise."

"'And if you kill an Arab,'" gasped Kanana, "'that moment I will set your father free!' Those were the prince's words! That was his promise, bound by all the powers of earth and heaven! He will keep it! He will not dare defy those powers, for I have killed an Arab!"

Clutching the sheepskin coat, Kanana tore it open, and, above a brilliant girdle, they saw a dagger buried in his bleeding breast. He tottered, reeled, stepped backward, and fell over the brink of the cliff. "You may as well go free," said Manuel, turning to the sheik. "A monstrous sacrifice has just been made to purchase your liberty."

Turning abruptly he entered his tent to consider, with his officers, the next result.

"I think they are flying," an officer reported, coming from the cliff. "The horsemen and camels are hurrying into the hills. Only foot soldiers seem remaining in the front."

"Let every soldier face them who has strength to stand!" commanded the prince. "Put everything to the front, and if they fly give them every possible encouragement."

The order was obeyed, and the forth day of battle began; but it was spiritless and slow.

The Bedouins, with their constantly thinning ranks, stood

with grim determination where their feet rested, but they made no effort to advance.

The wearied out and starving Grecian phalanx simply held its ground. The prince was not there to urge his soldiers on. The voice of Kahled did not sound among the Mussulmans.

An hour went by.

Suddenly there was an uproar in the rear of the army of Heraclius. There was a wild shout, a clash of arms, and the watchword of Islam rang above the tumult, in every direction.

Ten thousand horses and twenty thousand war camels poured in upon that defenseless rear, and even as Kanana had declared, in just one hour there were thirty thousand Arabs wielding their savage swords in the army of Heraclius.

Another hour went by. The battle cry of Kahled ceased. The shout of victory rang from the throats of the Mussulmans. Manuel and all his officers were slain. The magnificent army of Heraclius was literally obliterated.

Treasure without limit glutted the conquered camp. Arabia was saved.

Quickly the soldiers erected a gorgeous throne and summoned Kahled to sit upon it, while they feasted about him and did him honor as their victorious and invincible leader.

The veteran warrior responded to their call, but he came from his tent with his head bowed down, bearing in his arms a heavy burden. Slowly he mounted the platform, and upon the sumptuous throne he laid his burden down.

It was the bruised and lifeless body of Kanana.

With trembling hand the grim chief drew back the sheep-skin coat, and all men then beheld, bound about the Bedouin boy, the sacred girdle!

"I gave it to him," said Kahled solemnly; "and upon the fragments you have returned to me, he wrote the information by which we conquered Jababal and Manuel. You saw him throw his lance at me; you called him 'traitor!' but about the hand rest there was wound this strip. See! In blood—in his blood— these words are written here: 'Do not retreat. The infidels are starving and dying. Strike them in the rear.' It was his only means of reaching me. It was not the act of a traitor. No! It was the Lance of Kanana that rescued *Arabia*."

The Door in the Wall, *by Marguerite de An- geli, published by Doubleday & Co., Inc., and* Mickel and The Lost Ship, *by Olle Matt- son, published by Franklin Watts, Inc., are also stories of courage and loyalty in other times and other lands.*

Lassie Come-Home

BY ERIC KNIGHT

Illustrations by Thomas Victor Hall

> **When the family could no longer afford to keep her, Lassie was sold. But a dog cannot understand the money matters of humans, and Lassie felt she still belonged to the boy she loved.**

T HE dog had met the boy by the school gate for five years. Now she couldn't understand that times were changed and she wasn't supposed to be there any more. But the boy knew.

So when he opened the door of the cottage he spoke before he entered.

"Mother," he said, "Lassie's come home again."

He waited a moment, as if in hope of something. But the man and woman inside the cottage did not speak.

"Come in, Lassie," the boy said.

He held open the door, the tricolor collie walked in obediently. Going head down, as a collie when it knows something is wrong, it went to the rug and lay down before the hearth, a black-white-and-gold aristocrat. The man, sitting on a low stool by the fireside, kept his eyes turned away. The woman went to the sink and busied herself there.

"She was waiting at school for me, just like always," the boy went on. He spoke fast, as if racing against time. "She must ha' got away again. I thought, happen this time, we might just—"

"No!" the woman exploded.

The boy's carelessness dropped. His voice rose in pleading.

"But this time, mother! Just this time. We could hide her. They wouldn't ever know."

189

"Dogs, dogs, dogs!" the woman cried. The words poured from her as if the boy's pleading had been a signal gun for her own anger. "I'm sick o' hearing about tykes around this house. Well, she's sold and gone and done with, so the quicker she's taken back the better. Now get her back quick, or the first thing ye know we'll have Hynes round here again. Mr. Hynes!"

Her voice sharpened in imitation of the Cockney accent of the south: "Hi know you Yorkshiremen and yer come-'ome dogs. Training yer dogs to come 'ome so's yer can sell 'em hover and hover again.

"Well, she's sold, so ye can take her out o' my house and home to them as bought her!"

The boy's bottom lip crept out stubbornly, and there was silence in the cottage. Then the dog lifted its head and nudged the man's hand, as a dog will when asking for a patting. But the man drew away and stared silently into the fire.

The boy tried again, with the ceaseless guile of a child, his voice coaxing.

"Look, feyther, she wants thee to bid her welcome. Aye, she's that glad to be home. Happen they don't tak' good care on her up there? A bit o' linseed strained through her drinking water—that's what I'd gi' her."

Still looking in the fire, the man nodded. But the woman, as if perceiving the boy's new attack, sniffed.

"Aye, tha wouldn't be a Carraclough if tha didn't know more about tykes nor breaking eggs wi' a stick. Nor a Yorkshireman. My goodness, it seems to me sometimes that chaps in this village thinks more on their tykes nor they do o' their own flesh and blood. They'll sit by their firesides and let their own bairns starve so long as t' dog gets fed."

The man stirred, suddenly, but the boy cut in quickly.

"But she does look thin. Look, truly—they're not feeding her right. Just look!"

"Aye," the woman chattered. "I wouldn't put it past Hynes to steal t' best part o' t' dog meat for himself. And Lassie always was a strong eater."

"She's fair thin now," the boy said.

Almost unwillingly the man and woman looked at the dog for the first time.

"My gum, she is off a bit," the woman said. Then she caught herself. "Ma goodness, I suppose I'll have to fix her a bit o' summat. She can do wi' it. But soon as she's fed, back she goes. And never another dog I'll have in my house. Never another. Cooking and nursing for 'em, and as much trouble to bring up as a bairn!"

So, grumbling and chatting as a village woman will, she moved about, warming a pan of food for the dog. The man and boy watched the collie eat. When it was done, the boy took from the mantelpiece a folded cloth and a brush, and began prettying the collie's coat. The man watched for several minutes, and then could stand it no longer.

"Here," he said.

He took the cloth and brush from the boy and began working expertly on the dog, rubbing the rich, deep coat, then brushing the snowy whiteness of the full ruff and the apron, bringing out the heavy leggings on the forelegs. He lost himself in his work, and the boy sat on the rug, watching contentedly. The woman stood it as long as she could.

"Now will ye please tak' that tyke out o' here?"

The man flared in anger.

"Well, ye wouldn't have me tak' her back looking like a mucky Monday wash, wouldta?"

He bent again, and began fluffing out the collie's petticoats.

"Joe!" the woman pleaded. "Will ye tak' her out o' here? Hynes'll be nosing round afore ye know it. And I won't have that man in my house. Wearing his hat inside, and going on like he's the duke himself—him and his leggings!"

"All right, lass."

"And this time, Joe, tak' young Joe wi' ye."

"What for?"

"Well, let's get the business done and over with. It's him that Lassie runs away for. She comes for young Joe. So if he went wi' thee, and told her to stay, happen she'd be content and not run away no more, and then we'd have a little peace and quiet in the home—though heaven knows there's not much hope o' that these days, things being like they are." The woman's voice trailed away, as if she would soon cry in weariness.

The man rose. "Come, Joe," he said. "Get thy cap."

The Duke of Rudling walked along the gravel paths of his place with his granddaughter, Philippa. Philippa was a bright and knowing young woman, allegedly the only member of the duke's family he could address in unspotted language. For it was also alleged that the duke was the most irascible, vile-tempered old man in the three Ridings of Yorkshire.

"Country going to pot!" the duke roared, stabbing at the walk with his great blackthorn stick. "When I was a young man! Hah! Women today not as pretty. Horses today not as fast. As for dogs—ye don't see dogs today like—"

Just then the duke and Philippa came round a clump of rhododendrons and saw a man, a boy and a dog.

"Ah," said the duke, in admiration. Then his brow knotted. "Damme, Carraclough! What're ye doing with my dog?"

He shouted it quite as if the others were in the next county, for it was also the opinion of the Duke of Rudling that people were not nearly so keen of hearing as they used to be when he was a young man.

"It's Lassie," Carraclough said. "She's runned away again and I brought her back."

Carraclough lifted his cap, and poked the boy to do the same, not in any servile gesture, but to show that they were as well brought up as the next.

"Damme, ran away again!" the duke roared. "And I told that utter nincompoop Hynes to—where is he? Hynes! Hynes! Damme, Hynes, what're ye hiding for?"

"Coming, your lordship!" sounded a voice, far away behind the shrubberies. And soon Hynes appeared, a sharp-faced man in check coat, riding breeches, and the cloth leggings that grooms wear.

"Take this dog," roared the duke, "and pen her up! And damme, if she breaks out again, I'll—I'll—"

The duke waved his great stick threateningly, and then, without so much as a thank you or kiss the back of my hand to Joe Carraclough, he went stamping and muttering away.

"I'll pen 'er up," Hynes muttered, when the duke was gone. "And if she ever gets awye agyne, I'll—"

He made as if to grab the dog, but Joe Carraclough's hob-nailed boot trod heavily on Hynes' foot.

"I brought my lad wi' me to bid her stay, so we'll pen her up this time—Eigh—sorry! I didn't see I were on thy foot. Come, Joe, lad."

They walked down the crunching gravel path, along by the neat kennel buildings. When Lassie was behind the closed door, she raced into the high wire run where she could see them as they went. She pressed close against the wire, waiting.

The boy stood close, too, his fingers through the meshes touching the dog's nose.

"Go on, lad," his father ordered. "Bid her stay!"

The boy looked around, as if for help that he did not find. He swallowed, and then spoke, low and quickly.

"Stay here, Lassie, and don't come home no more," he said. "And don't come to school for me no more. Because I don't want to see ye no more. 'Cause tha's a bad dog, and we don't love thee no more, and we don't want thee. So stay here for-ever and leave us be, and don't never come home no more."

Then he turned, and because it was hard to see the path plainly, he stumbled. But his father, who was holding his head very high as they walked away from Hynes, shook him savage-ly, and snapped roughly: "Look where tha's going!"

Then the boy trotted beside his father. He was thinking that he'd never be able to understand why grownups sometimes

were so bad-tempered with you, just when you needed them
most.

After that, there were days and days that passed, and the
dog did not come to the school gate any more. So then it was
not like old times. There were so many things that were not
like old times.

The boy was thinking that as he came wearily up the path
and opened the cottage door and heard his father's voice,
tense with anger: ". . . walk my feet off. If tha thinks I like—"

Then they heard his opening of the door and the voice
stopped and the cottage was silent.

That's how it was now, the boy thought. They stopped talking in front of you. And this, somehow, was too much for him
to bear.

He closed the door, ran out into the night, and onto the
moor, that great expanse of land where all the people of that
village walked in lonesomeness when life and its troubles
seemed past bearing.

A long while later, his father's voice cut through the darkness.

"What's tha doing out there, Joe lad?"

"Walking."

"Aye."

They went on together, aimlessly, each following his own
thoughts. And they both thought about the dog that had been
sold.

"Tha maun't think we're hard on thee, Joe," the man said at
last. "It's just that a chap's got to be honest. There's that to it.
Sometimes, when a chap doesn't have much, he clings right
hard to what he's got. And honest is honest, and there's no
two ways about it.

"Why, look, Joe. Seventeen year I worked in that Clarabelle
Pit till she shut down, and a good collier, too. Seventeen year!
And butties I've had by the dozen, and never a man of 'em
can ever say that Joe Carraclough kept what wasn't his, nor
spoke what wasn't true. Not a man in this riding can ever
call a Carraclough dishonest.

"And when ye've sold a man summat, and ye've taken his

brass, and ye've spent it—well, then done's done. That's all. And ye've got to stand by that."

"But Lassie was—"

"Now, Joe! Ye can't alter it, ever. It's done—and happen it's for t' best. No two ways, Joe, she were getting hard to feed. Why, ye wouldn't want Lassie to be going around getting peaked and pined, like some chaps round here keep their tykes. And if ye're fond of her, then just think on it that now she's got lots to eat, and a private kennel, and a good run to herself, and living like a varritable princess, she is. Ain't that best for her?"

"We wouldn't pine her. We've always got lots to eat."

The man blew out his breath angrily. "Eigh, Joe, nowt pleases thee. Well, then, tha might as well have it. Tha'll never see Lassie no more. She run home once too often, so the duke's taken her wi' him up to his place in Scotland, and there she'll stay. So it's good-by and good luck to her, and she'll never come home no more, she won't. Now, I weren't off to tell thee, but there it is, so put it in thy pipe and smoke it, and let's never say a word about it no more—especially in front of thy mother."

The boy stumbled on in the darkness. Then the man halted.

"We ought to be getting back, lad. We left thy mother alone."

He turned the boy about, and then went on, but as if he were talking to himself.

"Tha sees, Joe, women's not like men. They have to stay at home and manage best they can, and just spend the time in wishing. And when things don't go right, well, they have to take it out in talk and give a man hades. But it don't mean nowt, really, so tha shouldn't mind when thy mother talks hard.

"Ye just got to learn to be patient and let 'em talk, and just let it go up t' chimney wi' th' smoke."

Then they were quiet, until, over the rise, they saw the lights of the village. Then the boy spoke: "How far away is Scotland, feyther?"

"Nay, lad, it's a long, long road."

"But how far, feyther?"

"I don't know—but it's a longer road than thee or me'll ever

walk. Now, lad. Don't thee fret no more, and try to be a man—
and don't plague thy mother no more, wilta?"

Joe Carraclough was right. It is a long road, as they say in
the North, from Yorkshire to Scotland. Much too far for a man
to walk—or a boy. And though the boy often thought of it, he
remembered his father's words on the moor, and he put the
thought behind him.

But there is another way of looking at it; and that's the distance from Scotland to Yorkshire. And that is just as far as from
Yorkshire to Scotland. A matter of about four hundred miles,
it would be, from the Duke of Rudling's place far up in the
Highlands, to the village of Holdersby. That would be for a
man, who could go fairly straight.

To an animal, how much farther would it be? For a dog
can study no maps, read no signposts, ask no directions. It
could only go blindly, by instinct, knowing that it must keep
on to the south, to the south. It would wander and err, quest
and quarter, run into firths and lochs that would send it side-
tracking and back-tracking before it could go on its way—
south.

A thousand miles, it would be going that way—a thousand
miles over strange terrain.

There would be moors to cross, and burns to swim. And
then those great, long lochs that stretch from one side of that
dour land to the other would bar the way and send a dog
questing a hundred miles before it could find a crossing that
would allow it to go south.

And, too, there would be rivers to cross, wide rivers like the
Forth and the Clyde, the Tweed and the Tyne, where one
must go miles to find bridges. And the bridges would be in
towns. And in the towns there would be officials—like the one
in Lanarkshire. In all his life he had never let a captured dog
get away—except one. That one was a gaunt, snarling collie
that whirled on him right in the pound itself, and fought and
twisted loose to race away down the city street—going south.

But there are kind people, too; ones knowing and understanding in the ways of dogs. There was an old couple in Dur-
ham who found a dog lying exhausted in a ditch one night—

lying there with its head to the south. They took that dog into
their cottage and warmed it and fed it and nursed it. And because it seemed an understanding, wise dog, they kept it in
their home, hoping it would learn to be content. But, as it grew
stronger, every afternoon toward four o'clock it would go to
the door and whine, and then begin pacing back and forth
between the door and the window, back and forth as the animals do in their cages at the zoo.

They tried every wile and every kindness to make it bide
with them, but finally, when the dog began to refuse food, the
old people knew what they must do. Because they understood
dogs, they opened the door one afternoon and they watched
the collie go, not down the road to the right, or to the left, but
straight across a field toward the south; going steadily at a trot,
as if it knew it still had a long, long road to travel.

Ah, a thousand miles of tor and brae, of shire and moor, of
path and road and plowland, of river and stream and burn
and brook and beck, of snow and rain and fog and sun, is a
long way, even for a human being. But it would seem too far—
much, much too far—for any dog to travel blindly and win
through.

And yet—and yet—who shall say why, when so many weeks
had passed that hope against hope was dying, a boy coming
out of school, out of the cloakroom that always smelled of damp
wool drying, across the concrete play yard with the black,
waxed slides, should turn his eyes to a spot by the school gate
from force of five years of habit, and see there a dog? Not a
dog, this one, that lifted glad eyes above a proud, slim head
with its black-and-gold mask; but a dog that lay weakly, trying
to lift a head that would no longer lift, trying to wag a tail that
was torn and blotched and matted with dirt and burs, and
managing to do nothing much except to whine in a weak,
happy, crying way as a boy on his knees threw arms about it,
and hands touched it that had not touched it for many a day.

Then who shall picture the urgency of a boy, running awkwardly, with a great dog in his arms, running through the village, past the empty mill, past the Labor Exchange, where the
men looked up from their deep ponderings on life and the
dole? Or who shall describe the high tones of a voice—a boy's

voice, calling as he runs up a path: "Mother! Oh, mother!
Lassie's come home! Lassie's come home!"

Nor does anyone who ever owned a dog need to be told the
sound a man makes as he bends over a dog that has been his
for years; nor how a woman moves quickly, preparing food—
which might be the family's condensed milk stirred into warm
water; nor how the jowl of a dog is lifted so that raw egg and

brandy, bought with precious pence, should be spooned in;
nor how bleeding pads are bandaged, tenderly.

That was one day. There was another day when the woman
in the cottage sighed with pleasure, for a dog lifted to its feet
for the first time to stand over a bowl of oatmeal, putting its
head down and lapping again and again while its pinched
flanks quivered.

And there was another day when the boy realized that,
even now, the dog was not to be his again. So the cottage rang
again with protests and cries, and a woman shrilling: "Is there
never to be no more peace in my house and home?" Long
after he was in bed that night the boy heard the rise and fall
of the woman's voice, and the steady, reiterative tone of the
man's. It went on long after he was asleep.

In the morning the man spoke, not looking at the boy, saying the words as if he had long rehearsed them.

"Thy mother and me have decided upon it that Lassie shall
stay here till she's better. Anyhow, nobody could nurse her
better than us. But the day that t' duke comes back, then back
she goes, too. For she belongs to him, and that's honest, too.
Now tha has her for a while, so be content."

In childhood, "for a while" is such a great stretch of days
when seen from one end. It is a terribly short time seen from
the other.

The boy knew how short it was that morning as he went to
school and saw a motorcar driven by a young woman. And in
the car was a gray-thatched, terrible old man, who waved a
cane and shouted: "Hi! Hi, there! Damme, lad! You, there!
Hi!"

Then it was no use running, for the car could go faster than
you, and soon it was beside you and the man was saying:
"Damme, Philippa, will you make this smelly thing stand still
a moment? Hi, lad!"

"Yes, sir."

"You're What's-'is-Name's lad, aren't you?"

"Ma feyther's Joe Carraclough."

"I know. I know. Is he home now?"

"No, sir. He's away to Allerby. A mate spoke for him at the
pit and he's gone to see if there's a chance."

"When'll he be back?"

"I don't know. I think about tea."

"Eh, yes. Well, yes. I'll drop round about fivish to see that father of yours. Something important."

It was hard to pretend to listen to lessons. There was only waiting for noon. Then the boy ran home.

"Mother! T' duke is back and he's coming to take Lassie away."

"Eigh, drat my buttons. Never no peace in this house. Is tha sure?"

"Aye. He stopped me. He said tell feyther he'll be round at five. Can't we hide her? Oh, mother!"

"Nay, thy feyther—"

"Won't you beg him? Please, please. Beg feyther to—"

"Young Joe, now it's no use. So stop thy teasing! Thy feyther'll not lie. That much I'll give him. Come good, come bad, he'll not lie."

"But just this once, mother. Please beg him, just this once. Just one lie wouldn't hurt him. I'll make it up to him. I will. When I'm growed up, I'll get a job. I'll make money. I'll buy him things—and you, too. I'll buy you both anything you want if you'll only—"

For the first time in his trouble the boy became a child, and the mother, looking over, saw the tears that ran openly down his contorted face. She turned her face to the fire, and there was a pause. Then she spoke.

"Joe, tha mustn't," she said softly. "Tha must learn never to want nothing in life like that. It don't do, lad. Tha mustn't want things bad, like tha wants Lassie."

The boy shook his clenched fists in impatience.

"It ain't that, mother. Ye don't understand. Don't ye see—it ain't me that wants her. It's her that wants us! Tha's wha made her come all them miles. It's her that wants us, so terrible bad!"

The woman turned and stared. It was as if, in that moment, she were seeing this child, this boy, this son of her own, for the first time in many years. She turned her head down toward the table. It was surrender.

"Come and eat, then," she said. "I'll talk to him. I will that, all right. I feel sure he won't lie. But I'll talk to him all right. I'll talk to Mr. Joe Carraclough. I will indeed."

At five that afternoon, the Duke of Rudling, fuming and muttering, got out of a car at a cottage gate to find a boy barring his way. This was a boy who stood, stubbornly, saying fiercely: "Away wi' thee! Thy tyke's net here!"

"Damme, Philippa, th' lad's touched," the duke said. "He is. He's touched."

Scowling and thumping his stick, the old duke advanced until the boy gave way, backing down the path out of the reach of the waving blackthorn stick.

"Thy tyke's net here," the boy protested.

"What's he saying?" the girl asked.

"Says my dog isn't here. Damme, you going deaf? I'm supposed to be deaf, and I hear him plainly enough. Now, ma lad, what tyke o' mine's net here?"

As he turned to the boy, the duke spoke in broadest Yorkshire, as he did always to the people of the cottages—a habit which the Duchess of Rudling, and many more members of the duke's family, deplored.

"Coom, coom, ma lad. Whet tyke's net here?"

"No tyke o' thine. Us hasn't got it." The words began running faster and faster as the boy backed away from the fearful old man who advanced. "No tyke could have done it. No tyke can come all them miles. It isn't Lassie. It's another one that looks like her. It isn't Lassie!"

"Why, bless ma heart and sowl," the duke puffed. "Where's thy father, ma lad?"

The door behind the boy opened, and a woman's voice spoke.

"If it's Joe Carraclough ye want, he's out in the shed—and been there shut up half the afternoon."

"What's this lad talking about—a dog of mine being here?"

"Nay," the woman snapped quickly. "He didn't say a tyke o' thine was here. He said it wasn't here."

"Well, what dog o' mine isn't here, then?"

The woman swallowed, and looked about as if for help. The duke stood, peering from under his jutting eyebrows. Her answer, truth or lie, was not spoken, for then they heard the rattle of a door opening, and a man making a pursing sound with his lips, as he will when he wants a dog to follow, and then Joe Carraclough's voice said: "This is t' only tyke us has here. Does it look like any dog that belongs to thee?"

With his mouth opening to cry one last protest, the boy turned. And his mouth stayed open. For there he saw his father, Joe Carraclough, the collie fancier, standing with a dog at his heels—a dog that sat at his left heel patiently, as any well-trained dog should do—as Lassie used to do. But this dog was not Lassie. It fact, it was ridiculous to think of it at the same moment as you thought of Lassie.

For where Lassie's skull was aristocratic and slim, this dog's head was clumsy and rough. Where Lassie's ears stood in twin-lapped symmetry, this dog had one ear draggling and the other standing up Alsatian fashion in a way to give any collie breeder the cold shivers. Where Lassie's coat was rich tawny gold, this dog's coat had ugly patches of black; and where Lassie's apron was a billowing stretch of snow-white, this dog had puddles of off-color blue-merle mixture. Besides, Lassie had four white paws, and this one had one paw white, two dirty-brown, and one almost black.

That is the dog they all looked at as Joe Carraclough stood there, having told no lie, having only asked a question. They all stood, waiting the duke's verdict.

But the duke said nothing. He only walked forward, slowly, as if he were seeing a dream. He bent beside the collie, looking with eyes that were as knowing about dogs as any Yorkshireman alive. And those eyes did not waste themselves upon twisted ears, or blotched marking, or rough head. Instead they were looking at a paw, that the duke lifted, looking at the underside of the paw, staring intently at five black pads, crossed and recrossed with scars where thorns had lacerated, and stones had torn.

For a long time the duke stared, and when he got up he did not speak in Yorkshire accents any more. He spoke as a gentleman should, and he said: "Joe Carraclough, I never owned this dog. 'Pon my soul, she never belonged to me. Never!"

Then he turned and went stumping down the path, thumping his cane and saying, "Bless my soul. Four hundred miles! Damme, wouldn't ha' believed it. Damme—five hundred miles!"

He was at the gate when his granddaughter whispered to him fiercely.

"Of course," he cried. "Mind your own business. Exactly what I came for. Talking about dogs made me forget. Carraclough! Carraclough! What're ye hiding for?"

"I'm still here, sir."

"Ah, there you are. You working?"

"Eigh, now. Working," Joe said. That's the best he could manage.

"Yes, working, working!" the duke fumed.

"Well, now—" Joe began.

Then Mrs. Carraclough came to his rescue, as a good housewife in Yorkshire will.

"Why, Joe's got three or four things that he's been considering," she said, with proper display of pride. "But he hasn't quite said yes or no to any of them yet."

"Then say no, quick," the old man puffed. "Had to sack Hynes. Didn't know a dog from a drunken filly. Should ha' known all along no Londoner could handle dogs fit for Yorkshire taste. How much, Carraclough?"

"Well, now," Joe began.

"Seven pounds a week, and worth every penny," Mrs. Carraclough chipped in. "One o' them offers may come up to eight," she lied, expertly. For there's always a certain amount of lying to be done in life, and when a woman's married to a man who has made a life-long cult of being honest, then she's got to learn to do the lying for two.

"Five," roared the duke—who, after all, was a Yorkshireman, and couldn't help being a bit sharp about things that pertained to money.

"Six," said Mrs. Carraclough.

"Five pounds ten," bargained the duke, cannily.

"Done," said Mrs. Carraclough, who would have been willing

to settle for three pounds in the first place. "But, o' course, us gets the cottage, too."

"All right," puffed the duke. "Five pounds ten and the cottage. Begin Monday. But—on one condition. Carraclough, you can live on my land, but I won't have that thick-skulled, screw-lugged, gay-tailed eyesore of a misshapen mongrel on my property. Now never let me see her again. You'll get rid of her?"

He waited, and Joe fumbled for words. But it was the boy who answered, happily, gaily: "Oh, no, sir. She'll be waiting at school for me most o' the time. And, anyway, in a day or so we'll have her fixed up and coped up so's ye'd never, never recognize her."

"I don't doubt that," puffed the duke, as he went to the car. "I don't doubt ye could do just exactly that."

It was a long time afterward, in the car, that the girl said: "Don't sit there like a lion on the Nelson column. And I thought you were supposed to be a hard man."

"Fiddlesticks, m'dear. I'm a ruthless realist. For five years I've sworn I'd have that dog by hook or crook, and now, egad, at last I've got her."

"Pooh! You had to buy the man before you could get his dog."

"Well, perhaps that's not the worst part of the bargain."

Wilderness Champion, by Joseph Lippincott, published by J. B. Lippincott Co., is also about a dog's reunion with his master. Two more dog stories are Silver Chief, by John O'Brien, published by Holt, Rinehart & Winston, Inc., and Junket, by Anne H. White, published by The Viking Press, Inc.

The Riding Lesson

BY KATE SEREDY

Illustrations by the author

> *Young Jancsi lives with his mother and his father, the "Good Master," on a farm in Hungary. When his cousin Kate, from Budapest, comes to pay a visit she turns out to be a tomboy such as Jancsi has never seen or heard of.*

NOBODY ever found out just what had happened between Kate and Father that night, nobody ever spoke about it. Jancsi knew she didn't get a licking—lickings were noisy affairs. But for a few days peace and serenity reigned. Kate was left alone with Mother in the daytime. Mother never complained about her. Jancsi and Father were very busy. They had hired men to do the plowing and planting. Jancsi had full charge of the three milking cows, the pigs, and the poultry. At the crack of dawn he was up. He milked and fed the cows and strained the milk. Then he took corn and swill to the pigs, mush to the chickens. Next he drove the ducks and geese to a grassy inclosure with a brook running through it. On nice days he led the cows to a small pasture close to the barn. If breakfast wasn't ready, he helped Father in the stables. After breakfast Father rode out to the herds. His herds were scattered over a vast area. Horses across the river to the north, sheep to the south. They had to be far away from each other because sheep ruin the grass for horses, cropping it too close to the ground. The men who took care of the herds lived in little huts close to the corrals. Sometimes Jancsi rode along with Father. He loved the days when he was allowed to do so. The herdsmen were his friends; they told him stories, taught him to whittle, to play the tilinkó, rope a wild horse, and clip sheep. Best of all Jancsi loved the times when they were so far away from home that Father decided to stay overnight. They cooked supper on an open fire and ate it crouching around the embers, singing, swapping stories, or talking about the animals. Here he was one of the men and they never made him feel that he was just a young boy. Later on they made bunks right out in the open field, under the starry sky. The herdsmen had great big coats, called "bunda." The bunda is made of sheepskin, and the herdsmen wear it all the year round. They say it keeps them warm in the winter, when they wear it with the furry side in. With the furry side out, it keeps them cool in the summer. "My bunda is my house," they say, and that is true. No icy blast penetrates it, no rain soaks through it. Jancsi loved to snuggle down into the furry warmth of this great coat; loved the keen smell of grass, the stir of animals close by, the song of the nightingale, the friendly companionship of it all.

On the days when he had to stay home, life wasn't so interesting before Kate came. Chopping wood, helping Mother in the dairy, carrying water, had been his share.

The first few days after Kate's hectic arrival the relation between the cousins was rather strained. Kate couldn't get over the funny "petticoats" Jancsi was wearing. Catching her amused glances, Jancsi paid her back by gazing solemnly at the rafters, muttering something about "outlandish rats that get into people's sausages." Finally it was Kate who broke the ice. One afternoon she was waiting at the gate when Father and Jancsi returned from the day's ride. Jancsi was riding his favorite, a skittish two-year-old horse. It was dancing and prancing now, eager to get to the stable and hungry for its oats. Kate followed them and watched Jancsi unsaddle the horse and feed it.

"He's beautiful. May I pat his neck?" she asked.

"Watch out, he's ticklish," warned Jancsi.

"Takes a real boy to ride a horse like you do," said Kate with admiration, but hastened to add, "even if you do wear petticoats."

"Petticoats! Can't you see they're split?" Jancsi demonstrated, spreading his pleated pants.

"M-m-m," said Kate. "Do you think I could ride if I split my skirts?"

"I could teach you, Kate. I bet you'd make a good rider with your long legs."

"Will you, Jancsi? Honest? And then I could ride with you and Uncle instead of messing around with old embroideries, trying to be good."

"Well . . . maybe you could. I'll teach you anyway," promised Jancsi.

Next day Father rode alone. Jancsi was working like fury, trying to finish his chores quickly. He had a surprise for Kate. There were twelve brand-new ducklings in the poultry yard. He finished his work quicker than he expected. Mother was in the vegetable patch, spading up the soil for her seedlings. He walked back to the house and called Kate. She emerged from the bedroom, walking primly and awkwardly. She looked like a very, very good little girl! The warning flashed through Jancsi's mind: "When she looks like an angel, she is contemplating something disastrous." He made up his mind to be extra careful.

He took her to the chicken coop first. He showed her the nests where the hens were sitting on eggs. Kate was bound to break some eggs to see whether there were really little chicks inside. Only his solemn promise that he would call her when the chickens began to break through saved the lives of several future chicks.

The pigsty was a total failure as an entertainment. Kate just held her nose and walked away. Then Jancsi took her to see the cows.

"Can you ride a cow?" asked Kate.

Jancsi laughed. "No, you silly, they're milk cows."

"Milk cows? Don't tell me stories, they're chocolate cows. Why, they're all brown!"

When she finally understood that you have to milk a cow to get milk, she didn't want to believe it. "Why," she said, "milk grows in bottles!" But she wasn't interested enough to argue about it—she hated milk.

The geese and ducks were more interesting to her. She giggled at the funny way the ducks waddled and shook their tails. When Jancsi finally took her to see the baby ducks, Kate clapped her hands, exclaimed over them. She was fairly dancing with joy.

"See, they're only a day old, but they can swim like nobody's

business," explained Jancsi proudly. Kate wanted to pick them up, but he told her that she must never handle very young animals; they might die. Surprisingly Kate listened to him. She said: "You know what they are like? Like little bunches of dandelions, all yellow and fuzzy. Let's pick dandelions and make believe they're duckies."

When they had a heap of the fuzzy yellow flowers, they sat down on the bank and tied them into small bunches. Kate threw some of them into the brook, where they floated, looking surprisingly like the ducklings. Then something unexpected happened. The mother duck got very excited, cocked her head to one side, then the other side. She peered at these yellow bunches suspiciously. Then she began to swim toward them, quack-quacking loudly.

"Look, Kate!" exclaimed Jancsi. "She thinks the flowers are baby ducks. Oh, how funny!"

It was funny indeed. Poor mother duck called and scolded, she tried to round up her strange brood, all in vain. The dandelions floated serenely down the brook. She got mad and pecked at one of the bunches, which promptly came to pieces. She was frantic now. She kept turning this way, that way, not knowing what had happened.

Kate and Jancsi rolled on the grass; they were weak with laughter. Then something caught Jancsi's eye. He sat up and gazed at Kate who was lying on her stomach, kicking her legs, giggling and moaning in her amusement. There was something very wrong with Kate's costume. Her dark blue skirt was spread out on both sides on the grass, but there wasn't any skirt on Kate proper, only long white bloomers. He shook her shoulder. "Kate! What—what happened to your dress?"

Kate turned her head and peered at herself. "I split my skirt because you said you'd teach me to ride," she announced calmly. She scrambled to her feet, dragging the horrified Jancsi with her. "Come on to the stable, let's start the lesson."

Jancsi was too shocked. "But, Kate, your good dress. It's ruined!"

"Phoo. Your petticoats are split and they aren't ruined," scoffed Kate.

"But you're a girl—it looks awful queer," mumbled Jancsi, trailing reluctantly after her. He wished Father would come home so he could put off the riding lesson. He picked an old fat mare for Kate. He was just puttering around with the saddles, playing for time. She watched him with interest, asking questions about saddle, harness, reins. Then Jancsi led out the horses and, casting a last hopeful glance toward the gate, gave up waiting for Father. He proceeded to show Kate how to mount. He did it first, then dismounted again, and, holding both reins, explained every move.

"Stand at the left side of the horse. Put your left hand on the pommel, your right hand on the stirrup to steady it. Step in the stirrup with your left foot and swing over the saddle." He made Kate mount and dismount several times. Then he handed her the reins, and mounted his own horse.

They started walking the horses slowly around the yard. "Please, Kate," Jancsi said, seeing her excited face and gleaming eyes, "please, Kate, don't scream. It frightens the horses. Just in case anything should happen, kick loose from the stirrups and jump."

Kate nodded her head solemnly, clinging to the pommel with both hands.

"Let go of the pommel," instructed Jancsi. "Only gypsies ride that way. Sit up straight."

"But the horse keep bobbing up and down, and I'm so high up," complained Kate, eying the ground suspiciously.

"High up! You were higher up on the rafters," giggled Jancsi.

"They didn't bob!" was the troubled answer.

It took quite a while before Kate got used to the bobbing and learned to sit straight and loose. Then she rewarded Jancsi with a gleaming smile. "I got it. Let's go fast now."

"Not today, Kate, you'll be sore all over anyway, not being used to the saddle."

But Kate wouldn't dismount. She coaxed and begged and wheedled until Jancsi made the horses trot. This was as far as he would go, however. He stopped the horses in spite of her dark and sulky look.

"Whee-ee!" She let out a long, loud scream. Jancsi's horse immediately went into the most violent action. He turned round and round like a spinning top. He dug his hoofs in the ground, trying to throw Jancsi. He rose on his hind legs, thrashing the air viciously with his front hoofs. Jancsi clung to the plunging animal, talking to him in a soft, reassuring voice. He finally succeeded in bringing the horse to a shivering stop. Dismounting, he looked around for Kate. The incredible child sat on her old mare, watching him with great interest.

"You screaming monkey," panted Jancsi. "Just you wait till I go riding with you again. Get off that horse!"

Kate didn't seem to notice that he was mad. "Gee, Jancsi, but you can ride! It was wonderful. This old armchair"— pointing to her horse—"just stood here while you had all the fun. Let me ride your horse now."

Jancsi, slightly pacified by her admiration, suddenly smiled. "If you dismount and walk over here, I'll let you." This wasn't a rash promise. He knew what would happen. Kate rolled off her horse—and just crumpled on the ground.

"My legs," she cried. "I haven't any legs!"

"Come on, Kate, walk over here!" teased Jancsi.

"Don't grin at me, I can't stand up. Oooh, I hurt all over!" moaned Kate.

"You sit there then until somebody picks you up," said Jancsi, leaving the puzzled Kate to rub her numb legs.

He was just putting away the saddles when Father rode in. Jancsi saw him stop and talk to Kate. He was laughing when he came into the stable.

"How long did you keep her in the saddle, anyway?" he asked.

Jancsi told him the story of the afternoon—except about the split skirt. He was very uneasy about that.

On their way back to the house, Father picked Kate up and carried her in. In the kitchen he put her on her shaking feet.

Mother, who was bending over a pot of stew, turned around to greet them.

"Supper's ready," she started to say, but suddenly threw up her hands. "Oh, my goodness gracious! What did you do to the child?" The split skirt was in full evidence now. Kate, balancing stiffly and awkwardly, was a queer sight indeed. She wasn't disturbed, however. "Had to split it to ride like Jancsi," she said.

"Split it? On purpose? Why, you look positively indecent, Kate," exclaimed Mother. "Hurry up and change your dress."

"Can't hurry and haven't any other dress!" was the calm answer.

"Well, then sit down. I'm ashamed to see such lack of modesty," cried Mother.

"Can't sit, either!" wailed Kate.

Poor Kate. She had to eat her supper, balancing on her unsteady pins, conscious of the amused glances of Father and Jancsi and the shocked looks of Mother. It was a willing and meek Kate who was carried to bed right after supper.

When Mother returned to the kitchen, Father said: "We'd better lend her Jancsi's outgrown clothes."

Jancsi approved of the idea. Mother was doubtful, but finally agreed that, Kate being what she was, she would be much better off in pants.

Kate Seredy continues this story in The Singing Tree, *also published by Viking. In the continuation, young Jancsi must serve as the "Good Master" while his father is away with the army during the war.*

Men of Iron

BY HOWARD PYLE

Illustrations by the author

> *In England, during the fourteenth century, when men seemed "made of iron," young Myles Falworth must make his way in the world as best he can, for his father, blind Lord Gilbert, has been unjustly accused of treason. After many struggles, Myles becomes a knight and wins the opportunity of defending his father's honor in combat.*

IN the days of King Edward III a code of laws relating to trial by battle had been compiled for one of his sons, Thomas of Woodstock. In this work each and every detail, to the most minute, had been arranged and fixed, and from that time judicial combats had been regulated in accordance with its mandates.

It was in obedience to this code that Myles Falworth appeared at the east gate of the lists (the east gate being assigned by law to the challenger), clad in full armor of proof, attended by Gascoyne, and accompanied by two of the young knights who had acted as his escort from Scotland Yard.

At the barriers he was met by the attorney Willingwood, the chief lawyer who had conducted the Falworth case before the High Court of Chivalry, and who was to attend him during the administration of the oaths before the King.

As Myles presented himself at the gate he was met by the Constable, the Marshal, and their immediate attendants. The Constable, laying his hand upon the bridle-rein, said, in a loud voice: "Stand, Sir Knight, and tell me why thou art come thus armed to the gates of the lists. What is thy name? Wherefore art thou come?"

Myles answered, "I am Myles Falworth, a Knight of the Bath

From *Men of Iron*, by Howard Pyle. Published by Harper & Brothers.

by grace of his Majesty King Henry IV. and by his creation, and do come hither to defend my challenge upon the body of William Bushy Brookhurst, Earl of Alban, proclaiming him an unknightly knight and a false and perjured liar, in that he hath accused Gilbert Reginald, Lord Falworth, of treason against our beloved Lord, his Majesty the King, and may God defend the right!"

As he ended speaking, the Constable advanced close to his side, and formally raising the umbril of the helmet, looked him in the face. Thereupon, having approved his identity, he ordered the gates to be opened, and bade Myles enter the lists with his squire and his friends.

At the south side of the lists a raised scaffolding had been built for the King and those who looked on. It was not unlike that which had been erected at Devlen Castle when Myles had first jousted as belted knight—here were the same raised seat for the King, the tapestries, the hangings, the fluttering pennons, and the royal standard floating above; only here were no fair-faced ladies looking down upon him, but instead, stern-browed Lords and knights in armor and squires, and here were no merry laughing and buzz of talk and flutter of fans and kerchiefs, but all was very quiet and serious.

Myles riding upon his horse, with Gascoyne holding the bridle-rein, and his attorney walking beside him with his hand upon the stirrups, followed the Constable across the lists to an open space in front of the seat where the King sat. Then, having reached his appointed station, he stopped, and the Constable, advancing to the foot of the stair-way that led to the dais above, announced in a loud voice that the challenger had entered the lists.

"Then call the defendant straightway," said the King, "for noon draweth nigh."

The day was very warm, and the sun, bright and unclouded, shone fiercely down upon the open lists. Perhaps few men nowadays could bear the scorching heat of iron plates such as Myles wore, from which the body was only protected by a leathern jacket and hose. But men's bodies in those days were tougher and more seasoned to hardships of weather than they are in these our times. Myles thought no more of the burning iron plates that incased him than a modern soldier thinks of his dress uniform in warm weather. Nevertheless, he raised the umbril of his helmet to cool his face as he waited the coming of his opponent. He turned his eyes upward to the row of seats on the scaffolding above, and even in the restless, bewildering multitude of strange faces turned towards him recognized those that he knew: the Prince of Wales, his companions of the Scotland Yard household, the Duke of Clarence, the Bishop of Winchester, and some of the noblemen of the Earl of Mackworth's party, who had been buzzing about the Prince for the past month or so. But his glance swept over all these, rather perceiving than seeing them, and then rested upon a square box-like compartment not unlike a prisoner's dock in the courtroom of our day, for in the box sat his father, with the Earl of Mackworth upon one side and Sir James Lee upon the other. The blind man's face was very pale, but still wore its usual expression of calm serenity—the calm serenity of a blind face. The Earl was also very pale, and he kept his eyes fixed steadfastly upon Myles with a keen and searching look, as though to pierce to the very bottom of the young man's heart, and discover if indeed not one little fragment of dry-rot of fear or uncertainty tainted the solid courage of his knighthood.

Then he heard the cries calling the defendant at the four corners of the list: "Oyez! Oyez! Oyez! William Bushy Brookhurst, Earl of Alban, come to this combat, in which you be enterprised this day to discharge your sureties before the King, the Constable, and the Marshal, and to encounter in your defence Myles Falworth, knight, the accepted champion upon behalf of Gilbert Reginald Falworth, the challenger! Oyez! Oyez! Oyez! Let the defendant come!"

So they continued calling, until, by the sudden turning of all faces, Myles knew that his enemy was at hand.

Then presently he saw the Earl and his attendants enter the outer gate at the west end of the barrier; he saw the Constable and Marshal meet him; he saw the formal words of greeting pass; he saw the Constable raise the umbril of the helmet. Then the gate opened, and the Earl of Alban entered, clad *cap-a-pie* in a full suit of magnificent Milan armor without juppon or adornment of any kind. As he approached across the lists, Myles closed the umbril of his helmet, and then sat quite still and motionless, for the time was come.

So he sat, erect and motionless as a statue of iron, half hearing the reading of the long intricately-worded bills, absorbed in many thoughts of past and present things. At last the reading ended, and then he calmly and composedly obeyed, under the direction of his attorney, the several forms and ceremonies that followed; answered the various official questions, took the various oaths. Then Gascoyne, leading the horse by the bridlerein, conducted him back to his station at the east end of the lists.

As the faithful friend and squire made one last and searching examination of arms and armor, the Marshal and the clerk came to the young champion and administered the final oath by which he swore that he carried no concealed weapons.

The weapons allowed by the High Court were then measured and attested. They consisted of the long sword, the short sword, the dagger, the mace, and a weapon known as the hand-gisarm, or glavelot—a heavy swordlike blade eight palms long, a palm in breadth, and riveted to a stout handle of wood three feet long.

The usual lance had not been included in the list of arms, the hand-gisarm being substituted in its place. It was a fearful and murderous weapon, though cumbersome, unhandy, and ill adapted for quick or dexterous stroke; nevertheless, the Earl of Alban had petitioned the King to have it included in the list, and in answer to the King's expressed desire the Court had adopted it in the stead of the lance, yielding thus much to the royal wishes. Nor was it a small concession. The hand-gisarm had been a weapon very much in vogue in King Richard's day, and was now nearly if not entirely out of fashion with the younger generation of warriors. The Earl of Alban was, of course, well used to the blade; with Myles it was strange and new, either for attack or in defence.

With the administration of the final oath and the examination of the weapons, the preliminary ceremonies came to an end, and presently Myles heard the criers calling to clear the lists. As those around him moved to withdraw, the young knight drew off his mailed gauntlet, and gave Gascoyne's hand one last final clasp, strong, earnest, and intense with the close friendship of young manhood, and poor Gascoyne looked up at him with a face ghastly white.

Then all were gone; the gates of the principal list and that of the false list were closed clashing, and Myles was alone, face to face, with his mortal enemy.

There was a little while of restless, rustling silence, during which the Constable took his place in the seat appointed for him directly in front of and below the King's throne. A moment or two when even the restlessness and the rustling were quieted, and then the King leaned forward and spoke to the Constable, who immediately called out, in a loud, clear voice:

"Let them go!" Then again, "Let them go!" Then, for the third and last time, "Let them go and do their endeavor, in God's name!"

At this third command the combatants, each of whom had till that moment been sitting as motionless as a statue of iron, tightened rein, and rode slowly and deliberately forward without haste, yet without hesitation, until they met in the very middle of the lists.

In the battle which followed, Myles fought with the long sword, the Earl with the hand-gisarm for which he had asked. The moment they met, the combat was opened, and for a time nothing was heard but the thunderous clashing and clamor of blows, now and then rising with a ceaseless uproar and din, now and then beating intermittently, now and then pausing. Occasionally, as the combatants spurred together, checked, wheeled, and recovered, they would be hidden for a moment in a misty veil of dust, which, again drifting down the wind, perhaps revealed them drawn a little apart, resting their panting horses. Then, again, they would spur together, striking as they passed, wheeling and striking again.

Upon the scaffolding all was still, only now and then for the buzz of muffled exclamations or applause of those who looked on. Mostly the applause was from Myles's friends, for from the very first he showed and steadily maintained his advantage over the older man. "Hah! well struck! well recovered!" "Look ye! the sword bit that time!" "Nay, look, saw ye him pass the point of the gisarm?" Then, "Falworth! Falworth!" as some more than usually skilful stroke or parry occurred.

Meantime Myles's father sat straining his sightless eyeballs, as though to pierce his body's darkness with one ray of light that would show him how his boy held his own in the fight, and Lord Mackworth, leaning with his lips close to the blind man's ear, told him point by point how the battle stood.

"Fear not, Gilbert," said he at each pause in the fight. "He holdeth his own right well." Then, after a while: "God is with us, Gilbert. Alban is twice wounded and his horse faileth. One little while longer and the victory is ours!"

A longer and more continuous interval of combat followed this last assurance, during which Myles drove the assault fiercely and unrelentingly as though to overbear his enemy by the very power and violence of the blows he delivered. The Earl defended himself desperately, but was borne back, back, back, farther and farther. Every nerve of those who looked on was stretched to breathless tensity, when, almost as his enemy was against the barriers, Myles paused and rested.

"Out upon it!" exclaimed the Earl of Mackworth, almost shrilly in his excitement, as the sudden lull followed the crashing of blows. "Why doth the boy spare him? That is thrice he hath given him grace to recover; an he had pushed the battle that time he had driven him back against the barriers."

It was as the Earl had said; Myles had three times given his enemy grace when victory was almost in his very grasp. He had three times spared him, in spite of all he and those dear to him must suffer should his cruel and merciless enemy gain the victory. It was a false and foolish generosity, partly the fault of his impulsive youth—more largely of his romantic training in the artificial code of French chivalry. He felt that the battle was his, and so he gave his enemy these three chances to recover, as some chevalier or knight-errant of romance might have done, instead of pushing the combat to a mercifully speedy end—and his foolish generosity cost him dear.

In the momentary pause that had thus stirred the Earl of Mackworth to a sudden outbreak, the Earl of Alban sat upon his panting, sweating war-horse, facing his powerful young enemy at about twelve paces distant. He sat as still as a rock, holding his gisarm poised in front of him. He had, as the Earl of Mackworth had said, been wounded twice, and each time with the point of the sword, so much more dangerous than a direct cut with the weapon. One wound was beneath his armor, and no one but he knew how serious it might be; the other was under the overlapping of the épaulière, and from it a finger's-breadth of blood ran straight down his side and over the housings of his horse. From without, the still motionless iron figure appeared calm and expressionless; within, who knows what consuming blasts of hate, rage, and despair swept his heart as with a fiery whirlwind.

As Myles looked at the motionless, bleeding figure, his breast swelled with pity. "My Lord," said he, "thou art sore wounded and the fight is against thee; wilt thou not yield thee?"

No one but that other heard the speech, and no one but Myles heard the answer that came back, hollow, cavernous, "Never, thou dog! Never!"

Then in an instant, as quick as a flash, his enemy spurred straight upon Myles, and as he spurred he struck a last desperate, swinging blow, in which he threw in one final effort all the strength of hate, of fury, and of despair. Myles whirled his horse backward, warding the blow with his shield as he did so. The blade glanced from the smooth face of the shield, and, whether by mistake or not, fell straight and true, and with almost undiminished force, upon the neck of Myles's war-horse, and just behind the ears. The animal staggered forward, and then fell upon its knees, and at the same instant the other, as though by the impetus of the rush, dashed full upon it with all the momentum lent by the weight of iron it carried. The shock was irresistible, and the stunned and wounded horse was flung upon the ground, rolling over and over. As his horse fell, Myles wrenched one of his feet out of the stirrup; the other caught for an instant, and he was flung headlong with stunning violence, his armor crashing as he fell. In the cloud of dust that arose no one could see just what happened, but that what was done was done deliberately no one doubted. The Earl, at once checking and spurring his foaming charger, drove the iron-shod war-horse directly over Myles's prostrate body. Then, checking him fiercely with the curb, reined him back, the hoofs clashing and crashing, over the figure beneath. So he had ridden over the father at York, and so he rode over the son at Smithfield.

Myles, as he lay prostrate and half stunned by his fall, had seen his enemy thus driving his rearing horse down upon him, but was not able to defend himself. A fallen knight in full armor was utterly powerless to rise without assistance; Myles lay helpless in the clutch of the very iron that was his defence. He closed his eyes involuntarily, and then horse and rider were upon him. There was a deafening, sparkling crash, a glimmering faintness, then another crash as the horse was reined furiously back again, and then a humming stillness.

In a moment, upon the scaffolding all was a tumult of uproar and confusion, shouting and gesticulation; only the King sat calm, sullen, impassive. The Earl wheeled his horse and sat for a moment or two as though to make quite sure that he knew the King's mind. The blow that had been given was foul, unknightly, but the King gave no sign either of acquiescence or rebuke; he had willed that Myles was to die.

Then the Earl turned again, and rode deliberately up to his prostrate enemy.

When Myles opened his eyes after that moment of stunning silence, it was to see the other looming above him on his war-horse, swinging his gisarm for one last mortal blow—pitiless, merciless.

The sight of that looming peril brought back Myles's wandering senses like a flash of lightning. He flung up his shield, and met the blow even as it descended, turning it aside. It only protracted the end.

Once more the Earl of Alban raised the gisarm, swinging it twice around his head before he struck. This time, though the shield glanced it, the blow fell upon the shoulder-piece, biting through the steel plate and leathern jack beneath even to the bone. Then Myles covered his head with his shield as a last protecting chance for life.

For the third time the Earl swung the blade flashing, and then it fell, straight and true, upon the defenceless body, just below the left arm, biting deep through the armor plates. For an instant the blade stuck fast, and that instant was Myles's salvation. Under the agony of the blow he gave a muffled cry, and almost instinctively grasped the shaft of the weapon with both hands. Had the Earl let go his end of the weapon, he would have won the battle at his leisure and most easily; as it was, he struggled violently to wrench the gisarm away from Myles. In that short, fierce struggle Myles was dragged to his knees, and then, still holding the weapon with one hand, he clutched the trappings of the Earl's horse with the other. The next moment he was upon his feet. The other struggled to thrust him away, but Myles, letting go the gisarm, which he held with his left hand, clutched him tightly by the sword-belt in the intense, vise-like grip of despair. In vain the Earl strove to beat him loose with the shaft of the gisarm, in vain he spurred and reared his horse to shake him off. Myles held him tight, in spite of all his struggles.

He felt neither the streaming blood nor the throbbing agony of his wounds; every faculty of soul, mind, body, every power of life, was centred in one intense, burning effort. He neither felt, thought, nor reasoned, but clutching, with the blindness

of instinct, the heavy, spiked, iron-headed mace that hung at
the Earl's saddle-bow, he gave it one tremendous wrench that
snapped the plaited leathern thongs that held it as though they
were skeins of thread. Then, grinding his teeth as with a spasm,
he struck as he had never struck before—once, twice, thrice full
upon the front of the helmet. Crash! crash! And then, even as
the Earl toppled sidelong, crash! And the iron plates split and
crackled under the third blow. Myles had one flashing glimpse
of an awful face, and then the saddle was empty.

Then, as he held tight to the horse, panting, dizzy, sick to
death, he felt the hot blood gushing from his side, filling his
body armor, and staining the ground upon which he stood. Still
he held tightly to the saddle-bow of the fallen man's horse until,

through his glimmering sight, he saw the Marshal, the Lieutenant, and the attendants gather around him. He heard the Marshal ask him, in a voice that sounded faint and distant, if he was dangerously wounded. He did not answer, and one of the attendants, leaping from his horse, opened the umbril of his helmet, disclosing the dull, hollow eyes, the ashy, colorless lips, and the waxy forehead, upon which stood great beads of sweat.

"Water! water!" he cried, hoarsely; "give me to drink!" Then, quitting his hold upon the horse, he started blindly across the lists towards the gate of the barrier. A shadow that chilled his heart seemed to fall upon him. "It is death," he muttered; then he stopped, then swayed for an instant, and then toppled headlong, crashing as he fell.

But Myles was not dead. Those who had seen his face when the umbril of the helmet was raised, and then saw him fall as he tottered across the lists, had at first thought so. But his faintness was more from loss of blood and the sudden unstringing of nerve and sense from the intense furious strain of the last few moments of battle than from the vital nature of the wound. Indeed, after Myles had been carried out of the lists and laid upon the ground in the shade between the barriers, Master Thomas, the Prince's barber-surgeon, having examined the wounds, declared that he might be even carried on a covered litter to Scotland Yard without serious danger. The Prince was extremely desirous of having him under his care, and so the venture was tried. Myles was carried to Scotland Yard, and perhaps was none the worse therefore.

The Prince, the Earl of Mackworth, and two or three others stood silently watching as the worthy shaver and leecher, assisted by his apprentice and Gascoyne, washed and bathed the great gaping wound in the side, and bound it with linen bandages. Myles lay with closed eyelids, still, pallid, weak as a little child. Presently he opened his eyes and turned them, dull and languid, to the Prince.

"What hath happed my father, my Lord?" said he, in a faint, whispering voice.

"Thou hath saved his life and honor, Myles," the Prince answered. "He is here now, and thy mother hath been sent for, and cometh anon with the priest who was with them this morn."

Myles dropped his eyelids again; his lips moved, but he made no sound, and then two bright tears trickled across his white cheek.

"He maketh a woman of me," the Prince muttered through his teeth, and then, swinging on his heel, he stood for a long time looking out of the window into the garden beneath.

"May I see my father?" said Myles, presently, without opening his eyes.

The Prince turned around and looked inquiringly at the surgeon.

The good man shook his head. "Not to-day," said he; "haply to-morrow he may see him and his mother. The bleeding is but new stanched, and such matters as seeing his father and mother may make the heart to swell, and so maybe the wound burst afresh and he die. An he would hope to live, he must rest quiet until to-morrow day."

But though Myles's wound was not mortal, it was very serious. The fever which followed lingered longer than common—perhaps because of the hot weather—and the days stretched to weeks, and the weeks to months, and still he lay there, nursed by his mother and Gascoyne and Prior Edward, and now and again by Sir James Lee.

One day, a little before the good priest returned to Saint Mary's Priory, as he sat by Myles's bedside, his hands folded, and his sight turned inward, the young man suddenly said, "Tell me, holy father, is it always wrong for man to slay man?"

The good priest sat silent for so long a time that Myles began to think he had not heard the question. But by-and-by he answered, almost with a sigh, "It is a hard question, my son, but I must in truth say, meseems it is not always wrong."

"Sir," said Myles, "I have been in battle when men were slain, but never did I think thereon as I have upon this matter. Did I sin in so slaying my father's enemy?"

"Nay," said Prior Edward, quietly, "thou didst not sin. It was for others thou didst fight, my son, and for others it is pardonable to do battle. Had it been thine own quarrel, it might haply have been more hard to have answered thee."

Who can gainsay, even in these days of light, the truth of

this that the good priest said to the sick lad so far away in the past?

One day the Earl of Mackworth came to visit Myles. At that time the young knight was mending, and was sitting propped up with pillows, and was wrapped in Sir James Lee's cloak, for the day was chilly. After a little time of talk, a pause of silence fell.

"My Lord," said Myles, suddenly, "dost thou remember one part of a matter we spoke of when I first came from France?"

The Earl made no pretence of ignorance. "I remember," said he, quietly, looking straight into the young man's thin white face.

"And have I yet won the right to ask for the Lady Alice de Mowbray to wife?" said Myles, the red rising faintly to his cheeks.

"Thou hast won it," said the Earl, with a smile.

Myles's eyes shone and his lips trembled with the pang of sudden joy and triumph, for he was still very weak. "My Lord," said he, presently, "belike thou camest here to see me for this very matter?"

The Earl smiled again without answering, and Myles knew that he had guessed aright. He reached out one of his weak, pallid hands from beneath the cloak. The Earl of Mackworth took it with a firm pressure, then instantly quitting it again, rose, as if ashamed of his emotion, stamped his feet, as though in pretence of being chilled, and then crossed the room to where the fire crackled brightly in the great stone fireplace.

Little else remains to be told; only a few loose strands to tie, and the story is complete.

Though Lord Falworth was saved from death at the block, though his honor was cleansed from stain, he was yet as poor and needy as ever. The King, in spite of all the pressure brought to bear upon him, refused to restore the estates of Falworth and Easterbridge—the latter of which had again reverted to the crown upon the death of the Earl of Alban without issue—upon the grounds that they had been forfeited not because of the attaint of treason, but because of Lord Falworth having refused to respond to the citation of the courts. So the business dragged along for month after month, until in January the King died suddenly in the Jerusalem Chamber at Westminster. Then matters went smoothly enough, and Falworth and Mackworth swam upon the flood-tide of fortune.

So Myles was married, for how else should the story end? And one day he brought his beautiful young wife home to Falworth Castle, which his father had given him for his own, and at the gate-way of which he was met by Sir James Lee and by the newly-knighted Sir Francis Gascoyne.

One day, soon after this home-coming, as he stood with her at an open window into which came blowing the pleasant Maytime breeze, he suddenly said, "What didst thou think of me when I first fell almost into thy lap, like an apple from heaven?"

"I thought thou wert a great, good-hearted boy, as I think thou art now," said she, twisting his strong, sinewy fingers in and out.

"If thou thoughtst me so then, what a very fool I must have looked to thee when I so clumsily besought thee for thy favor for my jousting at Devlen. Did I not so?"

"Thou didst look to me the most noble, handsome young knight that did ever live; thou didst look to me Sir Galahad, as they did call thee, withouten taint or stain."

Myles did not even smile in answer, but looked at his wife with such a look that she blushed a rosy red. Then, laughing, she slipped from his hold, and before he could catch her again was gone.

I am glad that he was to be rich and happy and honored and beloved after all his hard and noble fighting.

Howard Pyle, a remarkable story-teller and artist, has given us many fine books, among which are Otto of the Silver Hand, *published by Scribner, a tale of the days of the robber barons; and* Howard Pyle's Book of Pirates, *published by Harper.*

Black Beauty

BY ANNA SEWELL

Illustrations by Katharine Pyle

Anna Sewell was a Quaker girl who protested the thoughtless cruelties people often inflicted upon their horses. This "autobiography of a horse" is a powerfully moving plea for fair and gentle treatment.

THE first place that I can well remember, was a large, pleasant meadow with a pond of clear water in it. Some shady trees leaned over it, and rushes and water lilies grew at the deep end. Over the hedge on one side we looked into a plowed field, and on the other we looked over a gate at our master's house, which stood by the roadside; at the top of the meadow was a plantation of fir trees, and at the bottom a running brook overhung by a steep bank.

While I was young I lived upon my mother's milk, as I could not eat grass. In the daytime I ran by her side, and at night I lay down close by her. When it was hot, we used to stand by the pond in the shade of the trees, and when it was cold, we had a nice, warm shed near the plantation.

As soon as I was old enough to eat grass, my mother used to go out to work in the daytime, and come back in the evening.

There were six young colts in the meadow besides me; they were older than I was; some were nearly as large as grown-up horses. I used to run with them, and had great fun; we used to gallop all together round and round the field, as hard as we could go. Sometimes we had rather rough play, for they would frequently bite and kick as well as gallop.

One day, when there was a good deal of kicking, my mother whinnied to me to come to her, and then she said:

"I wish you to pay attention to what I am going to say to you.

From *Black Beauty*, by Anna Sewell.

The colts who live here are very good colts, but they are cart-horse colts, and, of course, they have not learned manners. You have been well bred and well born; your father has a great name in these parts, and your grandfather won the cup two years at the Newmarket races; your grandmother had the sweetest temper of any horse I ever knew, and I think you have never seen me kick or bite. I hope you will grow up gentle and good, and never learn bad ways; do your work with a good will, lift your feet up well when you trot, and never bite or kick even in play."

I have never forgotten my mother's advice; I knew she was a wise old horse, and our master thought a great deal of her. Her name was Duchess, but he often called her Pet.

Our master was a good, kind man. He gave us good food, good lodging, and kind words; he spoke as kindly to us as he did to his little children. We were all fond of him, and my mother loved him very much. When she saw him at the gate, she would neigh with joy, and trot up to him. He would pat and stroke her and say, "Well, old Pet, and how is your little Darkie?" I was a dull black, so he called me Darkie; then he would give me a piece of bread, which was very good, and sometimes he brought a carrot for my mother. All the horses would come to him, but I think we were his favorites. My mother always took him to the town on a market day in a light gig.

There was a plowboy, Dick, who sometimes came into our field to pluck blackberries from the hedge. When he had eaten all he wanted, he would have what he called fun with the colts, throwing stones and sticks at them to make them gallop. We did not much mind him, for we would gallop off; but sometimes a stone would hit and hurt us.

One day he was at this game, and did not know that the master was in the next field; but he was there, watching what was going on; over the hedge he jumped in a snap, and catching Dick by the arm, he gave him such a box on the ear as made him roar with the pain and surprise. As soon as we saw the master, we trotted up nearer to see what went on.

"Bad boy!" he said, "bad boy! to chase the colts. This is not the first time, nor the second, but it shall be the last—there—

take your money and go home, I shall not want you on my farm again." So we never saw Dick any more. Old Daniel, the man who looked after the horses, was just as gentle as our master, so we were well off.

Before I was two years old, a circumstance happened which I have never forgotten. It was early in the spring; there had been a little frost in the night, and a light mist still hung over the plantations and meadows. I and the other colts were feeding at the lower part of the field when we heard, quite in the distance, what sounded like the cry of dogs. The oldest of the colts raised his head, pricked his ears, and said, "There are the hounds!" and immediately cantered off, followed by the rest of us to the upper part of the field, where we could look over the hedge and see several fields beyond. My mother, and an old riding horse of our master's were also standing near, and seemed to know all about it.

"They have found a hare," said my mother, "and if they come this way, we shall see the hunt."

And soon the dogs were all tearing down the field of young wheat next to ours. I never heard such a noise as they made. They did not bark, nor howl, nor whine, but kept on a "yo! yo, o, o! yo! yo, o, o!" at the top of their voices. After them came a number of men on horseback, some of them in green coats, all galloping as fast as they could. The old horse snorted and looked eagerly after them, and we young colts wanted to be galloping with them, but they were soon away into the fields lower down; here it seemed as if they had come to a stand; the dogs left off barking, and ran about every way with their noses to the ground.

"They have lost the scent," said the old horse; "perhaps the hare will get off."

"What hare?" I said.

"Oh! I don't know *what* hare; likely enough it may be one of our own hares out of the plantation; any hare they can find will do for the dogs and men to run after." And before long the dogs began their "yo! yo, o, o!" again, and back they came all together at full speed, making straight for our meadow at the part where the high bank and hedge overhang the brook.

"Now we shall see the hare," said my mother; and just then a hare wild with fright rushed by, and made for the plantation. On came the dogs; they burst over the bank, leaped the stream, and came dashing across the field, followed by the huntsmen. Six or eight men leaped their horses clean over, close upon the dogs. The hare tried to get through the fence; it was too thick, and she turned sharp round to make for the road, but it was too late; the dogs were upon her with their wild cries; we heard one shriek, and that was the end of her. One of the huntsmen rode up and whipped off the dogs, who would soon have torn her to pieces. He held her up by the leg, torn and bleeding, and all the gentlemen seemed well pleased.

As for me, I was so astonished that I did not at first see what was going on by the brook; but when I did look, there was a sad sight; two fine horses were down, one was struggling in the stream, and the other was groaning on the grass. One of the riders was getting out of the water covered with mud, the other lay quite still.

"His neck is broken," said my mother.

"And serves him right, too," said one of the colts.

I thought the same, but my mother did not join with us.

"Well, no," she said, "you must not say that; but though I am an old horse, and have seen and heard a great deal, I never yet could make out why men are so fond of this sport. They often hurt themselves, often spoil good horses, and tear up the fields, and all for a hare or a fox, or a stag, that they could get more easily some other way; but we are only horses, and don't know."

While my mother was saying this, we stood and looked on. Many of the riders had gone to the young man; but my master, who had been watching what was going on, was the first to raise him. His head fell back and his arms hung down, and everyone looked very serious. There was no noise now; even the dogs were quiet, and seemed to know that something was wrong. They carried him to our master's house. I heard afterwards that it was young George Gordon, the squire's only son, a fine, tall young man, and the pride of his family.

There was now riding off in all directions to the doctor's, to the farrier's, and no doubt to Squire Gordon's, to let him know about his son. When Mr. Bond, the farrier, came to look at the

black horse that lay groaning on the grass, he felt him all over, and shook his head; one of his legs was broken. Then someone ran to our master's house and came back with a gun; presently there was a loud bang and a dreadful shriek, and then all was still; the black horse moved no more.

My mother seemed much troubled; she said she had known that horse for years, and that his name was "Rob Roy"; he was a good bold horse, and there was no vice in him. She never would go to that part of the field afterwards.

Not many days after, we heard the church bell tolling for a long time; and looking over the gate we saw a long, strange black coach that was covered with black cloth and was drawn by black horses; after that came another and another and another, and all were black; while the bell kept tolling, tolling. They were carrying young Gordon to the churchyard to bury him. He would never ride again. What they did with Rob Roy I never knew; but 'twas all for one little hare.

I was now beginning to grow handsome; my coat had grown fine and soft, and was bright black. I had one white foot, and a pretty white star on my forehead. I was thought very handsome; my master would not sell me till I was four years old; he said lads ought not to work like men, and colts ought not to work like horses till they were quite grown up.

When I was four years old, Squire Gordon came to look at me. He examined my eyes, my mouth, and my legs; he felt them all down; and then I had to walk and trot and gallop before him; he seemed to like me, and said, "When he has been well broken in, he will do very well." My master said he would break me in himself, as he should not like me to be frightened or hurt, and he lost no time about it, for the next day he began.

Everyone may not know what breaking in is, therefore I will describe it. It means to teach a horse to wear a saddle and bridle and to carry on his back a man, woman, or child; to go just the way they wish, and to go quietly. Besides this, he has to learn to wear a collar, a crupper, and a breeching, and to stand still while they are put on; then to have a cart or a chaise fixed behind him, so that he cannot walk or trot without dragging it after him; and he must go fast or slow, just as his driver wishes. He must never start at what he sees, nor speak to other horses, nor bite, nor kick, nor have any will of his own; but always do his master's will, even though he may be very tired or hungry; but the worst of all is, when his harness is once on, he may neither jump for joy nor lie down for weariness. So you see this breaking in is a great thing.

I had of course long been used to a halter and a headstall,

and to be led about in the field and lanes quietly, but now I
was to have a bit and a bridle; my master gave me some oats as
usual, and after a good deal of coaxing, he got the bit into my
mouth, and the bridle fixed, but it was a nasty thing! Those who
have never had a bit in their mouths cannot think how bad it
feels; a great piece of cold hard steel as thick as a man's finger
to be pushed into one's mouth, between one's teeth and over
one's tongue, with the ends coming out at the corner of your
mouth, and held fast there by straps over your head, under
your throat, round your nose, and under your chin; so that no
way in the world can you get rid of the nasty hard thing; it is
very bad! yes, very bad! at least I thought so; but I knew my
mother always wore one when she went out, and all horses did
when they were grown up; and so, what with the nice oats, and
what with my master's pats, kind words, and gentle ways, I
got to wear my bit and bridle.

Next came the saddle, but that was not half so bad; my master put it on my back very gently, whilst old Daniel held my
head; he then made the girths fast under my body, patting and
talking to me all the time; then I had a few oats, then a little
leading about, and this he did every day till I began to look for
the oats and the saddle. At length, one morning my master got
on my back and rode me round the meadow on the soft grass.
It certainly did feel queer; but I must say I felt rather proud to
carry my master, and as he continued to ride me a little every
day, I soon became accustomed to it.

The next unpleasant business was putting on the iron shoes;
that too was very hard at first. My master went with me to the
smith's forge, to see that I was not hurt or got any fright. The
blacksmith took my feet in his hand one after the other, and cut
away some of the hoof. It did not pain me, so I stood still on
three legs till he had done them all. Then he took a piece of iron
the shape of my foot, and clapped it on, and drove some nails
through the shoe quite into my hoof, so that the shoe was firmly
on. My feet felt very stiff and heavy, but in time I got used to it.

And now having got so far, my master went on to break me
to harness; there were more new things to wear. First, a stiff
heavy collar just on my neck, and a bridle with great sidepieces
against my eyes called blinkers, and blinkers indeed they were,

for I could not see on either side, but only straight in front of me; next there was a small saddle with a nasty stiff strap that went right under my tail; that was the crupper. I hated the crupper—to have my long tail doubled up and poked through that strap was almost as bad as the bit. I never felt more like kicking, but of course I could not kick such a good master, and so in time I got used to everything, and could work as well as my mother.

I must not forget to mention one part of my training, which I have always considered a very great advantage. My master sent me for a fortnight to a neighboring farmer's, who had a meadow which was skirted on one side by the railway. Here were some sheep and cows, and I was turned in among them.

I shall never forget the first train that ran by. I was feeding quietly near the pales which separated the meadow from the railway, when I heard a strange sound at a distance, and before I knew whence it came—with a rush and a clatter, and a puffing out of smoke—a long black train of something flew by, and was gone almost before I could draw my breath. I turned, and galloped to the farther side of the meadow as fast as I could go, and there I stood snorting with astonishment and fear. In the course of the day many other trains went by, some more slowly; these drew up at the station close by, and sometimes made an awful shriek and groan before they stopped. I thought it very dreadful, but the cows went on eating very quietly, and hardly raised their heads as the black, frightful thing came puffing and grinding past.

For the first few days I could not feed in peace; but as I found that this terrible creature never came into the field, or did me any harm, I began to disregard it, and very soon I cared as little about the passing of a train as the cows and sheep did.

Since then I have seen many horses much alarmed and restive at the sight or sound of a steam engine; but thanks to my good master's care, I am as fearless at railway stations as in my own stable.

Now if anyone wants to break in a young horse well, that is the way.

My master often drove me in double harness with my mother, because she was steady, and could teach me how to go better than a strange horse. She told me the better I behaved, the better I should be treated, and that it was wisest always to do my best to please my master; "but," said she, "there are a great many kinds of men; there are good, thoughtful men like our master, that any horse may be proud to serve; but there are bad, cruel men, who never ought to have a horse or dog to call their own. Besides, there are a great many foolish men, vain, ignorant, and careless, who never trouble themselves to think; these spoil more horses than all, just for want of sense; they don't mean it, but they do it for all that. I hope you will fall into good hands; but a horse never knows who may buy him, or who may drive him; it is all a chance for us, but still I say, do your best whatever it is, and keep up your good name."

At this time I used to stand in the stable, and my coat was brushed every day till it shone like a rook's wing. It was early in May, when there came a man from Squire Gordon's, who took me away to the Hall. My master said, "Good-bye, Darkie; be a good horse, and always do your best." I could not say "good-bye," so I put my nose into his hand; he patted me kindly, and I left my first home. As I lived some years with Squire Gordon, I may as well tell something about the place.

Squire Gordon's Park skirted the village of Birtwick. It was entered by a large iron gate, at which stood the first lodge, and then you trotted along on a smooth road between clumps of large old trees; then another lodge and another gate, which brought you to the house and the gardens. Beyond this lay the home paddock, the old orchard, and the stables. There was accommodation for many horses and carriages; but I need only describe the stable into which I was taken; this was very roomy, with four good stalls; a large swinging window opened into the yard, which made it pleasant and airy.

The first stall was a large square one, shut in behind with a wooden gate; the others were common stalls, good stalls, but not nearly so large; it had a low rack for hay and a low manger for corn; it was called a loose box, because the horse that was put into it was not tied up, but left loose, to do as he liked. It is a great thing to have a loose box.

Into this fine box the groom put me; it was clean, sweet, and airy. I never was in a better box than that, and the sides were not so high but that I could see all that went on through the iron rails that were at the top. He gave me some very nice oats, he patted me, spoke kindly, and then went away.

When I had eaten my corn, I looked around. In the stall next to mine stood a little fat gray pony, with a thick mane and tail, a very pretty head, and a pert little nose.

I put my head up to the iron rails at the top of my box and said, "How do you do? What is your name?"

He turned round as far as his halter would allow, held up his head, and said, "My name is Merrylegs; I am very handsome, I carry the young ladies on my back, and sometimes I take our mistress out in the low chair. They think a great deal of me, and so does James. Are you going to live next door to me in the box?"

I said, "Yes."

"Well, then," he said, "I hope you are good-tempered; I do not like anyone next door who bites."

Just then a horse's head looked over from the stall beyond; the ears were laid back, and the eye looked rather ill-tempered. This was a tall chestnut mare, with a long handsome neck; she looked across to me and said:

"So it is you who have turned me out of my box; it is a very strange thing for a colt like you to come and turn a lady out of her own home."

"I beg your pardon," I said, "I have turned no one out; the man who brought me put me here, and I had nothing to do with it; and as to my being a colt, I am turned four years old, and am a grown-up horse; I never had words yet with horse or mare, and it is my wish to live at peace."

"Well," she said, "we shall see; of course I do not want to have words with a young thing like you." I said no more.

In the afternoon when she went out, Merrylegs told me all about it.

"The thing is this," said Merrylegs; "Ginger has a bad habit of biting and snapping; that is why they call her Ginger, and when she was in the loose box, she used to snap very much. One day she bit James in the arm and made it bleed, and so Miss Flora and Miss Jessie, who are very fond of me, were afraid to come into the stable. They used to bring me nice things to eat, an apple or a carrot, or a piece of bread, but after Ginger stood in that box they dare not come, and I missed them very much. I hope they will now come again, if you do not bite."

I told him I never bit anything but grass, hay, and corn, and could not think what pleasure Ginger found it.

"Well, I don't think she does find pleasure," said Merrylegs; "it is just a bad habit; she says no one was ever kind to her, and why should she not bite? Of course it is a very bad habit; but I am sure, if all she says be true, she must have been very ill-used before she came here. John does all he can to please her, and James does all he can, and our master never uses a whip if a horse acts right; so I think she might be good-tempered here. You see," he said with a wise look, "I am twelve years old; I know a great deal, and I can tell you there is not a better place for a horse all round the country than this. John is the best groom that ever was, he has been here fourteen years; and you never saw such a kind boy as James is, so that it is all Ginger's own fault that she did not stay in that box."

The name of the coachman was John Manly; he had a wife and one little child, and they lived in the coachman's cottage, very near the stables.

The next morning, he took me into the yard and gave me a good grooming, and just as I was going into my box with my coat soft and bright, the Squire came in to look at me, and seemed pleased. "John," he said, "I meant to have tried the new horse this morning, but I have other business. You may as well take him around after breakfast; go by the common and the Highwood, and back by the watermill and the river; that will show his paces."

"I will, sir," said John. After breakfast he came and fitted me with a bridle. He was very particular in letting out and taking in the straps, to fit my head comfortably; then he brought the saddle; that was not broad enough for my back; he saw it in a minute and went for another, which fitted nicely. He rode me first slowly, then a trot, then a canter, and when we were on the common he gave me a light touch with his whip, and we had a splendid gallop.

"Ho-ho! my boy," he said, as he pulled me up, "you would like to follow the hounds, I think, wouldn't you?"

As we came back through the Park we met the Squire and Mrs. Gordon walking; they stopped, and John jumped off.

"Well, John, how does he go?"

"First-rate, sir," answered John, "he is as fleet as a deer, and has a fine spirit, too; but the lightest touch of the rein will guide him. Down at the end of the common we met one of those traveling carts hung all over with baskets, rugs, and such like; you know, sir, many horses will not pass those carts quietly; he just took a good look at it, and then went on as quietly and pleasant as could be. They were shooting rabbits near the Highwood, and a gun went off close by; he pulled up a little and looked, but did not stir a step to right or left. I just held the rein steady and did not hurry him, and it's my opinion he has not been frightened or ill-used while he was young."

"That's well," said the Squire, "I will try him myself tomorrow."

The next day I was brought up for my master. I remembered my mother's counsel and my good old master's, and I tried to do exactly what he wanted me to do. I found he was a very good rider, and thoughtful for his horse, too. When we came home, the lady was at the hall door as he rode up.

"Well, my dear," she said, "how do you like him?"

"He is exactly what John said," he replied; "a pleasanter creature I never wish to mount. What shall we call him?"

"Would you like Ebony?" said she. "He is as black as ebony."

"No, not Ebony."

"Will you call him Blackbird, like your uncle's old horse?"

"No, he is far handsomer than old Blackbird ever was."

"Yes," she said, "he is really quite a beauty, and he has such a sweet, good-tempered face and such a fine, intelligent eye— what do you say to calling him Black Beauty?"

"Black Beauty—why, yes, I think that is a very good name. If you like, it shall be his name," and so it was.

When John went into the stable, he told James that the master and mistress had chosen a good sensible English name for me, that meant something, not like Marengo, or Pegasus, or Abdallah. They both laughed, and James said, "If it was not for bringing back the past, I should have named him Rob Roy, for I never saw two horses more alike."

"That's no wonder," said John; "didn't you know that Farmer Grey's old Duchess was the mother of them both?"

I had never heard that before, and so poor Rob Roy who was killed at that hunt was my brother! I did not wonder that my mother was so troubled. It seems that horses have no relations; at least, they never know each other after they are sold.

John seemed very proud of me; he used to make my mane and tail almost as smooth as a lady's hair, and he would talk to me a great deal; of course I did not understand all he said, but I learned more and more to know what he *meant*, and what he wanted me to do. I grew very fond of him, he was so gentle and kind, he seemed to know just how a horse feels, and when he cleaned me, he knew the tender places, and the ticklish places; when he brushed my head, he went as carefully over my eyes as if they were his own, and never stirred up any ill temper.

James Howard, the stable boy, was just as gentle and pleasant in his way, so I thought myself well off. There was another man who helped in the yard, but he had very little to do with Ginger and me.

A few days after this, I had to go out with Ginger in the carriage. I wondered how we should get on together; but except laying her ears back when I was led up to her, she behaved very well. She did her work honestly, and did her full share, and I never wish to have a better partner in double harness. When we came to a hill, instead of slackening her pace, she would throw her weight right into the collar, and pull away straight up. We had both the same sort of courage at work, and John had oftener to hold us in than to urge us forward; he never had to use the whip with either of us; then our paces were much the same, and I found it very easy to keep step with her when trotting, which made it pleasant, and master always liked it when we kept step well, and so did John. After we had been out two or three times together we grew quite friendly and sociable, which made me feel very much at home.

As for Merrylegs, he and I soon became great friends; he was such a cheerful, plucky, good-tempered little fellow, that he was a favorite with everyone, and especially with Miss Jessie and Flora, who used to ride him about in the orchard, and have fine games with him and their little dog Frisky.

Our master had two other horses that stood in another stable. One was Justice, a roan cob, used for riding, or for the luggage cart; the other was an old brown hunter, named Sir Oliver; he was past work now, but was a great favorite with the master, who gave him the run of the park; he sometimes did a little light carting on the estate, or carried one of the young ladies when they rode out with their father; for he was very gentle, and could be trusted with a child as well as Merrylegs. The cob was a strong, well-made, good-tempered horse, and we sometimes had a little chat in the paddock, but of course I could not be so intimate with him as with Ginger, who stood in the same stable.

I was quite happy in my new place, and if there was one thing that I missed, it must not be thought I was discontented; all who had to do with me were good, and I had a light, airy stable and the best of food. What more could I want? Why, liberty! For three years and a half of my life I had had all the liberty I could wish for; but now, week after week, month after month, and no doubt year after year, I must stand up in a stable night and day except when I am wanted, and then I must be just as steady and quiet as any old horse who has worked twenty years. Straps here and straps there, a bit in my mouth, and blinkers over my eyes. Now, I am not complaining, for I know it must be. I only mean to say that for a young horse full of strength and spirits who has been used to some large field or plain, where he can fling up his head and toss up his tail and gallop away at full speed, then round and back again with a snort to his companions—I say it is hard never to have a bit more liberty to do as you like. Sometimes, when I have had less exercise than usual, I have felt so full of life and spring that when John has taken me out to exercise I really could not keep quiet; do what I would, it seemed as if I must jump, or dance, or prance, and many a good shake I know I must have given him, specially at the first; but he was always good and patient.

"Steady, steady, my boy," he would say; "wait a bit, and we'll have a good swing, and soon get the tickle out of your feet."

Then as soon as we were out of the village, he would give me a few miles at a spanking trot, and then bring me back as fresh as before, only clear of the fidgets, as he called them. Spirited horses, when not enough exercised, are often called skittish, when it is only play; and some grooms will punish them, but our John did not, he knew it was only high spirits. Still, he had his own ways of making me understand by the tone of his voice or the touch of the rein. If he was very serious and quite determined, I always knew it by his voice, and that had more power with me than anything else, for I was very fond of him.

I ought to say that sometimes we had our liberty for a few hours; this used to be on fine Sundays in the summertime. The carriage never went out on Sundays, because the church was not far off.

It was a great treat to us to be turned out into the home paddock or the old orchard. The grass was so cool and soft to our feet; the air so sweet, and the freedom to do as we liked was so pleasant; to gallop, to lie down, and roll over on our backs, or to nibble the sweet grass. Then it was a very good time for talking, as we stood together under the shade of the large chestnut tree.

One day when Ginger and I were standing alone in the shade we had a great deal of talk; she wanted to know all about my bringing up and breaking in, and I told her.

"Well," said she, "if I had had your bringing up I might have had as good a temper as you, but now I don't believe I ever shall."

"Why not?" I said.

"Because it has been all so different with me," she replied; "I never had anyone, horse or man, that was kind to me, or that I cared to please, for in the first place I was taken from my mother as soon as I was weaned, and put with a lot of other young colts; none of them cared for me, and I cared for none of them. There was no kind master like yours to look after me, and talk to me, and bring me nice things to eat. The man that had the care of us never gave me a kind word in my life. I do not mean that he ill-used me, but he did not care for us one bit further than to see that we had plenty to eat and shelter in the winter. A footpath ran through our field, and very often the great boys passing through would fling stones to make us gallop. I was never hit, but one fine colt was badly cut in the face, and I should think it would be a scar for life. We did not care for them, but of course it made us more wild, and we settled it in our minds that boys were our enemies. We had very good fun in the free meadows, galloping up and down and chasing each other round and round the field; then standing still under the shade of the trees. But when it came to breaking in, that was a bad time for me; several men came to catch me, and when at last they closed me in at one corner of the field, one caught me by the forelock, another caught me by the nose, and held it so tight I could hardly draw my breath; then another took my under jaw in his hard hand and wrenched my mouth open, and so by force they got on the halter, and the bar into my mouth; then one dragged me along by the halter, another flogging behind, and this was the first experience I had of men's kindness; it was all force. They did not give me a chance to know what they wanted. I was high bred and had a great deal of spirit, and was very wild, no doubt, and gave them, I daresay, plenty of trouble, but then it was dreadful to be shut up in a stall day after day instead of having my liberty, and I fretted and pined and wanted to get loose. You know yourself, it's bad enough when you have a kind master and plenty of coaxing, but there was nothing of that sort for me.

"There was one—the old master, Mr. Ryder, who I think could soon have brought me round, and could have done anything with me, but he had given up all the hard part of the trade to his son and to another experienced man, and he only came at times to oversee. His son was a strong, tall, bold man; they called him Samson, and he used to boast that he had never found a horse that could throw him. There was no gentleness in him as there was in his father, but only hardness, a hard voice, a hard eye, a hard hand, and I felt from the first that what he wanted was to wear all the spirit out of me, and just make me into a quiet, humble, obedient piece of horseflesh. 'Horseflesh!' Yes, that is all that he thought about," and Ginger stamped her foot as if the very thought of him made her angry. And she went on: "If I did not do exactly what he wanted, he

would get put out, and make me run round with that long rein in the training field till he had me tired out. I think he drank a good deal, and I am quite sure that the oftener he drank the worse it was for me. One day he had worked me hard in every way he could, and when I lay down I was tired and miserable, and angry; it all seemed so hard. The next morning he came for me early, and ran me round again for a long time. I had scarcely had an hour's rest, when he came again for me with a saddle and bridle and a new kind of bit. I could never quite tell how it came about; he had only just mounted me on the training ground, when something I did put him out of temper, and he chucked me hard with the rein. The new bit was very painful, and I reared up suddenly, which angered him still more, and he began to flog me. I felt my whole spirit set against him, and I began to kick, and plunge, and rear as I had never done before, and we had a regular fight; for a long time he stuck to the saddle and punished me cruelly with his whip and spurs, but my blood was thoroughly up, and I cared for nothing he could do if only I could get him off. At last, after a terrible struggle, I threw him off backwards. I heard him fall heavily on the turf, and without looking behind me, I galloped off to the other end of the field; there I turned round and saw my persecutor slowly rising from the ground and going into the stable. I stood under an oak tree and watched, but no one came to catch me. The time went on, the sun was very hot, the flies swarmed round me and settled on my bleeding flanks where the spurs had dug in. I felt hungry, for I had not eaten since the early morning, but there was not enough grass in that meadow for a goose to live on. I wanted to lie down and rest, but with the saddle strapped tightly on, there was no comfort, and there was not a drop of water to drink. The afternoon wore on, and the sun got low. I saw the other colts led in, and I knew they were having a good feed.

"At last, just as the sun went down, I saw the old master come out with a sieve in his hand. He was a very fine old gentleman with quite white hair, but his voice was what I should know him by among a thousand. It was not high, nor yet low, but full, and clear, and kind; and when he gave orders, it was so steady and decided that everyone knew, both horses and men, that he expected to be obeyed. He came quietly along, now and then shaking the oats about that he had in the sieve, and speaking cheerfully and gently to me, 'Come along, lassie, come along, lassie; come along, come along.' I stood still and let him come up; he held the oats to me and I began to eat without fear; his voice took all my fear away. He stood by, patting and stroking me while I was eating, and seeing the clots of blood on my side he seemed very vexed. 'Poor lassie! it was a bad business, a bad business!' then he quietly took the rein and led me to the stable. Just at the door stood Samson. I laid my ears back and snapped at him. 'Stand back,' said the master, 'and keep out of her way; you've done a bad day's work for this filly.' He growled out something about a vicious brute. 'Hark ye,' said the father, 'a bad-tempered man will never make a good-tempered horse. You've not learned your trade yet, Samson.' Then he led me into my box, took off the saddle and bridle with his own hands, and tied me up; then he called for a pail of warm water and a sponge, took off his coat, and while the stableman held the pail, he sponged my sides a good while so tenderly that I was sure he knew how sore and bruised they were. 'Whoa! my pretty one,' he said, 'stand still, stand still.' His very voice did me good, and the bathing was very comfortable. The skin was so broken at the corners of my mouth that I could not eat the hay, the stalks hurt me. He looked closely at it, shook his head, and told the man to fetch a good bran mash and put some meal into it. How good that mash was! and so soft and healing to my mouth. He stood by all the time I was eating, stroking me and talking to the man. 'If a high-mettled creature like this,' said he, 'can't be broken in by fair means, she will never be good for anything.'

"After that he often came to see me, and when my mouth was healed, the other breaker, Job, they called him, went on training me; he was steady and thoughtful, and I soon learned what he wanted."

The next time that Ginger and I were together in the paddock, she told me about her first place.

"After my breaking in," she said, "I was bought by a dealer to match another chestnut horse. For some weeks he drove us together, and then we were sold to a fashionable gentleman, and were sent up to London. I had been driven with a bearing rein by the dealer, and I hated it worse than anything else; but in this place we were reined far tighter; the coachman and his master thinking we looked more stylish so. We were often driven about in the park and other fashionable places. You who never had a bearing rein on don't know what it is, but I can tell you it is dreadful.

"I like to toss my head about, and hold it as high as any horse; but fancy, now, yourself, if you tossed your head up high and were obliged to hold it there, and that for hours together, not able to move it at all, except with a jerk still higher, your neck aching till you did not know how to bear it. Besides that, to have two bits instead of one; and mine was a sharp one, it hurt my tongue and my jaw, and the blood from my tongue colored the froth that kept flying from my lips, as I chafed and fretted at the bits and rein; it was worst when we had to stand by the hour waiting for our mistress at some grand party or entertainment; and if I fretted or stamped with impatience the whip was laid on. It was enough to drive one mad."

"Did not your master take any thought for you?" I said.

"No," she said, "he only cared to have a stylish turnout, as they call it; I think he knew very little about horses, he left that to his coachman, who told him I had an irritable temper; that I had not been well broken to the bearing rein, but I should soon get used to it; but *he* was not the man to do it, for when I was in the stable, miserable and angry, instead of being soothed and quieted by kindness, I got only a surly word or a blow. If he had been civil, I would have tried to bear it. I was willing to work, and ready to work hard, too; but to be tormented for nothing but their fancies angered me. What right had they to make me suffer like that? Besides the soreness in my mouth and the pain in my neck, it always made my windpipe feel bad, and if I had stopped there long, I know it would have spoiled my breathing; but I grew more and more restless and irritable, I could not help it; and I began to snap and kick when anyone came to harness me; for this, the groom beat me, and one day, as they had just buckled us into the carriage, and were straining my head up with that rein, I began to plunge and kick with all my might. I soon broke a lot of harness, and kicked myself clear; so that was an end of that place.

"After this, I was sent to Tattersall's to be sold; of course I could not be warranted free from vice, so nothing was said about that. My handsome appearance and good paces soon brought a gentleman to bid for me, and I was bought by another dealer; he tried me in all kinds of ways with different bits, and soon found out what I could bear. At last he drove me quite without a bearing rein, and then sold me as a perfectly quiet horse to a gentleman in the country; he was a good master, and I was getting along very well, but his old groom left him and a new one came. This man was as hard-tempered and hard-handed as Samson; he always spoke in a rough, impatient voice, and if I did not move in the stall the moment he wanted me, he would hit me above the hocks with his stable broom or the fork, whichever he might have in his hand. Everything he did was rough, and I began to hate him; he wanted to make me afraid of him, but I was too high-mettled for that; and one day when he had aggravated me more than usual, I bit him, which of course put him in a great rage, and he began to hit me about the head with a riding whip. After that, he never dared to come into my stall again, either my heels or my teeth were ready for him, and he knew it. I was quite quiet with my master, but of course he listened to what the man said, and so I was sold again.

"The same dealer heard of me, and said he thought he knew one place where I should do well. ' 'Twas a pity,' he said, 'that such a fine horse should go to the bad, for want of a real good chance,' and the end of it was that I came here not long before you did; but I had then made up my mind that men were my natural enemies, and that I must defend myself. Of course it is very different here, but who knows how long it will last? I wish I could think about things as you do; but I can't, after all I have gone through."

"Well," I said, "I think it would be a real shame if you were to bite or kick John or James."

"I don't mean to," she said, "while they are good to me. I did bite James once pretty sharp; but John said, 'Try her with kindness,' and instead of punishing me as I expected, James came to me with his arm bound up, and brought me a bran mash and stroked me; and I have never snapped at him since, and I won't either."

I was sorry for Ginger, but of course I knew very little then, and I thought most likely she made the worst of it; however, I found that as the weeks went on, she grew much more gentle and cheerful, and had lost the watchful, defiant look that she used to turn on any strange person who came near her; and one day James said, "I do believe that mare is getting fond of me, she quite whinnied after me this morning when I had been rubbing her forehead."

"Ay, ay, Jim, 'tis the Birtwick balls," said John, "she'll be as good as Black Beauty by and by; kindness is all the physic she wants, poor thing!" Master noticed the change too, and one day when he got out of the carriage and came to speak to us as he often did, he stroked her beautiful neck. "Well, my pretty one, well, how do things go with you now? You are a good bit happier than when you came to us, I think."

She put her nose up to him in a friendly, trustful way, while he rubbed it gently.

"We shall make a cure of her, John," he said.

"Yes, sir, she's wonderfully improved, she's not the same creature that she was; it's the Birtwick balls, sir," said John, laughing.

This was a little joke of John's; he used to say that a regular course of the Birtwick horse balls would cure almost any vicious horse; these balls, he said, were made up of patience and gentleness, firmness and petting, one pound of each to be mixed up with half a pint of common sense, and given to the horse every day.

Mr. Blomefield, the Vicar, had a large family of boys and girls; sometimes they used to come and play with Miss Jessie and Flora. One of the girls was as old as Miss Jessie; two of the boys were older, and there were several little ones. When they came, there was plenty of work for Merrylegs, for nothing pleased them so much as getting on him by turns and riding him all about the orchard and the home paddock, and this they would do by the hour together.

One afternoon he had been out with them a long time, and when James brought him in and put on his halter, he said:

"There, you rogue, mind how you behave yourself, or we shall get into trouble."

"What have you been doing, Merrylegs?" I asked.

"Oh!" said he, tossing his little head, "I have only been giving those young people a lesson. They did not know when they had had enough, nor when I had had enough, so I just pitched them off backward; that was the only thing they could understand."

"What?" said I, "you threw the children off? I thought you

did know better than that! Did you throw Miss Jessie or Miss Flora?"

He looked very much offended, and said:

"Of course not, I would not do such a thing for the best oats that ever came into the stable; why, I am as careful of our young ladies as the master could be, and as for the little ones, it is I who teach them to ride. When they seem frightened, or a little unsteady on my back, I go as smooth and as quiet as old pussy when she is after a bird; and when they are all right, I go on again faster, you see, just to use them to it; so don't you trouble yourself preaching to me; I am the best friend, and the best riding master those children have. It is not them, it is the boys; boys," said he, shaking his mane, "are quite different; they must be broken in, as we were broken in when we were colts, and just be taught what's what. The other children had ridden me about for nearly two hours, and then the boys thought it was their turn, and so it was, and I was quite agreeable. They rode me by turns, and I galloped them about up and down the fields and all about the orchard for a good hour. They had each cut a great hazel stick for a riding whip, and laid it on a little too hard; but I took it in good part, till at last I thought we had had enough so I stopped two or three times by way of a hint. Boys, you see, think a horse or pony is like a steam engine or a thrashing machine, and can go on as long and as fast as they please; they never think that a pony can get tired, or have any feelings; so as the one who was whipping me could not under-stand, I just rose up on my hind legs and let him slip off behind —that was all; he mounted me again, and I did the same. Then the other boy got up, and as soon as he began to use his stick I laid him on the grass, and so on, till they were able to under-stand that was all. They are not bad boys; they don't wish to be cruel. I like them very well; but you see I had to give them a lesson. When they brought me to James and told him, I think he was very angry to see such big sticks. He said they were only fit for drovers or gypsies, and not for young gentlemen."

"If I had been you," said Ginger, "I would have given those boys a good kick, and that would have given them a lesson."

"No doubt you would," said Merrylegs, "but then I am not quite such a fool (begging your pardon) as to anger our master

or make James ashamed of me; besides, those children are under my charge when they are riding; I tell you they are entrusted to me. Why, only the other day I heard our master say to Mrs. Blomefield, 'My dear madam, you need not be anxious about the children, my old Merrylegs will take as much care of them as you or I could; I assure you I would not sell that pony for any money, he is so perfectly good-tempered and trustworthy'; and do you think I am such an ungrateful brute as to forget all the kind treatment I have had here for five years, and all the trust they place in me, and turn vicious because a couple of ignorant boys used me badly? No! no! You never had a good place where they were kind to you; and so you don't know, and I'm sorry for you, but I can tell you good places make good horses. I wouldn't vex our people for anything; I love them, I do," said Merrylegs, and he gave a low "ho, ho, ho," through his nose as he used to do in the morning when he heard James's footstep at the door.

"Besides," he went on, "if I took to kicking where should I be? Why, sold off in a jiffy, and no character, and I might find myself slaved about under a butcher's boy, or worked to death at some seaside place where no one cared for me, except to find out how fast I could go, or be flogged along in some cart with three or four great men in it going out for a Sunday spree, as I have often seen in the place I lived in before I came here; no," said he, shaking his head, "I hope I shall never come to that."

Ginger and I were not of the regular tall carriage horse breed, we had more of the racing blood in us. We stood about fifteen and a half hands high; we were therefore just as good for riding as we were for driving, and our master used to say that he disliked either horse or man that could do but one thing; and as he did not want to show off in London parks he preferred a more active and useful kind of horse. As for us, our greatest pleasure was when we were saddled for a riding party, the master on Ginger, the mistress on me, and the young ladies on Sir Oliver and Merrylegs. It was so cheerful to be trotting and cantering all together that it always put us in high spirits. I had the best of it, for I always carried the mistress; her weight was little, her voice was sweet, and her hand was so light on the rein that I was guided almost without feeling it.

Oh! if people knew what a comfort to horses a light hand is, and how it keeps a good mouth and a good temper, they surely would not chuck, and drag, and pull at the rein as they often do. Our mouths are so tender that where they have not been spoiled or hardened with bad or ignorant treatment they feel the slightest movement of the driver's hand, and we know in an instant what is required of us. My mouth had never been spoiled, and I believe that was why the mistress preferred me to Ginger, although her paces were certainly quite as good. She used often to envy me, and said it was all the fault of breaking in, and the gag bit in London, that her mouth was not so perfect as mine; and then old Sir Oliver would say, "There, there! don't vex yourself; you have the greatest honor; a mare that can carry a tall man of our master's weight, with all your spring and sprightly action, does not need to hold her head down because she does not carry the lady; we horses must take things as they come, and always be contented and willing so long as we are kindly used."

I had often wondered how it was that Sir Oliver had such a very short tail; it really was only six or seven inches long, with a tassel of hair hanging from it; and on one of our holidays in the orchard I ventured to ask him by what accident it was that he had lost his tail. "Accident," he snorted, with a fierce look, "it was no accident! It was a cruel, shameful, cold-blooded act! When I was young I was taken to a place where these cruel things were done. I was tied up and made fast so that I could not stir, and then they came and cut off my long, beautiful tail, through the flesh, and through the bone, and took it away."

"How dreadful!" I exclaimed.

"Dreadful! Ah! It was dreadful; but it was not only the pain, though that was terrible and lasted a long time; it was not only the indignity of having my best ornament taken from me, though that was bad; but it was this, how could I ever brush the flies off my sides and my hind legs any more? You who have tails just whisk the flies off without thinking about it, and you can't tell what a torment it is to have them settle upon you and sting and sting, and have nothing in the world to lash them off with. I tell you, it is a lifelong wrong, and a lifelong loss; but thank Heaven! they don't do it now."

"What did they do it for then?" said Ginger.

"For fashion!" said the old horse with a stamp of his foot; "for fashion! if you know what that means. There was not a well-bred young horse in my time that had not his tail docked in that shameful way, just as if the good God that made us did not know what we wanted and what looked best."

"I suppose it is fashion that makes them strap our heads up

with those horrid bits that I was tortured with in London,"
said Ginger.

"Of course, it is," said he; "to my mind, fashion is one of the
wickedest things in the world. Now look, for instance, at the
way they serve dogs, cutting off their tails to make them look
plucky, and shearing up their pretty little ears to a point to
make them look sharp, forsooth! I had a dear friend once, a
brown terrier—Skye, they called her; she was so fond of me
that she never would sleep out of my stall; she made her bed
under the manger, and there she had a litter of five as pretty
little puppies as need be; none were drowned, for they were a
valuable kind, and how pleased she was with them! And when
they got their eyes open and crawled about, it was a real pretty
sight. But one day the man came and took them all away. I
thought he might be afraid I should tread upon them. But it
was not so; in the evening poor Skye brought them back again,
one by one, in her mouth; not the happy little things that they
were, but bleeding and crying pitifully. They had all had a
piece of their tails cut off, and the soft flap of their pretty little
ears was cut quite off. How their mother licked them, and
how troubled she was, poor thing! I never forgot it. They
healed in time, and they forgot the pain, but the nice, soft flap
that, of course, was intended to protect the delicate part of
their ears from dust and injury was gone forever. Why don't
they cut their own children's ears into points to make them
look sharp? Why don't they cut the end off their noses to make
them look plucky? One would be just as sensible as the other.
What right have they to torment and disfigure God's creatures?"

Sir Oliver, though he was so gentle, was a fiery old fellow,
and what he said was all so new to me and so dreadful that I
found a bitter feeling toward men rise up in my mind that I
had never had before. Of course, Ginger was much excited;
she flung up her head with flashing eyes and distended nos-
trils, declaring that men were both brutes and blockheads.

"Who talks about blockheads?" said Merrylegs, who just
came up from the old apple tree, where he had been rubbing
himself against the low branch. "Who talks about blockheads?
I believe that is a bad word."

"Bad words were made for bad things," said Ginger, and she

told him what Sir Oliver had said. "It is all true," said Merry-legs sadly, "and I've seen that about the dogs over and over again where I lived first; but we won't talk about it here. You know that master, and John, and James are always good to us, and talking against men in such a place as this doesn't seem fair or grateful, and you know there are good masters and good grooms besides ours, though, of course, ours are the best." This wise speech of good little Merrylegs, which we knew was quite true, cooled us all down, specially Sir Oliver, who was dearly fond of his master; and to turn the subject I said, "Can anyone tell me the use of blinkers?"

"No!" said Sir Oliver shortly, "because they are no use."

"They are supposed," said Justice in his calm way, "to pre-vent horses from shying and starting, and getting so frightened as to cause accidents."

"Then what is the reason they do not put them on riding horses; especially on ladies' horses?" said I.

"There is no reason at all," said he quietly, "except the fash-ion; they say that a horse would be so frightened to see the wheels of his own cart or carriage coming behind him that he would be sure to run away, although, of course, when he is ridden he sees them all about him if the streets are crowded. I admit they do sometimes come too close to be pleasant, but we don't run away; we are used to it, and understand it, and if we had never blinkers put on, we should never want them; we should see what was there, and know what was what, and be much less frightened than by only seeing bits of things that we can't understand."

Of course, there may be some nervous horses who have been hurt or frightened when they were young, and may be the better for them, but as I never was nervous I can't judge.

"I consider," said Sir Oliver, "that blinkers are dangerous things in the night; we horses can see much better in the dark than man can, and many an accident would never have hap-pened if horses might have had the full use of their eyes. Some years ago, I remember, there was a hearse with two horses returning one dark night, and just by Farmer Sparrow's house, where the pond is close to the road, the wheels went too near the edge, and the hearse was overturned into the water; both the horses were drowned, and the driver hardly escaped. Of course, after this accident a stout white rail was put up that might be easily seen, but if those horses had not been partly blinded they would of themselves have kept farther from the edge, and no accident would have happened. When our master's carriage was overturned, before you came here, it was said that if the lamp on the left side had not gone out John would have seen the great hole that the road makers had left; and so he might, but if old Colin had not had blinkers on he would have seen it, lamp or no lamp, for he was far too knowing an old horse to run into danger. As it was, he was very much hurt, the carriage was broken, and how John escaped nobody knew."

"I should say," said Ginger, curling her nostril, "that these men, who are so wise, had better give orders that in future all foals should be born with their eyes set just in the middle of their foreheads, instead of on the side; they always think they can improve upon Nature and mend what God has made."

Things were getting rather sore again, when Merrylegs held up his knowing little face and said, "I'll tell you a secret; I believe John does not approve of blinkers; I heard him talking with master about it one day. The master said that if horses had been used to them it might be dangerous in some cases to leave them off, and John said he thought it would be a good thing if all colts were broken in without blinkers, as was the case in some foreign countries; so let us cheer up, and have a run to the other end of the orchard; I believe the wind has blown down some apples, and we might just as well eat them as the slugs."

Merrylegs could not be resisted, so we broke off our long conversation, and got up our spirits by munching some very sweet apples which lay scattered on the grass.

The longer I lived at Birtwick, the more proud and happy I felt at having such a place. Our master and mistress were respected and beloved by all who knew them; they were good and kind to everybody and everything; not only men and women, but horses and donkeys, dogs and cats, cattle and birds. There was no oppressed or ill-used creature that had not a friend in them, and their servants took the same tone. If any of the village children were known to treat any creature cruelly, they soon heard about it from the Hall.

The Squire and Farmer Grey had worked together, as they said, for more than twenty years to get bearing reins on the cart horses done away with, and in our parts you seldom saw them; but sometimes if mistress met a heavily laden horse, with his head strained up, she would stop the carriage and get out, and reason with the driver in her sweet serious voice, and try to show him how foolish and cruel it was. I don't think any man could withstand our mistress. I wish all ladies were like her.

Our master, too, used to come down very heavy sometimes. I remember he was riding me toward home one morning when we saw a powerful man driving toward us in a little pony chaise, with a beautiful little bay pony, with slender legs and a high-bred, sensitive head and face. Just as he came to the Park gates the little thing turned toward them; the man, without word or warning, wrenched the creature's head round with such a force and suddenness that he nearly threw it on its haunches; recovering itself, it was going on when he began to lash it furiously; the pony plunged forward, but the strong, heavy hand held the pretty creature back with force almost enough to break its jaw, while the whip still cut into him. It was a dreadful sight to me, for I knew what fearful pain it gave the delicate little mouth; but master gave me the word, and we were up with him in a second.

"Sawyer," he cried in a stern voice, "is that pony made of flesh and blood?"

"Flesh and blood and temper," he said; "he's too fond of his own will, and that won't suit me." He spoke as if he was in a strong passion; he was a builder who had often been to the Park on business. "And do you think," said master sternly, "that treatment like this will make him fond of your will?"

"He had no business to make that turn; his road was straight on!" said the man roughly.

"You have often driven that pony up to my place," said the master; "it only shows the creature's memory and intelligence; how did he know that you were not going there again? But that has little to do with it. I must say, Mr. Sawyer, that more unmanly, brutal treatment of a little pony it was never my painful lot to witness; and by giving way to such passion you injure your own character as much, nay, more, than you injure your horse, and remember, we shall all have to be judged according to our works, whether they be toward man or toward beast."

Master rode me home slowly, and I could tell by his voice how the thing had grieved him. He was just as free to speak to gentlemen of his own rank as to those below him; for another day, when we were out, we met a Captain Langley, a friend of our master's; he was driving a splendid pair of grays in a kind of break. After a little conversation the Captain said:

"What do you think of my new team, Mr. Douglas? You know, you are the judge of horses in these parts, and I should like your opinion."

The master backed me a little, so as to get a good view of them. "They are an uncommonly handsome pair," he said, "and if they are as good as they look I am sure you need not wish for anything better; but I see you still hold that pet scheme of yours for worrying your horses and lessening their power."

"What do you mean," said the other, "the bearing reins? Oh, ah! I know that's a hobby of yours; well, the fact is, I like to see my horses hold their heads up."

"So do I," said master, "as well as any man, but I don't like to see them *held up;* that takes all the shine out of it. Now, you are a military man, Langley, and no doubt like to see your regiment look well on parade, 'Heads up,' and all that; but you would not take much credit for your drill if all your men had their heads tied to a backboard! It might not be much harm on parade except to worry and fatigue them, but how would it be in a bayonet charge against the enemy, when they want the free use of every muscle and all their strength thrown forward? I would not give much for their chance of victory, and it is just the same with horses; you fret and worry their tempers and decrease their power; you will not let them throw their weight against their work, and so they have to do too much with their joints and muscles, and, of course, it wears them up faster. You may depend upon it, horses were intended to have their heads free, as free as men's are; and if we could act a little more according to common sense, and a good deal less according to fashion, we should find many things work easier; besides, you know as well as I that if a horse makes a false step he has much less chance of recovering himself if his head and neck are fastened back. And now," said the master, laughing, "I have given my hobby a good trot out, can't you make up your mind to mount him, too, Captain? Your example would go a long way."

"I believe you are right in theory," said the other, "and that's rather a hard hit about the soldiers; but—well—I'll think about it," and so they parted.

One day late in the autumn, my master had a long journey to go on business. I was put into the dogcart, and John went with his master. I always liked to go in the dogcart, it was so light and the high wheels ran along so pleasantly. There had been a great deal of rain, and now the wind was very high and blew the dry leaves across the road in a shower. We went along merrily till we came to the toll bar and the low wooden bridge. The river banks were rather high, and the bridge, instead of rising, went across just level, so that in the middle, if the river was full, the water would be nearly up to the woodwork and planks; but as there were good, substantial rails on each side people did not mind it.

The man at the gate said the river was rising fast, and he feared it would be a bad night. Many of the meadows were under water, and in one low part of the road the water was half-way up to my knees; the bottom was good, and master drove gently, so it was no matter.

When we got to the town, of course, I had a good bait, but as the master's business engaged him a long time we did not start for home till rather late in the afternoon. The wind was then much higher, and I heard the master say to John he had never been out in such a storm; and so I thought, as we went along the skirts of a wood, where the great branches were swaying about like twigs, and the rushing sound was terrible.

"I wish we were well out of this wood," said my master.

"Yes, sir," said John, "it would be rather awkward if one of these branches came down upon us."

The words were scarcely out of his mouth when there was a groan, and a crack, and a splitting sound; and tearing, crashing down among the other trees came an oak, torn up by the roots, and it fell right across the road just before us. I will never say I was not frightened, for I was. I stopped still, and I believe I trembled; of course, I did not turn round or run away; I was not brought up to that. John jumped out and was in a moment at my head.

"That was a very near touch," said my master. "What's to be done now?"

"Well, sir, we can't drive over that tree nor yet get round it; there will be nothing for it but to go back to the four cross-ways, and that will be a good six miles before we get round to the wooden bridge again; it will make us late, but the horse is fresh."

So back we went, and round by the crossroads; but by the time we got to the bridge it was very nearly dark. We could just see that the water was over the middle of it; but as that happened sometimes when the floods were out, master did not stop. We were going along at a good pace, but the moment my feet touched the first part of the bridge I felt sure there was something wrong. I dare not go forward, and I made a dead stop. "Go on, Beauty," said my master, and he gave me a touch with the whip, but I dare not stir; he then gave me a sharp cut; I jumped, but I dare not go forward.

"There's something wrong, sir," said John, and he sprang out of the dogcart and came to my head and looked all about. He tried to lead me forward. "Come on, Beauty, what's the matter?" Of course, I could not tell him, but I knew very well that the bridge was not safe.

Just then, the man at the tollgate on the other side ran out of the house, tossing a torch about like one mad.

"Hoy, hoy, hoy, halloo, stop!" he cried.

"What's the matter?" shouted my master.

"The bridge is broken in the middle, and part of it is carried away; if you come on you'll be into the river."

"Thank God!" said my master. "You Beauty!" said John, and took the bridle and gently turned me round to the right-hand road by the river side. The sun had set some time, the wind seemed to have lulled off after that furious blast which tore up the tree. It grew darker and darker, stiller and stiller. I trotted quietly along, the wheels hardly making a sound on the soft road. For a good while neither master nor John spoke, and then master began in a serious voice. I could not understand much of what they said, but I found they thought, if I had gone on as the master wanted me, most likely the bridge would have given away under us, and horse, chaise, master, and man would have fallen into the river; and as the current was flowing very strongly, and there was no light and no help at hand, it was more than likely we should all have been drowned. Master said God had given men reason by which they could find out things for themselves, but He had given animals knowledge which did not depend on reason, and which was much more prompt and perfect in its way, and by which they had often saved the lives of men. John had many stories to tell of dogs and horses, and the wonderful things they had done; he thought people did not value their animals half enough, nor make friends of them as they ought to do. I am sure he makes friends of them if ever a man did.

At last we came to the Park gates, and found the gardener looking out for us. He said that mistress had been in a dreadful way ever since dark, fearing some accident had happened, and that she had sent James off on Justice, the roan cob, toward the wooden bridge to make inquiry after us.

We saw a light at the hall door and at the upper windows, and as we came up mistress ran out, saying, "Are you really safe, my dear? Oh! I have been so anxious, fancying all sorts of things. Have you had no accident?"

"No, my dear; but if your Black Beauty had not been wiser than we were, we should all have been carried down the river at the wooden bridge." I heard no more, as they went into the house, and John took me to the stable. Oh! what a good supper he gave me that night, a good bran mash and some crushed beans with my oats, and such a thick bed of straw, and I was glad of it, for I was tired.

One day when John and I had been out on some business of our master's, and were returning gently on a long, straight road, at some distance we saw a boy trying to leap a pony over a gate; the pony would not take the leap, and the boy cut him with the whip, but he only turned off on one side. He whipped him

again, but the pony turned off on the other side. Then the boy
got off and gave him a hard thrashing, and knocked him about
the head; then he got up again and tried to make him leap the
gate, kicking him all the time shamefully, but still the pony refused. When we were nearly at the spot, the pony put down
his head and threw up his heels and sent the boy neatly over
into a broad, quickset hedge, and with the rein dangling from
his head he set off home at a full gallop. John laughed out quite
aloud. "Served him right," he said.

"Oh! oh! oh," cried the boy, as he struggled about among the
thorns; "I say, come and help me out."

"Thank ye," said John, "I think you are quite in the right
place, and maybe a little scratching will teach you not to leap
a pony over a gate that is too high for him," and so with that
John rode off. "It may be," he said to himself, "that young
fellow is a liar as well as a cruel one; we'll just go home by
Farmer Bushby's, Beauty, and then if anybody wants to know
you and I can tell 'em, ye see"; so we turned off to the right,
and soon came up to the stack yard, and within sight of the
house. The farmer was hurrying out into the road, and his wife
was standing at the gate, looking very frightened.

"Have you seen my boy?" said Mr. Bushby, as we came up.
"He went out an hour ago on my black pony, and the creature
is just come back without a rider."

"I should think, sir," said John, "he had better be without a
rider, unless he can be ridden properly."

"What do you mean?" said the farmer.

"Well, sir, I saw your son whipping and kicking and knocking that good little pony about shamefully, because he would
not leap a gate that was too high for him. The pony behaved
well, sir, and showed no vice; but at last he just threw up his
heels and tipped the young gentleman into the thorn hedge;
he wanted me to help him out; but I hope you will excuse me,
sir, I did not feel inclined to do so. There's no bones broken,
sir, he'll only get a few scratches. I love horses, and it riles me
to see them badly used; it is a bad plan to aggravate an animal
till he uses his heels; the first time is not always the last."

During this time the mother began to cry, "Oh! my poor Bill,
I must go and meet him, he must be hurt."

"You had better go into the house, wife," said the farmer; "Bill wants a lesson about this, and I must see that he gets it; this is not the first time nor the second time he has ill-used that pony, and I shall stop it. I am obliged to you, Manly. Good evening."

So we went on, John chuckling all the way home. Then he told James about it, who laughed and said, "Serve him right. I knew that boy at school; he took great airs on himself because he was a farmer's son; he used to swagger about and bully the little boys; of course, we elder ones would not have any of that nonsense, and let him know that in the school and the playground farmers' sons and laborers' sons were all alike. I well remember one day, just before afternoon school, I found him at the large window catching flies and pulling off their wings. He did not see me, and I gave him a box on the ears that laid him sprawling on the floor. Well, angry as I was, I was almost frightened, he roared and bellowed in such a style. The boys rushed in from the playground, and the master ran in from the road to see who was being murdered. Of course, I said fair and square at once what I had done, and why; then I showed the master the poor flies, some crushed and some crawling about helpless, and I showed him the wings on the window sill. I never saw him so angry before; but as Bill was still howling and whining, like the coward that he was, he did not give him any more punishment of that kind, but set him up on a stool for the rest of the afternoon, and said that he should not go out to play for that week. Then he talked to all the boys very seriously about cruelty, and said how hardhearted and cowardly it was to hurt the weak and helpless; but what stuck in my mind was this, he said that cruelty was the Devil's own trade-mark, and if we saw anyone who took pleasure in cruelty we might know who he belonged to, for the devil was a murderer from the beginning and a tormentor to the end. On the other hand, where we saw people who loved their neighbors, and were kind to man and beast, we might know that was God's mark, for 'God is Love.'"

"Your master never taught you a truer thing," said John; "there is no religion without love, and people may talk as much as they like about their religion, but if it does not teach them to be good and kind to man and beast, it is all a sham—all a

sham, James, and it won't stand when things come to be turned
inside out and put down for what they are."

One morning, early in December, John had just led me into
my box after my daily exercise, and was strapping my cloth on,
and James was coming in from the corn chamber with some
oats, when the master came into the stable; he looked rather
serious, and held an open letter in his hand. John fastened the
door of my box, touched his cap, and waited for orders.

"Good morning, John," said the master; "I want to know if you
have any complaint to make of James?"

"Complaint, sir? No, sir."

"Is he industrious at his work and respectful to you?"

"Yes, sir, always."

"You never find he slights his work when your back is turned?"

"Never, sir."

"That's well; but I must put another question: Have you any
reason to suspect that when he goes out with the horses to exercise them, or to take a message, he stops about talking to his
acquaintances, or goes into houses where he has no business,
leaving the horses outside?"

"No, certainly not, and if anybody has been saying that about
James, I don't believe it, and I don't mean to believe it unless I
have it fairly proved before witnesses; it's not for me to say who
has been trying to take away James's character, but I will say
this, sir, that a steadier, pleasanter, honester, smarter young
fellow I never had in this stable. I can trust his word and I can
trust his work; he is gentle and clever with the horses, and I
would rather have them in his charge than in that of half the
young fellows I know in laced hats and liveries; and whoever
wants a character of James Howard," said John, with a decided
jerk of his head, "let them come to John Manly."

The master stood all this time grave and attentive, but as
John finished his speech a broad smile spread over his face, and
looking kindly across at James, who all this time had stood still
at the door, he said, "James, my lad, set down the oats and
come here; I am very glad to find that John's opinion of your
character agrees so exactly with my own. John is a cautious
man," he said, with a droll smile, "and it is not always easy to
get his opinion about people, so I thought if I beat the bush on

this side the birds would fly out, and I should learn what I wanted to know quickly; so now we will come to business. I have a letter from my brother-in-law, Sir Clifford Williams, of Clifford Hall; he wants me to find him a trustworthy young groom, about twenty or twenty-one, who knows his business. His old coachman, who has lived with him twenty years, is getting feeble, and he wants a man to work with him and get into his ways, who would be able, when the old man was pensioned off, to step into his place. He would have eighteen shillings a week at first, a stable suit, a driving suit, a bedroom over the coach house, and a boy under him. Sir Clifford is a good master, and if you could get the place it would be a good start for you. I don't want to part with you, and if you left us I know John would lose his right hand."

"That I should, sir," said John, "but I would not stand in his light for the world."

"How old are you, James?" said master.

"Nineteen next May, sir."

"That's young; what do you think, John?"

"Well, sir, it is young; but he is as steady as a man, and is strong, and well grown, and though he has not had much experience in driving, he has a light, firm hand and a quick eye, and he is very careful, and I am quite sure no horse of his will be ruined for want of having his feet and shoes looked after."

"Your word will go the furthest, John," said the master, "for Sir Clifford adds in a postscript, 'If I could find a man trained by your John, I should like him better than any other'; so James, lad, think it over, talk to your mother at dinner time, and then let me know what you wish."

In a few days after this conversation it was fully settled that James should go to Clifford Hall in a month or six weeks, as it suited his master, and in the meantime he was to get all the practice in driving that could be given to him. I never knew the carriage to go out so often before; when the mistress did not go out, the master drove himself in the two-wheeled chaise; but now, whether it was master or the young ladies, or only an errand, Ginger and I were put into the carriage and James drove us. At the first John rode with him on the box, telling him this and that, and after that James drove alone.

Then it was wonderful what a number of places the master would go to in the city on Saturday, and what queer streets we were driven through. He was sure to go to the railway station just as the train was coming in, and cabs and carriages, carts and omnibuses were all trying to get over the bridge together; that bridge wanted good horses and good drivers when the railway bell was ringing, for it was narrow, and there was a very sharp turn up to the station, where it would not have been at all difficult for people to run into each other if they did not look sharp and keep their wits about them.

After this it was decided by my master and mistress to pay a visit to some friends who lived about forty-six miles from our home, and James was to drive them. The first day we traveled thirty-two miles; there were some long, heavy hills, but James drove so carefully and thoughtfully that we were not at all harassed. He never forgot to put on the drag as we went downhill, nor to take it off at the right place. He kept our feet on the smoothest part of the road, and if the uphill was very long he set the carriage wheels a little across the road, so as not to run back, and gave us a breathing. All these little things help a horse very much, particularly if he gets kind words into the bargain.

We stopped once or twice on the road, and just as the sun was going down we reached the town where we were to spend the night. We stopped at the principal hotel, which was in the Market Place; it was a very large one; we drove under an archway into a long yard, at the farther end of which were the stables and coach houses. Two ostlers came to take us out. The head ostler was a pleasant, active little man, with a crooked leg and a yellow striped waistcoat. I never saw a man unbuckle harness so quickly as he did, and with a pat and a good word he led me to a long stable, with six or eight stalls in it and two or three horses. The other man brought Ginger; James stood by while we were rubbed down and cleaned.

I never was cleaned so lightly and quickly as by that little old man. When he had done, James stepped up and felt me over, as if he thought I could not be thoroughly done, but he found my coat as clean and smooth as silk.

"Well," he said, "I thought I was pretty quick, and our John quicker still, but you do beat all I ever saw for being quick and thorough at the same time."

"Practice makes perfect," said the crooked little ostler, "and 'twould be a pity if it didn't; forty years' practice and not perfect! ha, ha! that would be a pity; and as to being quick, why, bless you! that is only a matter of habit; if you get into the habit of being quick, it is just as easy as being slow; easier, I should say; in fact, it don't agree with my health to be hulking about over a job twice as long as it need take. Bless you! I couldn't whistle if I crawled over my work as some folks do! You see, I have been about horses ever since I was twelve years old, in hunting stables and racing stables; and being small, ye see, I was jockey for several years; but at the Goodwood, ye see, the turf was very slippery and my poor Larkspur got a fall, and I broke my knee, and so, of course, I was of no more use there; but I could not live without horses, of course I couldn't, so I took to the hotels, and I can tell ye it is a downright pleasure to handle an animal like this, well bred, well mannered, well cared for; bless ye! I can tell how a horse is treated. Give me the handling of a horse for twenty minutes, and I'll tell you what sort of a groom he has had. Look at this one, pleasant, quiet, turns about just as you want him, holds up his feet to be cleaned out, or anything else you please to wish; then you'll find another, fidgety, fretty, won't move the right way, or starts across the stall, tosses up his head as soon as you come near him, lays his ears, and seems afraid of you; or else squares about at you with his heels. Poor things! I know what sort of treatment they have had. If they are timid, it makes them start or shy; if they are high mettled, it makes them vicious or dangerous; their tempers are mostly made when they are young. Bless you! they are like children, train 'em in the way they should go, as the good Book says, and when they are old they will not depart from it, if they've a chance, that is."

"I like to hear you talk," said James. "That's the way we lay it down at home, at our master's."

"Who is your master, young man? if it be a proper question. I should judge he is a good one, from what I see."

"He is Squire Gordon, of Birtwick Park, the other side the Beacon hills," said James.

"Ah! so, so, I have heard tell of him; fine judge of horses, ain't he? The best rider in the county?"

"I believe he is," said James, "but he rides very little now, since the poor young master was killed."

"Ah! poor gentleman; I read all about it in the paper; a fine horse killed, too, wasn't there?"

"Yes," said James, "he was a splendid creature, brother to this one, and just like him."

"Pity! pity!" said the old man. " 'Twas a bad place to leap, if I remember; a thin fence at top, a steep bank down to the stream, wasn't it? no chance for a horse to see where he is going. Now, I am for bold riding as much as any man, but still there are some leaps that only a very knowing old huntsman has any right to take; a man's life and a horse's life are worth more than a fox's tail; at least I should say they ought to be."

During this time the other man had finished Ginger, and had brought our corn, and James and the old man left the stable together.

Later on in the evening a traveler's horse was brought in by the second ostler, and while he was cleaning him a young man with a pipe in his mouth lounged into the stable to gossip awhile.

"I say, Towler," said the ostler, "just run up the ladder into the loft and put some hay down into this horse's rack, will you? Only lay down your pipe."

"All right," said the other, and went up through the trap door; and I heard him step across the floor overhead and put down the hay. James came in to look at us the last thing, and then the door was locked.

I cannot say how long I had slept, nor what time in the night it was, but I woke up very uncomfortable, though I hardly knew why. I got up, the air seemed all thick and choking. I heard Ginger coughing, and one of the other horses moved about restlessly; it was quite dark, and I could see nothing, but the stable was full of smoke and I hardly knew how to breathe.

The trap door had been left open, and I thought that was the place it came through. I listened and heard a soft rushing sort of noise, and a low crackling and snapping. I did not know what it was, but there was something in the sound so strange

that it made me tremble all over. The other horses were now all awake; some were pulling at their halters, others were stamping.

At last I heard steps outside, and the ostler who had put up the traveler's horse burst into the stable with a lantern, and began to untie the horses, and try to lead them out; but he seemed in such a hurry and so frightened himself that he frightened me still more. The first horse would not go with him; he tried the second and third; they, too, would not stir. He came to me next and tried to drag me out of the stall by force; of course, that was of no use. He tried us all by turns and then left the stable.

No doubt, we were very foolish, but danger seemed to be all round, and there was nobody we knew to trust in, and all was strange and uncertain. The fresh air that had come in through the open door made it easier to breathe, but the rushing sound overhead grew louder, and as I looked upward through the bars of my empty rack, I saw a red light flickering on the wall. Then I heard a cry of "Fire!" outside, and the old ostler quietly and quickly came in; he got one horse out, and went to another, but the flames were playing round the trap door, and the roaring overhead was dreadful.

The next thing I heard was James's voice, quiet and cheery, as it always was.

"Come, my beauties, it is time for us to be off, so wake up and come along." I stood nearest the door, so he came to me first, patting me as he came in.

"Come, Beauty, on with your bridle, my boy, we'll soon be out of this smother." It was on in no time; then he took the scarf off his neck and tied it lightly over my eyes, and patting and coaxing he led me out of the stable. Safe in the yard, he slipped the scarf off my eyes and shouted, "Here, somebody! take this horse while I go back for the other."

A tall, broad man stepped forward and took me, and James darted back into the stable. I set up a shrill whinny as I saw him go. Ginger told me afterwards that whinny was the best thing I could have done for her, for had she not heard me outside she would never have had courage to come out.

There was much confusion in the yard; the horses being got out of other stables, and the carriages and gigs being pulled out of houses and sheds, lest the flames should spread farther. On the other side the yard windows were thrown up, and people were shouting all sorts of things; but I kept my eye fixed on the stable door, where the smoke poured out thicker than ever, and I could see flashes of red light. Presently I heard above all the stir and din a loud, clear voice, which I knew was master's:

"James Howard! James Howard! are you there?" There was no answer, but I heard a crash of something falling in the stable, and the next moment I gave a loud, joyful neigh, for I saw James coming through the smoke leading Ginger with him; she was coughing violently, and he was not able to speak.

"My brave lad!" said master, laying his hand on his shoulder. "Are you hurt?"

James shook his head, for he could not yet speak.

"Ay," said the big man who held me, "he is a brave lad, and no mistake."

"And now," said master, "when you have got your breath, James, we'll get out of this place as quickly as we can," and we were moving toward the entry, when from the Market Place there came a sound of galloping feet and loud, rumbling wheels.

" 'Tis the fire engine! the fire engine!" shouted two or three voices. "Stand back, make way!" and clattering and thundering over the stones two horses dashed into the yard with the heavy engine behind them. The firemen leaped to the ground; no need to ask where the fire was—it was torching up in a great blaze from the roof.

We got out as fast as we could into the broad, quiet Market Place; the stars were shining, and except the noise behind us all was still. Master led the way to a large hotel on the other side, and as soon as the ostler came he said, "James, I must now hasten to your mistress; I trust the horses entirely to you, order whatever you think is needed," and with that he was gone. The master did not run, but I never saw mortal man walk so fast as he did that night.

There was a dreadful sound before we got into our stalls; the shrieks of those poor horses that were left burning to death in the stable—it was very terrible! and made both Ginger and me feel very bad. We were taken in and well done by.

The next morning the master came to see how we were and to speak to James. I did not hear much, for the ostler was rubbing me down, but I could see that James looked very happy, and I thought the master was proud of him. Our mistress had been so much alarmed in the night that the journey was put off till the afternoon, so James had the morning on hand, and went first to the inn to see about our harness and the carriage, and then to hear more about the fire. When he came back, we heard him tell the ostler about it. At first no one could guess how the fire had been caused, but at last a man said he saw Dick Towler go into the stable with a pipe in his mouth, and when he came out he had not one, and went to the tap for another. Then the under ostler said he had asked Dick to go up the ladder to put down some hay, but told him to lay down his pipe first. Dick denied taking the pipe with him, but no one believed him. I remember our John Manly's rule, never to allow a pipe in the stable, and thought it ought to be the rule everywhere.

James said the roof and floor had all fallen in, and that only the black walls were standing; the two poor horses that could not be got out were buried under the burned rafters and tiles.

The rest of our journey was very easy, and a little after sunset we reached the house of my master's friend. We were taken into a clean, snug stable; there was a kind coachman, who made us very comfortable, and who seemed to think a good deal of James when he heard about the fire.

"There is one thing quite clear, young man," he said, "your horses know who they can trust; it is one of the hardest things in the world to get horses out of a stable when there is either fire or flood. I don't know why they won't come out, but they won't—not one in twenty."

We stopped two or three days at this place, and then returned home. All went well on the journey; we were glad to be in our own stable again, and John was equally glad to see us.

Before he and James left us for the night, James said, "I wonder who is coming in my place."

"Little Joe Green at the Lodge," said John.

"Little Joe Green! why, he's only a child!"

"He is fourteen and a half," said John.

"But he is such a little chap!"

"Yes, he is small, but he is quick, and willing, and kindhearted, too, and then he wishes very much to come, and his father would like it, and I know the master would like to give him the chance. He said if I thought he would not do he would look out for a bigger boy; but I said I was quite agreeable to try him for six weeks."

"Six weeks!" said James, "why, it will be six months before he can be of much use! It will make you a deal of work, John."

"Well," said John with a laugh, "work and I are very good friends; I never was afraid of work yet."

"You are a very good man," said James, "I wish I may ever be like you."

"I don't often speak of myself," said John, "but as you are going away from us out into the world to shift for yourself I'll tell you just how I look on these things. I was just as old as Joseph when my father and mother died of the fever within ten days of each other, and left me and my crippled sister Nelly alone in the world, without a relation that we could look to for help. I was a farmer's boy, not earning enough to keep myself, much less both of us, and she must have gone to the workhouse but for our mistress (Nelly calls her Angel, and she has good right to do so). She went and hired a room for her with old Widow Mallet, and she gave her knitting and needlework when she was able to do it; and when she was ill, she sent her dinners and many nice, comfortable things, and was like a mother to her. Then the master, he took me into the stable under old Norman, the coachman that was then. I had my food at the house, and my bed in the loft, and a suit of clothes and three shillings a week, so that I could help Nelly. Then there was Norman; he might have turned round and said that at his age he could not be troubled with a raw boy from the plowtail; but he was like a father to me, and took no end of pains with me. When the old man died some years after, I stepped into his place, and now, of course, I have top wages, and can lay by for a rainy day or a sunny day, as it may happen, and Nelly is as happy as a bird. So, you see, James, I am not the man that should turn up his nose at a little boy and vex a good, kind master. No! no! I shall miss you very much, James, but we shall pull through, and there's nothing like doing a kindness when 'tis put in your way, and I am glad I can do it."

"Then," said James, "you don't hold with that saying, 'Everybody look after himself and take care of number one.'"

"No, indeed," said John, "where should I and Nelly have been if master and mistress and old Norman had only taken care of number one? Why—she in the workhouse and I hoeing turnips!

Where would Black Beauty and Ginger have been if you had only thought of number one? Why, roasted to death! No, Jim, no! that is a selfish, heathenish saying, whoever uses it, and any man who thinks he has nothing to do but take care of number one, why, it's a pity but what he had been drowned like a puppy or a kitten, before he got his eyes open, that's what I think," said John, with a very decided jerk of his head.

James laughed at this; but there was a thickness in his voice when he said, "You have been my best friend except my mother. I hope you won't forget me."

"No, lad, no!" said John, "and if ever I can do you a good turn I hope you won't forget me."

The next day Joe came to the stable to learn all he could before James left. He learned to sweep the stable, to bring in the straw and hay; he began to clean the harness, and helped to wash the carriage. As he was quite too short to do anything in the way of grooming Ginger and me, James taught him upon Merrylegs, for he was to have full charge of him, under John. He was a nice little bright fellow, and always came whistling to his work.

Merrylegs was a good deal put out at being "mauled about," as he said, "by a boy who knew nothing"; but at the end of the second week he told me confidentially that he thought the boy would turn out well.

At last the day came when James had to leave us; cheerful as he always was, he looked quite downhearted that morning.

"You see," he said to John, "I am leaving a great deal behind; my mother and Betsy, and you, and a good master and mistress, and then the horses, and my old Merrylegs. At the new place there will not be a soul that I shall know. If it were not that I shall get a higher place, and be able to help my mother better, I don't think I should have made up my mind to it; it's a real pinch, John."

"Ay, James, lad, so it is, but I should not think much of you if you could leave your home for the first time and not feel it; cheer up, you'll make friends there, and if you get on well—as I am sure you will—it will be a fine thing for your mother, and she will be proud enough that you have got into such a good place as that."

So John cheered him up, but everyone was sorry to lose James; as for Merrylegs, he pined after him for several days, and went quite off his appetite. So John took him out several mornings with a leading rein, when he exercised me, and trotting and galloping by my side got up the little fellow's spirits again, and he was soon all right.

Joe's father would often come in and give a little help, as he understood the work, and Joe took a great deal of pains to learn, and John was quite encouraged about him.

One night, a few days after James had left, I had eaten my hay and was lying down in my straw fast asleep when I was suddenly awakened by the stable bell ringing very loud. I heard the door of John's house open, and his feet running up to the Hall. He was back in no time; he unlocked the stable door and came in, calling out, "Wake up, Beauty, you must go well now, if ever you did"; and almost before I could think he had got the saddle on my back and the bridle on my head; he just ran round for his coat, and then took me at a quick trot up to the Hall door. The Squire stood there with a lamp in his hand.

"Now, John," he said, "ride for your life, that is, for your mistress' life; there is not a moment to lose; give this note to Doctor White; rest your horse at the inn and be back as soon as you can."

John said, "Yes, sir," and was on my back in a minute. The gardener who lived at the lodge had heard the bell ring, and was ready with the gate open, and away we went through the Park and through the village, and down the hill till we came to the tollgate. John called very loudly and thumped upon the door; the man was soon out and flung open the gate.

"Now," said John, "do you keep the gate open for the Doctor; here's the money," and off we went again.

There was before us a long piece of level road by the river side; John said to me, "Now, Beauty, do your best," and so I did; I wanted no whip nor spur, and for two miles I galloped as fast as I could lay my feet to the ground; I don't believe that my old grandfather who won the race at Newmarket could have gone faster. When we came to the bridge, John pulled me up a little and patted my neck. "Well done, Beauty! good old fellow," he said. He would have let me go slower, but my spirit was up, and I was off again as fast as before. The air was frosty, the moon was bright, it was very pleasant; we came through a village, then through a dark wood, then uphill, then downhill, till after eight miles' run we came to the town, through the streets and into the Market Place. It was all quite still except the clatter of my feet on the stones—everybody was asleep. The church clock struck three as we drew up at Doctor White's door. John rang the bell twice, and then knocked at the door like thunder. A window was thrown up, and Doctor White, in his nightcap, put his head out and said, "What do you want?"

"Mrs. Gordon is very ill, sir; master wants you to go at once, he thinks she will die if you cannot get there—here is a note."

"Wait," he said. "I will come."

He shut the window, and was soon at the door.

"The worst of it is," he said, "that my horse has been out all day and is quite done up; my son has just been sent for, and he has taken the other. What is to be done? Can I have your horse?"

"He has come at a gallop nearly all the way, sir, and I was to give him a rest here; but I think my master would not be against it if you think fit, sir."

"All right," he said, "I will soon be ready."

John stood by me and stroked my neck. I was very hot. The Doctor came out with his riding whip.

"You need not take that, sir," said John. "Black Beauty will go till he drops; take care of him, sir, if you can; I should not like any harm to come to him."

"No! no! John," said the Doctor, "I hope not," and in a minute we had left John far behind.

I will not tell about our way back; the Doctor was a heavier man than John, and not so good a rider; however, I did my very best. The man at the tollgate had it open. When we came to the hill, the Doctor drew me up. "Now, my good fellow," he said, "take some breath." I was glad he did, for I was nearly spent, but that breathing helped me on, and soon we were in the Park. Joe was at the lodge gate, my master was at the Hall door, for he had heard us coming. He spoke not a word; the Doctor went into the house with him, and Joe led me to the

stable. I was glad to get home, my legs shook under me, and I
could only stand and pant. I had not a dry hair on my body;
the water ran down my legs, and I steamed all over—Joe used
to say, like a pot on the fire. Poor Joe! he was young and small,
and as yet he knew very little, and his father, who would have
helped him, had been sent to the next village; but I am sure he
did the very best he knew. He rubbed my legs and my chest,
but he did not put my warm cloth on me; he thought I was so
hot I should not like it. Then he gave me a pail full of water to
drink; it was cold and very good, and I drank it all; then he

gave me some hay and some corn, and thinking he had done right he went away. Soon I began to shake and tremble, and turned deadly cold, my legs ached, my loins ached, and my chest ached, and I felt sore all over. Oh! how I wished for my warm, thick cloth as I stood and trembled. I wished for John, but he had eight miles to walk, so I lay down in my straw and tried to go to sleep. After a long while I heard John at the door; I gave a low moan, for I was in great pain. He was at my side in a moment, stooping down by me; I could not tell him how I felt; but he seemed to know it all; he covered me up with two or three warm cloths, and then ran to the house for some hot water; he made me some warm gruel, which I drank, and then I think I went to sleep.

John seemed to be very much put out. I heard him say to himself, over and over again, "Stupid boy! stupid boy! no cloth put on, and I dare say the water was cold, too; boys are no good," but Joe was a good boy after all.

I was now very ill; a strong inflammation had attacked my lungs and I could not draw my breath without pain. John nursed me night and day, he would get up two or three times in the night to come to me; my master, too, often came to see me. "My poor Beauty," he said one day, "my good horse, you saved your mistress' life, Beauty! Yes, you saved her life." I was very glad to hear that, for it seems the Doctor had said if we had been a little longer it would have been too late. John told my master he never saw a horse go so fast in his life, it seemed as if the horse knew what was the matter. Of course I did, though John thought not; at least, I knew as much as this, that John and I must go at the top of our speed, and that it was for the sake of the mistress.

I do not know how long I was ill. Mr. Bond, the horse doctor, came every day. One day he bled me; John held a pail for the blood; I felt very faint after it, and thought I should die, and I believe they all thought so, too.

Ginger and Merrylegs had been moved into the other stable, so that I might be quiet, for the fever made me very quick of hearing; any little noise seemed quite loud, and I could tell everyone's footstep going to and from the house. I knew all

that was going on. One night John had to give me a draught;
Thomas Green came in to help him. After I had taken it and
John had made me as comfortable as he could, he said he should
stay half an hour to see how the medicine settled. Thomas said
he would stay with him, so they went and sat on a bench that
had been brought into Merrylegs' stall, and put the lantern at
their feet that I might not be disturbed with the light.

For a while both men sat silent, and then Tom Green said in
a low voice: "I wish, John, you'd say a bit of a kind word to
Joe; the boy is quite brokenhearted, he can't eat his meals, and
he can't smile. He says he knows it was all his fault, though he
is sure he did the best he knew, and he says, if Beauty dies, no
one will ever speak to him again. It goes to my heart to hear
him. I think you might give him just a word; he is not a bad
boy."

After a short pause, John said slowly, "You must not be too
hard upon me, Tom. I know he meant no harm, I never said he
did; I know he is not a bad boy, but, you see, I am sore myself.
That horse is the pride of my heart, to say nothing of his being
such a favorite with the master and mistress; and to think that
his life may be flung away in this manner is more than I can
bear; but if you think I am hard on the boy I will try to give
him a good word tomorrow—that is, I mean, if Beauty is better."

"Well, John! thank you. I knew you did not wish to be too
hard, and I am glad you see it was only ignorance."

John's voice almost startled me as he answered, "*Only* ignorance; only *ignorance!* how can you talk about *only* ignorance?
Don't you know that it is the worst thing in the world, next to
wickedness?— and which does the most mischief Heaven only
knows. If people can say, 'Oh! I did not know, I did not mean
any harm,' they think it is all right. I suppose Martha Mul-
wash did not mean to kill that baby when she dosed it with
Dalby and soothing syrups; but she did kill it, and was tried for
manslaughter."

"And serve her right, too," said Tom. "A woman should not
undertake to nurse a tender little child without knowing what
is good and what is bad for it."

"Bill Starkey," continued John, "did not mean to frighten his brother into fits when he dressed up like a ghost and ran after him in the moonlight; but he did; and that bright, handsome little fellow, that might have been the pride of any mother's heart, is just no better than an idiot, and never will be, if he live to be eighty years old. You were a good deal cut up your-self, Tom, two weeks ago, when those young ladies left your hothouse door open, with a frosty east wind blowing right in; you said it killed a good many of your plants."

"A good many!" said Tom. "There was not one of the tender cuttings that was not nipped off; I shall have to strike all over again, and the worst of it is that I don't know where to go to get fresh ones. I was nearly mad when I came in and saw what was done."

"And yet," said John, "I am sure the young ladies did not mean it; it was only ignorance!"

I heard no more of this conversation, for the medicine did well and sent me to sleep, and in the morning I felt better; but I often thought of John's words when I came to know more of the world.

Joe Green went on very well; he learned quickly, and was so attentive and careful that John began to trust him in many things; but, as I have said, he was small of his age, and it was seldom that he was allowed to exercise either Ginger or me; but it so happened one morning that John was out with Justice in the luggage cart, and the master wanted a note to be taken immediately to a gentleman's house, about three miles distant, and sent his orders for Joe to saddle me and take it, adding the caution that he was to ride carefully.

The note was delivered, and we were quietly returning till we came to the brickfield. Here we saw a cart heavily laden with bricks; the wheels had stuck fast in the stiff mud of some deep ruts, and the carter was shouting and flogging the two horses unmercifully. Joe pulled up. It was a sad sight. There were the two horses straining and struggling with all their might to drag the cart out, but they could not move it; the sweat streamed from their legs and flanks, their sides heaved, and every muscle was strained, while the man, fiercely pulling at the head of the forehorse, swore and lashed most brutally.

"Hold hard," said Joe, "don't go on flogging the horses like that; the wheels are so stuck that they cannot move the cart." The man took no heed, but went on lashing.

"Stop! Pray stop," said Joe; "I'll help you to lighten the cart, they can't move it now."

"Mind your own business, you impudent young rascal, and I'll mind mine." The man was in a towering passion, and the worse for drink, and laid on the whip again. Joe turned my head, and the next moment we were going at a round gallop toward the house of the master brickmaker. I cannot say if John would have approved of our pace, but Joe and I were both of one mind, and so angry that we could not have gone slower.

The house stood close by the roadside. Joe knocked at the door and shouted, "Hulloa! is Mr. Clay at home?" The door was opened, and Mr. Clay himself came out.

"Hulloa! young man! you seem in a hurry; any orders from the squire this morning?"

"No, Mr. Clay, but there's a fellow in your brickyard flogging two horses to death. I told him to stop and he wouldn't; I said I'd help him to lighten the cart, and he wouldn't; so I have come to tell you; pray, sir, go." Joe's voice shook with excitement.

"Thank ye, my lad," said the man, running in for his hat; then pausing for a moment—"Will you give evidence of what you saw if I should bring the fellow up before a magistrate?"

"That I will," said Joe, "and glad, too." The man was gone, and we were on our way home at a smart trot.

"Why, what's the matter with you, Joe? You look angry all over," said John, as the boy flung himself from the saddle.

"I am angry all over, I can tell you," said the boy, and then in hurried, excited words he told all that had happened. Joe was usually such a quiet fellow that it was wonderful to see him so roused.

"Right, Joe! You did right, my boy, whether the fellow gets a summons or not. Many folks would have ridden by and said 'twas not their business to interfere. Now, I say that with cruelty and oppression it is everybody's business to interfere when they see it; you did right, my boy."

Joe was quite calm by this time, and proud that John approved of him, and he cleaned out my feet, and rubbed me down with a firmer hand than usual.

They were just going home to dinner when the footman came down to the stable to say that Joe was wanted directly in master's private room; there was a man brought up for ill-using horses, and Joe's evidence was wanted. The boy flushed up to his forehead, and his eyes sparkled. "They shall have it," said he.

"Put yourself a bit straight," said John. Joe gave a pull at his necktie and a twitch at his jacket, and was off in a moment. Our master being one of the county magistrates, cases were often brought to him to settle, or say what should be done. In the stable we heard no more for some time, as it was the men's dinner hour, but when Joe came next into the stable I saw he was in high spirits; he gave me a good-natured slap and said, "We won't see such things done, will we, old fellow?" We heard afterwards that he had given his evidence so clearly, and the horses were in such an exhausted state, bearing marks of such brutal usage, that the carter was committed to trial, and might possibly be sentenced to two or three months in prison.

It was wonderful what a change had come over Joe. John laughed and said he had grown an inch taller in that week, and I believe he had. He was just as kind and gentle as before, but there was more purpose and determination in all that he did—as if he had jumped at once from a boy into a man.

I had now lived in this happy place three years, but sad changes were about to come over us. We heard from time to time that our mistress was ill. The Doctor was often at the house, and the master looked grave and anxious. Then we heard that she must leave her home at once and go to a warm country for two or three years. The news fell on the household like the tolling of a death bell. Everybody was sorry; but the master began directly to make arrangements for breaking up his estab-lishment and leaving England. We used to hear it talked about in our stable; indeed, nothing else was talked about.

John went about his work silent and sad, and Joe scarcely whistled. There was a deal of coming and going; Ginger and I had full work.

The first of the party who went were Miss Jessie and Flora, with their governess. They came to bid us good-bye. They hugged poor Merrylegs like an old friend, and so, indeed, he was. Then we heard what had been arranged for us. Master had sold Ginger and me to his old friend, the Earl of W——, for he thought we should have a good place there. Merrylegs he had given to the Vicar, who was wanting a pony for Mrs. Blomefield, but it was on condition he should never be sold, and when he was past work he should be shot and buried.

Joe was engaged to take care of him and to help in the house, so I thought that Merrylegs was well off. John had the offer of several good places, but he said he should wait a little and look around.

The evening before they left, the master came into the stable to give some directions and to give his horses the last pat. He seemed very low-spirited; I knew that by his voice. I believe we horses can tell more by the voice than many men can.

"Have you decided what to do, John?" he said. "I find you have not accepted any of those offers."

"No, sir. I have made up my mind that if I could get a situation with some first-rate colt breaker and horse trainer that it would be the right thing for me. Many young animals are frightened and spoiled by wrong treatment, which need not be if the right man took them in hand. I always get on well with horses, and if I could help some of them to a fair start I should feel as if I was doing some good. What do you think of it, sir?"

"I don't know a man anywhere," said master, "that I should think so suitable for it. You understand horses, and somehow they understand you, and in time you might set up for yourself; I think you could not do better. If in any way I can help you, write me; I shall speak to my agent in London, and leave your character with him."

Master gave John the name and address, and then he thanked him for his long and faithful service; but that was too much for John. "Pray don't, sir, I can't bear it; you and my dear mistress have done so much for me that I could never repay it; but we shall never forget you, sir, and please God we may some day see mistress back again like herself; we must keep up hope, sir."

Master gave John his hand, but he did not speak, and they both left the stable.

The last sad day had come; the footman and the heavy luggage had gone off the day before, and there was only master and mistress and her maid. Ginger and I brought the carriage up to the Hall door for the last time. The servants brought out cushions and rugs and many other things, and when all were arranged master came down the steps carrying the mistress in his arms (I was on the side next the house and could see all that went on); he placed her carefully in the carriage, while the house servants stood round crying.

"Good-bye again," he said, "we shall not forget any of you," and he got in—"Drive on, John." Joe jumped up, and we trotted slowly through the Park and through the village where the people were standing at their doors to have a last look and to say, "God bless them."

When we reached the railway station, I think mistress walked from the carriage to the waiting room. I heard her say in her own sweet voice, "Good-bye, John, God bless you." I felt the rein twitch, but John made no answer, perhaps he could not speak. As soon as Joe had taken the things out of the carriage, John called him to stand by the horses, while he went on the platform. Poor Joe! he stood close up to our heads to hide his tears. Very soon the train came puffing up into the station; then two or three minutes, and the doors were slammed to; the guard whistled, and the train glided away, leaving behind it only clouds of white smoke, and some heavy hearts.

When it was quite out of sight, John came back."We shall never see her again," he said—"never." He took the reins, mounted the box, and with Joe drove slowly home; but it was not our home now.

Two more classic horse stories are National Velvet, *by Enid Bagnold, published by Morrow, William & Co., and* My Friend Flicka, *by Mary O'Hara, published by J. B. Lippincott Co.*

The Adventure
of the Blue Carbuncle

BY SIR ARTHUR CONAN DOYLE

Illustrations by Lewis Zacks

Perhaps the best-known and best-loved detective in all fiction, the indomitable Sherlock Holmes graciously shares his popularity with his friend and confidant Dr. Watson. These two gentlemen have many thrilling adventures in which they match wits with criminals, as in this tale, given in its entirety.

I HAD called upon my friend Sherlock Holmes upon the second morning after Christmas, with the intention of wishing him the compliments of the season. He was lounging upon the sofa in a purple dressing-gown, a pipe-rack within his reach upon the right, and a pile of crumpled morning papers, evidently newly studied, near at hand. Beside the coach was a wooden chair, and on the angle of the back hung a very seedy and disreputable hard-felt hat, much the worse for wear, and cracked in several places. A lens and a forceps lying upon the seat of the chair suggested that the hat had been suspended in this manner for the purpose of examination.

"You are engaged," said I; "perhaps I interrupted you."

"Not at all. I am glad to have a friend with whom I can discuss my results. The matter is a perfectly trivial one" (he jerked his thumb in the direction of the old hat), "but there are points in connection with it which are not entirely devoid of interest and even of instruction."

I seated myself in his arm-chair and warmed my hands before his crackling fire, for a sharp frost had set in, and the windows were thick with the ice crystals. "I suppose," I remarked, "that homely as it looks, this thing has some deadly story linked on to

From *The Adventures of Sherlock Holmes,* by Sir Arthur Conan Doyle.

it—that it is the clew which will guide you in the solution of some mystery and the punishment of some crime."

"No, no. No crime," said Sherlock Holmes, laughing. "Only one of those whimsical little incidents which will happen when you have four million human beings all jostling each other within the space of a few square miles. Amid the action and reaction of so dense a swarm of humanity, every possible combination of events may be expected to take place, and many a little problem will be presented which may be striking and bizarre without being criminal. We have already had experience of such."

"So much so," I remarked, "that of the last six cases which I have added to my notes, three have been entirely free of any legal crime."

"Precisely. You allude to my attempt to recover the Irene Adler papers, to the singular case of Miss Mary Sutherland, and to the adventure of the man with the twisted lip. Well, I have no doubt that this small matter will fall into the same innocent category. You know Peterson, the commissionaire?"

"Yes."

"It is to him that this trophy belongs."

"It is his hat."

"No, no; he found it. Its owner is unknown. I beg that you will look upon it, not as a battered billycock, but as an intellectual problem. And, first, as to how it came here. It arrived upon Christmas morning, in company with a good fat goose, which is, I have no doubt, roasting at this moment in front of Peterson's fire. The facts are these: about four o'clock on Christmas morning, Peterson, who, as you know, is a very honest fellow, was returning from some small jollification, and was making his way homeward down Tottenham Court Road. In front of him he saw, in the gaslight, a tallish man, walking with a slight stagger, and carrying a white goose slung over his shoulder. As he reached the corner of Goodge Street, a row broke out between this stranger and a little knot of roughs. One of the latter knocked off the man's hat, on which he raised his stick to defend himself, and, swinging it over his head, smashed the shop window behind him. Peterson had rushed forward to protect the stranger from his assailants; but the man, shocked at having broken the window, and seeing an official-looking person in uniform rushing towards him, dropped his goose, took to his heels, and vanished amid the labyrinth of small streets which lie at the back of Tottenham Court Road. The roughs had also fled at the appearance of Peterson, so that he was left in possession of the field of battle, and also of the spoils of victory in the shape of this battered hat and a most unimpeachable Christmas goose."

"Which surely he restored to their owner?"

"My dear fellow, there lies the problem. It is true that 'For Mrs. Henry Baker' was printed upon a small card which was tied to the bird's left leg, and it is also true that the initials 'H. B.' are legible upon the lining of this hat; but as there are some thousands of Bakers, and some hundreds of Henry Bakers in this city of ours, it is not easy to restore lost property to any one of them."

"What, then, did Peterson do?"

"He brought round both hat and goose to me on Christmas morning, knowing that even the smallest problems are of in-

terest to me. The goose we retained until this morning, when
there were signs that, in spite of the slight frost, it would be well
that it should be eaten without unnecessary delay. Its finder has
carried it off, therefore, to fulfil the ultimate destiny of a goose,
while I continue to retain the hat of the unknown gentleman
who lost his Christmas dinner."

"Did he not advertise?"

"No."

"Then, what clue could you have as to his identity?"

"Only as much as we can deduce."

"From his hat?"

"Precisely."

"But you are joking. What can you gather from this old battered felt?"

"Here is my lens. You know my methods. What can you gather
yourself as to the individuality of the man who has worn this
article?"

I took the tattered object in my hands and turned it over
rather ruefully. It was a very ordinary black hat of the usual
round shape, hard, and much the worse for wear. The lining had
been of red silk, but was a good deal discolored. There was no
maker's name; but, as Holmes had remarked, the initials "H. B."
were scrawled upon one side. It was pierced in the brim for a
hat-securer, but the elastic was missing. For the rest, it was
cracked, exceedingly dusty, and spotted in several places, although there seemed to have been some attempt to hide the
discolored patches by smearing them with ink.

"I can see nothing," said I, handing it back to my friend.

"On the contrary, Watson, you can see everything. You fail,
however, to reason from what you see. You are too timid in
drawing your inferences."

"Then, pray tell me what it is that you can infer from this hat?"

He picked it up and gazed at it in the peculiar introspective
fashion which was characteristic of him. "It is perhaps less
suggestive than it might have been," he remarked, "and yet
there are a few inferences which are very distinct, and a few
others which represent at least a strong balance of probability.
That the man was highly intellectual is of course obvious upon
the face of it, and also that he was fairly well-to-do within the

last three years, although he has now fallen upon evil days. He
had foresight, but has less now than formerly, pointing to a moral
retrogression, which, when taken with the decline of his fortunes, seems to indicate some evil influence, probably drink,
at work upon him. This may account also for the obvious fact
that his wife has ceased to love him."

"My dear Holmes!"

"He has, however, retained some degree of self-respect," he
continued, disregarding my remonstrance. "He is a man who
leads a sedentary life, goes out little, is out of training entirely,
is middle-aged, has grizzled hair which he has had cut within
the last few days, and which he anoints with lime-cream. These
are the more patent facts which are to be deduced from his
hat. Also, by-the-way, that it is extremely improbable that he
has gas laid on in his house."

"You are certainly joking, Holmes."

"Not in the least. Is it possible that even now, when I give you
these results, you are unable to see how they are attained?"

"I have no doubt that I am very stupid; but I must confess
that I am unable to follow you. For example, how did you deduce that this man was intellectual?"

For answer Holmes clapped the hat upon his head. It came
right over the forehead and settled upon the bridge of his nose.
"It is a question of cubic capacity," said he; "a man with so
large a brain must have something in it."

"The decline of his fortunes, then?"

"This hat is three years old. These flat brims curled at the
edge came in then. It is a hat of the very best quality. Look at
the band of ribbed silk and the excellent lining. If this man
could afford to buy so expensive a hat three years ago, and has
had no hat since, then he has assuredly gone down in the world."

"Well, that is clear enough, certainly. But how about the foresight and the moral retrogression?"

Sherlock Holmes laughed. "Here is the foresight," said he,
putting his finger upon the little disk and loop of the hat-securer.
"They are never sold upon hats. If this man ordered one, it is a
sign of a certain amount of foresight, since he went out of his
way to take this precaution against the wind. But since we see
that he has broken the elastic, and has not troubled to replace

it, it is obvious that he has less foresight now than formerly, which is a distinct proof of a weakening nature. On the other hand, he has endeavored to conceal some of these stains upon the felt by daubing them with ink, which is a sign that he has not entirely lost his self-respect."

"Your reasoning is certainly plausible."

"The further points, that he is middle-aged, that his hair is grizzled, that it has been recently cut, and that he uses lime-cream, are all to be gathered from a close examination of the lower part of the lining. The lens discloses a large number of hair-ends, clean cut by the scissors of the barber. They all appear to be adhesive, and there is a distinct odor of lime-cream. This dust, you will observe, is not the gritty, gray dust of the street, but the fluffy brown dust of the house, showing that it has been hung up in-doors most of the time; while the marks of moisture upon the inside are proof positive that the wearer perspired very freely, and could, therefore, hardly be in the best of training."

"But the wife—you said that she had ceased to love him."

"This hat has not been brushed for weeks. When I see you, my dear Watson, with a week's accumulation of dust upon your hat, and when your wife allows you to go out in such a state, I shall fear that you also have been unfortunate enough to lose your wife's affection."

"But he might be a bachelor."

"Nay, he was bringing home the goose as a peace-offering to his wife. Remember the card upon the bird's leg."

"You have an answer to everything. But how on earth do you deduce that the gas is not laid on in his house?"

"One tallow stain, or even two, might come by chance; but when I see no less than five, I think that there can be little doubt that the individual must be brought into frequent contact with burning tallow—walks up-stairs at night probably with his hat in one hand and a guttering candle in the other. Anyhow, he never got tallow-stains from a gas-jet. Are you satisfied?"

"Well, it is very ingenious," said I, laughing; "but since, as you said just now, there has been no crime committed, and no harm done, save the loss of a goose, all this seems to be rather a waste of energy."

Sherlock Holmes had opened his mouth to reply, when the door flew open, and Peterson, the commissionaire, rushed into the apartment with flushed cheeks and the face of a man who is dazed with astonishment.

"The goose, Mr. Holmes! The goose, sir!" he gasped.

"Eh? What of it, then? Has it returned to life and flapped off through the kitchen window?" Holmes twisted himself round upon the sofa to get a fairer view of the man's excited face.

"See here, sir! See what my wife found in its crop!" He held out his hand and displayed upon the centre of the palm a brilliantly scintillating blue stone, rather smaller than a bean in size, but of such purity and radiance that it twinkled like an electric point in the dark hollow of his hand.

Sherlock Holmes sat up with a whistle. "By Jove, Peterson!" said he, "this is treasure trove indeed. I suppose you know what you have got?"

"A diamond, sir? A precious stone. It cuts into glass as though it were putty."

"It's more than a precious stone. It is *the* precious stone."

"Not the Countess of Morcar's blue carbuncle!" I ejaculated.

"Precisely so. I ought to know its size and shape, seeing that I have read the advertisement about it in *The Times* every day lately. It is absolutely unique, and its value can only be conjectured, but the reward offered of £1000 is certainly not within a twentieth part of the market price."

"A thousand pounds! Great Lord of mercy!" The commissionaire plumped down into a chair, and stared from one to the other of us.

"That is the reward, and I have reason to know that there are sentimental considerations in the background which would induce the countess to part with half her fortune if she could but recover the gem."

"It was lost, if I remember aright, at the 'Hotel Cosmopolitan,'" I remarked.

"Precisely so, on December 22d, just five days ago. John Horner, a plumber, was accused of having abstracted it from the lady's jewel-case. The evidence against him was so strong that the case has been referred to the Assizes. I have some account of the matter here, I believe." He rummaged amid his newspapers, glancing over the dates, until at last he smoothed one out, doubled it over, and read the following paragraph:

" 'Hotel Cosmopolitan Jewel Robbery. John Horner, 26, plumber, was brought up upon the charge of having upon the 22d inst. abstracted from the jewel-case of the Countess of Morcar the valuable gem known as the blue carbuncle. James Ryder, upper-attendant at the hotel, gave his evidence to the effect that he had shown Horner up to the dressing-room of the Countess of Morcar upon the day of the robbery, in order that he might solder the second bar of the grate, which was loose. He had remained with Horner some little time, but had finally been called away. On returning, he found that Horner had disappeared, that the bureau had been forced open, and that the small morocco casket in which, as it afterwards transpired, the countess was accustomed to keep her jewel, was lying empty upon the dressing-table. Ryder instantly gave the alarm, and Horner was arrested the same evening; but the stone could not be found either upon his person or in his rooms. Catherine Cusack, maid to the countess, deposed to have heard Ryder's cry of dismay on discovering the robbery, and to have rushed into the room, where she found matters as described by the last witness. Inspector Bradstreet, B division, gave evidence as to the arrest of Horner, who struggled frantically, and protested his innocence in the strongest terms. Evidence of a previous conviction for robbery having been given against the prisoner, the magistrate refused to deal summarily with the offence, but referred it to the Assizes. Horner, who had shown signs of intense emotion during the proceedings, fainted away at the conclusion, and was carried out of court.'

"Hum! So much for the police-court," said Holmes, thoughtfully, tossing aside the paper. "The question for us now to solve is the sequence of events leading from a rifled jewel-case at one end to the crop of a goose in Tottenham Court Road at the other. You see, Watson, our little deductions have suddenly assumed a much more important and less innocent aspect. Here is the stone; the stone came from the goose, and the goose came from Mr. Henry Baker, the gentleman with the bad hat and all the other characteristics with which I have bored you. So now we must set ourselves very seriously to finding this gentleman, and ascertaining what part he played in this little mystery. To do this, we must try the simplest means first, and these lie undoubtedly in an advertisement in all the evening papers. If this fail, I shall have recourse to other methods."

"What will you say?"

"Give me a pencil and that slip of paper. Now, then: 'Found at the corner of Goodge Street, a goose and a black felt hat. Mr. Henry Baker can have the same by applying at 6.30 this evening at 221B, Baker Street.' That is clear and concise."

"Very. But will he see it?"

"Well, he is sure to keep an eye on the papers, since, to a poor man, the loss was a heavy one. He was clearly so scared by his mischance in breaking the window and by the approach of Peterson, that he thought of nothing but flight; but since then he must have bitterly regretted the impulse which caused him to drop his bird. Then, again, the introduction of his name will cause him to see it, for every one who knows him will direct his attention to it. Here you are, Peterson, run down to the advertising agency, and have this put in the evening papers."

"In which, sir?"

"Oh, in the *Globe, Star, Pall Mall, St. James's, Evening News, Standard, Echo,* and any others that occur to you."

"Very well, sir. And this stone?"

"Ah, yes, I shall keep the stone. Thank you. And, I say, Peterson, just buy a goose on your way back, and leave it here with me, for we must have one to give to this gentleman in place of the one which your family is now devouring."

When the commissionaire had gone, Holmes took up the stone and held it against the light. "It's a bonny thing," said he. "Just see how it glints and sparkles. Of course it is a nucleus and focus of crime. Every good stone is. They are the devil's pet baits. In the larger and older jewels every facet may stand for a bloody deed. This stone is not yet twenty years old. It was found in the banks of the Amoy River in Southern China, and is remarkable in having every characteristic of the carbuncle, save that it is blue in shade, instead of ruby red. In spite of its youth, it has already a sinister history. There have been two murders, a vitriol-throwing, a suicide, and several robberies brought about for the sake of this forty-grain weight of crystallized charcoal.

Who would think that so pretty a toy would be a purveyor to the gallows and the prison? I'll lock it up in my strong box now, and drop a line to the countess to say that we have it."

"Do you think that this man Horner is innocent?"

"I cannot tell."

"Well, then, do you imagine that this other one, Henry Baker, had anything to do with the matter?"

"It is, I think, much more likely that Henry Baker is an absolutely innocent man, who had no idea that the bird which he was carrying was of considerably more value than if it were made of solid gold. That, however, I shall determine by a very simple test, if we have an answer to our advertisement."

"And you can do nothing until then?"

"Nothing."

"In that case I shall continue my professional round. But I shall come back in the evening at the hour you have mentioned, for I should like to see the solution of so tangled a business."

"Very glad to see you. I dine at seven. There is a woodcock, I believe. By-the-way, in view of recent occurrences, perhaps I ought to ask Mrs. Hudson to examine its crop."

I had been delayed at a case, and it was a little after half-past six when I found myself in Baker Street once more. As I approached the house I saw a tall man in a Scotch bonnet with a coat which was buttoned up to his chin, waiting outside in the bright semicircle which was thrown from the fanlight. Just as I arrived, the door was opened, and we were shown up together to Holmes's room.

"Mr. Henry Baker, I believe," said he, rising from his armchair, and greeting his visitor with the easy air of geniality which he could so readily assume. "Pray take this chair by the fire, Mr. Baker. It is a cold night, and I observe that your circulation is more adapted for summer than for winter. Ah, Watson, you have just come at the right time. Is that your hat, Mr. Baker?"

"Yes, sir, that is undoubtedly my hat."

He was a large man, with rounded shoulders, a massive head, and a broad, intelligent face, sloping down to a pointed beard of grizzled brown. A touch of red in nose and cheeks, with a slight tremor of his extended hand, recalled Holmes's surmise as to his habits. His rusty black frock-coat was buttoned right up in front, with the collar turned up, and his lank wrists protruded from his sleeves without a sign of cuff or shirt. He spoke in a slow staccato fashion, choosing his words with care, and gave the impression generally of a man of learning and letters who had had ill-usage at the hands of fortune.

"We have retained these things for some days," said Holmes, "because we expected to see an advertisement from you giving your address. I am at a loss to know now why you did not advertise."

Our visitor gave a rather shamefaced laugh. "Shillings have not been so plentiful with me as they once were," he remarked. "I had no doubt that the gang of roughs who assaulted me had carried off both my hat and the bird. I did not care to spend more money in a hopeless attempt at recovering them."

"Very naturally. By-the-way, about the bird, we were compelled to eat it."

"To eat it!" Our visitor half rose from his chair in his excitement.

"Yes, it would have been of no use to any one had we not done so. But I presume that this other goose upon the sideboard, which is about the same weight and perfectly fresh, will answer your purpose equally well?"

"Oh, certainly, certainly," answered Mr. Baker, with a sigh of relief.

"Of course, we still have the feathers, legs, crop, and so on of your own bird, so if you wish—"

The man burst into a hearty laugh. "They might be useful to me as relics of my adventure," said he, "but beyond that I can hardly see what use the *disjecta membra* of my late acquaintance are going to be to me. No, sir, I think that, with your permission, I will confine my attentions to the excellent bird which I perceive upon the sideboard."

Sherlock Holmes glanced sharply across at me with a slight shrug of his shoulders.

"There is your hat, then, and there your bird," said he. "By-the-way, would it bore you to tell me where you got the other one from? I am somewhat of a fowl fancier, and I have seldom seen a better grown goose."

"Certainly, sir," said Baker, who had risen and tucked his newly-gained property under his arm. "There are a few of us who frequent the 'Alpha Inn,' near the Museum—we are to be found in the Museum itself during the day, you understand. This year our good host, Windigate by name, instituted a goose club, by which, on consideration of some few pence every week, we were each to receive a bird at Christmas. My pence were duly paid, and the rest is familiar to you. I am much indebted to you, sir, for a Scotch bonnet is fitted neither to my years nor my gravity." With a comical pomposity of manner he bowed solemnly to both of us and strode off upon his way.

"So much for Mr. Henry Baker," said Holmes, when he had closed the door behind him. "It is quite certain that he knows nothing whatever about the matter. Are you hungry, Watson?"

"Not particularly."

"Then I suggest that we turn our dinner into a supper, and follow up this clew while it is still hot."

"By all means."

It was a bitter night, so we drew on our ulsters and wrapped cravats about our throats. Outside, the stars were shining coldly in a cloudless sky, and the breath of the passers-by blew out into smoke like so many pistol shots. Our footfalls rang out crisply and loudly as we swung through the Doctors' quarter, Wimpole Street, Harley Street, and so through Wigmore Street into Oxford Street. In a quarter of an hour we were in Bloomsbury at the "Alpha Inn," which is a small public-house at the corner of one of the streets which runs down into Holborn. Holmes pushed open the door of the private bar, and ordered two glasses of beer from the ruddy-faced, white-aproned landlord.

"Your beer should be excellent if it is as good as your geese," said he.

"My geese!" The man seemed surprised.

"Yes. I was speaking only half an hour ago to Mr. Henry Baker, who was a member of your goose club."

"Ah! yes, I see. But you see, sir, them's not *our* geese."

"Indeed! Whose, then?"

"Well, I got the two dozen from a salesman in Covent Garden."

"Indeed? I know some of them. Which was it?"

"Breckinridge is his name."

"Ah! I don't know him. Well, here's your good health, landlord, and prosperity to your house. Good-night."

"Now for Mr. Breckinridge," he continued, buttoning up his coat, as we came out into the frosty air. "Remember, Watson, that though we have so homely a thing as a goose at one end of this chain, we have at the other a man who will certainly get seven years' penal servitude unless we can establish his innocence. It is possible that our inquiry may but confirm his guilt; but, in any case, we have a line of investigation which has been missed by the police, and which a singular chance has placed in our hands. Let us follow it out to the bitter end. Faces to the south, then, and quick march!"

We passed across Holborn, down Endell Street, and so through a zigzag of slums to Covent Garden Market. One of the largest stalls bore the name of Breckinridge upon it, and the proprietor, a horsey-looking man, with a sharp face and trim side whiskers, was helping a boy to put up the shutters.

"Good-evening. It's a cold night," said Holmes.

The salesman nodded, and shot a questioning glance at my companion.

"Sold out of geese, I see," continued Holmes, pointing at the bare slabs of marble.

"Let you have 500 to-morrow morning."

"That's no good."

"Well, there are some on the stall with the gas-flare."

"Ah, but I was recommended to you."

"Who by?"

"The landlord of the 'Alpha.'"

"Oh, yes; I sent him a couple of dozen."

"Fine birds they were, too. Now where did you get them from?"

To my surprise the question provoked a burst of anger from the salesman.

"Now, then, mister," said he, with his head cocked and his arms akimbo, "what are you driving at? Let's have it straight, now."

"It is straight enough. I should like to know who sold you the geese which you supplied to the 'Alpha.'"

"Well, then, I sha'n't tell you. So now!"

"Oh, it is a matter of no importance; but I don't know why you should be so warm over such a trifle."

"Warm! You'd be as warm, maybe, if you were as pestered as I am. When I pay good money for a good article there should be an end of the business; but it's 'Where are the geese?' and 'Who did you sell the geese to?' and 'What will you take for the geese?' One would think they were the only geese in the world, to hear the fuss that is made over them."

"Well, I have no connection with any other people who have been making inquiries," said Holmes, carelessly. "If you won't tell us the bet is off, that is all. But I'm always ready to back my opinion on a matter of fowls, and I have a fiver on it that the bird I ate is country bred."

"Well, then, you've lost your fiver, for it's town bred," snapped the salesman.

"It's nothing of the kind."

"I say it is."

"I don't believe it."

"D'you think you know more about fowls than I, who have handled them ever since I was a nipper? I tell you, all those birds that went to the 'Alpha' were town bred."

"You'll never persuade me to believe that."

"Will you bet, then?"

"It's merely taking your money, for I know that I am right. But I'll have a sovereign on with you, just to teach you not to be obstinate."

The salesman chuckled grimly. "Bring me the books, Bill," said he.

The small boy brought round a small thin volume and a great greasy-backed one, laying them out together beneath the hanging lamp.

"Now then, Mr. Cocksure," said the salesman, "I thought that I was out of geese, but before I finish you'll find that there is still one left in my shop. You see this little book?"

"Well?"

"That's the list of the folk from whom I buy. D'you see? Well, then, here on this page are the country folk, and the numbers after their names are where their accounts are in the big ledger. Now, then! You see this other page in red ink? Well, that is a list of my town suppliers. Now, look at that third name. Just read it out to me."

"Mrs. Oakshott, 117, Brixton Road—249," read Holmes.

"Quite so. Now turn that up in the ledger."

Holmes turned to the page indicated. "Here you are, 'Mrs. Oakshott, 117, Brixton Road, egg and poultry supplier.'"

"Now, then, what's the last entry?"

" 'December 22. Twenty-four geese at 7s. 6d.' "

"Quite so. There you are. And underneath?"

" 'Sold to Mr. Windigate of the "Alpha" at 12s.' "

"What have you to say now?"

Sherlock Holmes looked deeply chagrined. He drew a sovereign from his pocket and threw it down upon the slab, turning away with the air of a man whose disgust is too deep for words. A few yards off he stopped under a lamp-post, and laughed in the hearty, noiseless fashion which was peculiar to him.

"When you see a man with whiskers of that cut and the 'pink 'un' protruding out of his pocket, you can always draw him by a bet," said he. "I dare say that if I had put £100 down in front of him, that man would not have given me such complete information as was drawn from him by the idea that he was doing me on a wager. Well, Watson, we are, I fancy, nearing the end of our

quest, and the only point which remains to be determined is whether we should go on to this Mrs. Oakshott to-night, or whether we should reserve it for to-morrow. It is clear from what that surly fellow said that there are others besides ourselves who are anxious about the matter, and I should—"

His remarks were suddenly cut short by a loud hubbub which broke out from the stall which we had just left. Turning round we saw a little rat-faced fellow standing in the centre of the circle of yellow light which was thrown by the swinging lamp, while Breckinridge the salesman, framed in the door of his stall, was shaking his fists fiercely at the cringing figure.

"I've had enough of you and your geese," he shouted. "I wish you were all at the devil together. If you come pestering me any more with your silly talk I'll set the dog at you. You bring Mrs. Oakshott here and I'll answer her, but what have you to do with it? Did I buy the geese off you?"

"No; but one of them was mine all the same," whined the little man.

"Well, then, ask Mrs. Oakshott for it."

"She told me to ask you."

"Well, you can ask the King of Proosia, for all I care. I've had enough of it. Get out of this!" He rushed fiercely forward, and the inquirer flitted away into the darkness.

"Ha! this may save us a visit to Brixton Road," whispered Holmes. "Come with me, and we will see what is to be made of this fellow." Striding through the scattered knots of people who lounged round the flaring stalls, my companion speedily overtook the little man and touched him upon the shoulder. He sprang round, and I could see in the gaslight that every vestige of color had been driven from his face.

"Who are you, then? What do you want?" he asked, in a quavering voice.

"You will excuse me," said Holmes, blandly, "but I could not help overhearing the questions which you put to the salesman just now. I think that I could be of assistance to you."

"You? Who are you? How could you know anything of the matter?"

"My name is Sherlock Holmes. It is my business to know what other people don't know."

"But you can know nothing of this?"

"Excuse me, I know everything of it. You are endeavoring to trace some geese which were sold by Mrs. Oakshott, of Brixton Road, to a salesman named Breckinridge, by him in turn to Mr. Windigate, of the 'Alpha,' and by him to his club, of which Mr. Henry Baker is a member."

"Oh, sir, you are the very man whom I have longed to meet," cried the little fellow, with outstretched hands and quivering fingers. "I can hardly explain to you how interested I am in this matter."

Sherlock Holmes hailed a four-wheeler which was passing. "In that case we had better discuss it in a cosey room rather than in this windswept market-place," said he. "But pray tell me, before we go farther, who it is that I have the pleasure of assisting."

The man hesitated for an instant. "My name is John Robinson," he answered, with a sidelong glance.

"No, no; the real name," said Holmes, sweetly. "It is always awkward doing business with an *alias*."

A flush sprang to the white cheeks of the stranger. "Well, then," said he, "my real name is James Ryder."

"Precisely so. Head attendant at the 'Hotel Cosmopolitan.' Pray step into the cab, and I shall soon be able to tell you everything which you would wish to know."

The little man stood glancing from one to the other of us with half-frightened, half-hopeful eyes, as one who is not sure whether he is on the verge of a windfall or of a catastrophe. Then he stepped into the cab, and in half an hour we were back in the sitting-room at Baker Street. Nothing had been said during our drive, but the high, thin breathing of our new companion, and the clasping and unclasping of his hands, spoke of the nervous tension within him.

"Here we are!" said Holmes, cheerily, as we filed into the room. "The fire looks very seasonable in this weather. You look cold, Mr. Ryder. Pray take the basket-chair. I will just put on my slippers before we settle this little matter of yours. Now, then! You want to know what became of those geese?"

"Yes, sir."

"Or rather, I fancy, of that goose. It was one bird, I imagine, in which you were interested—white, with a black bar across the tail."

Ryder quivered with emotion. "Oh, sir," he said, "can you tell me where it went to?"

"It came here."

"Here?"

"Yes, and a most remarkable bird it proved. I don't wonder that you should take an interest in it. It laid an egg after it was dead—the bonniest, brightest little blue egg that ever was seen. I have it here in my museum."

Our visitor staggered to his feet and clutched the mantelpiece with his right hand. Holmes unlocked his strong-box, and held up the blue carbuncle, which shone out like a star, with a cold, brilliant, many-pointed radiance. Ryder stood glaring with a drawn face, uncertain whether to claim or to disown it.

"The game's up, Ryder," said Holmes, quietly. "Hold up, man, or you'll be into the fire! Give him an arm back into his chair, Watson. He's not got blood enough to go in for felony with impunity. Give him a dash of brandy. So! Now he looks a little more human. What a shrimp it is, to be sure!"

For a moment he had staggered and nearly fallen, but the brandy brought a tinge of color into his cheeks, and he sat staring with frightened eyes at his accuser.

"I have almost every link in my hands, and all the proofs which I could possibly need, so there is little which you need tell me. Still, that little may as well be cleared up to make the case complete. You had heard, Ryder, of this blue stone of the Countess of Morcar's?"

"It was Catherine Cusack who told me of it," said he, in a crackling voice.

"I see—her ladyship's waiting-maid. Well, the temptation of sudden wealth so easily acquired was too much for you, as it has been for better men before you; but you were not very scrupulous in the means you used. It seems to me, Ryder, that there is the making of a very pretty villain in you. You knew that this man Horner, the plumber, had been concerned in some such matter before, and that suspicion would rest the more readily upon him. What did you do, then? You made some small job in my lady's room—you and your confederate Cusack—and you managed that he should be the man sent for. Then, when he had left, you rifled the jewel-case, raised the alarm, and had this unfortunate man arrested. You then—"

Ryder threw himself down suddenly upon the rug and clutched at my companion's knees. "For God's sake, have mercy!" he shrieked. "Think of my father! of my mother! It would break their hearts. I never went wrong before! I never will again. I swear it. I'll swear it on a Bible. Oh, don't bring it into court! For Christ's sake, don't!"

"Get back into your chair!" said Holmes, sternly. "It is very well to cringe and crawl now, but you thought little enough of this poor Horner in the dock for a crime of which he knew nothing."

"I will fly, Mr. Holmes. I will leave the country, sir. Then the charge against him will break down."

"Hum! We will talk about that. And now let us hear a true account of the next act. How came the stone into the goose, and how came the goose into the open market? Tell us the truth, for there lies your only hope of safety."

Ryder passed his tongue over his parched lips. "I will tell you

it just as it happened, sir," said he. "When Horner had been
arrested, it seemed to me that it would be best for me to get
away with the stone at once, for I did not know at what moment
the police might not take it into their heads to search me and my
room. There was no place about the hotel where it would be
safe. I went out, as if on some commission, and I made for my
sister's house. She had married a man named Oakshott, and
lived in Brixton Road, where she fattened fowls for the market.
All the way there every man I met seemed to me to be a policeman or a detective; and, for all that it was a cold night, the
sweat was pouring down my face before I came to the Brixton
Road. My sister asked me what was the matter, and why I was
so pale; but I told her that I had been upset by the jewel robbery
at the hotel. Then I went into the back yard and smoked a pipe,
and wondered what it would be best to do.

"I had a friend once called Maudsley, who went to the bad,
and has just been serving his time in Pentonville. One day he
had met me, and fell into talk about the ways of thieves, and
how they could get rid of what they stole. I knew that he would
be true to me, for I knew one or two things about him; so I made
up my mind to go right on to Kilburn, where he lived, and take
him into my confidence. He would show me how to turn the
stone into money. But how to get to him in safety? I thought of
the agonies I had gone through in coming from the hotel. I
might at any moment be seized and searched, and there would
be the stone in my waistcoat pocket. I was leaning against the
wall at the time, and looking at the geese which were waddling
about round my feet, and suddenly an idea came into my head
which showed me how I could beat the best detective that ever
lived.

"My sister had told me some weeks before that I might have
the pick of her geese for a Christmas present, and I knew that
she was always as good as her word. I would take my goose now,
and in it I would carry my stone to Kilburn. There was a little
shed in the yard, and behind this I drove one of the birds—a
fine big one, white, with a barred tail. I caught it, and, prying
its bill open, I thrust the stone down its throat as far as my finger
could reach. The bird gave a gulp, and I felt the stone pass
along its gullet and down into its crop. But the creature flapped

and struggled, and out came my sister to know what was the matter. As I turned to speak to her the brute broke loose and fluttered off among the others.

" 'Whatever were you doing with that bird, Jem?' says she.

" 'Well,' said I, 'you said you'd give me one for Christmas, and I was feeling which was the fattest.'

" 'Oh,' says she, 'we've set yours aside for you—Jem's bird, we call it. It's the big white one over yonder. There's twenty-six of them, which makes one for you, and one for us, and two dozen for the market.'

" 'Thank you, Maggie,' says I; 'but if it is all the same to you, I'd rather have that one I was handling just now.'

" 'The other is a good three pound heavier,' said she, 'and we fattened it expressly for you.'

" 'Never mind. I'll have the other, and I'll take it now,' said I.

" 'Oh, just as you like,' said she, a little huffed. 'Which is it you want, then?'

" 'That white one with barred tail, right in the middle of the flock.'

" 'Oh, very well. Kill it and take it with you.'

"Well, I did what she said, Mr. Holmes, and I carried the bird all the way to Kilburn. I told my pal what I had done, for he was a man that it was easy to tell a thing like that to. He laughed until he choked, and we got a knife and opened the goose. My heart turned to water, for there was no sign of the stone, and I knew that some terrible mistake had occurred. I left the bird, rushed back to my sister's and hurried into the back yard. There was not a bird to be seen there.

" 'Where are they all, Maggie?' I cried.

" 'Gone to the dealer's, Jem.'

" 'Which dealer's?'

" 'Breckinridge, of Covent Garden.'

" 'But was there another with a barred tail?' I asked, 'the same as the one I chose?'

" 'Yes, Jem; there were two barred-tailed ones, and I could never tell them apart.'

"Well, then, of course I saw it all, and I ran off as hard as my feet would carry me to this man Breckinridge; but he had sold the lot at once, and not one word would he tell me as to where they had gone. You heard him yourselves to-night. Well, he has always answered me like that. My sister thinks that I am going mad. Sometimes I think that I am myself. And now—and now I am myself a branded thief, without ever having touched the wealth for which I sold my character. God help me! God help me!" He burst into convulsive sobbing, with his face in his hands.

There was a long silence, broken only by his heavy breathing, and by the measured tapping of Sherlock Holmes's finger-tips upon the edge of the table. Then my friend rose and threw open the door.

"Get out!" said he.

"What, sir! Oh, heaven bless you!"

"No more words. Get out!"

And no more words were needed. There was a rush, a clatter upon the stairs, the bang of a door, and the crisp rattle of running footfalls from the street.

"After all, Watson," said Holmes, reaching up his hand for his clay pipe, "I am not retained by the police to supply their deficiencies. If Horner were in danger it would be another thing; but this fellow will not appear against him, and the case must collapse. I suppose that I am commuting a felony, but it is just possible that I am saving a soul. This fellow will not go wrong again; he is too terribly frightened. Send him to jail now, and you make him a jail-bird for life. Besides, it is the season of forgiveness. Chance has put in our way a most singular and whimsical problem, and its solution is its own reward. If you will have the goodness to touch the bell, doctor, we will begin another investigation, in which, also, a bird will be the chief feature."

Sir Arthur Conan Doyle's Sherlock Holmes stories appeared separately over the years 1887 to 1905. Attractive modern editions include The Boys' Sherlock Holmes: A Selection from the Works of A. Conan Doyle, *arranged by Howard Haycraft, published by Harper; and* Sherlock Holmes: The Complete Adventures, *published by both Dial and Heritage.*

Call It Courage

BY ARMSTRONG SPERRY

Illustrations by the author

> Rather than cringe in the face of his terrible
> fear of the sea, Mafatu, son of a Polynesian
> chief, decides to conquer his weakness. With
> only his dog Uri for companionship, the boy
> sets out in a small boat. For a while, Kivi the
> albatross seems to guide the little craft.

DAY broke over a gray and dismal world. The canoe lifted
and fell idly on the glassy swells. Mafatu looked back over his
shoulder, searching the horizon for a last glimpse of Hikueru;
but the atoll had vanished, as if to hide itself forever from his
concern.

The matting sail slatted uselessly. But there seemed to be
no need of a sail: the little canoe was riding one of the mysterious ocean currents that flow in their courses through the
length and breadth of the Pacific: the *Ara Moana,* Paths of the
Sea, as the Ancients called them. They were the ocean currents
that had carried the Polynesian navigators from island to island
in the childhood of the world. Mafatu was drifting farther and
farther away from his homeland.

With wide-flapping wings Kivi rose from the bow of the
canoe. In ascending spirals the bird climbed higher and higher,
until at last he was no more than a gray speck against the
lighter gray of the sky. Mafatu watched his albatross disappear
and felt a desolation flood his heart. Now there was only Uri
to keep him company in this hostile world of sky and sea. Uri.
. . . The yellow dog lay curled up in the shadow of the bow,
opening one eye from time to time to look at his master.
Wherever Mafatu went, Uri, too, would go.

All around, as far as the eye could reach, were wastes of leaden water. The canoe was the moving center of a limitless circle of sea. The boy shuddered. His fingers gripped the paddle convulsively. He thought of Kana and the other boys—what would they say when they learned that he had disappeared? And Tavana Nui—would there be sorrow in his father's heart? Would he believe that Moana, the Sea God, had claimed his son at last?

It was an ominous, oppressive world at this season of storm. Half a mile distant a whale heaved its varnished hulk to the surface, to throw a jet of vapory mist high into the air; then it submerged, leaving scarcely a ripple to mark its passage. A shoal of flying fishes broke water, skimming away in a silver shimmer of flight. A dolphin sped after them, smooth-rolling in pursuit, so close that the boy could hear the sound of its breathing. This world of the sea was ruled by Nature's harsh law of survival. Mafatu knew the sea with an intimacy given to few. He had seen fleets of giant mantas whipping the lagoon of Hikueru to a boiling fury; he had seen the mighty cachalot set upon by killer-whales and torn to ribbons almost in the blink of an eye; once he had seen an octopus as large as the trunk of a tamanu, with tentacles thirty feet long, rise from the mile-deep water beyond the barrier-reef. . . . *Ai*, this sea!

Mafatu opened one of the green drinking nuts and tilted back his head to let the cool liquid trickle down his parched throat; more refreshing than spring water, cool on the hottest days, and as sustaining as food. The boy scooped out the gelatinous meat for Uri and the dog ate it gratefully.

The ocean current which held the canoe in its grip seemed to have quickened. There was a wind rising, too, in little puffs and gusts. Now the canoe heeled over under the sudden attack, while Mafatu scrambled onto the outrigger to lend his weight for ballast; then the wind dropped as suddenly as it appeared, while the canoe righted itself and the boy breathed freely once again. He searched the skies for Kivi. His albatross might have been one of a thousand sea birds flying against the roof of the sky, or he might have vanished utterly, leaving his friends here in solitary space. The bird had led Mafatu out through the reef-passage at Hikueru into the open ocean, and now, it seemed, had deserted him.

A storm was making, moving in out of those mysterious belts which lie north and south of the equator, the home of hurricanes. The wind shifted a point, bringing with it a heavy squall. Mafatu lowered the sail on the run and gripped the steering paddle with hands that showed white at the knuckles. All

around him now was a world of tumbling water, gray in the hollows, greenish on the slopes. The wind tore off the combing crests and flung the spray at the sky. Like advance scouts of an oncoming army, wind gusts moved down upon the canoe, struck at it savagely. So busy was Mafatu with the paddle that there was no time for thought. He called a prayer to Maui, God of the Fishermen:

"*Maui é! E matai tu!*"

Somehow the sound of his own voice reassured him. Uri lifted his head, cocked his ears, thumped his tail for a second. The canoe rose to the swells as lightly as a gull and coasted like a sled down the frothing slopes. What skill had wrought this small canoe! This dugout, hewn from the mighty tamanu tree. It swooped and yielded, bucked and scudded, one with the fierce element whose back it rode.

The sky darkened. A burst of lightning lit up the sea with supernatural brilliance. An instantaneous crack of thunder shattered the world. Lightning again, striking at the hissing water. Mafatu watched it with fascinated eyes. Now it was all about him. It ran to the end of the boom in globes of fire that exploded and vanished, and in the awful moment of its being it revealed mountain shapes of dark water, heaving, shouldering.

. . . . How long could this frail craft of wood and sennit resist? Under the combined attack of wind and sea it seemed that something must inevitably give way. The wind shrilled a fiercer note. Spray stung the boy's flesh, blinded his eyes, chilled his marrow.

The sail went first—with a split and a roar. Fragments swept off on the back of the wind. The cords that held the mast hummed like plucked wires. Then with a rending groan the mast cracked. Before Mafatu could leap to cut it clear, it

snapped off and disappeared in a churn of black water. The
boy clung to the paddle, fighting to keep his canoe from turning
broadside. Water swept aboard and out again. Only the buoy-
ancy of tamanu kept the craft afloat. Uri cowered in the bow,
half submerged, his howls drowned by the roar of the elements.
Mafatu gripped his paddle for very life, an unreasoning terror
powering his arms. This sea that he had always feared was
rising to claim him, just as it had claimed his mother. How
rightly he had feared it! Moana, the Sea God, had been biding
his time. . . . "Someday, Mafatu, I will claim you!"

The boy lost all sense of time's passage. Every nerve became
dulled by tumult. The wind howled above his head and still
Mafatu clung to the lashed steering paddle; clung fast long after
strength had vanished and only the will to live locked his strong
fingers about the shaft. Even death would not loose the grip
of those fingers. He held his little craft true to the wind.

There was a wave lifting before the canoe. Many the boy
had seen, but this was a giant—a monster livid and hungry.
Higher, higher it rose, until it seemed that it must scrape at
the low-hanging clouds. Its crest heaved over with a vast sigh.
The boy saw it coming. He tried to cry out. No sound issued
from his throat. Suddenly the wave was upon him. Down it
crashed. *Chaos!* Mafatu felt the paddle torn from his hands.
Thunder in his ears. Water strangling him. Terror in his soul.
The canoe slewed round into the trough. The boy flung himself
forward, wound his arms about the mid-thwart. It was the end
of a world.

The wave passed. Stunned, gasping, Mafatu raised his head
and looked about. For a second he could not believe that he
still breathed and had being. He saw Uri wedged under the
bow, choking for air. He pulled the dog free. Then he saw
that his string of drinking nuts had vanished. His fish spear
was gone. The knife that hung about his neck by a twist of
bark had been torn away. Even his *pareu* of fiber tapa fell from
his body as water soaked it through. He was naked, defenseless,
without food or weapon, hurled forward on the breath of the
hurricane. Numb of all feeling, empty as a shell, still he clung
to life, and the hours droned by. . . .

So gradual was the storm's easing that at first the boy was

unaware of it. The wind was blowing itself out, moving off into the empty spaces of the world. Uri crept toward the prostrate boy, quailing beside him, whimpering softly.

Night came and passed.

There was no morning mist to dim the splendor of the sun-burst across the swinging seas. Far away the wings of an albatross caught its gold as it wheeled and planed against the roof of heaven. The only hint of recent storm lay in the rough and tumbling waters. As the sun climbed through the hot hours of morning, it burned into the boy's body like the sacred fires of the great marae of Hikueru. Mafatu's skin blistered and cracked. His tongue swelled in his throat. He tried to call out a prayer to Maui, but his voice was thick; the sounds which came forth were no more than a hoarse cry. The canoe, stripped of sail and mast, without a paddle to guide it in the swift-racing current, twisted and shifted in the rushing waters.

As one hour merged into another there came moments of fitful, choking slumber, a growing agony of thirst for the boy and his dog. The sun burned into them like an inescapable eye. The current which held Mafatu's canoe fast in its grip was bearing it swiftly on toward its mysterious destination.

And thus the day passed, while night once more descended, bringing blessed release from the sun.

Now the air was luminous with promise of another day. Out of the sultry mists the sea emerged, blue and violent. With the coming of this new day terror raised its head. Mafatu tried to fight it back, to deny its existence; but it gripped his heart with clammy fingers, tightened his throat. He flung himself flat on the floor of the canoe and buried his face in his arms. He must have cried out then. His voice was but a hoarse croak, yet it stirred Uri to life: the dog's ragged tail gave one feeble thump. With the ghost of a whimper the animal laid his hot nose against the boy's hand.

The brave thump of his dog's tail touched Mafatu profoundly. He caught the animal to him, while a new assurance, a new strength, flooded his being. If Uri could have courage to die, surely he, Mafatu, could not do less! In that instant he heard

a whir and fury in the sky above, a beat of wide wings. . . .
Looking upward, the boy's dulled eyes made out the widespread
wings of an albatross, circling above the canoe.

"Kivi!" Mafatu cried hoarsely. "*Ai*, Kivi!"

Even as he spoke, the bird wheeled slowly, then flew off
straight ahead for the distant horizon. The boy noticed then
that the sea current was carrying him almost due southwest.
Kivi's flight moved in exact parallel. Once more it seemed as
if his albatross were leading him onward, just as he had led
the canoe out of the passage of Hikueru.

Mafatu scanned the rim of the horizon; it looked as hard as
the cut edge of a stone. But suddenly the boy's heart gave a
great leap and he started forward. *It couldn't be!* It was a cloud.
. . . But the sky was cloudless. Far off in the sea-shimmer lay
something that was neither sea nor sky. The swells, lifting higher, now revealed, now concealed it. That shadow on the horizon
—it was land! The boy flung himself forward, shaking uncon-
trollably.

He seized Uri in his arms and lifted him up, laughing, crying:
"Uri! Uri! It's land. *Land!*"

The dog sniffed at the air and a little whimper broke from
him.

What island could this be? Was it Tahiti, the golden island,
whose language was akin to that of Hikueru? Or was it, perhaps, one of the terrible dark islands of the eaters-of-men?

Now the current had a westward drift, and it was to the west
that the dark islands lay. . . .

All day, as the canoe drifted onward, the boy watched the
distant shadow-shape of land, not daring to take his eyes from
it lest it vanish into the sea. Hunger and thirst were lulled into
forgetfulness. There was only this one reality, land—escape
from the sea. Weak as he was, he still clung to the thwart, his
lips whispering a silent prayer of gratitude. With waning afternoon, the island took more distinct form as the canoe drifted
nearer. It was high and peaked, its valleys blue-shadowed
against the paler tone of the sky. Hour by hour, with every lift
of the swells, the island rose higher and higher, filling Mafatu's
soul with wonder. Hikueru, the only land he had ever seen, was

as flat as his hand; but a great single peak crowned this strange island. Trees rose green and fair, tier upon tier of them, from the shoreline into the foothills of the purple mountain. Uri had caught the scent of the land now and was quivering with delight.

Then from far off came the first muffled thunder of the reef: the boom of the surf high-bursting on the barrier coral. That sound—was it the voice of Moana? "Someday, Mafatu, someday." . . . Involuntarily the boy shuddered. Would his ears never be free of the Sea God's threat?

Mafatu was powerless to guide his craft. He sensed that the current had quickened. He could only watch helplessly as the little canoe, swift as the following gulls, rushed to meet the tides of the island where they met and churned in a cross sea of conflict. Now across the swells came a sound like a chorus of ghostly fishermen weary with their day's toil: sea birds, always complaining, never at rest; while softer, yet rising above it was another sound—the voice of the reef itself, quieting with sundown, like the reassuring hush of a mother to her child.

Night stole up from the face of the sea, enveloping the world. There was no moon, but the black sky was spangled with unguessed millions of stars: other worlds, other suns. To the watching boy, with land in the offing, they seemed closer and more friendly. The bottom star of the Southern Cross pointed to the end of the world. . . . A soft land breeze, heavy with a scent of flowers, wafted out across the dark waters, tantalizing, bitter-sweet.

Weak with thirst, the boy drifted now into a merciful sleep. He struggled against it, like a weary swimmer fighting a rip-tide, but his head drooped and his eyes closed.

He was aroused at midnight by a thunderous tumult in his ears. Of a sudden he felt the canoe under him lifted and flung high into the air. Then down it crashed into splinters upon the reef. Boy and dog were hurled headlong into the boiling surf.

The shock of cold water brought Mafatu half back to consciousness. Blindly he struck out, fighting for survival. Uri—where was he? No sign of the dog. The boy was aware that the canoe must have been flung over the barrier-reef, for here the water was scarcely troubled by wind or tide. Now he was

swimming, swimming. . . . Somewhere ahead a strip of beach, salt-white in the darkness, lured him onward. His muscles did it of themselves. Only a will to live. A strip of sand white in the night. . . . He caught the gleam of a shark's belly, close at hand, but on he swam. His unhampered limbs moved freely through the water.

Of a sudden there was something solid beneath his feet. Sand. Mafatu stumbled, staggered, fell to his knees in the shallows. His lips moved in dry, soundless speech. Lying there with the water rippling and breaking over him, he pulled himself half upright, swayed onward. The palms, trooping to the edge of the beach, were motionless in the night air. All the world seemed to hold its breath as this boy climbed up out of the sea.

He fell to the sand once more, then, guided by he knew not what impulse, he dragged himself to the edge of the jungle. A murmur of water reached his ears, soft as a chuckle of pleasant laughter. Water, sweet water. . . . Down the face of an age-worn rock a small cascade lost itself amid ferns and cool mosses. A ragged, strangling cry broke from Mafatu's throat. He stood upright to full height. Then he crashed to the mossy bank. One cheek lay in the cool water.

The moon lifted above the rim of the palms. It outlined in silver the form of a boy thin with hunger, naked as the daystar. It revealed a small wet dog, dragging himself across the beach to his master's side.

Mafatu lay without moving. Before Uri drank, he touched the boy's cheek with his hot muzzle.

Call It Courage *was awarded the Newbery Medal in 1941. Among the many other thrilling stories by author-artist Armstrong Sperry are* Black Falcon (Holt, Rinehart and Winston), *based on the life of Jean Lafitte, the pirate;* Rain Forest (Macmillan), *which is laid in New Guinea; and* Thunder Country (Macmillan), *the account of a scientific expedition to Venezuela.*

The Witch Trial

BY ELIZABETH GEORGE SPEARE

Illustrations by Nicholas Angelo

When sixteen-year-old Kit Tyler comes from Barbados to live with her Puritan relatives in Connecticut in 1687, she rebells against many things, but especially against the persecution of so-called witches. And then Kit herself is accused of witchcraft and brought to trial.

T HE sun had been slanting through the chinks in the shed wall for hours when Kit heard the heavy bolt withdrawn and the shed door opened. This time it was the constable's wife, with a wooden trencher of mush. In spite of its dubious appearance it sent a faint curl of steam into the frosty air, and Kit forced herself to take a few spoonfuls while the woman stood watching, hands on her hips.

"I reckoned you'd be half froze," the woman observed. "To tell the truth I couldn't sleep half the night thinking of you out here. 'Tis good enough for thieves and drunkards, I says to my man, but 'tis no place for a female, witch or no. I've seen the girl in Meeting, I says, sitting there decent as you please,. and it goes against reason she could be a witch. There's some folks in this town always bent on stirring up trouble."

Kit looked up at her gratefully. " 'Twas good of you to send the quilt," she said. "How long will they keep me here, do you think?"

"My man has orders to take you to the Town House in an hour."

So soon! Kit put down the spoon, her stomach curling. "What will happen there?"

"The magistrate and the ministers will examine you. If they

think you be guilty they'll send you on to Hartford to wait trial. At any rate, you'll be off our hands. My man and I, we don't relish this work much. We'll be glad when his term is up."

Kit laid down the trencher in dismay. "But I can't go like this! I've been sitting in the dirt all night!" The face she lifted to the woman was even sorrier than she realized, streaked with mud and tears.

"You're no treat to look at, that's sure," the woman admitted. "If they took you for a witch right now I'd scarce blame them. Wait a minute."

She went away, taking the precaution of bolting the door securely, and returned presently with a basin of water and a rough wooden comb. Gratefully, Kit did what she could to make herself respectable. The dress, dirty and crumpled, could not be helped.

It required the constable and two sturdy members of the Watch to conduct a timid witch up Carpenter's Lane, along Broad Street, up Hungry Hill to the Town House. The small building seemed full of people as she entered. Benches and chairs along the two walls were crowded with men from the town, with here and there a sharp-faced woman, cronies of Goodwife Cruff. At a table at the end of the room sat Captain Samuel Talcott, Magistrate from Wethersfield to the General Court of Connecticut, and a group of men whom Kit knew as the town selectmen. Her uncle sat in his place among them, his lips tight, his eyebrows drawn fiercely together. What anguish it must cost him, Kit thought with shame, to have to sit here and pass judgment on a member of his own household. At the opposite end of the table sat the two ministers, Reverend John Woodbridge and Dr. Gershom Bulkeley, both famed for their relentless sermons against witchcraft. Kit's heart sank. There was no one, no one in the whole room, save her uncle, who would speak a word in her defense. William had not come.

Captain Talcott rapped on the table and a hush fell over the room. "Good folk, we will proceed at once to the business at hand. We have come here in order to inquire and search into the matter of Mistress Katherine Tyler, lately of Barbados, who is accused by sundry witnesses of the practice of witchcraft. Mistress Tyler will come forward."

Prompted by the constable's elbow, Kit got to her feet and moved haltingly across the room to stand facing the magistrate across the table.

"You will listen to the charge against you."

A clerk read from a parchment, giving full weight and due to every awful word.

"Katherine Tyler, thou art here accused that not having the fear of God before thine eyes thou hast had familiarity with Satan the grand enemy of God and man, and that by his instigation and help thou hast in a preternatural way afflicted and done harm to the bodies and estates of sundry of His Majesty's subjects, in the third year of His Majesty's reign, for which by the law of God and the law of the Colony thou deservest to die."

There was a murmur along the benches. Kit's hands felt icy, but she kept her eyes steadily on the magistrate.

"Mistress Tyler, you are accused by Adam Cruff with the following actions. Firstly that you were the familiar friend and companion of the Widow Hannah Tupper of Blackbird Pond, an alleged witch who has within the past week disappeared in a suspicious manner. Such friendship is a lawful test of guilt, inasmuch as it is well known that witchcraft is an art that may be learned and conveyed from one person to another, and that it has often fallen out that a witch, upon dying, leaveth some heir to her witchcraft.

"Secondly, that you are guilty of actions and works which infer a court with the devil, which have caused illness and death to fall upon many innocent children in this town."

The clerk sat down. Captain Talcott eyed the girl before him. Quite plainly he had a distaste for the duty at hand, but his stern soldierly countenance did not soften.

"Mistress Tyler," he said, "you have heard the complaints against you. We will proceed with the first accusation. Is it true that you were a friend and companion of the Widow Tupper?"

For a moment Kit feared that her voice would not come. "Yes, sir," she managed shakily.

"Is it true that on sundry occasions during the summer you have entered her house and visited with her?"

"Yes, sir."

"Is it true that you were also acquainted with a certain cat which the widow entertained as a familiar spirit?"

"It—it was just an ordinary cat, sir, like any cat."

"You will answer yes or no. Is it true that you have engaged with the Widow Tupper in various enchantments with the direct intent of causing mischief to certain people?"

"Oh no, sir! I don't know what you mean by enchantments."

"Do you deny that on a certain day in August last, on passing the pasture of Goodman Whittlesley you cast a spell upon his cattle so that they were rooted to the ground where they stood and refused to answer his call or to give any milk on that evening?"

"I—I don't understand, sir. How could I do such a thing?"

"Goodman Whittlesley, will you repeat your complaint for this assembly?"

Her head reeling, Kit stood helpless as, one after the other, they rose and made their complaints, these men and women whom she scarcely recognized. The evidence rolled against her like a dark wave.

One man's child had cried aloud all night that someone was sticking pins into him. Another child had seen a dark creature with horns at the foot of her bed. A woman who lived along South Road testified that one morning Kit had stopped and spoken to her child and that within ten minutes the child had fallen into a fit and lain ill for five days. Another woman testified that one afternoon last September she had been sitting in the window, sewing a jacket for her husband, when she had looked up and seen Kit walking past her house, staring up at the window in a strange manner. Whereupon, try as she would, the sleeve would never set right in the jacket. A man swore he had seen Kit and Goody Tupper dance round a fire in the meadow one moonlit night, and that a great black man, taller than an Indian, had suddenly appeared from nowhere and joined in the dance.

Matthew Wood leaped suddenly to his feet. "I protest this mockery!" he roared, in a voice that silenced every whisper. "Not one word of this nonsense could be proved in the Court of Assistants. There is not one shred of lawful evidence in the lot! I beg you, Sam Talcott, make an end of it!"

"Do I infer that you are willing to vouch for your niece's good character, Matthew Wood?"

"Certainly. I will vouch for it."

"We are to understand then that these visits to the Widow Tupper were taken with your approval?"

Taken aback, Matthew glared at the magistrate. "No, I had no knowledge of them," he admitted.

"Did you ever, at any time, indicate to your niece that she was not to associate with this woman?"

"Yes, I forbade her to go."

"Then the girl has been disobedient and deceitful."

Matthew clenched his fists in frustration. "The girl has been thoughtless and headstrong at times. But her upbringing has been such as to encourage that."

"You admit then that her education has been irregular?"

"You can twist what I say as you will, Sam Talcott," said Matthew in steely anger. "But I swear before all present, on my word as a freeman of the colony, that the girl is no witch."

"We are obliged to listen to the testimony, Matthew," said Captain Talcott reasonably. "I will thank you to keep silent. What is your opinion of the case, Dr. Bulkeley?"

Dr. Bulkeley cleared his throat. "In my opinion," he said deliberately, "it is necessary to use the greatest caution in the matter of testimony. Since the unnatural events so far recounted appear to rest in each case upon the word of but one witness, the legality of any one of them is open to question."

"It is ridiculous to talk of legality," interrupted Matthew. "There has not one word been spoken that makes sense!"

For the last few moments Goodwife Cruff had been vehemently prodding her husband. He rose now obediently. "Sir, I've summat to say as makes sense," he announced, assuming a bold tone, "and there's more than one witness to prove it. I've got summat here as was found in the widow's house that night."

With a sinking heart Kit watched as he drew an object from his pocket. It was not the hornbook, as she expected. It was the little copybook. At sight of it Goodwife Cruff's anger burst through all restraints.

"Look at that!" she demanded. "What do you say about that?

My Prudence's name, written over and over. 'Tis a spell, that's
what it is! A mercy the child is alive today. Another hour and
she'd have been dying like the others!"

The magistrate accepted the copybook reluctantly, as though
it were tainted.

"Do you recognize this book, Mistress Tyler?"

Kit could barely stand upright. She tried to answer, but only a hoarse whisper came out.

"Speak up, girl!" he ordered sharply. "Does this book belong to you?"

"Yes sir," she managed.

"Did you write this name?"

Kit could barely swallow. She had vowed she would never deceive her uncle again! Then, remembering, she looked back at the copybook. Yes, the name on the first line was in her own hand, large and clear for Prudence to copy. "Yes sir," she said, her voice loud with relief. "I wrote the name."

Matthew Wood passed a hand over his eyes. He looked old, old and ill as he had looked that day beside Mercy's bed.

"Why should you write a child's name over and over like that?"

"I—I can't tell you sir."

Captain Talcott looked perplexed. "There are no other children's names here," he said. "Why did you choose to write the name of Prudence Cruff?"

Kit was silent.

"Mistress Tyler." The magistrate spoke to her directly. "I had considered this morning's inquiry merely a formality. I did not expect to find any evidence worthy of carrying to the court. But this is a serious matter. You must explain to us how this child's name came to be written."

As Kit looked back at him mutely, the restraints that held the tensely waiting crowd gave way. Men and women leaped to their feet, screaming.

"She won't answer! That proves she's guilty!"

"She's a witch! She's as good as admitted it!"

"We don't need a jury trial. Put her to the water test!"

"Hanging's too good for her!"

In the midst of the pandemonium Gershom Bulkeley quietly reached for the copybook, studied it carefully, and turned a shrewd, deliberative eye upon Kit. Then he whispered something to the magistrate. Captain Talcott nodded.

"Silence!" he barked. "This is the Colony of Connecticut! Every man and woman is entitled to a trial before a jury. This case will be turned over to the General Session in Hartford. The inquiry is dismissed."

"Hold a minute, Captain!" called a voice. A commotion near the door had been scarcely noticed. "There's a fellow here says he has an important witness for the case."

Every voice was suddenly stilled. Almost paralyzed with dread, Kit turned slowly to face a new accuser. On the threshold of the room stood Nat Eaton, slim, straight-shouldered, without a trace of mockery in his level blue eyes.

Nat! The wave of joy and relief was so unexpected that she almost lost her balance, but almost instantly it drained away and left a new fear. For she saw that beside him, clinging tightly to his hand, was Prudence Cruff.

Goodwife Cruff let out a piercing scream. "Take her out of here! The witch will put an evil eye on her!" She and her husband both started forward.

"Stand back!" ordered the magistrate. "The child is protected here. Where is the witness?"

Nat put his hands on the child's shoulders and gently urged her forward. With one trusting look up at his face, Prudence walked steadily toward the magistrate's table.

Suddenly Kit found her voice. "Oh please sir!" she cried, the tears rushing down her face, "let them take her away! It is all my fault! I would do anything to undo it if I could! I never meant any harm, but I'm responsible for all of it. Please—take me to Hartford. Do what you want with me. But—oh, I beg you—send Prudence away from this horrible place!"

The magistrate waited till this outburst was over.

"'Tis a trifle late to think about the child," he said coldly. "Come here, child."

Kit sank on her knees and buried her face in her hands. The buzz in the room roared like a swarm of bees around her head. Then there was a waiting hush. She could scarcely bear to look at Prudence, but she forced herself to raise her head. The child was barefoot and her snarled hair was uncovered. Her thin arms, under the skimpy jumper, were blue with cold. Then Kit stared again. There was something strange about Prudence.

"Will you stand there, child, in front of the table?" Captain Talcott spoke reassuringly.

Watching Prudence, Kit suddenly felt a queer prickling along her spine. There *was* something different about her. The child's head was up. Her eyes were fastened levelly on the magistrate. Prudence was not afraid!

"We will ask you some questions, Prudence," said the magistrate quietly. "You will answer them as truthfully as you possibly can. Do you understand?"

"Yes sir," whispered Prudence.

"Do you know this young woman?"

"Oh yes, sir. She is my teacher. She taught me to read."

"You mean at the dame school?"

"No, I never went to the dame school."

"Then where did she teach you?"

"At Hannah's house in the meadow."

A loud scream from Goodwife Cruff tore across the room.

"You mean Mistress Tyler took you to Hannah Tupper's house?"

"The first time she took me there. After that I went by myself."

"The little weasel!" cried Goodwife Cruff. "That's where she was all those days. I'll see that girl hung!"

It is all over, thought Kit, with a wave of faintness.

Gershom Bulkeley still held the little copybook. He spoke now, under his breath, and passed the book to Captain Talcott.

"Have you ever seen this book before?" the magistrate questioned.

"Oh yes, sir. Kit gave it to me. I wrote my name in it."

"That's a lie!" cried Goodwife Cruff. "The child is bewitched!"

Captain Talcott turned to Kit. "Is it true," he asked her, "that the child wrote her own name in this book?"

Kit dragged herself to her feet. "'Tis true," she answered dully. "I wrote it for her once and then she copied it."

"You can't take her word for anything, sir," protested Goodman Cruff timidly. "The child don't know what she's saying. I might as well tell it, Prudence has never been what you'd call bright. She never could learn much."

The magistrate paid no attention. "Could you write your name again, do you think?"

"I—I think so, sir."

He dipped the quill pen carefully in the ink and handed it to the child. Leaning over the table, Prudence set the pen on the copybook. For a moment there was not a single sound in the room but the hesitant scratching.

Goodman Cruff was on his feet. Propelled by a curiosity greater than any awe for the magistrate, he came slowly across the room and peered over his child's shoulder.

"Is that proper writing?" he demanded in unbelief. "Prudence Cruff, does it say, right out as it should?"

The magistrate glanced at the writing and handed the copy-book to Gershom Bulkeley.

"Very proper writing, I should say," Dr. Bulkeley commented, "for a child with no learning."

The magistrate leaned to take the pen out of the small fingers. Goodman Cruff tiptoed back to the bench. The bluster was gone from him. He looked dazed.

"Now Prudence," the magistrate continued. "You say that Mistress Tyler taught you to read?"

"What sort of reading?" Goodwife Cruff rose in a frenzy. "Magic signs and spells I tell you! The child would never know the difference."

Gershom Bulkeley also rose to his feet. "That at least will be easy to prove," he suggested reasonably. "What can you read, child?"

"I can read the Bible."

Dr. Bulkeley picked up the Great Bible from the table and turned the pages thoughtfully. Then, moving to hand the Book to Prudence, he realized that it was too heavy for her to hold and laid it carefully on the table beside her. "Read that for us, child, beginning right there."

Kit held her breath. Was it the tick of the great clock that sounded so frightening, or her own heart? Then across the silence came a whisper.

> "Buy the truth, and sell it not; also wis-wisdom, and in-in-instruction, and understanding."

The childish voice slowly gained strength and clarity till it reached every corner of the room.

> "The father of the right-righteous shall greatly rejoice; and he that begetteth a wish child shall have joy of him. Thy father and thy mother shall be glad, and she that bare thee shall rejoice."

In the warm rush of pride that welled up in her, Kit forgot her fear. For the first time she dared to look back at Nat Eaton where he stood near the door. Across the room their eyes met, and suddenly it was as though he had thrown a line straight into her reaching hands. She could feel the pull of it, and over its taut span strength flowed into her, warm and sustaining.

When finally she looked away she realized that everyone in the room was staring at the two parents. They had both leaned forward, their mouths open in shock and unbelief. As she listened, Goodwife Cruff's face darkened and her eyes narrowed. She saw now that she had been tricked. The fresh anger that was gathering would be vented on her child.

On the father's face a new emotion seemed to be struggling. As the thin voice ended, Goodwife Cruff drew in her breath through her teeth in a venomous hiss. But before she could release it her husband sprang forward.

"Did you hear that?" he demanded widely, of everyone present. All at once his shoulders straightened. "That was real good reading. I'd like to see any boy in this town do better!"

"It's a trick!" denied his wife. "That child could never read a word in her life! She's bewitched, I tell you!"

"Hold your tongue, woman," shouted her husband unexpectedly. "I'm sick and tired of hearing about Prudence being bewitched. All these years you been telling me our child was half-witted. Why, she's smart as a whip. I bet it warn't much of a trick to teach her to read."

Goodwife Cruff's jaw dropped. For one moment she was struck utterly dumb, and in that moment her husband stepped into his rightful place. There was a new authority in his voice.

"All my life I've wished I could read. If I'd had a son, I'd of seen to it he learned his letters. Well, this is a new country over here, and who says it may not be just as needful for a woman to read as a man? Might give her summat to think about besides witches and foolishness. Any rate, I got someone now to read the Good Book to me of an evening, and if that's the work of the devil, then I say 'tis a mighty queer thing for the devil to go working against himself!"

The magistrate had not interrupted this speech. There was a glint of amusement in his eye as he asked, "I take it then, Goodman Cruff, that you withdraw your charges against this young woman?"

"Yes," he answered loudly. "Yes. I'll withdraw the charges."

"Adam Cruff!" His wife had found her voice. "Have ye lost your senses? The girl has bewitched you too!"

In the back of the room someone tittered. A man's laugh rang out—was it Nat? All at once, like a clap of thunder, the tension of the room broke into laughter that shook the timbers and rattled the windows. Every man in the room was secretly applauding Adam Cruff's declaration of independence. Even the magistrate's stern lips twisted slightly.

"There seems to be no evidence of witchcraft," he announced, when order had been restored. "The girl has admitted her wrong in encouraging a child to willful disobedience. Beyond that I cannot see that there is any reasonable charge against her. I pronounce that Mistress Katherine Tyler is free and innocent."

But suddenly Goodwife Cruff's anger found a new outlet. "That man!" she shrilled. "Isn't he the seaman? The one who was banished for setting fire to houses? Thirty lashes they promised him if he showed his face here again!"

There was renewed uproar. The constable looked to the magistrate for orders. Captain Talcott hesitated, then shrugged his shoulders. "Arrest him," he snapped. "The sentence still stands."

"Oh no!" Kit pleaded in alarm. "You can't arrest him, when he only came back to help me."

With a shrewd look at his niece, Matthew Wood interceded for her. " 'Tis the truth, Sam," he observed. "The lad risked the penalty to see justice done. I suggest you remit the sentence."

"A good suggestion," agreed the magistrate, relieved to have an end to the matter. But Nat had slipped out of the room and his halfhearted pursuers reported not a single trace of him.

"They won't find him," a voice whispered in Kit's ear. A small hand crept into hers. "He's got a fast little pinnace hidden on the riverbank. He told me to say goodbye to you if he had to hurry away."

"Prudence!" Kit's knees had suddenly turned to water. "How— how did it all happen?"

"He came and found me this morning. He said he got worrying about you and came back and sort of spied around till he heard about the meeting. He said I was the only one could save you, and he promised he would stay right here and help as long as we needed him."

"Oh I'm so grateful to both of you!" Kit's tears started again. "And I'm so proud of you, Prudence! Will you be all right, do you think?"

"She'll be all right." Goodman Cruff, coming to claim his daughter, had overheard. "Time somebody looked after her so's she won't need to run off any more. Next summer she'll go to your school, like I always wanted."

"Goodwife Cruff," the magistrate called back the departing woman. "I remind you that the penalty for slander is heavy. A fine of thirty pounds or three hours in the stocks. Mistress Tyler would be within her rights to press her own charges."

"Oh no!" gasped Kit.

Matthew Wood stood beside her. "Let us make an end of this," he said. "We have no desire to press charges. With your permission, Captain, I shall take Katherine home."

The Witch of Blackbird Pond *was awarded the Newbery Medal in 1959 as the most distinguished contribution to literature for American children. Mrs. Speare has also written* Calico Captive, *published by Houghton Mifflin, the story of a girl who was kidnapped by Indians.*

Outside

BY ANN NOLAN CLARK

Illustrations by Jean Charlot

Cusi, a young Inca Indian boy, has spent most of his life in a beautiful mountain valley high in the Andes learning from old Chuto how to care for the precious llama flock. The day comes when Cusi must go "outside" and make his own decision as to what he will do with his life.

CUSI needed no one to waken him. He had been awake long before Chuto motioned him to follow along as the Old One walked yesterday's trail to the place of the Sunrise Call. The way did not seem as long this morning as it had the day before, or as difficult, or as dark. Cusi kept within touching distance of Chuto's swiftly moving shadow slipping through the dawn. The boy was pleased that the trail was easier to follow. Just once walking over it and I know it well, he thought. My feet learn quickly, or maybe it's these new sandals Chuto made yesterday. Maybe some of the minstrel's music went into the making. The boy chuckled at the thought, but as Chuto turned his head to listen Cusi stopped his laughter. Perhaps this was not the time for letting thoughts go straying. Perhaps he should be thinking of the Great Sun Father.

Cusi shivered. This morning the wind was very cold. It was filled with the chill breath of the snowbanks. It was not a day wind, loud and lusty. It was a dawn wind of the high sierras, low and slow and cold. Only the sun could warm the world and make it right for living.

The man and the boy had now reached the rock circle and stood waiting, facing the eastern sky. Slowly the sky colored, heralding the coming day. Slowly Cusi felt happiness fill his body warmly. This had never happened to him before. Never before had he felt happiness flowing with his blood to make his body warm and light with captured laughter and delight.

Then the sun came. Chuto's voice rose to meet the sun, and Cusi knew forever the joy of welcoming the coming of the Great Father who lightened and warmed the world.

After the call was finished Chuto stood for a minute with head bowed, lost in thinking. For a brief time he had touched the Spirit World, and he hated to return to the realness of living. But it was only for a moment. With a sigh the old man raised his head, straightened his thin shoulders, and turned to the homeward trail.

The way back was even more swift than the coming had been. Chuto was troubled. Cusi felt it, and he knew what was troubling the Old One. He does not want to leave our llamas. He does not want to see the outside world, the boy thought and felt guilt at his own excitement in going.

Breakfast was quiet. The minstrel sat deep in thought. His face was closed this morning. No flashing smile came to lighten its darkness and to soften its sternness. More than ever he bore the look of an eagle ready for flight. His songs had stilled themselves. His pipes lay silent on the ychu grass. Only his body was with them. His mind and his heart were traveling another trail.

Suncca whined and whined, and the day wind began blowing. Misti kept close beside his young master. Chuto ate, looking only at the food set before them.

Cusi would have liked to talk. He needed to talk. Going to the Salt Pits was an event that needed to be talked about. But the boy did not talk. The silence of the two men was too heavy to cut through with words.

The breakfast corn and potatoes eaten, Chuto began to pack. The minstrel stirred and looked around. Then he spoke. "Perhaps I know more than my songs," he said. "Perhaps I, too, have been sent along the path I follow. Are you certain, brother, that you want this salt you journey to get? Are you sure it is what you want to do?"

Chuto nodded but did not speak or stop his work of getting the possessions together.

After a time the minstrel spoke again. "Hidden Valley takes care of its flock and the keepers of its flock. Not so the world outside. The outside world is filled with people who are strange to you. They are people of two bloods. They are and they are not. They know and they do not know. They care and they do not care. Think, brother. Are you certain that you want to ford this river of people whose blood runs fresh and salt in never-mixing streams?"

Chuto answered simply, "I do not want to go. There is need to go. It has been asked of me. Once I received a like request and I refused it. The cost of that refusal lies heavy in my heart."

To this the minstrel had no answer. Instead he went into the hut and brought out his pack. "This," he said, handing Chuto a small package, "is food fit for a journey. It is brown sugar and parched corn. Eat it as you walk along and your feet will not stumble because of hunger."

Chuto was pleased. He took the package offered him. "I know this food. I carried it always when I too journeyed over the mountain trails."

Cusi had been whispering to Misti, but now he looked at Chuto in surprise. He had not known that Chuto had traveled the mountain trails. He had never thought about it, really, but if he had he would have thought that Chuto always had lived in Hidden Valley. He felt a flash of jealousy that Chuto had known another world than this they shared together. He must know more about it. All about it. Where had Chuto been?

The boy began a question, but the minstrel stopped him. "Look how pleased Misti is that you are going to see the world beyond the swinging bridge," he said jokingly.

Cusi's eyes danced with delight. "Are we going by the narrow trail? Are we going over the swinging bridge? Is it possible?" he asked. His words tumbled over themselves in his excitement.

Chuto nodded, and the minstrel laughed, "Why not? It is the shortest way down the mountain, especially if you should fall." He was teasing now. Cusi laughed with him.

Chuto counted the bundles aloud. "These two rolled mats for sleeping. I take one. One for Cusi. Inside them—so—I put the squares of woven cloth for the salt. The coils of rope to tie them. Two for me and one for Cusi. The gift package of food I will divide. We will need to eat it as we walk along. The extra sandals and the ponchos I will take. The gourds for drinking I tie here to this. The spun yarn for trading goes in Cusi's pack, all except that which we spin as we walk along. It is all here, I think. Yes, it is all here."

Chuto stood up and looked around with satisfaction. It was good to know that everything that was needed was in its place, ready for the taking.

Quickly he rolled the mats. The smaller one was Cusi's. He tied it across the boy's shoulders. The larger one he took upon his own back. Then he tied his coca bag full of dried coca leaves and lime lumps made of seashell to the sash at his side where his poncho opened. The small coca bag he gave to Cusi, who tied it to his own sash. Then the Old One looped his sling-shot over his shoulder. It was his only weapon. He was not a hunter; he was a shepherd. The slingshot was all he needed.

They were ready to go. Everything was ready. There was nothing more to do.

They said good-by.

Misti looked after them. His sharp pointed ears with the red woolen tassels stood straight up in surprise. Could it be that he was being left behind? Quietly and deliberately he spat—at nothing in particular, just to show his displeasure. It made him feel better.

Suncca whined. It was the only thing he could do. It did not make him feel better. He whined too much and too often.

Chuto and Cusi had begun their journey. They walked across the meadow of ychu grass, a thin old man and a thinner, younger boy. They were dressed alike, knitted woolen caps of bright llama yarn on their heads, blue ponchos with red em- broidered stripes woven of llama wool on their shoulders, white shin-length cotton trousers, and tied llama sandals. Their rolled mat bundles moved as their shoulders moved.

They did not look back. They had begun their journey. They were on their way.

They passed the opening of the llama trail down into the valley where the Indian family were clearing the underbrush for their new home. In a way, Cusi would have liked to take this trail. If they had done so, he could have seen the family

close by. He could, perhaps, have talked with them. Then he would have known so much more about them than he possibly could learn just by watching. Also, if they had gone by way of the llama trail, he could have taken Misti. Since Misti had been old enough to leave his mother, Yellow-Ears, he had been the boy's companion by day and by night. Cusi felt strange to be going off without the beautiful black llama walking proudly beside him.

But quickly the young Indian boy forgot Misti in his excitement over the trail they were taking. This trail lay behind the ruins of the stone corral, behind the grass-thatched hut, behind the mountain meadow where the llamas grazed. It was hidden from view by a clump of trees hung heavily with vines and covered thickly with velvet green moss and white feathered lichens.

Cusi knew about this trail, but he had never traveled it before. At once it led steeply a hundred feet downward to the knifelike edge of a sheer rock cliff. Two thousand feet below them tumbled and stormed the roaring rapids of a wide, swiftly moving river. The deep thunder roar of the rapids could be heard distinctly on the cliff crest where Chuto and Cusi stood. Beneath them white spray shot upward like a lacy veil, partly hiding the dark green water of the river and giant tree trunks that were being tossed and splintered against sharp boulders in the mighty current.

The boy lifted his eyes from the wild, angry scene below him and let them travel to the opposite cliff that loomed just as sharply and just as sheer on the far side of the wide, wide river.

Over the gorge, above the rapids, connecting cliff to cliff, swung a slender bridge. This was the swinging bridge the minstrel had teased about. This was the bridge that they must cross.

The bridge was made of rope vines of maguey plant. These vines had been twisted and plaited together into two cables as thick as Chuto's body. They were tied into holes that had been drilled in the cliff walls. Between the rope cables planks had been tied. Higher up was a smaller vine rope to be used as a handrail.

Cusi had looked at this swinging bridge before, but he had

never thought of crossing it. Now terror touched him with its cold fingers, and hot excitement filled him with the thought of what he was about to do. He felt that he never could move a sandaled foot a half-pace forward. Yet he knew that he would move. He knew that he would cross the bridge. He knew that nothing could hinder that first step that would lead forward.

Chuto looked at the boy once, briefly, then stepped upon the first plank. Cusi watched him. He was terrified. He was fascinated. He was at once impatient and yet frightened for his own starting. Step by step, hand by hand, the old man crossed the canyon. The frail-looking bridge swayed and swung. Far below it the rapids leaped upward in icy frenzy.

Chuto became but a small speck moving along the rocking vine cable. Slowly, slowly, slowly he moved farther along. He reached the middle, and the bridge dipped hammock-like. Cusi never took his eyes from the black dot on the slender line. Breathlessly he watched. He waited. He watched.

Ah! Chuto had reached the far cliff ledge. He stood there, gaining his balance on the firm rock cliff!

Then he turned, raising a hand as signal for Cusi's starting.

Not for nothing had Chuto trained the boy to obey his commands. This was reward for his years of patient teaching. Cusi put one foot on the first plank and moved his body forward. He was on the bridge now. He must keep going. Move a foot and move a hand. Inch forward. Never look backward. Never look downward. Never look anywhere but the opposite cliff where good, kind Chuto waited.

Suddenly Cusi was not afraid. He felt bold and brave and strong and tall. This was adventure. This was fun. He was at the middle now. The bridge was not dipping as much as it had done when Chuto crossed. It was swinging. It was swaying. It was rocking, but it was not dipping. Keep going. Keep going. Step by step. Hand by hand. Never look down. Keep looking at Chuto. He was bigger now. Chuto was bigger. He could see him plainly. He was his everyday size.

The bridge stopped moving underfoot. Cusi had reached the firm rock ledge. He had reached the other side. The world danced crazily around him. Around and around. Dizzily he leaned forward. He shut his eyes to clear his dizziness. Chuto said mildly, "A few coca leaves can be chewed now, I think.

Yes, we will sit here with our backs against the cliff wall and chew some coca leaves."

Cusi was glad to sit down. He did not look again at the bridge across the chasm. He did not need to see it. He had crossed it. That was enough.

Far below the rapids sprayed and foamed. The dark green river flowed its way through the heart of a mountain made of granite.

A condor soared and swerved and circled in graceful, lazy curves against the tropic sky.

White clouds tore themselves on the jagged crested mountains and hung in gray wisps upon the pointed peaks of deeper, whiter glistening snow.

Chuto stood up, stretching himself, and motioned with his lips that this was the way that they would go. The cliff where they were was a rounded pillar of granite. There was no trail up its smooth, hard sides. There was no trail down.

Cusi watched Chuto as the Indian swung upward, catching the end of a narrow ladder made of tied tree branches. Then he boosted Cusi up so that the boy could catch the ladder ends, could hold them tightly in his hands, could get a foothold on the ladder. Cusi began climbing. He had to climb. He could not get down. There was only space beneath him.

The granite rock was in layers of color, beautiful colors, rich and dark and aged with weather and with years. Cusi dared not look up or down or sideways. There was no Chuto to watch, for the old man had been left far below him.

Across the cliff face the boy climbed steadily. Sweat ran into his eyes, stinging them with its salt. His hands were wet against the ladder rungs.

But he climbed on and on. At last he reached safety behind the granite wall. The mountain here sloped gently into a lush, green valley. Vines and ferns, bushes and flowers and orchid plants made a world more beautiful than a dream. There was no ychu grass or bare, brown hills. Only by looking far, far above in the blue painted sky could he see the pointed peaks of snow.

Below him in the valley a gentle rain was falling. The wetness of the raindrops made the greenness of the jungle fresher, greener, and more vivid.

"Hidden Valley lies behind us." Cusi turned at the sound. Chuto was jumping lightly from the top of the ladder to the sloping trail.

The Indian untied the gourd drinking cups, and he and the boy drank mountain water from a crystal pool. They bathed their faces in its coolness and rested in the shade, munching the minstrel's gift of parched corn and caked brown sugar. The sun was high in the sky. There were no shadows. It was midday.

In about an hour the man and the boy started down the mountain trail. They walked slowly. This was a new world for Cusi. Everything was strange and interesting to the boy. Chuto was patient and kind. He explained everything. He knew the names of the flowers and gathered a handful to show the boy. There were purple columbine and purple munca flowers. There were the yellow-white dead-man's-shoes and the golden-yellow teardrops-of-the-sun. He gathered bunches of punga-punga. These flowers he would dry and use as medicine when they returned to their Hidden Valley.

He showed the boy tracks of the puma, mountain lion, and of atoc, the fox. By a fern-clad streamlet they found the heart-shaped hoofprints of the small deer of the Andes.

The air was hot and heavy and thick and difficult to breathe. Cusi felt slow and stupid and sleepy. He had never felt like this in the thin, cold air of the mountaintops. The air, too, was sweet with flower scent and dank with the smell of tree mold and earth mold. There was no wind, no movement of any kind. The jungle kept its own secrets in the green silences of its shaded depths.

Chuto named the trees for Cusi. Eucalyptus from Australia, willow and poplar brought from Europe. The trees and their names and the countries they came from meant nothing to Cusi. They were strange to sight and sound. They left no memory in his mind, no echo in his heart. He saw them. That was all.

By midafternoon they had begun climbing again. Chuto hurried. "We must get to the crest before evening falls," he explained to Cusi. "We have friends yonder. Do you see their clearing away up the mountain slope, a tiny patch of brown?"

Cusi looked, but he saw no brown—only green, every shade of green and every hue of green. His eyes ached with the unfamiliar color. Even in closing them, green seeped through his squinted lids. He was so sleepy. His feet felt heavy and as if they did not belong to him. "My feet are two heavy somethings that I pick up and put down and pick up and put down," he told Chuto.

Chuto laughed. "It is because we are in lower country. You must remember that our home is thousands of feet above us."

Cusi was interested. He had not thought about altitude before. He had not needed to think about it. In the world he knew everything was high or higher. "Is low altitude what makes it so warm and so green and so thick with plants and trees?" he asked.

Chuto nodded. "Partly," he said. "But save your breath for climbing. I feel safer in the mountains at nighttime than in the jungle valley. Besides, there are several places we must cross while there is light enough to see our footing."

"Are there more bridges or more ladders?" Cusi wanted to know.

"No," Chuto told him, "but the trail is rocky and steep and there may have been landslides."

Cusi knew about landslides. They had them often in the highlands. He had seen tons and tons of snow and earth and boulders slide down a mountain slope, taking trees and rocks and whatever living thing was in the path of its sliding. He hurried his steps to match Chuto's. He knew about mountain slides. He agreed with Chuto that when darkness fell he would feel safer on the mountain crest than deep in this valley walled with green.

Soon they came to several scattered huts in a small clearing. A woman was threshing pigweed by the door of the largest hut. On a square of blanket on the ground she had placed the canihua stalks. With a wooden flail she was beating them. She stopped when she saw strangers on the trail and called to someone within the hut. A boy about Cusi's age came to the door and silently stared at the two visitors. Chuto asked for water, and the boy brought two gourds of cool fresh spring water. At a word from the woman he went again into the hut and brought out goat's milk, yellow and rich and warm. Cusi tasted the milk from the gourd handed him, but he did not like it. He handed the gourd to Chuto and drank more of the cool spring water. It

tasted better. Besides, he knew what it was. He would have
liked to talk to the boy, but shyness overcame his desire. The
woman asked, not looking at them, where they were going and
from whence they had come. Chuto pointed backward over the
trail they had come and said, "We come from the highlands. We
travel to the Salt Pits." That was all. There seemed nothing else
to say. Chuto thanked them for the refreshments, and he and
Cusi started on the trail again. The boy and the woman
watched them go. They saw no one else in the clearing. Soon
all trace of it was swallowed in the dense green background.

The trail grew steep and rocky. At times they went up narrow stone steps. Once they came to a gigantic boulder. Cusi
looked upward worriedly. He could see no ladder. As they
approached the immense rock, Chuto turned abruptly. They
entered a low, narrow, winding tunnel. It was as black as night
and felt damp and clammy. Smell of wet earth, so thick it left
Cusi panting, hung heavy throughout the long way. Cusi felt
relief when suddenly they were in sunlight again. The mountains now were bare and bleak and brown. A steady wind blew
against them, making the going difficult. Night was coming
across the highlands. The sun with its warmth and light was
gone. It had not lingered to paint the sky in memory of its
passing. It just was gone, sinking its brilliancy quickly in the
soft lush green beneath them.

Another stairway, a trail on a crest where straight down on
either side there was nothing but space, filled now with the
purple shadows of night.

Cusi smelled fire smoke before he saw it. He knew that
smell—llama dung. How homelike, how good, how safe it
smelled! High on the brown, bare mountain they came to an
ancient ruin. On a cliff crest were the walls of stone, and up
to it, across terraces, up stairways, through arches the travelers
plodded wearily.

Chuto began to shout, "Ay—e, Ay—e, Ay—e," and the
brown mountains called back, "Ah–y—e, Ah–y—e, Ah–y—e,"
in echoed refrain.

Two men and several women and three or four children
appeared as if by magic. The men raised their hands in glad
salute. They called a warm welcome. They knew Chuto. They
were friends.

"Welcome to Condor Kuncca," the older man said, meeting Chuto at the foot of the last terrace. "What brings our brother to us?" he asked and continued, "Whatever it is, we are honored by the visit." Then he added, placing a kind hand on Cusi's shoulder, "This one, of course, is one of the Chosen! The other one did not return?"

Chuto replied, "Death has no returning. Yes, this time a good choice, I think."

Cusi looked at him. Why is it, he wondered, that Chuto talks in riddles to other men, but to me, Cusi, his words are simple and plain. However, the Indian seemed to understand. He was smiling at Chuto and nodding his head. They shook hands.

Chuto spoke again. "A man learns, I think, with the passing of his days. This time I myself open the gate. If it is closed, his hand, not mine, shall close it."

They had reached the stone building now. The younger Indian came forward to shake Chuto's hand in welcome and to welcome also the young boy with him. The women were shy. They laughed behind their hands, but Cusi knew that was their way. No one had told him, but he understood that a welcome does not need to be expressed by words or gestures. If the heart speaks to the stranger, the stranger feels at home.

Cusi was interested in the stone building at the top of the terraces and stairways. The younger Indian sensed his interest and said, "Perhaps you wonder why we call this Condor Kuncca? But see, is it not like an eagle's nest here on the crest of a rock cliff?"

Cusi looked and nodded. It was like an eagle's nest. It was like home too. He knew this stonework; it was the masterpiece of ancient builders. He knew the smell of the smoke; it was llama dung. These men were herdsmen.

Presently he saw the llamas. There were perhaps a dozen of them resting by the shelter of the stone corrals. He wondered why there were not more. There were hundreds in his flock at Hidden Valley.

The women went in to prepare the evening meal. They had a different kind of food from what Cusi had at home. They had roasted guinea pig and sweet potatoes. Cusi was hungry. He liked the taste of this food.

The children were small and were afraid of strangers. They

hid in the wide skirts of their mothers. Cusi could see only their big black eyes watching him, watching him, watching him.

When the men had finished eating, the women and the children disappeared within the shelter. The men were left by the fire to sip chicha and talk. Cusi tried to listen, but their words were strange. He did not understand their meaning. He was tired. Unrolling his sleeping mat, he curled up in the shelter of the wall. Chuto put the extra poncho over him, but the tired young boy did not know it. He was asleep.

The next morning, directly after sunrise, they left. The women had given them packages of dried meat and dried sweet potatoes. The men had given Chuto a gourd of chicha to carry with him. Now they stood on the top terrace, waving to them —the men, the women, and even the children. They were so friendly. Cusi looked back at them and smiled and waved. Now that he was going, his shyness had left him. He called good-by.

Chuto was far on the trail. Cusi hastened to overtake him. He could hear the lead llama bell tinkling merrily as the llamas began their morning grazing. Cusi called good-by to them in passing.

The mountain on this far side was not steep. There was no swinging bridge to cross nor frail ladder to climb. I know why we call our valley Hidden Valley, the boy thought. The mountains hide it so well. It's almost as if no one is supposed to find it.

The trail led through an open meadow. Chuto pointed out a hacienda in the distance. It was a long, low building of brown adobe mud. It had a sloping roof of bright red tile. As they came nearer, they could see its many doorways and other openings. Chuto called these openings windows, and explained their use to the highland boy.

The hacienda was enclosed by a low mud wall. There was a blue gate in the wall. Cusi looked over it and saw a patio filled with growing flowers of many colors.

At the back of the low adobe building were green fields sloping down to a lazy river. Men were working the fields with oxen, huge white, slow-moving, patient beasts. They kept their great heads lowered, looking at the ground and never at the sun. They seemed to say, "We have been conquered. We have nothing to hope for." Looking at them made Cusi sad. They were so big, so dull, so broken.

The trail widened into a roadway paved with cobblestones. The stones were rounded and smooth, polished for centuries by passing feet, animal feet and feet of men their masters.

Men were on the road now. Most of them were walking, but some were riding small brown burros. The burros were not at all like the oxen. They were small and frisky and saucy and gay. Cusi laughed at the funny burros whose long ears seemed too big for them to manage. He laughed again when he saw women riding sidesaddle on the fat brown donkeys. The women did not mind. They laughed back at him and called to him in a tongue he did not know.

"Do these people in this country not know how to say words of intelligence?" he asked Chuto in surprise.

It was Chuto's turn to laugh. "They know how to talk. It is you who do not know how to listen," he teased the boy.

Cusi was indignant, and Chuto stopped teasing to explain. "These are Spanish people. They are not Indian. Their words are Spanish words, not Indian," he said. "Perhaps I should teach you Spanish. Yes, that is what I should do. Perhaps."

"Do you speak Spanish?" Cusi asked. "I have not heard you."

Chuto laughed shortly. "With whom would I speak? The llamas know Indian."

Chuto pointed to a nearby field where people were planting. "There are some Indians," he said. "The people of the hacienda and those who work the oxen and ride on burros are not Indian. They are Spanish."

"Why don't they have llamas instead of burros?" Cusi asked. "Llamas are better."

The old man answered proudly, "No one who has a drop of blood not Indian can manage a llama. The llama remembers," he added darkly.

In the potato field a long line of men were working. Each man had a long-handled spade with a foothold tied to it. They worked together and in rhythm. At the call of the leader each man jumped upward with a shout. Then they came down together, plunging the sharp spade points into the earth of the field. Kneeling on the earth before them was a long line of women. As the men dug the earth the women turned it with their strong brown hands.

Cusi would have liked to stay a long time watching the people working. Chuto was impatient. Their journey was almost at an end. He wanted to get there, to get the salt and to go home again.

At the ruins of the Sacred Baths of the Inca they rested. They bathed in the cold water that bubbled in a spring and came from the melted snows of the high sierras. Chuto told Cusi to sit in the high throne seat carved from solid rock. It was where the Inca had sat in the long ago when the Inca was mighty ruler of a vast and loyal kingdom. Now a young boy sat there and pulled thoughtfully at his golden earplugs. Was he of the ancient nobility? Was that what the minstrel had meant when he and Chuto talked together? Did the royal blood of ancient kings still flow in the veins of his people? Again Cusi felt a vague unknown trouble like a cloud over the sun of a happy day. Again he felt a longing in his heart. Was it for kinship? Was it for family? How could he miss what he had not known?

Chuto too seemed troubled. He sat on a rock seat above the babbling spring that lay in its carved basin of pure white stone. He did not seem impatient now to meet whatever lay before him. He seemed rather to be going backward into days that were gone. "You are old for your age, my Cusi, and wise, too, I think. Wiser than I when I had your years. Wiser perhaps than that other who chose another way."

Cusi could feel his heart beat wildly as he listened to the words Chuto was saying to him. There had been someone else, then. Had it been another boy? Cusi wondered. What had happened to this other one? Where was he now? Cusi decided to find out. He said, "You speak of someone that I do not know. What other one do you talk about?"

Chuto got to his feet. He answered hurriedly, "Not now. Not now. My heart does not say that this is the time to tell you things that some day you must know." He looked around worriedly for something new to talk about. Pointing to a distant opening between the faraway mountain peaks, he said, "In that direction Cuzco lies—Cuzco the Holy City, divided into four

parts by three rivers, and from its heart four great roads lead
to the four corners of the world that is Peru." The old man
looked at the boy to see if he were listening, to see if he were
interested. He tried again. "Four roads there were in the days
of the Inca: to the mountains, to the valleys, to the pampas, to
the sea."

But Cusi felt stubborn. "Why do you know these things?
Where did you learn them? Why do you never tell me what I
want to know? Chuto, respected one, tell me who I am."

The old man looked pleadingly at the boy seated above him.
"I must be sure that you have understanding before I speak.
Bear with me, my Cusi," he said softly. "I do the best I know."

Cusi was embarrassed. He felt ashamed of his fretful questions. Chuto's words made him feel uneasy. What Chuto must
tell him, he must be ready to hear. He could learn to wait.

He jumped from the Inca seat where he had been sitting. He
flashed a quick smile at the worried Old One, who smiled in
return in fondness and in gratitude.

Glad of an opportunity to change their conversation, both
Indians, the old one and the young one, turned away from the
ruins of the Inca Bath and onto the trail again.

They walked along in silence, a comfortable silence. They
were companions. Companions have no need for constant
talking.

It was not long before the two Indians entered the Valley of
the Salt. This too had been used in ancient times and was still
being used in much the same manner. The Valley of the Salt
was a wide, open, flat valley, terraced in sections by low walls
made of perfectly fitted stone.

Here and there in the terraces men could be seen, working
busily in the hot sun of afternoon. They dug shallow holes in
the loose grainy soil. These were filled shortly with water from
some underground source. Chuto, who knew so many things,
did not know just what it was that caused this water to be salty.
But salty it was, and it was this sandy, salty brine that the men
scooped out of the shallow holes into hollowed stone traylike
vessels that were lying about in great numbers. Under the hot
tropical sun it would not be many hours before the water evap-

orated. The coarse, gray, sandy salty substance that remained
was the salt they used.

When Chuto and Cusi arrived at the pits they spent no time
resting. They began working immediately. Chuto dug the shallow holes. Cusi dipped the salt brine into the stone trays.

The sun burned down in glaring fierceness. When Cusi
would have stopped, Chuto pointed to the boy's coca bag.
"Chew some," he ordered briefly. "We must get our supply
today so that it will be dry enough to take tomorrow." Cusi was
glad that they would not stay long at this place. He liked it
even less than he had the wooded jungle places they had seen
yesterday.

The coca he chewed made him feel less tired. He bent to his
task again. After another hour of working the sun sank below
the distant hills. For a short time it was breathlessly hot. Then
the night wind came over the flat land, bringing sharp, stinging
cold. Chuto helped Cusi finish scooping the sandy brine into
the trays. Then they went over to join the other salt diggers,
who had stopped work also and were now sitting around a small
supper fire.

Chuto brought the yarn he had carried down the mountain
to barter. While they ate parched corn and dried meat, Chuto
bargained. The other men examined the yarn, noting its quality
and the evenness of its spinning. "The women of your village
spin good yarn," one man told him. Chuto did not answer. He
did not say there were no women in his village. He did not say
he had no village. He did not say that he had spun the yarn
and under his patient teaching Cusi had spun some of it. Although spinning is chiefly women's work, men and boys know
how to spin. Occasionally they can be seen spinning yarn as
they walk along the highland trails.

But Chuto said none of this. He merely looked pleased, and
the men took that for answer. The women of his village were
good spinners. That was what they thought. Chuto let them
think it. He was a good bargainer. Cusi was proud of him as
the value of the yarn went up and up. When the trading was
finished everyone was pleased. Chuto had a pile of peanuts and
a stack of dried fish. The men had yarn spun evidently by a
village of expert weavers.

Besides, bargaining was fun. It eased the strangeness of meeting. It gave them something to talk about. Each man showed his wits, his cleverness, and his smartness. It made for laughter. It gained respect. These men knew one another now as men of similar abilities. They were acquainted. Now they could talk together of many things.

At the opposite side of the valley a narrow steep road led into the sloping hills. Along this road there now appeared two round glaring eyes. They would appear and disappear and appear again, each time rounder, more glaring, larger. Cusi was terrified. It must be an animal from another world. He looked fearfully at the men, but in the gathering dusk he could not see their faces plainly. They did not seem frightened. He could not feel their fear. They were leaning forward, watching the lights, but more in expectancy and interest than in fear. The lights came nearer and nearer with strange noise and a still stranger smell. Then they disappeared completely. The men waited. Cusi saw two men walking across the gray-blanketed terraces.

Chuto chuckled, looking down at Cusi's set face. "Come," he said to the boy. "Come with me. We will see what this thing is that comes with such a clamor." Cusi made himself follow the old Indian across the terraces to the beginning of the road.

"They call this thing a truck," Chuto explained. "It has wheels instead of feet. It has a motor instead of a heart. It has evil-smelling blood by name of gasoline." Chuto knew everything!

When Cusi could get his breath, he asked, "What pulls it? Where are its eyes? It had them open. I saw them." Chuto laughed and quietly, patiently explained the mysteries of a thing that lived and moved but was not alive. It took a while. Cusi was not one to believe merely because he saw it. He must understand.

Chuto sighed. The world outside of Hidden Valley was so strange, so fascinating, so full of interest and of wonder, so very big. This was what he had been dreading, but it was why he had come. He knew what Cusi was experiencing. Had it not happened to him? Had it not happened to that other one? It happened to each in his lifetime. It must happen. It was the law. And each reacted to it in his own way. That too was a part of the pattern. Chuto sighed again and again explained the mystery and the magic of this thing here before them that they could see and touch.

By and by they returned to the group. The supper fire was completely dead. Fuel was too scarce to burn for pleasure or for warmth. It was gathered slowly. It was hoarded carefully. It was burned frugally and only when necessary.

The men were bartering with the newcomers, the men of the truck. This truck was full of coca leaves for the highland markets. They had come from the eastern slopes of the Andes, where coca is grown. In between their trading talk they told of other things. They told about coca-growing. How it grows only in the wettest lands, how it grows in low, small bushes and must be lovingly tended. They told of the skill and care needed in picking the leaves four times each year. They explained how it was dried and packed in woven net bags. "Eighteen pounds to the bag," they said, "no more, no less."

From coca-growing to other things the talk lazily drifted into the wind and into the night.

One of the men had come up from the fishing villages on the seacoast. He had dried fish to trade along the way to the market at Cuzco. Cusi listened wide-eyed to his tales of the sea. The man described the waves of a storm-swept sea to be as high as mountain peaks. Cusi tried to picture mountains of water pointing up to the sky, but he couldn't do it. A bottomless pool of still, black water, a swirling river cutting its way through granite, white foaming rapids breaking trees into splinters—these things he could picture. He had seen them in life. He could see them in memory. But mountains of water, rolling and tossing and pitching on a sea of water, he could not imagine. Finally he gave up and sat listening to the tales, entertained but unbelieving.

He did not remember sleeping, but he must have slept. He wakened in the gray dawn, cramped and cold. The men were where he had left them, huddled around a tiny fire. Only this was morning. This was breakfast fire. The men were eating again, but this morning no one talked. Last night they had shared talk and experiences; this morning each was bent upon his own individual task.

Chuto thought it would take an hour more of sunshine to dry the salt enough for packing. It took longer. It was midday before they were packed and on the trail again.

Just before they departed, two men and a boy about Cusi's age came to the pits. The two boys eyed each other and would have liked to talk and get acquainted. Cusi thought, I think I like that boy. I wish he lived in Hidden Valley. I could show him Misti. But there was no time to break down shyness, nor even to speak.

The boy was scooping brine from the holes the men dug when Cusi went by him, packed with salt to take the homeward trail. The boy looked up, and his eyes met Cusi's. They were not Indian eyes; they were Spanish eyes. He could not talk with me even if there was time, Cusi thought. He would not know my Indian language. Never in my whole life have I talked with a boy, Cusi thought with despair. He looked back once, but the boy was bent over the salt hole, dipping salt brine.

It was night again when they arrived at Condor Kuncca, the Indian shelter. Cusi had thought that surely this time he could make friends with the small children there. But they were asleep. In a clay bed not much larger than a shelf they were rolled in little knots, noisily sleeping. Cusi looked at them. How cunning they were, and little and brown. Brothers and sisters! Family!

The boy slept again near the llama corral while Chuto and the other men talked.

Early next morning they were far along the trail before the sun rose and Chuto put down his pack to greet it with his ancient prayer.

The way home was uneventful. There was no one at all at the hut where the woman had been threshing pigweed. The place had a lonely, unfriendly look. Cusi was glad when Chuto did not stop.

It was midafternoon when they reached the place of the tree-tied ladder. Cusi was surprised when Chuto put down his pack and prepared to stay. The boy had thought that if they hurried they could be home not too long after dark. He could see Misti and Yellow-Ears and the rest of the flock. He could hear Suncca whine. He could tell the minstrel all the things that had happened on the journey. He could be home for the night. Now that he was so close he wanted to go on, to be really home again.

Chuto said, "No," and then to the boy's look of disappointment added, "The swinging bridge needs not the shadows of evening but the brightness of day for its crossing."

Cusi was not pleased. He set his pack down with a thud. He sat himself down and wound his arms around his knees and tried to see around the cliff and along the trail and over the rapids to home.

Home. What a wonderful place it was. He would never leave it again, or if he did it would be for a short time only.

Chuto sighed. "Is your heart going back over the trail your feet have traveled?" he asked tiredly.

Cusi shook his head. "That way," he said, pointing his lips on the way toward home. Chuto laughed, and his laughter held the precious tones of gladness.

> Secret of the Andes *received the Newbery Medal in 1953. Mrs. Clark has also given us a story of a Guatemalan Indian boy in* Santiago *and of a Costa Rican boy in* Magic Money, *both published by Viking.*

Circum-Terra

BY ROBERT HEINLEIN

Illustrations by Clifford Geary

In the far future, when most nations of the universe are members of an Interplanetary Federation, nineteen-year-old Don finds himself caught in a revolution started by Venus. He makes friends with a scientist-dragon from that planet, a weird creature affectionately called "Sir Isaac Newton."

THE weight of acceleration was no worse than it had been the day before in the *Santa Fé Trail* but the drive persisted for more than five minutes, minutes that seemed like an endless hour. After they passed the speed of sound the compartment was relatively quiet. Don made a great effort and managed to turn his head a little. "Sir Isaac Newton's" great bulk was flattened to the deck, making Don think unpleasantly of a lizard crushed into a road. His eyestalks drooped like limp asparagus. He looked dead.

Don strained for breath and called out, "Are you all right?"

The Venerian did not stir. His voder instrument was covered by the sagging folds of his neck; it seemed unlikely that his tendrils could have managed the delicate touch required for its keys even had it been free. Nor did he reply in his own whistling speech.

Don wanted to go to him, but he was as immobilized by the blast weight as is the bottommost player in a football pile up. He forced his head back where it belonged so that he might breathe less painfully and waited.

When the blast died away his stomach gave one protesting flipflop, then quieted down; either the anti-nausea shot had worked or he had his space balance again—or both. Without

waiting for permission from the control room he quickly un-
strapped and hurried to the Venerian. He steadied himself in
the air, holding with one hand to the steel bands restraining his
companion.

The dragon was no longer crushed to the deckplates; only
the steel hoops kept him from floating around the compartment. Behind him his giant tail waved loosely, brushing the
ship's plates and knocking off paint chips.

The eyestalks were still limp and each eye filmed over. The
dragon stirred only in the meaningless motion of string in
water; there was nothing to show that he was alive. Don
clenched a fist and pounded on the creature's flat skull. "Can
you hear me? Are you all right?"

All he got out of it was a bruised hand; Sir Isaac made no
response. Don hung for a moment, wondering what to do. That
his acquaintance was in a bad way he felt sure, but his training
in first aid did not extend to Venerian pseudo-saurians. He dug
back into his childhood memories, trying to think of something.

The same ship's officer who had rearranged the berthing appeared at the forward or "upper" hatch, floating head "down."
"All okay this deck?" he inquired perfunctorily and started to
back out.

"No!" Don shouted. "Case of blast shock."

"Huh?" The officer swam on into the compartment and looked
at the other passenger. He swore unimaginatively and looked
worried. "This is beyond me; I never carried one before. How
the deuce do you give artificial respiration to a thing as big
as that?"

"You don't," Don told him. "His lungs are completely enclosed in his armor box."

"He looks dead. I think he's stopped breathing."

A memory floated to the top in Don's mind; he snatched it.
"Got a cigarette?"

"Huh? Don't bother me! Anyhow the smoking lamp is out."

"You don't understand," Don persisted. "If you've got one,
light it. You can blow smoke at his nostril plate and see whether
or not he's breathing."

"Oh. Well, maybe it's a good idea." The spaceman got out a
cigarette and struck it.

"But be careful," Don went on. "They can't stand nicotine. One big puff and then put it out."

"Maybe it's not such a good idea," the ship's officer objected. "Say, you sound like a Venus colonial?"

Don hesitated, then answered, "I'm a Federation citizen." It seemed like a poor time to discuss politics. He moved over to the dragon's chin, braced his feet against the deckplates and shoved, thus exposing the Venerian's nostril plate which was located under the creature's head in the folds of his neck. Don could not have managed it, save that they were in free fall, making the bulky mass weightless.

The man blew smoke at the exposed opening. It eddied forward, then some of it curled inside; the dragon was still alive.

Still very much alive. Every eyestalk sprang to rigid attention; he lifted his chin, carrying Don with it, then he sneezed. The blast struck Don where he floated loosely and turned him over and over. He threshed in the air for a moment before catching a handhold on the hatch ladder.

The ship's officer was rubbing one wrist. "The beggar clipped me," he complained. "I won't try that again soon. Well, I guess he'll be all right."

Sir Isaac whistled mournfully; Don answered him. The spaceman looked at him. "You savvy that stuff?"

"Some."

"Well, tell him to use his squawk box. I don't!"

Don said, "Sir Isaac—use your voder."

The Venerian tried to comply. His tentacles hunted around, found the keys of the artificial voice box, and touched them. No sound came out. The dragon turned an eye at Don and whistled a series of phrases.

"He regrets to say that its spirit has departed," Don interpreted.

The ship's officer sighed. "I wonder why I ever left the grocery business? Well, if we can get it unlatched from him, I'll see if 'Sparks' can fix it."

"Let me," said Don and squirmed into the space between the dragon's head and the deckplates. The voder case, he found, was secured to four rings riveted to the Venerian's skin plates. He could not seem to find the combination; the dragon's ten-

drils fluttered over his hands, moved them gently out of the
way, unfastened the box, and handed it to him. He wiggled out
and gave it to the man. "Looks like he kind of slept on it," he
commented.

"A mess," the other agreed. "Well, tell him I'll have them fix
it if possible and that I'm glad he wasn't hurt."

"Tell him yourself; he understands English."

"Eh? Oh, of course, of course." He faced the Venerian who
immediately set up a long shrilling. "What's he say?"

Don listened. "He says he appreciates your good wishes but
that he is sorry to have to disagree; he is unwell. He says that
he urgently requires—" Don stopped and looked puzzled, then
whistled the Venerian equivalent of "Say that again, please?"

Sir Isaac answered him; Don went on, "He says he's just got
to have some sugar syrup."

"*Huh?*"

"That's what he says."

"I'll be— How much?"

There was another exchange of whistles; Don answered,
"Uh, he says he needs at least a quarter of a—there isn't any
word for it; it's an amount about equal to half a barrel, I'd
say."

"You mean he wants *half a barrel* of waffle juice?"

"No, no, a quarter of that—an eighth of a barrel. What would
that come to in gallons?"

"I wouldn't attempt it without a slipstick; I'm confused. I
don't even know that we have any on board." Sir Isaac set up
more frantic whistling. "But if we don't, I'll have the cook whop
up some. Tell him to hold everything and take it easy." He
scowled at the dragon, then left quite suddenly.

Don attached himself to one of the steel straps and asked,
"How are you feeling now?"

The dragon replied apologetically to the effect that he
needed to return to the egg for the moment. Don shut up and
waited.

The captain himself showed up to attend the sick passenger.
The ship, being in free trajectory for the satellite space station,
would not require his presence in the control room until well

past noon, New Chicago time; he was free to move around the ship. He arrived in company with the ship's doctor and followed by a man herding a metal tank.

The two conferred over the dragon, at first ignoring Don's presence. However neither of them knew the piping speech of the dragon tribe; they were forced to turn to Don. Through him Sir Isaac again insisted that he required sugar solution as a stimulant. The captain looked worried. "I've read somewhere that sugar gets them drunk the same as alcohol does us."

Don again translated for the Venerian; what he had asked for was simply a medicinal dose.

The captain turned to the medical officer. "How about it, surgeon?"

The doctor stared at the bulkhead. "Captain, this is as far outside my duties as tap dancing."

"Confound it, man, I asked for your official opinion!"

The medical officer faced him. "Very well, sir—I would say that if this passenger should die, you having refused him something he had asked for, it would look very, very bad indeed."

The captain bit his lip. "As you say, sir. But I'll be switched if I want several tons of intoxicated dragon banging around in my ship. Administer the dose."

"Me, sir?"

"*You*, sir."

The ship being in free fall it was quite impossible to pour out the syrup and let the Venerian lick it up, nor was he physically equipped to use the "baby bottle" drinking bladders used by humans when weightless. But that had been anticipated; the tank containing the syrup was a type used in the galley to handle soup or coffee in free fall. It had a hand pump and an attachable hose.

It was decided, Sir Isaac concurring, to place the end of the hose well down the dragon's throat. But nobody seemed to want the job. Granted that *Draco Veneris Wilsonii* is a civilized race, to stick one's head and shoulders between those rows of teeth seemed to be inviting a breach in foreign relations.

Don volunteered for the job and was sorry when they took him up on it. He trusted Sir Isaac but recalled times when

Lazy had stepped on his foot quite unintentionally. He hoped that the dragon had no unfortunate involuntary reflexes; apologies are no use to a corpse.

While he kept the end of the hose firmly in place he held his breath and was glad that he had taken that anti-nausea injection. Sir Isaac did not have halitosis, as dragons go, but dragons go rather far in that direction. The job done, he was happy to back out.

Sir Isaac thanked them all, via Don, and assured them that he would now recover rapidly. He seemed to fall asleep in the midst of whistling. The ship's doctor peeled one eyestalk and shined a hand torch at it. "The stuff has hit him, I think. We'll let him be and hope for the best."

They all left. Don looked his friend over, decided that there was no point in sitting up with him, and followed them. The compartment had no view port; he wanted at least one good look at Earth while they were still close by. He found what he sought three decks forward.

They were still only fifteen thousand miles out; Don had to crowd in close to the view port to see all of Earth at one time. It was, he had to admit, a mighty pretty planet; he was a little bit sorry to be leaving it. Hanging there against velvet black and pinpoint stars, drenched in sunlight so bright it hurt your eyes, it almost took your breath away.

The sunrise line had swung far into the Pacific past Hawaii, and North America was spread out to his gaze. Storm blanketed the Pacific Northwest, but the Midwest was fairly clear and the Southwest was sharp. He could make out where New Chicago was with ease; he could see the Grand Canyon and from it he could almost figure out where the ranch had to be. He was sure that with a small telescope he could have spotted it.

He gave up his place at last. He was soaking in the pleasant melancholy of mild homesickness and the comments of some of the other passengers were beginning to annoy him—not the cheerful inanities of tourists but the know-it-all remarks of self-appointed old timers, making their second trip out. He headed back to his own compartment.

He was startled to hear his name called. He turned and the ship's officer he had met before floated up to him. He had with him Sir Isaac's voder. "You seem to be chummy with that over-educated crocodile you're bunking with; how about taking this to him?"

"Why, certainly."

"The radio officer says it needs an overhaul but at least it's working again." Don accepted it and went aft. The dragon seemed to be sleeping, then one eye waved at him and Sir Isaac whistled a salutation.

"I've got your voice box," Don told him. "Want me to fasten it on for you?"

Sir Isaac politely refused. Don handed the instrument to the fidgeting tendrils and the dragon arranged it to suit him. He then ran over the keys as a check, producing sounds like frightened ducks. Satisfied, he began to speak in English: "I am enriched by the debt you have placed upon me."

"It was nothing," Don answered. "I ran into the mate a couple of decks forward and he asked me to fetch it along."

"I do not refer to this artificial voice, but to your ready help when I was in distress and peril. Without your quick wit, your willingness to share mud with an untested stranger, and—in passing—your knowledge of the true speech, I might have lost my chance to attain the happy death."

"Shucks," Don answered, feeling somewhat pink, "it was a pleasure." He noticed that the dragon's speech was slow and somewhat slurred, as if his tentacles lacked their customary dexterity. Besides that, Sir Isaac's talk was more pedantic than ever and much more Cockney-flavored—the voder was mixing aspirates with abandon and turning the *theta* sound into "f"; Don felt sure that the Earthman who had taught him to speak must have been born in earshot of Bow Bells.

He noticed as well that his friend could not seem to make up his mind which eye he wanted to use on him. He kept waggling one after another at Don, as if seeking one which would let him focus better. Don wondered if Sir Isaac had overestimated the proper size of a medicinal dose.

"Permit me," the Venerian went on, still with ponderous dignity, "to judge the worth of the service you have done me." He changed the subject. "This word 'shucks'—I do not recognize the use you made of it. Husks of plants?"

Don struggled to explain how little and how much "shucks" could mean. The dragon thought it over and tapped out an answer. "I believe that I gain a portion of understanding. The semantic content of this word is emotional and variable, rather than orderly and descriptive. Its referent is the state of one's spirits?"

"That's it," Don said happily. "It means just what you want it to mean. It's the way you say it."

"Shucks," the dragon said experimentally. "Shucks. I seem to be getting the feel of it. A delightful word. Shucks." He went on, "The delicate nuances of speech must be learned from the living users thereof. Perhaps I may return the favor by helping you in some small wise with your already great mastery of the speech of my people? Shucks."

This confirmed Don's suspicion that his own whistling had become so villainous that it might do for popcorn vending but not for regular communication. "I certainly would appreciate a chance to brush up," he answered. "I haven't had a chance to speak 'true speech' for years—not since I was a kid. I was taught by an historian who was working with my father on the (whistled) ruins. Perhaps you know him? His name was 'Professor Charles Darwin.'" Don added the whistled or true version of the Venerian scholar's name.

"You ask me if I know (whistled)? He is my brother; his grandmother, nine times removed, and my grandmother, seven times removed, were the same egg. Shucks!" He added, "A learned person, for one so young."

Don was a bit taken aback to hear "Professor Darwin" described as "young"; as a child he had classed him and the ruins as being about the same age. He now had to remind himself that Sir Isaac might see it differently. "Say, that's nice!" he answered. "I wonder if you knew my parents? Dr. Jonas Harvey and Dr. Cynthia Harvey?"

The dragon turned all eyes on him. "You are their egg? I have not had the honor of meeting them but all civilized persons know of them and their work. I am no longer surprised at your own excellence. Shucks!"

Don felt both embarrassment and pleasure. Not knowing what to say he suggested that Sir Isaac coach him for a while in "true speech," a suggestion to which the dragon readily assented. They were still so engaged when the warning signal sounded and a voice from the control room sang out, "Strap down for acceleration! Prepare to match trajectories!"

Don placed his hands against his friend's armored sides and shoved himself back to his couch. He paused there and said, "Are you going to be all right?"

The dragon made a sound which Don construed as a hiccup, and tapped out, "I feel sure of it. This time I am fortified."

"I hope so. Say—you don't want to bung up your voder again. Want me to take care of it?"

"If you will, please."

Don went back and got it, then fastened it to his bags. He had barely time to fasten his safety belts when the first surge of acceleration hit them. It was not so bad, this time, neither as many gravities as the blast-off from Earth nor of as long duration, for they were not breaking free of Earth's crushing grip but merely adjusting trajectories—modifying the outer end of the *Glory Road*'s elliptical path to make it agree perfectly with the circular orbit of Circum-Terra, the cross-roads station in space which was their destination.

The captain gave them one long powerful shove, waited, then blasted twice more for short intervals—without, Don noted, finding it necessary to invert and blast back. He nodded approval. Good piloting!—the captain knew his vectors. The bull horn sang out, "Contact! Unstrap at will. Prepare to disembark."

Don returned the voder to Sir Isaac, then lost track of him, for the dragon again had to be taken aft to be transferred through the cargo hatch. Don whistled goodbye and went forward, towing his bags behind him, to go out through the passenger tube.

Circum-Terra was a great confused mass in the sky. It had been built, rebuilt, added to, and modified over the course of years for a dozen different purposes—weather observation station, astronomical observatory, meteor count station, television relay, guided missile control station, high-vacuum strain-free physics laboratory, strain-free germ-free biological experiment station, and many other uses.

But most importantly it was a freight and passenger transfer

station in space, the place where short-range winged rockets
from Earth met the space liners that plied between the planets.
For this purpose it had fueling tanks, machine shops, repair
cages that could receive the largest liners and the smallest
rockets, and a spinning, pressurized drum—"Goddard Hotel"
—which provided artificial gravity and Earth atmosphere for
passengers and for the permanent staff of Circum-Terra.

Goddard Hotel stuck out from the side of Circum-Terra like
a cartwheel from a pile of junk. The hub on which it turned
ran through its center and protruded out into space. It was
to this hub that a ship would couple its passenger tube when
discharging or loading humans. That done, the ship would
then be warped over to a cargo port in the non-spinning major
body of the station. When the *Glory Road* made contact, there
were three other ships in at Circum-Terra, the *Valkyrie* in
which Don Harvey had passage for Mars, the *Nautilus,* just
in from Venus and in which Sir Isaac expected to return home,
and the *Spring Tide,* the Luna shuttle which alternated with its
sister the *Neap Tide.*

The two liners and the moon ship were already tied up to
the main body of the station; the *Glory Road* warped in at the
hub of the hotel and immediately began to discharge passengers. Don waited his turn and then pulled himself along by
handholds, dragging his bags behind him, and soon found himself inside the hotel, but still in weightless free fall in the cylin-
drical hub of the Goddard.

A man in coveralls directed Don and the dozen passengers
he was with to a point halfway along the hub where a large
lift blocked further progress. Its circular door stood open and
turned very slowly around, moving with the spinning hotel
proper. "Get in," he ordered. "Mind you get your feet pointed
toward the floor."

Don got in with the others and found that the inside of the
car was cubical. One wall was marked in big letters: FLOOR.
Don found a handhold and steadied himself so that his feet
would be on the floor when weight was applied. The man got
in and started the car out toward the rim.

There was no feeling of weight at first, at least not toward
the "floor." Don experienced a dizzy sensation as increasing
spin sloshed the liquid about in his inner ear. He knew that he

had ridden this elevator before, when he was eleven and heading for Earth and school, but he had forgotten its unpleasant aspects.

Soon the elevator stopped; the floor became the floor in earnest, though with considerably less than one gravity, and the upsetting sensation ceased. The operator opened the door and shouted, "Everybody out!"

Don walked into a large inner compartment, carrying his bags. It was already crowded with more than half of the ship's passengers. Don looked around for his dragon friend, then remembered that the ship would have to be moved around to a cargo port before the Venerian could disembark. He put his bags on the floor and sat down on them.

The crowd, for some reason, seemed unquiet. Don heard one woman say, "This is preposterous! We've been here at least half an hour and no one appears to know that we're here."

A man answered, "Be patient, Martha."

"'Patient' he says! Only one door out of the place and it locked—suppose there were a fire?"

"Well, where would you run to, dear? Nothing outside but some mighty thin vacuum."

She squealed. "Oh! We should have gone to Bermuda as I wanted to."

"As *you* wanted to?"

"Don't be petty!"

Another elevator load discharged and then another; the ship was empty. After many minutes more of grumbling, during which even Don began to wonder at the service, the only door other than the elevator door opened. Instead of a hotelman anxious to please his guests, in came three men in uniform. The two flank men were carrying mob guns cradled at their hips; the third man had only a hand pistol, still holstered. He stepped forward, planted his feet and set his fists on his hips. "Attention! Quiet, everybody."

He got it; his voice had the ring of command which is obeyed without thinking. He went on, "I am Assault Sergeant McMasters of the High Guard, Venus Republic. My commanding officer has directed me to advise you of the present situation."

There was an additional short moment of silence, then a rising mutter of surprise, alarm, disbelief, and indignation. "Pipe down!" the sergeant shouted. "Take it easy. Nobody's going to get hurt—if you behave." He went on, "The Republic has taken over this station and everybody is being cleared out. You groundhogs will be shipped back to Earth at once. Those of you who are headed home to Venus will go home—provided you pass our loyalty check. Now, let's get sorted out."

A fussy, plump man pushed his way forward. "Do you realize, sir, what you are saying? 'Venus Republic,' indeed. This is piracy!"

"Get back in line, fatty."

"You can't do this. I wish to speak to your commanding officer."

"Fatty," the sergeant said slowly, "back up before you get a boot in your belly." The man looked dumbfounded, then scuttled back into the crowd.

The sergeant continued, "Those of you going to Venus form a queue here at the door. Have your ID's and birth certificates ready."

The passengers, up to that time a friendly group of fellow travelers, split into hostile camps. Someone shouted, "Long live the Republic!", which was followed by the beefy sound of a fist striking flesh. One of the guards hurried into the crowd and stopped the impending riot. The sergeant drew his side-arm and said in a bored voice, "No politics, please. Let's get on with the job."

Somehow a line was formed. The second in line was the man who had cheered the new nation. His nose was dripping blood but his eyes were shining. As he offered his papers to the sergeant he said, "This is a great day! I've waited all my life for it."

"Who hasn't?" the sergeant answered. "Okay—on through the door for processing. Next!"

Don was busy trying to quiet down and arrange his whirling thoughts. He was forced at last to admit that this was it, this was war, the war that he had told himself was impossible. No cities had been bombed, not yet—but this was the Fort Sumter of a new war; he was smart enough to see that. He did not have to be threatened with a boot in the belly to see what was in front of his face.

He realized with nervous shock that he had just barely gotten away in time. The *Valkyrie* might be the last ship to Mars in a long, long time. With the transfer station in the hands of the rebels it might be the last one for years.

The sergeant had not said anything about passengers for Mars as yet; Don told himself that the sergeant's first effort must naturally be to sort out the citizens of the two belligerents. He decided that the thing to do was to keep his mouth shut and wait.

There was an interruption in the queue. Don heard the sergeant say, "You're in the wrong pew, bud. You go back to Earth."

The man he was speaking to answered, "No, no! Take a look at my papers; I'm emigrating to Venus."

"You're a leetle bit late to be emigrating. The situation has changed."

"Why? Sure, I know it has changed. I declare for Venus."

The sergeant scratched his head. "This one isn't in the book. Atkinson! Pass this man on through; we'll let the lieutenant figure it out."

When he had completed the group that wanted to go to Venus the sergeant went to a speech-only wall phone. "Jim? Mac speaking, from the nursery. They got that dragon out yet? No? Well, let me know when the *Road* is back at the chute; I want to load." He turned back to the crowd. "All right, you groundhogs—there'll be a delay so I'm going to move you into another room until we're ready to send you back to Earth."

"Just a moment, Sergeant!" called out a male passenger.

"Yeah? What do you want?"

"Where do passengers for Luna wait?"

"Huh? Service discontinued. You're going back to Earth."

"Now, Sergeant, let's be reasonable. I haven't the slightest interest in politics; it does not matter to me who administers this station. But I have business on the Moon. It is *essential* that I get to the Moon. A delay would cost millions!"

The sergeant stared at him. "Now isn't that just too bad! You know, brother, I've never had as much as a thousand at one time in my life; the thought of losing millions scares me." His manner suddenly changed. "You stupid jerk, have you ever thought what a bomb would do to the roof of Tycho City? Now line up, all of you, double file."

Don listened to this with disquiet. Still, the sergeant had not said anything about Mars. He got into line, but at the very end. When the tail of the line reached the door he stopped. "Get a move on, kid," said the sergeant.

"I'm not going back to Earth," Don told him.

"Huh?"

"I'm headed for Mars in the *Valkyrie*."

"Oh, I see. You mean you were—now you're headed back to Earth in the *Glory Road*."

Don said stubbornly, "Look, mister, I've *got* to get to Mars. My parents are there; they are expecting me."

The sergeant shook his head. "Kid, I feel sorry for you. I really do. The *Valkyrie* isn't going to Mars."

"What?"

"She's being recommissioned as a cruiser of the High Guard. She's going to Venus. So I guess you had better go back to Earth. I'm sorry you won't be able to join your folks, but war is like that."

Don breathed slowly and forced himself to count up to ten. "I'm not going back to Earth. I'll wait right here until a ship does go to Mars."

The sergeant sighed. "If you do, you'll have to chin yourself on a star while you wait."

"Huh? What do you mean?"

"Because," he said slowly, "a few minutes after we blast off there will be nothing in this neighborhood but a nice, pretty radioactive cloud. Want to play a leading role in a Geiger counter?"

Robert Heinlein is well known for his stories of outer space, which make use of authentic scientific material. Among the most popular are Rocket Ship Galileo, *about a flight to the moon, and* Red Planet, *concerning adventures on Mars, both published by Scribner.*

INDEX of Authors and Titles

ACKNOWLEDGMENTS

The publishers wish to express their appreciation to the following publishers, agents, authors, and artists who have granted permission to use material appearing in this book. Any errors or omissions are unintentional and will be corrected in future printings if notice is sent to The Crowell-Collier Publishing Company.

CURTIS BROWN, LTD. *Lassie Come-Home,* by Eric Knight, from *Saturday Evening Post,* copyright 1938 by The Curtis Publishing Company; reprinted by permission of Curtis Brown, Ltd.

DODD, MEAD & COMPANY, INC.   Illustrations by Katherine Pyle for the excerpt from *Black Beauty,* by Anna Sewell; reprinted by permission of Dodd, Mead & Company, Inc.

HARCOURT, BRACE & WORLD, INC.   Excerpt from *The Kid from Tomkinsville,* by John R. Tunis, illustrations by Jay Hyde Barnum, copyright 1940 by John R. Tunis; used by permission of Harcourt, Brace & World, Inc.

HOLT, RINEHART & WINSTON, INC.   "Service at the Point of a Rifle," from *Young Fu of the Upper Yangtze,* by Elizabeth Foreman Lewis, illustrated by Kurt Wiese, copyright 1932, 1959 by Holt, Rinehart & Winston, Inc.; reprinted by permission of Holt, Rinehart & Winston, Inc.

HOUGHTON MIFFLIN COMPANY   Excerpt from *Johnny Tremain,* by Esther Forbes, illustrated by Lynd Ward, copyright 1943 by Esther Forbes Hoskins; "The Witch Trial," from *The Witch of Blackbird Pond,* by Elizabeth George Speare, illustrated by Nicholas Angelo, copyright 1958 by Elizabeth George Speare; reprinted by permission of and arrangement with Houghton Mifflin Company, the authorized publishers.

LITTLE, BROWN & CO.   "Head Winds and a Rough Sea," from *The Dark Frigate,* by Charles Boardman Hawes, copyright 1923 by The Torbell Company & The Atlantic Monthly Press, Inc., copyright 1934 by Little, Brown & Co.; frontispiece illustration by Otto Fischer; by permission of Little, Brown & Co.

LOTHROP, LEE & SHEPARD COMPANY   Permission to use *The Lance of Kanana,* by Harry W. French.

THE MACMILLAN COMPANY   "Alas, Poor Annabelle," from *Caddie Woodlawn,* by Carol Ryrie Brink, illustrated by Kate Seredy, copyright 1935 by The Macmillan Company; excerpt from *Call It Courage,* written and illustrated by Armstrong Sperry, copyright 1940 by The Macmillan Company; "The Great Tarnov Crystal," from *The Trumpeter of Krakow,* by Eric P. Kelly, copyright 1928 by The Macmillan Company; used by permission of The Macmillan Company.

JOHN MURRAY, LTD.   *The Adventure of the Blue Carbuncle,* by Sir Arthur Conan Doyle; reprinted in Canada with permission of John Murray, Ltd.

CHARLES SCRIBNER'S SONS   "Circum-Terra," reprinted from and illustration reproduced from *Between Planets,* by Robert Heinlein, illustrated by Clifford Geary, copyright 1951 by McCall Corporation and Robert Heinlein; used with permission of Charles Scribner's Sons.

THE VIKING PRESS, INC.   "Adventure in Sheridan Square," from *The Bells of Bleecker Street,* written and illustrated by Valenti Angelo, copyright 1949 by Valenti Angelo; "Outside," from *Secret of the Andes,* by Ann Nolan Clark, illustrated by Jean Charlot, copyright 1952 by Ann Nolan Clark; "The Riding Lesson," from *The Good Master,* written and illustrated by Kate Seredy, copyright 1935 by Kate Seredy; reprinted by permission of The Viking Press, Inc.

MARY YOST ASSOCIATES   *The Adventure of the Blue Carbuncle;* reprinted by permission of The Estate of Sir Arthur Conan Doyle.